Mark Billingham has twice won the Theakston's Old Peculier Award for the Best Crime Novel of the Year, and has also won a Sherlock Award for the Best Detective created by a British writer. Each of the novels featuring Detective Inspector Tom Thorne has been a *Sunday Times* bestseller. *Sleepyhead* and *Scaredycat* were made into a hit TV series on Sky 1 starring David Morrissey as Thorne, and a series based on the novels *In the Dark* and *Time of Death* was broadcast on BBC1. Mark lives in north London with his wife and two children.

*Praise for the DI Tom Thorne series:*

'Morse, Rebus, and now Thorne. The next superstar detective is already with us. Don't miss him'
Lee Child

'Tom Thorne is the most interesting cop in British crime fiction at present'
*The Times*

'DI Thorne is a wonderful creation'
Karin Slaughter

'What is so impressive is how real the characters are, not least his physically battered and psychologically scarred Detective Inspector Tom Thorne'
*Guardian*

'With each of his books, Mark Billingham gets better and better. These are stories and characters you don't want to leave'
Michael Connelly

'If you haven't yet come across DI Thorne, treat yourself. You won't be disappointed'
*Sunday Express*

D0460547

## Also by Mark Billingham

# MARK BILLINGHAM

## — A TOM THORNE THRILLER —

# Buried

sphere

SPHERE

First published in Great Britain in 2006 by Little, Brown
Paperback published in 2007 by Sphere
This reissue published by Sphere in 2020

3 5 7 9 10 8 6 4

Copyright © Mark Billingham 2006

The moral right of the author has been asserted.

*All characters and events in this publication, other than those
clearly in the public domain, are fictitious and any resemblance
to real persons, living or dead, is purely coincidental.*

All rights reserved.
No part of this publication may be reproduced, stored in a
retrieval system, or transmitted, in any form or by any means, without
the prior permission in writing of the publisher, nor be otherwise circulated
in any form of binding or cover other than that in which it is published
and without a similar condition including this condition
being imposed on the subsequent purchaser.

A CIP catalogue record for this book
is available from the British Library.

ISBN 978-0-7515-4856-3

Typeset in Plantin by M Rules
Printed and bound in Great Britain by
Clays Ltd, Elcograf S.p.A.

Papers used by Sphere are from well-managed forests
and other responsible sources.

Sphere
An imprint of
Little, Brown Book Group
Carmelite House
50 Victoria Embankment
London EC4Y 0DZ

An Hachette UK Company
www.hachette.co.uk

www.littlebrown.co.uk

For Sarah Lutyens.

Without whom there wouldn't have been any at all.

# PROLOGUE

You think about the kids.

First and last, in this sort of situation, in this sort of *state*; when you can't decide if it's anger or agony that's all but doubling you up, and making it so hard for you to spit the words across the room. First and last, you think about them ...

'Why the hell, why the *fuck*, didn't you tell me this earlier?'

'It wasn't the right time. It seemed best to wait.'

'*Best?*' She takes a step towards the man standing on the far side of her living room.

He moves back instinctively until his calves are squashed against the edge of the sofa and he almost topples back on to the carefully plumped cushions. 'I think you should try to calm down,' he says.

The room smells of pot pourri. There are lines on the carpet showing that it has recently been vacuumed, and the carriage clock that can be heard ticking loudly when the shouting stops sits on a highly polished pine mantelpiece.

'What do you expect me to do?' she says. 'I'd really be interested to know.'

'I can't tell you what to do. It's your decision.'

'You think I've got a *choice*?'

'We need to sit down and talk about the best way forward—'

3

'Christ Almighty. You just march in here and tell me this. Casually, like it's just something you forgot to mention. You walk in here and tell me all this ... shit!' She's begun to cry again, but this time she does not lift a hand to her face. She shuts her eyes and waits for the moment to pass. For the fury to return, undiluted.

'Sarah—'

'I don't know you. I don't even fucking *know* you!'

For a few seconds there's just the ticking, and the distant traffic, and the noise bleeding in from a radio in the kitchen, turned down low when she'd heard the doorbell. Inside, the central heating's working overtime, but there's still plenty of sun streaming into the room through the net at the windows.

'I'm sorry.'

'You're *what*?' But she's heard him well enough. She smiles, then laughs. She gathers the material of her dress between her fingers as her fists clench at her sides. There's something starting to twitch in her belly now; a spasm takes hold at the top of her leg. 'I need to get to the school.'

'The kids'll be fine. Honestly, love. Absolutely fine.'

She repeats his last word; and then again, in a whisper. There's no stopping the tears this time or the scream that comes from deep inside; or the swell and the surge that take her fast across the room, her hands clawed and flying at the man's face.

The man raises his arms to protect himself. He grabs the fingers that stab at his eyes, and, once he has them, as soon as he is in control of her, he tries to keep her still; to guide her firmly away. 'You've got to stay calm.'

'You. Rotten. Fucker.' She snaps back her head.

'Please listen—' The spit hits him just above the lip and starts to run into his mouth. He swears at her; a word he rarely uses.

And he pushes her . . .

And suddenly she's dead weight, falling back, opening her mouth to cry out, and smashing down through the glass of the coffee table.

A few seconds' ticking. And traffic. And the buzz from the kitchen.

The man takes a step towards her, then stops dead. He can see what's happened straight away.

Her back hurts, and her ankle, where she's caught them on the edge of the table as she's fallen. She tries to sit up, but her head is suddenly as heavy as a wrecking ball. The moan rattles from her chest, and her shoulders grind glass into the carpet beneath her. She lies, breathless, across the ragged jewels and slivers, recognising a song from the distant radio at the same moment that she feels the warmth and the wetness at the back of her head. Spreading at her throat, and creeping down inside the neck of her sweater.

*Shard . . .*

She thinks for a second or two about that word; about what a stupid word it is when you say it to yourself repeatedly. About her bad luck. How bloody unlucky can you get? Must have caught an artery, or maybe two. And, though she can hear her name being spoken, though she is well aware of the desperation, of the *panic*, in the voice, she is already starting to fade and to focus; concentrating only on the faces of her children.

First and last.

As her life ebbs quickly away – running red across smoked glass – her final thought is a straightforward one. Simple and tender and vicious.

*If he's touched my kids, I'll kill him.*

# PART ONE

# THE PUNCH COMING

# LUKE

'I suppose all I'm really saying is try not to worry. OK, Mum? That you don't have to, I mean. Even sitting here saying that, I know how pointless it is, because it's something you've always done. Juliet and me reckon that if you weren't worried about something, you'd probably feel odd, or under the weather, like part of you wasn't working properly. You'd be disconcerted. Like when you know there's something important you've forgotten to do, or when you can't remember where you've put your keys, you know? If you weren't worried, we'd be worried that you weren't!

'It's all right, though. I'm doing pretty well. Better than "pretty well" actually. I'm not saying it's five-star or anything, but the food could be a damn sight worse, and they're being fairly nice to me. And it's only the second most uncomfortable bed I've ever slept in. Remember when we stayed in that shitty guest house in Eastbourne that time, when Juliet had her hockey tournament, and the bed felt like it had rocks in it? I'm even managing to get some sleep, amazingly enough.

'I don't really know what else to say. What else I'm *supposed* to say ...

'Except ... If you want to video the comedy shows I like, that'd be cool. And don't rent my room out straight away, and please tell everyone at school not to be too devastated. See? Well fed, sleeping OK, and I've still got my sense of humour. So, really, there's nothing to get yourself worked up about, all right, Mum? I'm fine. Tell you what – when this is all finally sorted out, how about that PS2 game I've been going on about? Can't blame a lad for trying, can you?

'Look, there's loads of other things to say, but I'd better not go on too long, and you know the stuff I mean anyway. Mum? You know what I'm trying to say, yeah?

'Right. That's it ... '

The boy's eyes slide away from the camera, and a man carrying a syringe steps quickly towards him. He sits up, tenses as the man reaches across, driving the bag down over the boy's head in the few seconds before the picture disappears.

# TUESDAY

# ONE

There *was* humour, of course there was; off colour usually, and downright black when the occasion demanded it. Still, the jokes had not exactly been flying thick and fast of late, and none had flown in Tom Thorne's direction.

But this was as good a laugh as he'd had in a while.

'Jesmond asked for *me*?' he said.

Russell Brigstocke leaned back in his chair, enjoying the surprise that his shock announcement had certainly merited. It was an uncertain world. The Metropolitan Police Service was in a permanent state of flux, and, while precious little could be relied upon, the less than harmonious relationship between DI Tom Thorne and the Chief Superintendent of the Area West Murder Squad was a reassuring constant. 'He was very insistent.'

'The pressure must be getting to him,' Thorne said. 'He's losing the plot.'

Now it was Brigstocke's turn to see the funny side. 'Why am I suddenly thinking about pots and kettles?'

'I've no idea. Maybe you've got a thing about kitchenware.'

'You've been going on about wanting something to get stuck into. So—'

'With bloody good reason.'

Brigstocke sighed, nudged at the frames of his thick, black glasses.

It was warm in the office, with spring kicking in but the radiators still chucking out heat at December levels. Thorne stood and slipped off his brown leather jacket. 'Come on, Russell, you know damn well that I haven't been given anything worth talking about for near enough six months.'

Six months since he'd worked undercover on the streets of London, trying to catch the man responsible for kicking three of the city's homeless to death. Six months spent writing up domestics, protecting the integrity of evidence chains, and double-checking pre-trial paperwork. Six months kept out of harm's way.

'This is something that *needs* getting stuck into,' Brigstocke said. 'Quickly.'

Thorne sat back down and waited for the DCI to elaborate.

'It's a kidnapping—' Brigstocke held up a hand as soon as Thorne began to shake his head; ploughed on over the groaning from the other side of his desk. 'A sixteen-year-old boy, taken from outside a school in north London three days ago.'

The shake of the head became a knowing nod. 'Jesmond doesn't want *me* on this at all, does he? It's sod all to do with what I can do, or what I might be good at. He's just been asked to lend the Kidnap Unit a few bodies, right? So he does what he's told like a good team player, and he gets me out of the way at the same time. Two birds with one stone.'

A spider plant stood on one corner of Brigstocke's desk, its dead leaves drooping across a photograph of his kids. He snapped off a handful of the browned and brittle stalks and began crushing them between his hands. 'Look, I know you've been pissed off and I know you've had good reason to be ...'

'*Bloody* good reason,' Thorne said. 'I'm feeling much better than I was, you know that. I'm ... up for it.'

'Right. But until the decision gets taken to give you a more active role on the team here, I thought you might appreciate the chance to get yourself "out of the way". And it wouldn't just be you, either. Holland's been assigned to this as well ...'

Thorne stared out of the window, across the grounds of the Peel Centre towards Hendon and the grey ribbon of the North Circular beyond. He'd seen prettier views, but not for some time.

'Sixteen?'

'His name's Luke Mullen.'

'So the kid was taken ... Friday, right? What's been happening for the last three days?'

'You'll be fully briefed at the Yard.' Brigstocke glanced down at a sheet of paper on the desktop. 'Your contact on the Kidnap Unit is DI Porter. Louise Porter.'

Thorne knew that Brigstocke was on his side; that he was caught between a loyalty to his team and a responsibility to the brass above him. These days, anyone of his rank was one part copper to nine parts politician. Many at Thorne's own level worked in much the same way, and Thorne would fight tooth and nail to avoid going down the same dreary route ...

'Tom?'

Brigstocke had certainly said the right things. The boy's age in itself was enough to spark Thorne's interest. The victims of those who preyed on children for sexual gratification were usually far younger. It wasn't that older children were not targeted, of course, but such abuse was often institutionalised or, most tragically of all, took place within the home itself. For a sixteen-year-old to be taken off the street was unusual.

'Trevor Jesmond getting involved means there's pressure to get a result,' Thorne said. If a shrug and a half smile could be signs of enthusiasm, then he looked mustard-keen. 'I reckon I could do with a bit of pressure at the minute.'

'You haven't heard all of it yet.'

'I'm listening.'

So Brigstocke enlightened him, and when it was

finished and Thorne got up to leave, he looked out of the window one last time. The buildings sat opposite, brown and black and dirty-white; office blocks and warehouses, with pools of dark water gathered on their flat roofs. Thorne thought they looked like the teeth in an old man's mouth.

Before the car had reached the gates on its way out of the car park, Thorne had slotted a Bobby Bare CD into the player, taken one look at Holland's face and swiftly ejected it again. 'I should make sure there's always a Simply Red album in the car,' Thorne said. 'So as not to offend your sensibilities.'

'I don't like Simply Red.'

'Whoever.'

Holland gestured towards the CD panel on the dash. 'I don't mind *some* of your stuff. It's just all that twangy guitar shit . . . '

Thorne turned the car on to Aerodrome Road and accelerated towards Colindale tube. Once they hit the A5 it would be a straight run through Cricklewood, Kilburn and south into town.

Having criticised Thorne's choice of music, Holland proceeded to score two out of two by turning his sarcastic attentions to the car itself. The yellow BMW – a 1971 three-litre CS – gave Thorne a good deal of pride and pleasure, but to DS Dave Holland it was little more than the starting point for an endless series of 'old banger' jokes.

For once, though, Thorne did not rise to the bait. There

17

was little anyone could have done to make his mood much worse. 'The boy's old man is an ex-copper,' he said. He jabbed at the horn as a scooter swerved in front of him, spoke as if he were describing something extremely distasteful. '*Ex-Detective Chief Superintendent* Anthony Mullen.'

Holland's dirty-blond hair was longer than it had been for a while. He pushed it back from his forehead. 'So?'

'So, it's a bloody secret-handshake job, isn't it? He's calling in favours from his old mates. Next thing you know, we're getting shunted across to another unit.'

'It's not like there was anything better to do, though, is it?' Holland said.

The look from Thorne was momentary, but it made its point firmly enough.

'For *either* of us, I mean. Not a lot of bodies on the books at the moment.'

'Right. *At the moment.* You never know when something major's going to come in though.'

'Sounds almost like you're hoping.'

'Sorry?'

'Like you don't want to miss out ...'

Thorne said nothing. His eyes drifted to the wing mirror, stayed there as he flicked up the indicator and waited to pull out.

Neither spoke again for several minutes. Rain had begun to streak the windows, through which Kilburn was giving way to the rather more gentrified environment of Maida Vale.

'Did you get any more from the DCI?' Holland asked.

Thorne shook his head. 'He knows as much as we do. We find out the rest when we get there.'

'You had much to do with SO7 before?'

Like many officers, Holland had not yet got used to the fact that SO units had officially been renamed SCD units, now that they were part of what had become known as the Specialist Crime Directorate. Most people still used the old abbreviations, knowing full well that the brass would change the name again soon enough, next time they were short of something to do. SO7 was the Specialist Operations department whose component command units dealt with everything from contract killings to serious drug crime. Aside from the Kidnap Unit, these OCUs included the Flying Squad, the Hostage and Extortion Team, and the Projects Team, with whom Thorne had worked on the joint gangland operation that had ended so badly the previous year.

'Not the Kidnap Unit, mercifully. They're high-flyers; they don't like to mingle with the likes of us. They like to stay a bit *mysterious*.'

'Well, I suppose there has to be an element of secrecy, bearing in mind what they do. They have to be a bit more discreet than the rest of us.'

Thorne looked unconvinced. 'They fancy themselves.' He leaned across and turned on the radio, tuned it in to Talk Sport.

'So this bloke Mullen knows Jesmond, does he?'

'Known him for years.'

19

'Same sort of age, then?'

'I think Mullen's a few years older,' Thorne said. 'They worked together on an old AMIP unit south of the river somewhere. The DCI reckons Mullen was the one responsible for bringing Jesmond on. Pulled our Trevor up through the ranks.'

'Right ...'

'Remind me to punch the fucker, would you?'

Holland smiled, but looked uncomfortable.

'What?'

'Someone's kidnapped his son ...' Holland said.

On the final stretch of the Edgware Road, approaching Marble Arch, the traffic began to snarl up. Thorne grew increasingly frustrated, thinking that if the congestion charge had made a difference, it was only to people's wallets. On the radio, they were talking about the game Spurs were due to play the following evening. The studio expert said they were favourites to take three points off Fulham, after three wins on the bounce.

'That's the kiss of bloody death,' Thorne said.

Holland was clearly still thinking about what had been said a few minutes earlier. 'I think you just see these things differently,' he said. 'Once you've got kids, you know?'

Thorne grunted.

'If something happens to somebody else's—'

'You think I was being insensitive?' Thorne asked. 'What I said.'

'Just a bit.'

'If I was *really* being insensitive, I'd say it was divine

20

retribution.' He glanced across and raised an eyebrow. This time, the smile he received in return was genuine, but it still seemed to sit less easily on Holland's face than Thorne might once have expected.

Holland had never been quite as fresh-faced, as green and keen, as Thorne remembered; but when he'd been drafted on to Thorne's team six years before as a twenty-five-year-old DC, there had certainly been a little more enthusiasm. And there had been belief. Of course, he and his girlfriend had been through domestic upheavals since then: there'd been the affair with a fellow officer who'd later been murdered on duty; then the birth of his daughter, who would be two years old later in the year.

And there'd been a good many bodies.

An ever-expanding gallery of those you only ever got to know once their lives had been taken from them. People whose darkest intimacies might be revealed to you, but whose voices you would never hear, whose thoughts you could never be privy to. An exhibition of the dead, running alongside another of the murderous living. And of those left behind; the pickers-up of lives.

Thorne and Holland, and others who came into contact with such things, were not *defined* by violence and grief. They did not walk and wake with it, but neither were they immune. It changed everything, eventually.

The belief became blunted . . .

'How's everything at home, Dave?'

For a second or two, Holland looked surprised, then pleased, before he closed up, just a little. 'It's good.'

'Chloe must be getting big.'

Holland nodded, relaxing. 'She's changing every five minutes. Discovering stuff, you know? Doing something different every time I get home. She's really into music at the moment, singing along with whatever's on.'

'Nothing with twangy guitars, though.'

'I keep thinking I'm missing it all. Doing this . . . '

Thorne guessed there was little point in asking about Holland's girlfriend. Sophie was not exactly Thorne's greatest fan. He knew very well that his name was far more likely to be shouted than spoken in the small flat Holland and Sophie shared in Elephant & Castle; that he might well have caused a fair number of the arguments in the first place.

The BMW finally hit thirty again on Park Lane. From here, they would continue down to Victoria, then cut across to St James's and the Yard.

Holland turned to Thorne as they slowed at Hyde Park Corner. 'Oh, by the way, Sophie told me to say "hello",' he said.

Thorne nodded, and nosed the car into the stream of traffic that was rushing around the roundabout.

This was not his favourite place.

It was here that he'd spent a few hideous weeks the year before; perhaps the most miserable he'd ever endured. Back then, when he'd been taken off the team, and given what was euphemistically called 'gardening leave', Thorne had known very well that he wasn't being himself, that he hadn't been coping since the death of his father. But hearing it from the likes of Trevor Jesmond had been something else; being told he was 'dead wood' and casually wafted away like a bad smell. It was the undercover job that had thankfully provided a means of escape, and the subsequent weeks spent sleeping on the streets had been infinitely preferable to those he'd spent stewing in a windowless cupboard at New Scotland Yard.

As they walked towards the entrance, Thorne scowled at a group of tourists taking photographs of each other in front of the famous revolving sign.

'What did you *do* when you were here?' Holland asked.

Thorne took out his warrant card and showed it to one of the officers on duty at the door. 'I tried to work out how many bottles would constitute a fatal dose of Tippex ...'

Kidnapping and Specialist Investigations was one of a number of SO units based in Central 3000, a huge, open-plan office that took up half of the fifth floor. Each unit's area was colour-coded, its territory marked out by a rectangular flag suspended from the low ceiling: the Tactical Firearms Unit was black; the Surveillance Unit was green; the Kidnap Unit was red. Elsewhere, other colours indicated the presence of the Technical Support and Intelligence units, either of which could make use of an enormous bank of TV monitors, each one able to tap into any CCTV camera in the metropolitan area or broadcast live pictures directly from any Met helicopter.

Thorne and Holland took it all in. 'And we were

wondering why we couldn't afford a new kettle at our place,' Holland said.

A short, dark-haired woman rose from a desk in the red area and introduced herself as DI Louise Porter. Holland ran the kettle line past her during the minute or two of small talk. He looked pleased that she seemed to find it funny. Thorne was impressed with the effort she put in to pretending.

Porter quickly ran through the set-up of the team, one of three on the unit. It was a more or less standard structure. She was one of two DIs heading things up, with a dozen or so other officers, all working to a detective chief inspector. 'DCI Hignett told me to apologise for not being here to meet you himself,' Porter said, 'but he'll catch up with you later. And it's *three* DIs now, of course.' She nodded towards Thorne. 'Thanks for mucking in.'

'No problem,' Thorne said.

'Not that you had any choice though, right?'

'None at all.'

'Sorry about that, but we can always do with the help.' She glanced down. 'Are you OK?'

Thorne stopped moving from foot to foot, realised that he was grimacing. 'Dodgy back,' he said. 'Must have twisted something.' The truth was that he'd been suffering badly for some time, the pain down his left leg far worse after any period spent sitting in a car or, God forbid, at a desk. At first he'd put it down to something muscular – a hangover from the nights spent sleeping outdoors, perhaps – but now he suspected that there was a more deep-seated problem. It would sort itself out, but in the meantime he was getting through a lot of painkillers.

Porter introduced Thorne and Holland to those members of the team who were around. Most of them seemed friendly enough. They all looked busy.

'Obviously a lot of the lads are out and about,' Porter said. 'Chasing up what we laughably call "leads".'

Holland leaned back against an empty desk. 'At least you've got some.'

'Just the one, really. A couple of witnesses saw Luke Mullen get into a car on the afternoon he disappeared.'

'Number plate?' Thorne asked.

'Bits of it. Blue or black. And it *might* be a Passat. This is from the other kids at the school, all just finished for the day, too busy talking about music or skateboards or whatever the hell they do.'

Holland grinned. 'Not got any yourself, then?'

'"*Get* into a car",' Thorne said. 'So it didn't look like he was being forced?'

'He got into the car with a young woman. Attractive. I think the other boys were too busy eyeing her up to pay much attention to the car.'

'Maybe Luke had a new girlfriend,' Holland suggested.

'That's what some of the boys think, certainly. They'd seen him with her before.'

'So, isn't it possible?' Thorne asked. 'He's a sixteen-year-old boy. Maybe he's just buggered off to a hotel somewhere with a glamorous older woman.'

'It's possible.' Porter began to gather a few things from

25

her desk, then grabbed a handbag from the back of a chair. 'But this was last Friday. Why hasn't he been in touch?'

'He's probably got better things to do.'

Porter cocked her head, acknowledging a theory that she had clearly dismissed. 'Who goes away for a dirty weekend with nothing but a school blazer and a sweaty games kit?' She let it sink in, then walked past Thorne and Holland towards the door, leaving them in little doubt that they were expected to follow.

Holland waited until she was out of earshot. 'Well, she doesn't seem to fancy herself *too* much . . .'

Outside, in the lobby, another member of the team stepped out of the lift. Porter introduced the woman to Thorne and Holland before the three of them took her place. Porter exchanged a few quick words with her colleague, then punched a button and glanced round at Thorne as the doors closed. 'She's one of two family liaison officers who've been at the house on rotation since we were brought in. You'll meet the other one when we get there.'

'Right.'

Porter's eyes shifted to the display of illuminated numbers above the doors. Thorne wondered if she was always this anxious; in this much of a hurry.

'I want to get a good couple of hours with the Mullens today if I can. These first few conversations with the family are the important ones, obviously.'

It took a second or two to sink in. '"*First few*"?' Thorne said.

Porter turned to look at him.

'I'm not clear about—'

'We only got brought into this yesterday afternoon,' she said. 'The kidnap wasn't reported straight away.'

Thorne caught a look from Holland, who was obviously every bit as confused as he was. 'Was there some kind of threat?' he asked. 'Were the family told not to involve the police?'

'Whoever took Luke has made no contact with the family whatsoever.'

The lift reached the ground floor and the doors opened, but Thorne made no move to go anywhere.

'At the moment, your guess is as good as mine,' Porter said.

'And what would that be?'

'What's the point in guessing? The simple fact is that Luke Mullen was kidnapped on Friday afternoon, but for reasons best known to themselves, his parents decided to wait a couple of days before telling anybody.'

# CONRAD

Say you're a dwarf, OK?

It doesn't mean that you only fancy other dwarves, does it? That you can't be excited about a fumble with someone you might have to stand on a chair to have a proper snog with? Actually, it's *normal* to want to be with someone different, isn't it? Just to see what it would be like.

He knew damn well that he was *meant* to be with a woman who worked on the till in Asda and wore fake Burberry and knock-off perfume, so when Amanda had come sniffing round, deliberately dropping her aitches and knocking back the alcopops like there was no tomorrow, he'd been in there like a rat up a drainpipe. Why wouldn't he? He'd always fantasised about a bit of posh, and even though he knew deep down she was only slumming it, everything had seemed to be working out very nicely.

Recently, though, he'd started to feel like something was

missing, and it wasn't just the sex falling off a bit, which it always did anyway a few months in. It was more than that. He'd started to feel like everything was a bit unreal. She could call herself Mandy all she liked, and dress down, but she would always be an 'Amanda' and he would never really be in her league when it came to breeding or brains. Not that he was stupid; far from it. He knew what was what, pretty much. But when it came to doing stuff, to making a living and all the rest of it, he tended to go where other people took him. That was fine, though, because he knew his limitations. Which made him clever enough, he reckoned.

Now, though, he'd started to think about other women. Nobody specific; just other types of woman. *His* types. He'd started to drift off, even in the middle of bloody important stuff like what to do with the kid and what have you, and imagine himself with women who had dirty bra straps and read crappy magazines. He thought about women who made a bit more noise in bed and treated him properly and didn't tell him where to put his fingers. It made him feel guilty at first, but lately he'd been telling himself that she probably felt exactly the same way. She probably dreamed about rugger-buggers called Giles or Nigel when they were doing it and maybe his accent was starting to put her teeth on edge as much as hers was doing to his ...

Maybe it was all down to this business with the kid. It had seemed like easy money at the time and it hadn't taken long to agree to it, but, Christ, it was a damn sight more

29

stressful than knocking over some old duffer or talking your way into a pensioner's flat. Both of them were acting a bit funny, and maybe, when this was all over and they had some real cash to play with, he'd start to feel more like himself again. Maybe they could get away somewhere.

What was he thinking? It would make bloody good *sense* to get away somewhere. And maybe then he'd stop thinking about those other girls . . .

When Amanda came into the room five minutes later, he thought for one horrible minute that she could see what he'd been thinking. That it was as obvious as the semi in his lap that he'd swiftly covered up with a *Daily Star*. But everything was cool. She asked him if he was OK and kissed him on the top of his head when he asked her the same thing. She walked over and helped herself to one of his fags, then had a quick look to see if there was anything decent on the box.

Then she sat on the edge of the bed and began to talk about what they were going to do with the boy.

# TWO

'He's not exactly a baby, is he?' Holland leaned forward, dropped a hand on to each of the front headrests. 'They were probably just waiting for him to come waltzing back home again.'

'That's more or less how they explained it.'

'He might have done this sort of thing before.'

'No, I don't think so,' Porter said. She took the unmarked Saab Turbo past a silver 4×4, glared hard at the driver, who was talking animatedly into her mobile phone. 'But like I said, we haven't spoken to the parents that much yet. Hopefully we'll find out a bit more over the next couple of hours.'

'Presuming we get there in one piece.' Thorne was sitting a little stiffly in the passenger seat, unnerved to discover that Porter was just as impatient behind the wheel as she had been back in the office. Her frequent glances into the rear-view mirror had more to do with the purpose of their journey than it did with road safety.

'Obviously, any kind of threat and we wouldn't be interviewing the family at home. We'd stay well clear; find some way of talking to them on neutral territory.'

'That can't always be easy,' Holland said.

'It isn't, but if you *have* to visit the home address, there are ways and means. You just need to be a bit inventive.'

'What, like disguises and stuff?'

Thorne turned, and pulled a face at Holland. '*Disguises?* How old are you, six?'

'Right,' Porter said. 'We've got a big dressing-up box back at the office. Gas Board uniforms and postmen's outfits.' She took a long look at the rear-view. 'There's no reason to believe that visiting the Mullens at home places Luke in any kind of extra danger, but there are procedures you follow whatever the circumstances. You make sure the lid stays on. You make sure there's no uniformed involvement.' Another check in the mirror. 'And you keep your bloody eyes open.'

The crash course in kidnap investigation techniques had lasted from the car park at the Yard as far as Arkley – a leafy Hertfordshire suburb a dozen or so miles north of the centre of London. It had become clear that the unit's protocols were infinitely flexible and that everything happened much faster than elsewhere. Though kidnapping was little different from murder – in that the unit would never have any such thing as a 'typical' case – Thorne was surprised at the enormous range of crimes that fell within its remit.

32

Though the majority of kidnaps were subject to a press blackout and so never became public knowledge, there could be no doubt that it was a growth industry.

'And a relatively safe one for the kidnappers,' Porter said. She told them that over half of all her cases involved hardcore foreign drug gangs, distributors and smugglers; that fewer than one in five ever resulted in a conviction. 'Most of the victims never testify, the ungrateful fuckers. We rescued an old guy last year who'd been tied up in a loft and tortured for a couple of weeks. They cut both the poor bastard's ears off and he still wouldn't give evidence in case others in the gang came after him.'

'You can understand him being scared,' Holland said. 'He wouldn't hear them coming.'

Thorne sighed, shifted in his seat. 'Sounds like you're all getting plenty of overtime,' he said.

Porter grunted her agreement. 'Heavy-duty dealers are getting lifted every other week. Yardies, Russians, Albanians, whatever. It's a quick way of scoring cash or merchandise – putting the shits up a rival. We're not short of jobs, but maybe the wheels don't turn quite so quickly when it comes to some of our less than law-abiding kidnap victims.'

Thorne knew very well what she meant. He'd worked on a case the year before; the case during which his father had died. The squad, and Thorne in particular, had found themselves caught in the middle of a vicious gang war. He explained to Porter that one side had been involved in a people-smuggling racket; that though a fair number of gang members had died, few could bring themselves to care a great deal, or argue that the city wasn't a better place without them.

'That stuff's down to us, too,' Porter said. 'If people are brought here and then used as slave labour, they've basically become hostages. They're held against their will and usually there's an implied threat to their families back at home.' She slowed the car to a stop a hundred yards from a driveway. 'It's also the main reason why people are queuing up to work on the unit,' she continued. 'So far this year I've been to China, Turkey, the Ukraine. It's all business class, *and* we get the air miles.'

Holland sucked his teeth. 'I went to Aberdeen to interview a rapist once . . . '

Porter took a good look at a Jag that drove past, waited a minute or two after it had disappeared around a corner, before moving the Saab slowly forward and turning it on to the driveway.

'This kind of case isn't common, though, is it?' Thorne asked. 'Snatching civilians?'

She shook her head. 'You can get the family of a bank employee being held until the safe's opened, but even that's pretty rare. You might get one like this in Spain and Italy every so often, but it's like rocking-horse shit here. Thank God.'

'So why no ransom with Luke Mullen?'

'I've no idea.'

'I still don't see why it has to be a kidnap.'

'It doesn't. There are other possibilities.'

34

'Like Luke going off voluntarily with the woman in the blue car?'

'Or just running away,' Porter said. 'But parents never like to admit that their precious kid might do that.'

Holland released his seatbelt. 'Like no parent ever thinks their kids are stupid, or ugly.'

'You've got kids?'

'I've got a little girl.' Holland grinned. 'She's gorgeous and *very* bright.'

'Maybe this isn't about money at all,' Thorne said.

Porter appeared to think about it as she killed the engine. 'It's certainly . . . unusual.'

'Who knows . . .' – Thorne opened the door and swung his legs out, let out a groan of pain as he lifted himself upright – 'if there *had* been a ransom demand, maybe the parents might have got on the phone a bit quicker.'

Holland got out and walked towards him, looking up at the detached, mock-Tudor house where Tony Mullen and his wife lived. 'It's a big place,' he said.

Porter locked the car and the three of them began moving together towards the front door. 'It's probably feeling that little bit bigger just at the moment,' she said.

A few minutes earlier, Thorne had seen the relief flood into Tony Mullen's face, but it had been purely temporary. Already, sitting across from Thorne in an uncomfortable-looking armchair, a damp pallor of desperation was smearing itself back across his features; the look of a man bracing himself.

He'd been at the front door before they were, staring out at the three of them as if he were urgently trying to read something in how they walked; to work out what they had come to tell him by the way they approached the house. Porter had shaken her head. A small movement, but it had been enough.

Mullen had let out a long breath and closed his eyes for a second or two. There was something approaching a smile when he opened them again, when he moved the hand that had been flat and white against the door frame and held it out, palm skyward, towards them.

'Your guts just go into your boots,' he said. 'Whenever the phone goes or the bloody doorbell rings, especially if it's you lot. It's like feeling the punch coming. You know?'

The introductions were made there on the doorstep.

'Trevor Jesmond said he'd sort out a few extra pairs of hands,' Mullen said. He touched Thorne's arm. 'Make sure you say "thanks" to him, will you?'

Thorne wondered if Jesmond had told Mullen what he really thought about the man those extra hands belonged to. If he had, Thorne guessed it was probably a less than honest assessment. If the request for help had come directly from Mullen himself, Jesmond would hardly want his old friend thinking he was palming him off with damaged goods. Thorne decided it was a subject best left alone; that he should keep things light for as long as it was appropriate.

He looked at Mullen. The man had less grey in his hair than Thorne himself did, and, though the circumstances had clearly taken their toll, the rest of him looked in pretty good shape, too. 'Well, either you're a lot older than you look or you retired early,' he said.

Mullen seemed taken aback for a second, but his tone was friendly enough as he led the three of them into a gloomy hallway. 'Can't you be both?'

'It's certainly what I'm aiming for,' Porter said, hanging up her coat.

'You're right, though. I did bow out early,' Mullen said. He looked Thorne up and down. 'What are you? Forty-seven, forty-eight?'

Thorne tried not to react. 'I'm forty-five in a few months.'

'Right, well, I'll be fifty this year, and I know I'd look a damn sight older than that if I'd stayed in the job. You know what it's like. I was starting to forget what Maggie and the kids looked like.'

Thorne nodded. There hadn't been anyone to forget for a fair few years, but he understood what Mullen meant well enough.

'I'd managed to squirrel a bit away, and it seemed as good a time as any. I fancied a move and Maggie was pretty keen for me to get out. She even got used to having me under her feet after a while.'

On cue, Maggie Mullen came down the stairs, with every one of the fifty-odd years Thorne guessed were behind her, showing on her face. The lines had become cracks. The freshly applied make-up had done precious little for eyes that were puffy and red-rimmed. 'I was catching up on some sleep,' she said.

It was Holland who prevented the pause becoming a silence. He nodded towards Mullen, picking up the thread of the previous exchange. 'It's what politicians always say, isn't it?'

Mullen looked at him. 'Sorry?'

'Whenever they leave the job, for whatever reason, they say they want to spend more time with their family.'

They stood around a little awkwardly, almost as though they were not the parents of a kidnapped child and those entrusted with finding him; as though they were waiting politely for someone to announce that dinner was served.

Now, in the living room, something of that odd formality lingered, not helped by the seating arrangements. It was a large room and the sofas and chairs had been positioned around a rectangular, Chinese-style rug. Thorne and Porter sat on a cream leather sofa with Mullen and his wife fifteen or more feet away on uncomfortable-looking armchairs, which were themselves a fair distance from each other. There was music playing somewhere upstairs, and noise too from the kitchen, where Holland and DC Kenny Parsons – the on-duty family liaison officer – had gone to make coffee.

Thorne looked out of the French windows at the garden. It was enormous compared with the postage-stamp-sized plots that graced most London properties. He turned back to Mrs Mullen. 'I can see why you moved here. I wouldn't fancy mowing it, mind you.'

It was Tony Mullen that responded. 'This place was a

38

compromise, really. I was all for upping sticks completely and getting out into the country, but Maggie didn't really want to leave London. It *feels* like you're in the country here, but you've got High Barnet tube a few minutes away, or you're twenty minutes from King's Cross on the overground.'

Thorne made the right noises, thinking: This is a world away from King's Cross.

'And the schools,' Maggie Mullen said. 'We moved because of the schools.'

Then, with that one meaningful word, the terrible reason for them all being there was finally in the room with them, and the small talk was well and truly done with.

Tony Mullen slapped his palms against his legs, the noise causing his wife to start slightly. 'We know it's not bad news, thank God, but I presume that there isn't any good news, either.'

Porter edged forward on the sofa. 'We're doing everything we can, but—'

'Don't.' Mullen raised a hand. 'I'm really not interested in the pat speeches. I know the game, remember. So let's not waste anyone's time, all right, Louise?'

Thorne could see that Porter was more than a little irked at the familiarity, but he thought she was probably not the type to react. Not the first time, anyway. Instead, she let her eyes drift across to Mullen's wife and spoke softly to her. 'It wasn't a speech.'

'I'm the new boy,' Thorne said, 'so you'll have to forgive

me if we go over some old ground, but I was wondering about the delay.'

Mullen stared right back at him. It was a grudging invitation for Thorne to elaborate.

'Luke went missing on Friday after school, but the first call to the police was made at a little after nine yesterday morning. Why the wait?'

'We've already explained all this,' Mullen said. The edge to his voice revealed traces of a Midlands accent. Thorne remembered Porter telling him that Mullen was originally from Wolverhampton. 'We just thought Luke was out and about somewhere.'

'Only on Friday evening, surely?'

'He could have gone to a club, then stayed over at a mate's or something. There was usually a certain amount of leeway on a Friday night.'

'It was me.' Maggie Mullen cleared her throat. 'I was the one who thought there was nothing to worry about. I was the one who persuaded Tony that we should just wait for Luke to come home.'

'Why didn't you say this yesterday?' Porter asked.

'Is it really important?' she said.

'I'm sure it isn't, but—'

'We waited. That's all that matters. We waited when we shouldn't have and I'll have to live with that.'

'There was an argument,' Mullen said.

Thorne's eyes stayed on Maggie Mullen. He watched her drop her head and stare at her feet.

Mullen sat up straight in his chair and continued. 'Luke

and I had a stupid row that morning. There was a lot of shouting and swearing, the usual kind of stuff.'

'What did you argue about?' Thorne asked.

'School,' Mullen said. 'I think maybe we were putting him under a bit of pressure. *I* was putting him under pressure.'

'Luke and his dad usually get on so well.' Maggie Mullen looked at Porter, spoke as though her husband were no longer in the room. '*Really* well. It's not normal for them to argue like that.'

Porter smiled. 'The fights I used to have with my mum and dad ...'

'Sometimes I think Luke's closer to his dad than he is to me, you know?'

'Don't be silly,' Mullen said.

'I get jealous sometimes, if I'm honest.'

'Come on, love ...'

Maggie Mullen was staring straight ahead.

Thorne followed her gaze to the elaborate fireplace; to the flame-effect gas fire and the half-life-sized ceramic cheetah sitting to one side of it. 'Was this row really that serious?' he asked. 'Serious enough for Luke to leave without a word?'

'No way.' Mullen was categorical. Said it again to ensure that Thorne and Porter got the message.

'Mrs Mullen?'

The drum and bass coming through the ceiling seemed louder for a few seconds. Still staring towards the fireplace, Maggie Mullen shook her head.

'Whether it's got anything to do with this argument or

41

not, Luke's disappearance may still have a simple explanation.' Porter waited until all faces were turned to her before carrying on. 'We've at least got to accept that possibility.'

Maggie Mullen stood up and smoothed down the back of her skirt. 'I'm happy to accept it, love. I'm *praying* for it.' She walked across to the fireplace, reached for a packet of Silk Cut on the mantelpiece.

'Obviously, we've checked out all his friends,' Porter said. 'But in the absence of any sort of communication from anyone who might be holding Luke, there has to be a possibility that he's gone away with someone.'

'You mean this woman?' Mullen said.

'He'd been spotted with "this woman" on other occasions.' Thorne stood up too and walked behind the sofa, the relief from the pain in his leg almost instantaneous. 'If Luke's seeing an older woman, he might have thought better about telling you.'

The boy's mother was clearly not convinced. 'I can't see it.' She fumbled for a cigarette. 'I can't imagine Luke with a girl his own age, let alone someone older. He isn't confident with girls. He's a bit awkward.'

'Come on, Maggie,' Mullen said. 'He could have been into all sorts of things. I don't mean drugs or anything like that, but kids have secrets, don't they?'

'Your husband's got a point,' Thorne said. 'How well does any parent know an adolescent?'

Maggie Mullen lit her cigarette, took in the first lungful like it was oxygen. 'I've been asking myself that quite a lot,' she said. 'Ever since I started to wonder if I was ever going to see my son again.'

In the kitchen, DC Kenny Parsons opened another cupboard and peered inside. 'Maybe we should just leave it.'

Holland was sitting at the table, idly turning the pages of a *Daily Express*. 'Don't be nervous, mate. As family liaison officer, you definitely get biscuit privileges.'

'*Result*. Here you go.' Parsons produced an unopened packet and placed it on a tray next to the mugs. Coffee had already been spooned into each. The kettle had boiled minutes ago, but been ignored.

'So how d'you reckon things are between them?' Holland asked, nodding towards the living room. 'Normally, I mean.'

Parsons flicked the kettle on again and carried the tray to the table. He was in his mid-thirties, Holland guessed, a dark-skinned black man with hair cut almost to the scalp, and the trick of looking untidy in a perfectly presentable suit. 'You know they split up for a while a few years back?'

Holland nodded; Porter had told them as much. The team were looking at the family, of course, but not as closely as they might have, had Luke been a bit younger; or if it had been more obviously an abduction rather than a kidnap. The family were certainly not under any suspicion, not this early on at any rate, but a few discreet enquiries had been made all the same.

'She was the one that walked out, right?' Holland asked.

'Yeah, but she wasn't gone for very long.'

'Old man playing away from home, d'you reckon?'

'Usually the way, isn't it?'

'So what about now?'

Parsons considered it. 'Things are pretty good, I think.'

Holland had discovered quickly that his new colleague was not short of opinions. He had plenty to say about those on his own team, and was far more relaxed when it came to talking about the Mullen family than he was about helping himself to their digestives.

Holland was happy enough to get another perspective on the case.

'Bear in mind that even splitting the shifts, we're not here twenty-four hours a day,' Parsons said. 'Mullen was fairly adamant early on that he didn't want anyone stopping overnight. Based on what I *have* seen, though, I reckon he rules the roost, give or take. He's used to people doing what he tells them to do, for obvious reasons.'

'And *do* they do what he tells them? The wife doesn't come across as any sort of doormat.'

'Oh no, she's not. Definitely.'

'She seems nice enough,' Holland said. 'I mean, she's obviously a bit shell-shocked just now ...'

'She's tougher than she looks, if you ask me.' Parsons moved the mugs around on the tray, lining them up, making room for milk and sugar. 'Ex-teacher, right?' He held up his hands, as if the point were self-evident.

'Right.'

'So I reckon she can give as good as she gets. I bet there are times she tells him *exactly* what to do.' He waited in vain for a reaction to the vaguely lewd suggestion before continuing. 'I think the family's learned how to look like they do what the old man tells them, know what I mean? They're good at making him feel like he's in charge. Probably no different to when he was on the Job, right?'

Notwithstanding Parsons' obvious taste for gossip and speculation, Holland could see the sense in what he was saying. His own father had been a police officer. In the few short years between retirement and an early death, his relationship with Holland's mother had fallen into exactly the pattern that Parsons was talking about.

'What about the kid?'

'You seen his room?'

'Not yet.'

'It's a lot different to my lad's, I can tell you that. I don't think we're talking about your average sixteen-year-old.'

'The average sixteen-year-old doesn't get kidnapped,' Holland said.

'It's all a touch too neat and tidy.' Parsons made a face, as if the very notion were somehow distasteful. 'And I wouldn't put a lot of money on finding any wank-mags under the bed.' He stopped as he saw Holland's expression change, and turned to see the girl standing in the doorway. 'Juliet ...'

Holland had no way of knowing how long Juliet Mullen had been standing outside the door, how much of their conversation she'd overheard. He couldn't tell if her manner and the tone of her voice were because she was angry with them or upset about what had happened to her brother, or simply down to the fact that she was an average fourteen-year-old.

The girl half turned to go, then nodded towards the tray and spoke casually, as if she were insulting them in code: 'I'll have tea. Milk and two.'

'What time does your post come?' Thorne asked.

'Excuse me?'

'What time in the morning? Mine's all over the bloody place. It's any time before lunchtime, really, and stuff gets lost right, left and centre.'

If Tony Mullen knew where Thorne was going, he showed no sign of it. 'Between eight and nine, usually. I don't see—'

'Your wife said that she stopped you from phoning the police straight away.'

'She didn't *stop* me . . .'

'That she didn't think there was anything to worry about.'

'I wouldn't have called immediately anyway. There was no reason to.'

Thorne strolled around the sofa, walked to the opposite side of the fireplace to where Maggie Mullen was crushing her cigarette butt into an ashtray. 'Sorry, I may have got the wrong end of the stick, but your wife certainly implied that you were worried; or at least concerned. That's why I was asking about what time your post arrived.' Thorne caught Porter's eye; saw that she understood. 'I think you were expecting a ransom demand. I think you presumed that someone had snatched Luke and that you'd hear from them yesterday morning. I think you were probably waiting to find out exactly what they wanted and that you were planning to handle it yourself. When you didn't get anything in the post, that's when you *really* started to worry, when you started to wonder what might have happened. That's when you called us.'

Maggie Mullen walked across the room and sat down on the arm of her husband's chair. Her hand moved very briefly to his, then back into her lap. 'Tony tends to look on the blacker side of things a lot of the time.'

'The Job does that to most of us,' Porter said.

'Look, it's understandable.' Thorne was still trying to connect with Tony Mullen. 'I'm sure I would have thought the same thing.'

'I knew he'd been kidnapped before I went to bed on Friday night,' Mullen said. He looked up at Thorne, something like relief on his face. 'I was brushing my teeth and Maggie was sorting the dog out downstairs, and I knew someone had taken him. Was holding him. Luke wasn't the type to just go off, certainly not without letting us know where he was.'

'Like I said, it's understandable. In light of your career, you've got every reason to believe there might be people who would want to hurt you. Or hurt those close to you.'

Mullen said something, but Thorne couldn't make it out.

He couldn't hear much for a second or two.

47

He was straining to make out the voice of his father above the roar and hot spit of long-dead flames ...

'We'll need a list,' he said, finally. 'Anyone who might bear a grudge. Anyone who issued threats.'

Mullen nodded. 'I've been trying to work on one over the weekend.' His tone and the look he gave his wife were guilty, confessional, as though the fact that he'd been thinking about such things at all meant he'd been assuming the worst. 'But I don't think it'll be much help. Either my memory's going or I didn't make as many enemies as I thought.'

'Well, that makes our job easier,' Porter said.

'Right. Good.' Thorne was trying to sound equally positive, but he must have looked every bit as dubious as he felt.

Mullen's expression hardened. 'Would you remember every one?'

Thorne tried to stay composed and encouraging, tried to put the edge in Mullen's voice down to stress, to blame the aggression on guilt and panic. 'Probably not.'

'How many people have you seriously pissed off, Detective Inspector Thorne? You needn't include the ones you were supposed to be working with.'

Thorne thought then that perhaps Jesmond had been a little more candid in his description of him after all. Or perhaps Tony Mullen was just a good judge of character. He said nothing; just considered what Mullen had told him about putting a list together. Thorne himself would have much less trouble, and doubted that he was unique.

When it came to those who might have posed a serious threat to him, or to anyone he cared about, Thorne had no problem recalling every last one of them.

Holland and Parsons appeared in the doorway at the same moment that the phone rang. Everyone, Thorne included, jumped slightly, and Maggie Mullen was first to her feet.

'It's important to try and stay calm ...'

'Love ...'

If she heard what either Porter or her husband said, Maggie Mullen chose to ignore it. Her eyes were fixed only on the phone as she crossed to where it sat on a low table near the window.

A trace/intercept had, of course, been set up on the Mullens' home number as soon as the Kidnap Unit had been scrambled, with all incoming calls monitored by Technical Support back at the Yard. If, as was most likely, the all-important call were to come from an unregistered mobile, the Telephone Unit would immediately begin working on cell-site location, moving from place to place where required in a vehicle equipped with the necessary, state-of-the-art gadgetry.

When she reached the phone, Mrs Mullen held out a hand; she turned and looked first at her husband, then across at Porter and Thorne.

Porter nodded.

Mrs Mullen took a deep breath and picked up the phone. She spoke the number quickly, waited, then shook her head. Her eyes closed and she turned away, muttering into the mouthpiece, fingers dragging through her long brown hair for the few seconds before she hung up.

'Mags?'

She walked slowly towards her husband's chair, her voice splintering as she spoke, and Thorne could see relief and disappointment, inseparable, fighting it out in the fall of her face, and of her shoulders. He saw how well-matched, how brutal, the two feelings could be.

'Hannah. One of Juliet's friends.'

'It's OK, love.' Mullen was on his feet, moving to meet her.

'Obviously we told everyone we could not to call,' she said. 'We wanted to make sure the line stayed clear, you know, in case Luke got in touch. In case anyone who *had* him tried to contact us. We tried to think of everyone, but there are a few people we must have forgotten ...'

Then Mullen's arms were around her and pulling her close. Her own hung at her sides, as though she suddenly lacked the strength to lift them. Her head bowed as she sobbed hard into his neck.

Thorne beckoned Holland and Parsons into the room with the coffee tray, then glanced at Porter, who raised her eyes from the floor to meet his. He was heartened to see that she found watching the embrace just as difficult as he did.

# AMANDA

Everything changed the first time Conrad put a gun to her head in that petrol station in Tooting.

The set-up had certainly looked real, and she'd made a convincing enough hostage, so he hadn't needed to go such a long way over the top: to pull her hair quite so much, to press the barrel of the toy gun so hard into the side of her head. Later that night, after they'd counted the money and got completely wrecked, she'd read him the Riot Act. Yes, obviously they had to be convincing, but they weren't fucking method actors! He hadn't known exactly what she meant, of course, so she'd explained it to him in simpler terms until he did. He was terribly sorry and upset, and only too happy to listen when she told him how they could do things better the next time.

That was when she'd fully understood that she was the one in charge.

All she'd wanted in the beginning was someone to get heavy with a dealer she owed money to. Conrad had managed that easily enough, then they'd just carried on seeing each other. It helped that he was OK looking, that he knew his way around and that he seemed to like looking after her. He'd racked his brains for ways to come up with cash, to pay for what she needed. She was touched and relieved, happy to have found the first man who would really take care of her since her father. The fake robbery idea had been Conrad's, as it happened, but everything since had come from her.

To get your own way, of course, it helped if you knew what the other person was thinking. If you could predict which way they were liable to jump. Conrad had never been particularly good at pretending he was feeling one thing when what was really in his heart and head was written all over his face. She liked that about him. She'd always been wary of men who were better liars than she was.

Her daddy hadn't been a good liar, either. Didn't have it in him. Of course, he may have had some sordid secret life that he'd kept hidden from Amanda and her mother. He may have visited rent boys, or kept a string of mistresses – and, with the marriage he had, who could have blamed him? – but she preferred to imagine him as she remembered him: perfect, right until the day he left. As handsome as he'd been the moment before he went through the windscreen of his Mercedes.

Conrad hadn't gone for the kidnap idea straight away. He'd needed a little convincing. She'd told him that it would be easy money; that, more importantly, it would be far *bigger* money than they could get from any branch of Threshers or a BP station. She promised him that afterwards they could make a fresh start somewhere, that she could afford to get some proper help and maybe get herself cleaned up. That had sorted him out; those promises, and the ones she'd made in the dark with her skinny little body.

And now there was the boy. Their overgrown baby hostage.

He'd responded to promises, same as any other man: that he wouldn't be hurt if he behaved himself; that he would be home soon; that everything was going to be all right.

She looked across to where he lay sleeping, his head on the hands that she'd tied at the wrists with crêpe bandage. She wondered if she should give him another dose to keep him asleep, or let him wake up and see if he'd learned his lesson. The knife seemed to have calmed him down a bit, scared him into being a good lad. Like most blokes she'd ever known, if promises weren't enough, threats would usually do the trick.

He was a good-looking boy, she decided. His personality wasn't easy to read, given the circumstances, but he seemed nice enough. She thought he would probably break a heart or two, if he ever got the chance.

# THREE

'Shouldn't we be doing this in summer?' Hendricks suggested. 'I'm freezing my cobs off.'

'Put your coat on then.'

Whatever the Job euphemistically chose to call a sudden and inexplicable leave of absence, such as that imposed upon him the previous year, this had been about as close to 'gardening' as Thorne had come. Or was ever likely to. Half an hour in B & Q one Saturday afternoon and a weekend of self-assembly hell had been all the time necessary to work a small miracle on the few square feet of cracked and manky paving slabs behind his kitchen.

'I wanted a bit of sympathy, obviously,' Hendricks said. 'I mean, that's why I came. And beer's always a bonus. But I hadn't banked on double pneumonia.'

Thorne drank the last from a can of Sainsbury's own-label Belgian lager and looked across what any self-respecting estate agent – if that were not a contradiction in terms – would now describe as 'a small but well-appointed patio area'. A couple of plants in plastic pots, a wonky barbecue on wheels, a heater on a stand.

And a weeping pathologist . . .

In fact, Hendricks seemed to be past the worst of it, but his bloodshot eyes still looked as though they might brim and leak at any moment, and the tremble at the centre of his chin hadn't quite disappeared. Thorne had seen his friend cry before, and, though it was always uncomfortable, he could never help but be struck by the painful incongruity of the spectacle. He knew better than anyone how strongly the Mancunian could take things to heart, yet Phil Hendricks remained – in appearance at least – an imposing, even aggressive, figure. He was a shaven-headed Goth, with dark clothes and tattoos; with rings, studs and spikes through assorted areas of flesh. Watching him in genuine distress was like seeing pensioners touch tongues, or a Hell's Angel cradle a mewling newborn. It was disconcerting. It was like staring at an arty postcard.

'So, have I been sympathetic enough?' Thorne asked.

'Well, not straight away, no.'

'That's because I know what a bloody drama queen you are. You turn up on the doorstep wailing and it could mean anything. I don't know whether someone's died, or if you've just lost one of your George Michael CDs.'

Thorne got the smile he was aiming for. Hendricks was certainly no drama queen, but when he'd arrived an hour before it *had* taken a while for Thorne to realise how serious it was. Hendricks had told him that he and his boyfriend Brendan had had a major argument, that this was *definitely* the end, but Thorne had known both of them long enough to take such pronouncements of doom with a fistful of salt.

Thorne's first tactic had worked a time or two before: beer and distraction. Once the initial crying jag had abated and Thorne had got Hendricks settled down in the living room with a drink, he tried talking to him about work. Hendricks was a civilian member of Russell Brigstocke's Major Investigation Team at Homicide Command (West), and the pathologist Thorne had worked with most regularly in recent years. He had also become a close friend; probably the only person Thorne could think of who might donate a kidney should he ever need one. Certainly the only one who might actually have the odd one or two knocking around.

Their cosy chats about death and dismemberment were often perversely enjoyable, but this was one work conversation that was never destined to go anywhere. Though the two shared plenty of ancient history, Thorne's position on the sidelines in recent weeks meant that they hadn't a single ongoing investigation in common. Besides, the only dead thing Hendricks had seemed keen to talk about was his own relationship. 'It's not like the times before,' he'd said. 'He really fucking means it this time.'

Thorne had begun to see that the situation was more serious than he'd first thought; that this was more than just a spat. He'd done his best to calm down his friend.

He'd phoned out for pizza and dragged a couple of kitchen chairs into the garden.

'I can't feel my feet,' Hendricks said.

'Stop bloody moaning.' It *was* chilly, no question, and Thorne had never got around to buying a gas bottle for the heater, but he was enjoying being outside. 'I'm starting to see why Brendan's done a bunk.'

Hendricks didn't appear to find that crack quite so funny. He lifted his feet up on to the seat of his chair, wrapped his hands around his ankles.

'Maybe he just needs a bit of space to cool off,' Thorne said.

'I was the one doing most of the shouting.' When Hendricks sighed the breath hung in front of his face. 'He stayed pretty calm a lot of the time.'

'Maybe a day or two apart isn't such a bad idea, you know?'

Hendricks looked like he thought it was just about the *worst* idea anyone had ever come up with. 'He took a lot of his stuff. Said he's coming back for the rest tomorrow.'

In recent months, the couple had been living at Hendricks' place in Islington, but Brendan had kept his own flat. 'So he's got somewhere to fuck off back to when we split up,' Hendricks had joked once.

Up to this point it had all been about the *fact* of the argument, the ferocity and finality of it. Hendricks remained adamant that it had been terminal, yet did not seem particularly keen to talk about what had triggered the fight in the first place.

57

Thorne asked the question, then immediately wished he hadn't when he watched his friend turn his head away and lie to him.

'I can't even remember, to be honest, but I can tell you it was nothing important. It never really is, is it? You end up falling out over the stupidest things.'

'Right . . . '

'I think it's probably been brewing for a few weeks. We're both stressed at work, you know?'

Though Thorne guessed there was still something he wasn't being told, he knew that Hendricks was probably right about the stress. He'd seen what the work could take out of Hendricks on any number of occasions, and knew that his partner's job was far from being a walk in the park, either. Brendan Maxwell worked for the London Lift, an organisation that provided much-needed services for the city's homeless. Thorne had got to know him well during his investigations into the rough-sleeper killings the year before.

Thorne looked at his watch. 'What time did we order that pizza?'

'I'm not going to do much better, am I?' Hendricks stood up and leaned back against the wall next to the kitchen door. 'Better than Brendan, I mean.'

'Come on, Phil . . . '

'I'm not, though. There's no point kidding myself. I'm just trying to be realistic, that's all.'

'I give it a fortnight,' Thorne said. 'A tenner says you've got a new piercing within two weeks. You up for it?' This was one of their jokes: that Hendricks commemorated each new boyfriend with a piercing. A unique, if painful way of putting notches on his bedpost. It had been a *running* joke, until Brendan had come along.

'It's just the thought of being single again.'

'You aren't single yet.'

'Back on the scene. How depressing is that?'

'It's not going to happen, I'm telling you.'

'We were so grateful that we'd saved each other from that, you know? That we'd found each other. Fuck.'

Thorne watched Hendricks repeatedly drive the heel of his biker boot into the brick behind him. He saw the tears come again. It suddenly seemed like all he'd done that day was watch people trying, and failing, not to cry.

The powerful hit of relief he felt when he heard the phone ringing in the kitchen was quickly cancelled out by an equally strong pang of shame. He wondered if he should let it ring; what Hendricks would think of him if he got up and answered it; how much longer whoever was calling would bother hanging on.

When Hendricks gestured towards the kitchen, Thorne shrugged a *what-can-you-do?* and hurried inside.

There must have been something in his voice when he picked up.

'Not a good time?' Brigstocke asked.

Thorne's answer might have sounded vague, but was about as honest as he could be. 'Yes and no.'

'I just wanted to see how life on the Kidnap Unit was treating you.'

Thorne took the phone through to the living room. 'You just wanted to see if I fucked up on my first day, you mean.'

'Oh, I know you didn't fuck up. I've already spoken to the DCI.'

'And?'

'Gold stars all round, I reckon. You impressed DI Porter, by the sound of it. What did you make of her?'

Thorne dropped into the armchair, swiftly followed by his terminally confused cat, who jumped on to his lap and began digging in her claws. Thorne lifted Elvis up until she let go and tossed her back to the floor. 'She seemed OK,' he said. 'She certainly knows what she's doing.' He couldn't be sure why he was so reluctant to say what he really thought, especially when she'd obviously said such good things about him. The fact was that he'd been very impressed with Louise Porter. In every sense.

'Exciting enough for you?'

'Well, I'm not stuck behind a desk,' Thorne said. 'But I'm not sitting here waiting for my pulse to return to normal, either.' He could hear one of Brigstocke's kids in the background. The tone of the silence changed as a hand went over the mouthpiece, and he heard Brigstocke's muffled voice telling the child that he'd be with him in a few minutes.

'Sorry ...'

'I'm not even sure we're looking at a kidnap,' Thorne said. 'This business with the woman's bloody odd. And if someone *is* holding the kid, it doesn't make any sense that they haven't got in touch.'

'What does Porter think?'

'She thinks it's strange, too. We were talking about motivation, you know? About why *anybody* takes a hostage. There's always a reason. It might be drugs, or money, or some kind of political statement. But they always want something.'

'You think the boy's just left home?'

'God knows. I think we might be wasting a lot of time and effort, though.'

The doorbell rang, but almost as soon as Thorne was on his feet, Hendricks had come inside and was making his way to the door. Thorne reached into his leather jacket for his wallet but Hendricks waved him away.

'So I'd be right in thinking you wouldn't be keen on me making this transfer permanent, then?'

'This is going to sound weird, and I know that, whatever the reason turns out to be, there's still a missing kid, but I find it hard to get ... excited about it. There's an element of going through the motions. Does that make sense?'

'You're happier when there's a body, aren't you?' Brigstocke said. 'You want a killer to go after.'

Thorne thought about what Holland had said to him in the car that morning: 'Sounds almost like you're hoping.' He wondered if the pair of them might have a point; if perhaps there were a part of him that could only be described as 'ghoulish'. 'I just think we should do what we're good at,' he said. He knew, even as he spoke, that he was sounding sulky and defensive.

Brigstocke sniffed. 'I could say something deep and

meaningful here, about how some people care more about the dead than they do about the living, but I'm not sure I can be arsed.'

'I think you'd be doing the pair of us a favour if you didn't,' Thorne said.

Brigstocke said nothing. Just hummed, like he was thinking about it.

The front door slammed and Hendricks walked back towards the kitchen with the boxes. Thorne was eager to follow him. 'I need to go. I'm about to eat my dinner.'

'I know. I heard the doorbell,' Brigstocke said. 'Curry or pizza?'

Thorne laughed. 'You haven't lost it.'

A minute later he was taking two fresh cans of beer from the fridge, glad that the call from Brigstocke had ended on an upbeat note. It could easily have gone the other way. So many conversations he'd had of late had seemed dangerously poised, while Holland, Hendricks and a number of others had all used the phrase 'walking on eggshells' more than once. When Thorne got snappy, told them in no uncertain terms that they were being oversensitive, they just looked at him like he'd proved their point.

'Shall we eat this outside?' Thorne asked.

Hendricks was already picking at pepperoni slices. 'Are you kidding? It's even colder now. I'm young, free and single, mate, and if I'm going out on the pull, the last thing I need is my knob shrinking to the size of an acorn.' He picked up his pizza box and wandered into the living room.

Thorne was about to shout after him, ask if he fancied

62

putting some music on, then thought better of it. Hendricks might have been gagging it up, but the pain hadn't gone anywhere. He would almost certainly pull out an album with at least one unsuitable track on it; the make-up of Thorne's collection would make it hard not to. It was, as people never seemed to tire of telling him, the problem with country music: too many songs about dead dogs and lost love.

'Stick the TV on,' he shouted as an alternative. 'See if there's a game on Sky.'

He stepped back outside to bring in the kitchen chairs. It was a clear night, but there was no guarantee it wouldn't piss down before morning. He thought through what he'd said to Brigstocke about not feeling excited, and about what it might take to start the blood pumping that little bit faster. He wondered how bad he'd really feel if the body so many people accused him of wishing for turned up. He just hoped to Christ that if it did, it wasn't Luke Mullen's.

He looked up as a plane passed, winking and droning overhead. The sky was the colour of a dusty plum, and spattered with stars. He carried the chairs inside and shut the door. Hendricks was already shouting at the television.

In spite of his bad back, of the boredom and the morbid thoughts, Thorne was feeling pretty good. Relative to the recent past, at any rate. All the same, it was a welcome diversion to spend a few hours with someone who – if only for the time being – was in worse shape than he was.

# CONRAD

The kid was clever, no doubt about that. A bit of a smart-arse, in fact, but it didn't matter how brainy you were if you weren't the one in the driving seat. The kid had probably passed a ton more exams than he ever had, but it didn't count for much now, did it? Clever didn't mean a lot with a bag over your head.

Because he was the one calling the shots.

Even as the words formed in his mind, it struck him as a smart way of putting things. 'Shots' as in guns, and 'shots' like when you give someone an injection.

He'd always been tall and well built, and he'd always looked after himself, but he'd never been given any real respect. Not when he was younger, anyway. Back then he'd lacked the 'necessary', the something in the eyes or whatever, that made people take you seriously; that made them back off, try to smile, and say, 'All right, mate, whatever you want.' He'd wanted to make someone react like that ever since his balls had dropped, and he could still remember when it had happened for the first time. It was a few years ago now, but he could remember every single detail of it. It was like watching a film that he was starring in.

A poxy red Fiesta.

The spiky-haired ponce behind the wheel had cut in front of him at the lights, swerved across into his lane instead of turning right like he should have done. Then, to top it off, the arsehole had given him the finger when he'd leaned on his horn, as he'd every bloody right to do!

So he's chased the fucker. He's right up his arse, doing fifty and sixty through Dalston and Hackney, all the way to Bow. There's big puddles on the streets and precious little traffic around that time of the morning; just night buses and the odd dodgy minicab getting out of the way seriously fast.

The Fiesta pulls up hard and sharp somewhere round the back of Victoria Park, and the bloke gets out and starts waving a baseball bat around. Shaking his head and pointing a finger. Shouting his mouth off as he walks towards the car.

The next bit's in slow motion and the sound's really pumped up loud. He can feel his heart going mental underneath his Puffa, but it's excitement, not fear, and when he gets out of the car he gets the look he's been dreaming about for so long.

It's the moment when power shifts.

The tosser with the bat has obviously fancied it right up to that moment, because the bat gives him the edge, and he probably isn't afraid to use it either. It's made him braver than he's got any right to be. But then he sees the gun, and he shits himself.

He *shits* himself. Or he might just as well have done, judging by the look on his face as he walks away. As he puts down the bat, and puts up his hands, and says, 'All right, mate, no harm done.'

Of course, the gun was only a replica and, real or not, maybe it was the gun that was getting the respect rather than him, but still. It didn't matter. The feeling as he climbed back into his car was amazing, like nothing he'd known before, and it had stayed with him. Singing in his blood as he tore past the buses and ripped through the puddles, right up until the moment when everything had gone very tits up twenty minutes later . . .

Across the room, the boy was awake beneath the hood. He could tell by the position of him, by the way his head turned and his face pressed against the material.

'You hungry?'

They'd had a long discussion about whether to use a gag and Amanda had decided against it in the end. It was maybe a bit over the top. Anyway, the kid was drugged up most of the time and, even when he wasn't, they'd be on him like a rash if he tried screaming.

'You want something to eat?'

The boy said nothing, even though he could. Just

ignored the question. He chose to keep quiet for some reason, like he was protesting or something; like he was playing a game with them.

Trying to be clever.

# WEDNESDAY

# FOUR

His father had taken to coming by in the early hours of the morning.

Since the back problems, Thorne had been waking anywhere from 5 a.m. onwards. He'd lie there in the dark, in the only comfortable position he'd been able to find – his knees up to his chest – and think about his old man. Occasionally, he'd manage to drift back to sleep again, and then their encounters would be stranger, *richer*, as, in that hour or two before he would need to get up, he invariably dreamed.

In the dreams, Jim Thorne would appear as he had been in the final stages of the Alzheimer's; in the six months or so before the fire that had killed him. It was typical of his father, Thorne thought, to be so perverse, so bloody-minded. Why couldn't he have moved through the dreams as a younger man? Or a man whose mind was at least firing on the right cylinders? Instead, his father came to him belligerent and foul-mouthed, stumbling through their conversations, distracted, furious and lost.

Helpless . . .

Often, the old man would do nothing but sit on the edge of Thorne's bed, eager to ask questions. This was how it had been towards the end. The disregard for social niceties had gone hand in hand with an obsession for trivia, lists and quizzes.

'Name ten World War Two fighter planes. Which are the three biggest lakes in the world? That's freshwater lakes.'

Since passing on, he'd introduced the element of multiple choice.

'Was the cause of the fire that killed me: (A) accidental or (B) started deliberately?'

Often this would be followed by a question Thorne found a little easier to answer: 'Whose fault was it: (A) yours or (B) yours?'

This was usually when Thorne would wake, and for a while the question would stay with him. The feelings it stirred were unmistakable, yet hard to name or pin down. Not quite shame, but a shade of it. Like the relationship which 'coming down with something' has to the illness itself; to the symptoms that will eventually appear. He would move robotically through the rituals of the morning – ablutions, breakfast, getting dressed – until the memory of the dream began to dissolve. Feeling the water sizzle against his skin as he shaved, and the cereal turning to charcoal in his mouth.

72

He'd put Phil Hendricks into a minicab late the previous night. As always, the sofa-bed had been on offer, but Hendricks had wanted to get home. The big talk about cruising for someone to take his boyfriend's place had not lasted long. The beer had washed away the pretence of acceptance, and by the end of a long evening he was tearful again, and desperate to return to the flat in case Brendan had decided to come back.

In his kitchen, Thorne ate toast and marmalade standing up, listening to Greater London Radio and waiting for the early morning dose of painkillers to kick in.

It was five weeks until the first anniversary of his father's death.

Outside, it had started to rain gently, and on GLR the host was trying to get a word in as some woman ranted about the disgusting state of the capital's rail network.

He decided that he would call his Auntie Eileen – his father's younger sister – and Victor, the old man's best friend. Maybe they could all get together on the day. Have a drink or something.

His was not, had never been, a close family, and it was all so terribly British, this cleaving together after a loss. Yet, while he saw it for the gesture that in many ways it was, he still craved it; he needed the chance to measure his grief against that of others. He wanted to be with people who could talk to him without feeling like they were walking on eggshells.

On the radio, a man was saying that the previous caller

73

had been rude and overbearing, but that she'd been right about how crap the railways were.

Thorne wondered how the Mullens were doing. To lose someone but not know for sure if they were really gone was arguably the worst kind of loss, and they certainly seemed to be cleaving together. It was odd, he thought, that a word could have such opposite definitions: to cling together, and to split violently apart.

He was scooping food into a bowl for Elvis when the phone rang, and though the codeine hadn't quite taken effect, Porter's call was enough to make him forget the pain pulsing down his leg and into his foot.

They could now be certain that Luke Mullen had been kidnapped. Whoever was holding him had finally decided to get in touch.

At Central 3000, chairs had been hastily put out and a screen set up in a corner beneath the red flag. Officers from other departments cut their conversation, stood still or just worked in silence, as the team from the Kidnap Unit gathered round and watched the video that had come through the Mullens' front door first thing that morning.

When it had finished, Porter rewound the tape without a word and they watched it through again.

'Obviously the original's gone to the FSS,' she said when they'd finished. 'They'll fast-track it, along with the envelope it came in.'

The Forensic Science Service handled enquiries from all forty-three police forces in England and Wales, testing firearms and fibres, running toxicology screens, minutely analysing blood, drug or tissue samples. Their labs in Victoria would normally take a week or more to turn round comprehensive fingerprint or DNA results. A fast-track request could reduce that time significantly: with luck, they would hear back within a day, on the prints at least.

'Not that I can see us getting a great deal,' Porter said. She gestured towards the screen. The image was frozen at the point where, seen from behind with his face hidden from view, a man carrying a bag in one hand and a syringe in the other is moving purposefully towards Luke Mullen. 'It looks very much like they know what they're doing.'

'What do we think's in the syringe?' Holland asked.

A DS in front of him – a tall Scotsman with a mullet – turned around. 'Rohypnol maybe, or diazepam. Any benzo-diazepine, really.'

'How's he get hold of that kind of stuff?'

'With a computer and a credit card. It's pretty bloody simple these days. They shut down a site a couple of weeks ago that was selling a vial of ketamine and a couple of syringes in a smart leather case. Knocking them out at £19.99 as "date-rape kits".'

'Doesn't he need to know what he's doing, though? If he's going to keep the kid sedated all the time?'

Thorne listened to the exchange, but kept his eyes fixed on the television screen; on the frozen, flickering image of the boy and the man who was holding him. There was terror in the boy's eyes. It had been there throughout, of course, albeit partially hidden by the brave face he'd been putting on for his parents. But the mask had fallen quickly away when the man began walking towards him with the needle.

The Scottish officer shook his head. 'You can also find out how to do it on the Net. Plenty of teach-yourself guides out there. What size doses to use or whatever.'

'Or you learn from experience,' Thorne said.

There was a sizeable pause after that.

Then the ACTIONS were outlined and allocated. There was little of substance to work on other than the partial number plate of the blue or black car, and talking to a few more witnesses who'd seen Luke getting into it.

Porter waited until most of her team had been given tasks and those few who hadn't were clearing away chairs or paperwork before she talked to Thorne and Holland about their roles. 'I'm going back to the school this afternoon,' she said. 'I don't know which of you is better at talking to teenage boys ....'

Holland was the first to speak up, aware of a good, long look from Thorne as he answered. 'Yeah, I'll tag along.'

'Tom?'

'I thought I might have a word with one or two people Tony Mullen used to work with,' Thorne said. 'Show them the list. See if their memory's any better than his.'

At the end of the previous day, Mullen had handed over the list of all those who might have held a grudge against him.

'He *has* got quite a lot to think about,' Porter said.

Thorne could see she had a point, but he was not completely convinced. 'That's exactly why I thought it might be more ... comprehensive, I suppose. If my son was taken and there was no obvious reason why, I'd be sticking down the name of anyone who'd so much as looked at me funny.'

Mullen had come up with just five names. Five men who might, *at one time*, have had cause to wish or do him harm. Each had been run through the CRIMINT database within minutes, and once those traced to Australia, HMP Parkhurst and Kensal Green cemetery had been eliminated, they were down to two.

Porter was pulling papers from her desktop, bits and pieces from a drawer and sweeping them into her handbag. 'I'm going over to the house for an hour or two first. I'll probably head straight to the school from there. You never know, he's had a bit more time to think, he might have come up with another name or two overnight.'

She picked up her mobile phone and clipped it to her belt, then dropped a second handset into her handbag. The Airwave had been rolled out across the force over the previous year and a half, one handset issued to every officer. It was certainly an ingenious piece of kit: a phone *and* a radio, with a range that, for the first time, would allow the user to talk to a fellow officer anywhere in the UK at the touch of a button. Still, in spite of a blizzard of memos, some officers preferred to stick with their own phones. These were less flashy perhaps, but they were generally smaller, lighter and, most importantly, *didn't* have GPS capability built in. Mysteriously, a large number of these state-of-the-art Airwave handsets were getting lost, or left at home by officers who were none too keen on Control-room staff knowing exactly where they were at all times.

Thorne was interested to note that, as far as he could see, Porter's Airwave had not been switched on when she'd dropped it into her bag.

The team's DCI, a quietly spoken Geordie who needed to lose a few pounds, appeared at Porter's shoulder, brandishing a sheaf of papers and telling her that he needed five minutes with her before she disappeared. Though Barry Hignett had met Thorne and Holland briefly first thing, he took the chance to welcome them again, explaining that there was bugger-all room for niceties on the teeth of a case such as this one.

Hignett walked Porter to a nearby desk and spread out the papers in front of her. Holland watched for a minute, then turned around, his back to them, and spoke low to Thorne: 'Did you want to go to the school?'

Thorne looked at him as though he were speaking Chinese. 'What?'

'With Porter, I mean.' He lowered his voice further still. 'Only I thought you looked a bit pissed off before, when I said that I'd go.'

'Don't be so bloody silly,' Thorne said.

When Porter had finished with Hignett, she arranged to meet Holland later at the school. Then Thorne took the stairs with her down to ground level.

'*They're being fairly nice to me.*' Thorne said it quietly, nodding as an officer he'd spoken to once or twice moved past him, coming up. 'That's what Luke said on the tape.' It had been a dramatic moment when the figure with the syringe had emerged from behind the camera. The picture had remained unsteady, the camera clearly handheld rather than mounted on a tripod. Whatever Luke had said or not said, that was when it had become clear that he was being held by more than one person. That they were looking at a conspiracy to kidnap. 'Two of them, d'you reckon? Or more?'

'If it's just two, I'd put money on the other one being the woman Luke was seen with.'

'Is that common? A man and a woman working as a team?'

'I've come across it a few times,' Porter said. 'For obvious reasons, the woman's most often the one involved in the abduction itself. The trust figure.'

'Right.'

*For obvious reasons.*

Thorne wondered why, in the light of so many high-profile cases, those reasons remained obvious, but clearly they did. Hindley was always more hated than Brady. Maxine Carr, despite being found not guilty of even *knowing* that her boyfriend had murdered two young girls, was, if anything, the more vilified of the two.

'A couple of the kids reckoned they'd spotted them together before, didn't they?' Thorne said. 'Luke and this woman. She obviously took her time to get close to him.'

'It paid off,' Porter said. 'Talking of which, there's still no sign of a ransom demand. No talk of *anyone* getting paid off.'

'Maybe that'll be on the next tape.' But as they came out into the lobby on the ground floor, and moved towards the revolving doors, Thorne was still thinking about the 'how' rather than the 'why'. Imagining a woman getting close to her victim; smiling and touching and always attentive. Thinking that trust was nurtured, like bodies and minds; that it was abused at the same time that they were. He remembered the smile that faltered a little as the boy on the screen had done his best to crack jokes. He remembered the emptiness in the stare. He wondered if Luke Mullen would ever trust anyone again.

The drizzle hadn't stopped all morning, but there were still plenty of people milling around outside the entrance. A couple sat eating sandwiches, perched on adjacent concrete stumps. Rows of these bollards, installed to deter car-bombers, had sprung up outside most of the city's public buildings, and Thorne often wondered if cement companies might be secretly funding some of the terrorist groups. He shared the theory with Porter and they paused for a minute, enjoying the joke; Thorne, on his way towards the tube station at St James's Park and Porter headed for the Yard's underground garage.

'How much does it bother you?' Thorne asked. 'That nobody's asking the Mullens for any money. That nobody's asking for *anything*.'

'These cases are never predictable, I've learned that much. But yeah, it's bloody odd.'

'They've had Luke four days already.'

'Four days, five nights. Mind you, we were worried that they hadn't got in touch, and then they did.'

Thorne began to do up the buttons on his leather jacket. 'Something bothers me,' he said. 'Something on the tape.'

'What?'

'I wish I could tell you. Something's not right, though; something that he said, or maybe just the way he said it.'

'It'll come to you.'

'Maybe.'

'It's old age, mate. That's Alzheimer's kicking in.'

Thorne dug down deep for a smile.

'I'll catch up with you later on at Arkley,' she said. 'See how they're doing, OK?'

'Right.' He took a step backwards, half turned, on his way. 'What do you make of Mullen?'

'I think he needs to remember he's not a copper any more.'

Thorne fastened the top button of his jacket and stuffed his hands into the pockets. Thinking about memory, perfect and fucked-up. Thinking that his memories of the time before he was a copper were getting pushed for space; shunted aside by less pleasant recollections. 'You ever thought about getting out early?' he asked.

'Now and again. What about you?'

'There's times I think about it a fair bit.'

'What sort of times?' Porter asked.

'When I'm awake . . .'

*

Tony Mullen reached into the fridge for the wine bottle, pulled the glass across the counter-top and poured himself a decent measure. He moved over to where his daughter was making herself a sandwich. Stroked the back of her head as he drank.

Neither had spoken since he'd come into the kitchen a few minutes before, and they continued to stand, each busy in their own way, sharing the space in silence until Juliet Mullen picked up her plate and walked out.

He listened to his daughter's footsteps on the stairs, to the creak and click of her bedroom door, and to the music which escaped in the few seconds between those final two sounds. He strained to hear the murmur of Maggie's voice, and, though he could hear nothing, he knew very well that in some room or other of the house his wife would be deep in conversation. She'd been keeping the landline clear for obvious reasons, but somewhere she'd be sitting or lying down with the mobile pressed to her ear; talking it out and talking it through to her family, her friends, anyone willing to listen and pretend they understood what was happening.

He'd spoken when he'd had to. He'd given the necessary information when it had been required of him, but aside from that, he'd said next to nothing. That had always been the way between them if ever there was trouble, if ever the family unit had been threatened in any way. He'd always be the one to go into himself, bottle things up; the one to turn the problem every which way without saying a word while others did the screaming and shouting. Luke was like that, too: never one to get hysterical. Maggie was usually the one that wore her heart on her sleeve and it was never easy to tell what was going on inside Juliet's head.

It wasn't very inclusive or touchy-feely, he knew that. It was old fashioned and out of step. He guessed that in some ways it might have been better if they'd all sat around and opened up, if they'd *shared*, but it wasn't the way he or his family operated, and you couldn't help the way you were.

He moved his fingers back and forth across the smooth, cold surface of the counter-top and thought about DI Tom Thorne. The cheeky bastard had given him a hard time the day before, badgered him, even though only one person in that room had made DCI, and only one was ever likely to. He was grateful to Jesmond for laying on the extra men, but Thorne was one he'd have to watch. That type of copper – the 'bull in a china shop' type – didn't solve cases like this one. His son would be freed by doing what was simple and sound, and not by refusing to accept what you'd been told and banging on about how many names were on a fucking list.

Mullen emptied his glass and thought about the name he *hadn't* written down. He told himself that it was unimportant; that it was acceptable within the scheme of things; that he'd done it for the right reason. A silly reason perhaps, but one worth the very smallest of lies.

He would have loved to forget the man to whom that name belonged, but it would never slip his mind. It was a name with unhappy connotations, after all. But it was a name – and this was all that really counted – that he knew damn well had *nothing* to do with his son's disappearance. With who was holding Luke, or where, or what they wanted. So why did it matter, and what harm could come from leaving one name out of it?

He listened for a minute or two more, then moved back to the fridge.

What harm?

# AMANDA

It was a bag. Just a plastic bag, that had done all the damage; was still doing it if assorted shrinks and social workers knew what they were talking about.

Probably one of those really cheap, stripy ones that you picked up at late-night supermarkets and shitty corner shops. The driver of the second car had never gone so far as to describe the bag in court, but that was how she always imagined it. Fluttering across the street and up on to the windscreen, held there by the wind, blinding the driver for that crucial second or two and causing him to swerve. A shapeless piece of jetsam that made him drive into the silver Mercedes coming the other way. That floated up like smoke at the impact, and sent her daddy through the glass.

Cheap and insubstantial. Virtually weightless. Something so terrible coming from nothing . . .

The boy was dosed-up now and out of it, and Conrad was getting a bit of sleep in the next room. It was the middle of the day, but both their body clocks had gone haywire. The curtains were closed all the time; it could have been morning, noon or night. It didn't really matter one way or the other. It was boring, that was all. They just had to stay where they were for as long as the whole thing took; until they knew what was happening next.

When she dwelled on what had happened to her father, which was often, she never really thought about the other driver: unsighted and screaming behind the wheel; giving his evidence in a neck-brace; limping away down the steps outside the court while her mother shouted after him. She thought instead – and she knew how irrational it was – about the person who had sold the plastic bag. About the person who had filled it with fruit, or fish, or fuck-all worth talking about, and about all the hands the bag had passed through before it was finally tossed into the gutter. She thought about the people who would never know the part they had played in her father's death. She imagined all their faces. She gave each one a life, and a family to fill it. And in her darkest moments, of which there were many, she'd take a member of that family away, and watch the life she'd made for someone fall apart.

She walked across to the portable CD player in the corner of the bedroom, turned the music up just a little to drown out the boy's breathing. She took what she needed from her handbag and sat back down on the floor.

They'd argued again about the usual thing, Conrad

doing that low, disappointed voice he saved up for the drug conversations. He told her that she needed to keep a clear head. She pointed out that it was precisely because the situation they were in was so stressful that she needed the lift. He got angrier then, reminded her that she *always* needed it, and she told him that the last thing she needed was for him to be so self-righteous, and that she'd sort herself out afterwards, when they had the money.

Nodding her head to the music, she tipped out the powder; measured and scraped and cut. She rolled up the note and stared at the lines, at the flyaway grains that dotted the tabletop around their edges. Insubstantial. Virtually weightless.

Something so wonderful coming from nothing.

# FIVE

Fifteen minutes from the Mullen house, in the largely affluent suburb of Stanmore, Butler's Hall School had occupied its hundred-plus acres of lush parkland for a little under a century.

Holland read a potted history of the place, flicking through the school's lavish prospectus as he waited in a car at the end of a mile-long driveway. Of its 250-plus pupils – most of whom were fed in from a nearby prep school in the same foundation – almost a third were boarders. Of the total number, around 40 per cent were girls, first admitted as sixth-formers in the early eighties, then into the main body of the school ten years after that.

Kenny Parsons, who had gone in search of a toilet fifteen minutes earlier, knocked on the window. Holland looked up, wound down the window.

'It's a fair bet that if you can afford to send your kids here, you can afford to cough up a decent ransom,' Parsons said. 'These kids might as well have targets on their backs.'

'Wouldn't be allowed,' Holland said, lifting the brochure. 'There's a very strict uniform code.'

Parsons looked back towards the school. 'There's a very strict *everything* code.'

Holland got out of the car, tossed the brochure on to the back seat. He and Parsons began walking towards the school building. '"Falsehood dishonours me",' he said.

'Come again?'

'That's the translation from the Latin, apparently. "Lies shame me", or whatever. The school motto.'

Parsons nodded, vacant. 'The lower sixth should be out in a minute,' he said.

The end of the school day was staggered, with pupils from upper and lower years coming out at twenty-minute intervals. Porter and three colleagues, working in teams of two, were already elsewhere on the school premises, talking to children from the fourth and fifth forms in the presence of teachers or parents. As Holland and Parsons moved towards the school's main exit, they joined another pair of SO7 officers, falling in behind them as they walked across the car park, cutting through the massed ranks of silver or black people carriers: Porsche Cayennes, Volvos and BMW X5s. One of the officers, a skinny Essex boy with bad skin, put his face close to the tinted window of a Lexus as he passed, tried to see inside. 'What do these people *do*?' he said.

Holland, Parsons and the others stopped in the school quad, loitering outside a pair of vast wooden doors, which slammed open as the first of the students began to emerge. Like all those officers working on site, the four were smartly, though informally, dressed: khakis and casual jackets; suits over polo shirts. They could easily have been teachers, or even, in one or two cases, students out of uniform.

Parsons was clearly still thinking about his colleague's question as he watched the first wave of pupils emerge, and spoke above their chatter. 'Well, I don't think many of them are coppers. And I can't see any of their kids becoming coppers, either.'

'They do have scholarship places,' Holland said. 'Not everyone's dad's an oil billionaire or a footballer, you know.'

'That's a fair point,' the Essex boy said. 'Take Mullen for a kick-off. Unless he was seriously bent, I can't see how he'd be rolling in it.'

Parsons said something about a DCI's pension, about Mullen making seriously good money as a security consultant, but Holland had stopped listening. He was watching two girls, aged fifteen or so, heads together, whispering. He was thinking about Chloe. Deciding that, even though it was a long way off, he wouldn't argue if there was so much as a chance of her getting into a place like this. That he *would* argue until his last breath with the idea of her ever becoming a copper.

Officers had travelled to Butler's Hall late on the

Monday – the first day the unit had become involved – and taken more statements the day after that, but it was understandable that Barry Hignett was keen to speak to everyone who might have anything to add. Understandable in that, until the people holding Luke Mullen decided to let the police or his parents know exactly what they *wanted*, there was little else that could usefully be done.

Pupils had been spoken to in school. They were told that Luke Mullen was still missing and that there would be police officers waiting to talk to them if they felt they had anything useful to report. The headmaster had been at pains to remind them that neglecting to do so would be as good as falsehood, and every bit as dishonourable. They were urged to pass on any information they had, however trivial it might seem, about the Friday afternoon when Luke had been driven away.

The Essex boy and his partner paired off, taking up a position at the other end of the quad, but neither they nor Holland and Parsons were exactly swamped by the rush of eager young informants.

Those few pupils Holland and Parsons did speak to all told just about the same story. It became clear that over the previous few days the school jungle drums had been working overtime and that it would not be easy to sort out the fact from the hearsay.

One boy assured Holland that Luke Mullen had run off with a sexy older woman. Several sixth-form girls swore blind that they'd seen Luke and the mystery woman kissing two or three days earlier. One of Luke's classmates said that he thought Luke had a secret girlfriend; that he'd been dropping hints about going away somewhere with her. Spain, maybe, or France.

Nothing they were told took them any closer to identifying the car. It was still probably a Passat, and more likely dark blue than black, but the partial number plate had now become all but useless, with another dozen different letters and numbers passed on by those who swore they'd seen it drive away with Luke Mullen inside.

The descriptions they were given of the woman were much the same as they already had, though, again, such statements became less credible once it became clear that those giving them had been talking to each other. She was in her late twenties. She was dirty blonde. She was very skinny. 'Tasty, though,' one of Luke's classmates had said. 'Luke reckoned she was fit. Mind you, he hadn't got much to compare her to, had he?'

The emphasis in this, as in all similar dealings with the public, was on the search for a missing teenager. It was certainly not talked of as an abduction; and, in line with standard practice, the word 'kidnap' was never used by officers outside of Central 3000 or the Mullen house.

A school, however, was as perfect a breeding ground for conjecture as it was for stomach bugs or cold sores.

'This woman's the one who kidnapped Mullen, yes?' The boy was fifteen, a year below Luke, but his manner was that of a pupil three or four years older.

'I can't go into too many details, I'm afraid,' Holland said. The boy had neatly parted hair and was carrying a small briefcase. Holland guessed that he was probably not a big star on the rugby field.

'I understand.'

Holland saw straight away that it was best to speak to the boy as if he were genuinely as mature as he appeared. 'But she's certainly someone we're interested in tracing.'

'How much of a description do you have?' the boy asked.

Holland exchanged a look with Kenny Parsons, then gave the boy the basic facts. 'Obviously, if there's anything more you can add . . .'

'I'm doing S-level art,' the boy said. 'I'm one of the best in the year.'

Holland stared at him.

'I got a pretty good look at the woman with Luke. I could probably draw her, if you'd like.'

'We'll get that arranged as soon as we can,' Holland said.

Parsons made a note of the boy's name and address. They asked him a few more questions: ascertained exactly where he'd been standing the previous Friday afternoon; how far away he'd been; if there was anyone with him at the time.

'People have been saying that she was Luke's girlfriend or something,' the boy said out of the blue, 'but I can't say I'm convinced.'

'Why not?' Holland found it hard to believe that the boy could be an expert on such matters; that he was much beyond a crush on the dinner ladies.

'Body language.' He said it as though it were obvious, and as if he were becoming slightly bored with the conversation. Yet there was an authority and a confidence about him, which, to Holland at least, made what he said oddly credible.

'What about Luke? What did he seem like?'

'Happy enough, I suppose. They walked straight past me at one point and he was talking to her.'

'Did you—?'

'I didn't catch any of what was said I'm afraid, but he seemed ... content.'

'It didn't look like he was going anywhere under duress, then? He didn't seem frightened or apprehensive?'

'No, but *she* did.' The boy swung his briefcase distractedly. Stared past Holland and Parsons towards the school gates, as if he were looking for a friend. 'She looked scared to death.'

Thorne had certainly made good use of his Travelcard.

He'd been across to Barking to talk to a DI on the Intel Unit based there, then spent an hour and a half travelling up to Finchley to interview a DCI on the Flying Squad. Both men had told him what a great bloke Tony Mullen was, what a loss it had been when he'd retired so early, how terrible it was that his family had been targeted. One of them said he'd started a collection at the station, but then stopped and given the money back when he'd realised he didn't know what it was *for*.

They had looked at Mullen's already truncated list.

Neither had made much comment, but each had told a war story or two, remembering the part they'd played alongside Tony Mullen in catching and putting away the individuals named. Thorne had listened, laughed in all the right places, and encouraged each officer in turn to consider any other of Mullen's past cases that they felt might have a bearing on what was happening. To give him the name of any person they felt should be checked out, if only to be eliminated from any enquiry. Between them, another two names had been suggested; four altogether now on the list Thorne carried with him on the short journey to Colindale. To the meeting he had scheduled at the Peel Centre.

In the Major Incident Room on the third floor of Becke House, Thorne spent fifteen minutes catching up with a few of those he would normally have been working with: he shared a quick cup of coffee with Yvonne Kitson, who seemed a little preoccupied; he traded jokes with Samir Karim and Andy Stone, who assured him that no one had even noticed he was gone; and he stuck his head round Russell Brigstocke's door in the vain hope of some moral support.

Detective Chief Superintendent Trevor Jesmond made it clear from the second Thorne stepped across his threshold that they were not going to be talking for long.

'It shouldn't take long, Sir.'

'Good. I'm up to my bloody eyeballs.'

Thorne brought Jesmond up to speed on the Luke Mullen case as briskly as he could. He explained that they had to seriously consider revenge as the motive for kidnapping Tony Mullen's son; that they were looking at anyone who might be holding a grudge. As Jesmond knew Mullen better than anyone, Thorne said, and had worked closely with him over a number of years, nobody was better placed, or better qualified, to cast an expert eye across a list of the candidates. He laid it on good and thick, and though Thorne could see that Jesmond knew he was being flattered, it seemed to work.

'Naturally I'm keen to do anything I can to help,' Jesmond said.

Thorne reached into his pocket for the list. 'Of course . . .'

'Tony and Maggie are going through hell.'

'A couple more names have been added since we spoke on the phone . . .'

Jesmond stood and walked past Thorne to the door. He lifted an overcoat from a metal hat-stand. 'We'll continue this outside. Then I can be doing other things at the same time.'

'It's still not a long list—'

'What is it women like to say? That we blokes can't multi-task?'

Thorne said nothing, alarmed to see Jesmond's thin lips sliding back across his teeth in something approaching a smile.

One of the 'other things' turned out to involve trudging across to the centre's driving school, where, for no obviously good reason, they stood and watched those on the advanced driving course take cars around the track or turn inwards to career across a skid-pan.

Jesmond waved to one of the instructors, then shouted above the roar of an engine: 'Do you like motor sport, Thorne?'

Thorne pretended he hadn't heard, and asked Jesmond to repeat the question while he thought about whether to lie. He watched an Audi squealing between a series of bollards. 'Only the crashes,' he said.

And that was the end of that.

The driving school was directly opposite the athletics arena. When not captivated by the sight of cars swerving or being driven at high speed, Thorne could glance across and watch a gaggle of recruits jogging slowly around the asphalt perimeter. Each wore a pristine blue tracksuit, but several looked anything but athletic. Most looked as though they'd have preferred a nice riot, or maybe an armed siege.

'Tony Mullen had a decent strike rate,' Jesmond said. 'As good as anyone I can think of, as it happens. But you know as well as I do that most of the lowlife we put away treat being caught as part of the job. They don't take it personally. If they were going to try and get their own back on every copper who'd ever nicked them, they'd be far too fucking busy to reoffend.'

Thorne knew it was true, by and large, but he also knew better than most that there were some to whom the rules did not, *could not*, apply. When it came to the ones that killed, there were some for whom the offence was far from

occupational; whose reactions when they were caught –
when they were no longer able to act on their compul-
sions – were anything but predictable.

It was clear when Jesmond spoke again that, as usual,
the expression on Thorne's face had made it obvious what
he was thinking.

'Of course, there are always going to be headcases,'
Jesmond said, 'and I know you've had your fair share of
those over the last few years. But they can usually be discounted, because the majority of them end up in places
they're never coming out of again.'

*The majority of them.*

A few names and faces flashed through Thorne's mind:
*Nicklin, Foley, Zarif . . .*

'Thorne?'

Thorne nodded, not quite sure what he was being asked.
To his right, a mud-spattered meat wagon moved slowly
through the car wash. Three more brooded in line behind it.

'Let's have a look at this list, then,' Jesmond said.

Thorne passed the slip of paper across, waited.

'I wouldn't even *think* about Billy Campbell.' Jesmond
jabbed at the paper. 'He was just a gobshite. Told just
about every copper, judge and prison officer he ever ran
across that he'd come after them. Liked to shout his mouth
off, that's all, same as a lot of them.'

Campbell's was one of the two names added that morning. Thorne hadn't had a chance to run it through the
system. 'What about the others?' he asked.

'I've never heard of Wayne Anthony Barber.'

The other new name. 'Went down on two counts of rape in 1994. Liked to threaten his victims with a screwdriver. Went for Mullen in the interview room, by all accounts.'

Jesmond shrugged and pointed to the two names at the top of the list. 'These the ones Tony Mullen gave you?'

Thorne grunted a yes.

'Fair enough, I suppose. Cotterill and Quinn are both nasty pieces of work.' He stretched out an arm, waved the paper for Thorne to take. 'This case doesn't fit either of them, though.'

'Harry Cotterill took a building-society teller hostage in 1989 ...'

'It's not the same thing. These two aren't kidnappers.'

'They'll know people, though.'

'I can't see it.'

'They're both *around*, at any rate,' Thorne took the paper, folded it and put it back in his pocket. 'Worth having a look at, surely?'

'You asked me what I thought,' Jesmond said. 'It's an SO7 job, so it's Barry Hignett's call anyway.'

Thorne took a breath of diesel and burning rubber. Used it to say thank you, though it was very much for nothing.

Later, when Holland had seen him as one of a very different group, it became clear to him that the boy stood out, that he was the one you focused on, whomever he was with. There was a physicality that drew the eye; a look-at-me-if-you-want-to swagger. A confidence. A lot of them had *that*, of course; it went with the uniform, and the accent, and the knowledge that, barring disaster, they were going to do fairly well for themselves. This boy was different, though; he looked like he knew it and he couldn't care less.

Holland and Parsons had been talking to a group of girls. Sixteen- and seventeen-year-olds, confident in a different way still from their male counterparts. They answered questions succinctly and then posed a few of their own. They flirted and laughed. Holland had laughed right back, well aware that some of the girls were highly attractive and that they knew it. He watched them walking away, then turned to see Parsons staring at him, mock-stern, an eyebrow raised.

'Easy, tiger ...'

'Don't be so bloody silly!' As Holland snapped, he remembered Thorne saying exactly the same thing, in exactly the same way, when certain veiled suggestions had been made about DI Louise Porter. Then he turned back towards the door to the school and saw the boy.

He was with three others; not the tallest, nor the one at the front as they came out into the quad, but he was still the focal point. He made some comment and the others laughed, and Holland could see straight away that he was the leader. The one around whom the other boys moved.

As the group approached, Holland watched the boy make subtle alterations to his appearance: the daily change from classroom to street. The tie was loosened and low-ered, fingers pushed the blond hair into spikes, and when the hand had finished working at the side of the head a gold cross was dangling from the boy's left ear.

Holland stared at the earring. There was something familiar about it; something important.

Parsons held out a hand, beckoned the group towards them. 'We're talking to anyone who might have seen what happened to Luke Mullen last Friday afternoon.'

There was a good deal of shrugging and shuffling of feet. More than one pair of eyes settled on the boy with the earring.

'Presumably that's when you'd have been coming out of school,' Parsons said. 'Perhaps one of you saw Luke Mullen getting into a car.'

There was a pause before answers began to tumble out, clumsily, one on top of the other.

'Loads of kids are getting into cars ...'

'I was playing rugby last Friday ...'

'There was a meeting for next year's skiing trip ...'

'I don't think we can help you.'

Answering last, the boy with the earring spoke with that odd, almost mid-Atlantic accent that Holland had heard in many of the pupils already: an upward intonation at the end of every sentence, as if everything were a nice, easy question being asked of someone who really ought to know the answer. The boy spoke for the other three, and Holland could see that they were happy to let him do so. He was the one each of them was keen to hang around with and to emulate; the friend they wanted. Holland remembered the boy with the briefcase, the young artist they'd spoken to earlier. This boy was everything that one was not, and probably most wanted to be.

Holland, if he was honest, had been as neither boy himself. At secondary school in Kingston twenty years before, he'd slogged it out somewhere between the two extremes. Head down; unhappily anonymous.

The four boys were already starting to amble away, but Kenny Parsons walked quickly after them, moved ahead and halted their progress. 'Hang on, lads, we haven't finished.'

'Haven't we?' the boy with the earring asked.

'One of your friends is missing.'

'I barely know him.' One of the others laughed. The boy with the earring shot him a look, shut him up instantly.

'So you're not in the same class?'

'Correct. We're not.'

'Same year?'

'Also correct. I don't see how any of this is really helping, though, do you?' He was already on the move again, hitching his bag across his shoulder and walking towards the main road.

Holland watched the boy and his friends depart. Something familiar about the boy's face, too; something important. Thinking about the way he'd spoken to Parsons; the way he'd looked at a police officer.

A *black* police officer . . .

'Cheeky little fucker,' Parsons said.

It was a jolt, like the gut-lurch you feel driving over a humpback bridge, when Holland finally dragged the picture into focus. The cross dangling from the ear. A face he'd seen before.

'I thought these posh kids had better manners than that.'

Holland nodded, knowing that this was exactly the point; that, if he was right, 'cheeky' was not the half of it.

The boy with the earring could afford to be sure of himself. It went with the uniform and the accent, for sure, but it also went with the fact that people made judgements about character on the strength of how you looked and sounded. Most people believed what such things had always told them.

Holland collared the next kid who passed and pointed towards the boy with the spiky hair. He asked the question and was given a name. Then he watched the boy called Adrian Farrell turn to look at them and walk slowly backwards down the drive, the blond hair still visible as he was absorbed, uniform by uniform, into the exodus of blue and grey.

The boy could well afford to be confident, because appearances were just that. And police officers, just like everybody else, made stupid assumptions.

Thorne, though usually more likely to brood than complain, was not beyond a decent moan every so often; and Carol Chamberlain, if she was in the right mood, could be a good listener. He grumbled into the phone about his back, about being shifted to the Kidnap Unit, about the

103

fact that his only real avenue of investigation was rapidly turning into a cul-de-sac.

Carol Chamberlain was not in the right mood. 'You should go and see someone,' she said.

'What, like a psychiatrist?'

'That as well, but I'm talking about your back. Shut up about it and go and see a doctor.'

After the chat with Jesmond, Thorne had walked back to Becke House and run the two newest names on the list through CRIMINT. Billy Campbell was reported to be attending a drug and alcohol rehab centre in Scotland. Wayne Barber had finally got round to using that screwdriver and was serving life with a twenty-five-year tariff in Wakefield Prison. That left only Mullen's original two, and Jesmond had made it clear he thought they were both a waste of time.

Thorne had started to feel like he was wading through treacle. He'd grabbed a sandwich from the canteen and walked back up to the Major Incident Room. Wondered whom he could possibly call up and complain to while he ate his lunch.

He'd known ex-DCI Carol Chamberlain for a couple of years. She'd been brought out of retirement in her early fifties and recruited for the Area Major Review Unit, a small team comprising previously retired officers, put together to take a fresh look at cold cases. They were known – not always affectionately – as the Crinkly Squad.

Chamberlain was anything but crinkly.

Thorne had always known that she could be spiky, that

she was not a woman to get on the wrong side of, but the year before he'd seen a blackness seep and spill from her; a slick of poisonous rage every bit the equal of anything bubbling and slopping inside himself, which had threatened to envelop them both. Once its acrid shadow had lifted, there had been enough light for them both to see clearly, to get what was needed, but there had been a price to pay. If it hadn't been for those few terrible minutes of madness – never spoken of since – they would not have found the man responsible for setting fire to a young girl. And, though Chamberlain would never know it, Thorne's father might still be alive.

She was a friend, but like most people whom Tom Thorne respected, she frightened him a little.

'Maybe I should call back later,' Thorne said. 'Obviously you're busy worming the cat or doing a crossword or something.'

'Cheeky bastard. Just because I don't want to listen to you whingeing.'

'I called because *occasionally* you have some decent advice.'

'Right, and because I know Tony Mullen.'

'*Sorry?*' Thorne put down his sandwich.

'Didn't you know that?'

'If I had, I would have called you straight away. How long have you known him?'

'I worked with him in CID at Golders Green, twelve or thirteen years ago, something like that. He'd've been a DS then, probably, or maybe he was about to be made up. He

105

was being bumped up to chief inspector round about the time I retired, I think.'

Thorne grabbed a scrap of paper, began to scribble notes. 'So?'

'So ... he was decent enough, I suppose. Straight, as far as I could tell, but that doesn't mean a great deal. I've got a lot of people wrong one way or another over the years.'

'What about these two names then? Cotterill and Quinn.' Thorne could hear classical music in the background. Chamberlain's husband, Jack, was a keen listener.

'I know it's not what you want to hear, but I think Jesmond might be right. I can't see either of those two as kidnappers.' She paused. 'I don't suppose anybody mentioned Grant Freestone, did they?'

'Should they have?' Thorne wrote down the name.

'Well, not *everyone* maybe, but I'm surprised his name hasn't come up at all.'

'I'm listening.'

'Freestone sexually assaulted a number of kids, 1993 or '94, round there. Boys and girls, I don't think he was fussy. He kept them in a garage behind his flat.'

*Kept them ...*

Thorne tried to blink away the image of a bag coming down over a boy's face.

'I was only on it briefly,' Chamberlain said. 'But Tony Mullen was very much involved, might even have been the arresting officer. It was common knowledge that things got nasty, that Freestone was making threats more or less from the moment he was nicked until he got sent down.'

'Threats against Mullen?'

'He might well have threatened others, but it's Mullen I remember. I was in court one of the days and I can still see the look Freestone gave him: not aggressive exactly, but . . . Well, I can still remember it, so . . . '

'Thanks, Carol. I'll check it out.'

She said nothing for a second or two, then the music was turned down. 'Let me do it.'

Slowly, Thorne underlined Grant Freestone's name. 'I thought, you know, there were cats to worm.'

'I'm ignoring you. Seriously, Tom, why don't you let me do some asking around and get back to you?'

Thorne could hear the change in Chamberlain's voice immediately. The work she did for AMRU was irregular, and frustrating more often than not. He knew how much she relished feeling useful; how keen she was to get her teeth into something, into *anything*. He also knew that she still had a broad network of contacts and that she was bloody good at what she did. She might come up with a damn sight more than could be gleaned from any computer search.

'Also, Jack's had a dodgy back for years,' she said. 'He's got some fantastic stuff he rubs on at night. I can bring it next time I see you.'

'Thanks.'

'So you've had a double result.'

Thorne thought about the video, the man with the

syringe. He wondered if this could possibly be the same man whose face Carol Chamberlain still remembered from a courtroom a dozen years earlier. A man who'd taken children before.

With one hand, he reached for his discarded sandwich. The other put pen back to paper and began to scrawl.

Drew box after box after box around the man's name.

# CONRAD

He'd come to realise a long time ago that nearly everything came down to fish and ponds. To how big a fish you were and the size of the pond you swam around in. That and time, of course. He'd decided that time was a very weird thing to get your head round.

Obviously, he'd never read that book about it by the bloke in the wheelchair; the one who spoke through some machine he'd invented and sounded like a Dalek. He wouldn't have understood it if he had, he knew that much, but he was pretty bloody sure that it would have been interesting. Time never ceased to amaze him, the way it messed you around. How you always got back from somewhere quicker than you got there. How the first week of your summer holiday seemed to last for ages and then the second week flew by and was all over before your skin had started peeling. How time dragged

109

on and on when you were waiting for something to happen.

It didn't seem like five minutes since Amanda had danced across and stuck her tits out at him. Since she'd been happy to let him get his end away for a few Bacardi Breezers and the promise of a favour. Five minutes ... six months ... whatever ... and now they were shooting a kid full of drugs and sitting and waiting for something to happen.

To be honest, he'd been happier doing what they'd done before. It was easy – in and out – and if anyone got hurt it was only because they really asked for it. People who were stupid enough to get all heroic – with money that belonged to fucking Esso or whoever – deserved a kicking, as far as he was concerned. This was different, though. There was no guts in it, nothing to make you feel like you'd earned what you'd made. It felt shameful, like something only a pussy or a wanker would do. It was a weakling's crime.

Maybe he'd feel different when the two of them were sitting somewhere warm, spending the money. Maybe then he could forget how they'd come by it. He hoped so, anyway.

Amanda was in the kitchen. Cheese on toast, probably; baked beans or something. She kept telling him that they'd splash out on somewhere flashy, go to a place with a doorman and photographers outside when the money came through. He'd asked when that was likely to be; told her that he was getting fed up sitting around with his thumb up his arse. That he wanted it finished. She'd told him that it wouldn't be much longer. That it would be over and done with soon enough, one way or another. He'd thought that sounded a bit fucking ominous. He'd looked across at the boy then, slumped in a corner of the bedroom, and thought that it sounded very fucking scary . . .

That had been a while ago. Hours and hours. Days, even. Time dragging its feet like some poor bastard who knows he's got a beating coming.

He knew it was all his own fault. That he'd had the chance to say 'no' early on, to say that it was a stupid idea. He couldn't lay all this at Amanda's door; but still, he hated it.

Waiting and not knowing.

And feeling like a very small fish.

# SIX

There were posters covering almost every inch of the pale green Anaglypta: the Spurs team of 1975, with Steve Perryman in front holding the ball; a futuristic Roger Dean landscape; the female tennis player walking away from camera scratching at a bare buttock. In the corner of the room, a music centre sat on a shelf supported by house-bricks, Bowie and Deep Purple gatefolds spread out across its Perspex lid and leaning against its speakers. Books and piles of magazines were strewn across an old dining table, carried up from downstairs to be used as a desk: *Melody Maker*, *New Musical Express*, *Shoot!*, *Jaws*, *Chariots of the Gods*, a couple of tattered Sven Hassel paperbacks. A Jilly Johnson calendar and a Woolworth's dartboard on the wall next to the window ...

Thorne blinked and looked again at these newer walls. Smooth and orchid pale.

There were reproductions of ancient maps, architectural blueprints with elaborate French calligraphy, posters for exhibitions at the V & A and Tate Modern. Some had been mounted in simple clip-frames while others were stuck to the wall with Blu-Tack. Standing in the centre of a very different bedroom from the one that had once been his own, Thorne decided that what Parsons had said the day before was about right: Luke Mullen was hardly a typical sixteen-year-old.

He walked across to the metal and glass workstation, surprised to see an Arsenal diary on top of the papers stacked to one side. He reached for it, curious, and somewhat relieved that the boy – though clearly misguided in his choice of team – had at least one passion with which Thorne was able to identify. He flicked through the first few pages, saw immediately that it was no more than a homework diary.

There was a rectangular patch of dust on the glass, where Luke's laptop had sat. The tech boys were still working on the hard drive, digging around for anything that might have been well hidden by anyone who knew what they were doing. But from what they'd been able to establish thus far, there was no significant email correspondence, nothing on any computerised diary to suggest that Luke had been planning to go anywhere. He hadn't spent time in chat rooms, and it didn't appear that he'd struck up a recent relationship with anyone online.

Little more had been gleaned from the details of his

mobile-phone activity. The phone itself had been in Luke's possession when he'd gone missing, so it had not been possible to check his contacts list, but records of calls and text messages provided by the phone company had yet to reveal anything that looked important. Luke had called his sister more than anybody else.

Thorne stared at the dust, at the shape of it, marking the absence of something, and found himself holding his breath. He imagined a young, alert mind racing, and fighting hard as the drug took hold, as eyelids dropped and thoughts slipped into the wet. Sopping and inky-black . . .

He pulled down the sleeve of his jacket, gripped it between fingers and palm and leaned down to wipe away the marks from the glass.

'You won't find him in here.'

Thorne turned to see Juliet Mullen standing in the door-way of her brother's room. He slapped the grey dust marks from his sleeve. 'Actually, I've found quite a lot of him,' he said.

The girl rolled her eyes and walked past him into the room, clearly unimpressed, and unwilling to discuss anything as tedious as an abstract concept. She leaned back against a wall and slid slowly down it until she was sitting on the grey carpet. 'So . . . ?'

Thorne looked around, then back at Juliet. 'Well, Luke was certainly tidy.'

'Nothing gets past you, does it?'

'I *am* a detective.'

114

'Can you prove that?'

'I've taken exams.'

'They must have lowered the pass rate.'

She wasn't smiling, but Thorne sensed that behind the studied air of boredom and irritation, it was a struggle not to; that she was enjoying the banter. Her hair was long, the same charcoal as the make-up around her eyes and the hooded top she wore over baggy jeans. Skateboarder chic, Thorne thought it might be called. Or grunge, or something. He thought about asking her, then decided it wasn't such a great idea.

'What was on the video?' she said suddenly.

It took Thorne a moment to work out what she was talking about; a moment before deciding he would not answer.

'Mum and Dad watched it this morning, before they called Porter. Just the once, I think, but it was enough. Obviously they wouldn't let me see it. And they didn't want to talk about it afterwards, so . . . '

'So?'

'So . . . I thought it couldn't hurt to ask.'

Thorne watched her draw her knees up, shrinking into the corner of the room. He couldn't help but be reminded of the previous evening with Phil Hendricks. Now, as then, he could see the pain and the longing beneath the pose; the anguish, raw behind the flippant remark. It couldn't hurt to tell her.

'It was Luke. Just Luke on the tape.'

She nodded quickly, as though something she already

knew had been confirmed. It was a mature gesture, self-possessed, but in the next instant a tremor in the soft flesh around her mouth turned her back into a child again. 'What did he say? Did he say anything?'

'Juliet, I can't—'

'They were crying after they'd watched it, the pair of them. They pretended they weren't, which was a bit bloody pointless, if you ask me. I mean, I knew what it was, you know? I didn't think they were watching porno at nine o'clock in the morning.'

'They didn't want you to get upset,' Thorne said.

'Right, that's brilliant. So now all I can think about is what *might* have been on the tape. What whoever's got Luke *might* have been doing to him. How much pain he *might* have been in.'

'He's doing OK. Honestly.'

'Define "OK".'

Thorne took a deep breath.

'"OK" as in having a whale of a time?' She began plucking at the pile of the carpet. 'Or "OK" as in still breathing?'

It was as tough a question as had been thrown at Thorne in a long time. 'Nobody's hurting him.'

Her head dropped to her knees. When she heaved it up again fifteen or twenty seconds later, the eyeliner was beginning to run. 'He's got a year and a bit on me, but sometimes it's like I'm the older sister.' Her eyes roamed from one part of the room to another, like she was searching to prove her point. 'I have to look after him in loads of ways. You know what I mean?'

Thorne stepped across and sat down on the edge of the bed. The duvet was dark blue and neatly squared away. He guessed that Luke had probably made the bed himself before leaving for school on Friday. 'Yeah, I think I do,' he said.

She sniffed. 'Pain in the fucking arse . . . '

The silence that followed was probably more uncomfortable for the girl than it was for Thorne. It was less than half a minute before she pulled herself to her feet. 'Right . . . ' Like she had a lot to be getting on with.

Thorne stood, too. He cocked his head towards the doorway, towards the rest of the house. 'It's good that you're all so . . . close. At a time like this, you know?'

Juliet Mullen nodded, pushed her hair back behind her ears.

'What did they argue about?' Thorne walked back to the workstation and looked at the photograph pinned to a corkboard above it: Luke on his father's shoulders, eyes wide behind orange swimming goggles; the pair of them grinning like idiots and the sun bouncing off the blue water around them. 'Luke and your dad, last Friday morning.'

'Stupid stuff about school.'

'Work stuff?'

'About Luke not making the rugby team or something. It wasn't a big deal.'

'Your dad seems to think it was.'

'That's just because of what's happened. Because he's feeling guilty. Because the last time he saw Luke, the two of them were shouting at each other.' She took a pace towards the bed and leaned down to smooth out the duvet where Thorne had been sitting. 'Luke was already feeling bad about it by the time we got to school. He told me he was going to say "sorry" when he got home, that it was all his fault for being cheeky or whatever.'

'Was it?' Thorne asked.

'I can't even remember. It was just bloody silly because those two never argue, you know? They're really close. It's that whole father–son thing?' It sounded like a question at the end, as though she were making sure Thorne knew what she meant.

'Right.'

'See you later.'

Thorne watched her leave. He knew exactly what she'd meant and, more importantly, he now also knew what had bothered him about the video.

What it was that Luke had said . . . or hadn't said.

He stopped on his way out, seeing that the corner of a poster near the door had come unstuck, and when he reached across to press it back in place, he noticed the writing beneath. He peered at the words, at the small, neat letters written in black ink on the wallpaper. A stark and secret litany of frustration, impatience or rage.

Fuck off
Fuck off
Fuck off!

*

From the school, Holland had gone straight back to Central 3000 and found himself a desk out of the way. He needed ten or fifteen minutes to gather his thoughts, to get into the Police National Computer system and to go over the relevant material. It was only when he'd done both, when he was as certain as he could be that he had something worth shouting about, that he called Becke House and spoke to Yvonne Kitson.

'How's your kidnap going, Dave?'

'Fine.'

'Missing us?'

'Listen, Guv, I need to talk to you about the Amin Latif murder.'

It was a little over six months since the eighteen-year-old Asian, an engineering student at a local sixth-form college, had been beaten to death by three white youths at a bus stop in Edgware. It had been, for all the obvious reasons, a high-profile investigation, but despite the media coverage, an extensive enquiry and even a witness who had provided a detailed description of the main attacker, the case had quickly gone cold.

Cold, but still tender. Still embarrassing.

Russell Brigstocke had been the nominal senior investigating officer, but, day to day, Yvonne Kitson had run things. To all intents and purposes, it had been her case, and – at least as far as she was concerned – her failure. She'd known from the moment she'd first looked at the boy's body – at a bloodied hand, knuckles down in a puddle across double yellow lines – that his death would

119

stay with her, irrespective of whether she caught those responsible. Hate crimes tended to do that. And the Amin Latif murder was about as hateful as they came.

Holland had her attention immediately.

He told her that he'd seen a seventeen-year-old, *spoken* to a seventeen-year-old, whose resemblance to her chief murder suspect was simply too close to be ignored. As he described the boy he and Parsons had interviewed an hour or two earlier, he stared at the picture which he'd called up and printed out from the PNC. The E-fit had been based on the description given by a friend of Amin Latif, a fellow student who had been present at the time of the attack but had escaped with a few broken bones and six months of nightmares. The picture wasn't identical to the image in his mind's eye: the blond hair was lank and lay flat against the head, much as it would have done on a night in October when it had been pissing down with rain. But below the hairline, everything else was spot on.

The face was Adrian Farrell's.

'Shit ... shit!' The exclamation of surprise had quickly been followed by a far harsher one. By annoyance aimed at no one but herself. '*Butler's Hall?*'

'I know. Who'd've thought?'

'*We* should,' Kitson snapped. 'We fucking-well should have thought.'

Butler's Hall was several miles from the street where Amin Latif had died, but it was certainly close enough; well within the thick red circle that had been drawn on the map in the Major Incident Room. Well within the scheme of things. There would probably have been 'Can You Help?' posters near by, and perhaps a number of its pupils lived at addresses that were canvassed during the house-to-house enquiries. Of course, it would have been impossible to question every student at every school and college in the area, but plenty had been, and Yvonne Kitson would not have bet on too many of them being pupils at Butler's Hall.

Assumptions, by their very nature, went unspoken. And racist thugs did not go to public school.

'What was he like, Dave? I don't mean physically . . . '

'Arrogant, aggressive. Full of himself.'

'You sure you weren't just seeing that? Projecting it? Are you positive you weren't making this boy's behaviour fit because of what you thought?'

'It wasn't until afterwards that I thought *anything*,' Holland said. 'I was watching the little fucker walk away from us, and when he turned round I knew he was the kid in the picture. The kid with the earring.'

Kitson said nothing for a few moments. Holland could hear her slurping her coffee, swallowing, *deciding*. There was a flutter of panic as he realised that, in the past, he'd watched her, Brigstocke and others judging similar pronouncements of certainty from Tom Thorne. He'd also seen the fallout later, when such certainty had proved to be horribly misguided.

'Fair enough,' Kitson said.

Holland let out the breath he'd been unconciously holding. 'What should we do?'

'*You're* still working on a kidnap, as far as I know, but *I* want to have a look at him.'

'You going to bring him in?'

'I want to see him first, just to double-check you're right to be so worked up about it.'

Holland had been afraid that talking to Kitson, or anybody else, might shake his conviction a little, but it had done the opposite. As he ran through each detail of the conversation with Adrian Farrell, as he described the look the boy had given Kenny Parsons, he could feel his certainty settling into determination. And now that her initial anger had worn off, he could hear the exhilaration in Kitson's voice too.

And she had every right to be excited.

Finding a murderer was one thing of course, and convicting him was quite another, but what had made this particular killing so uniquely barbaric was also what gave them their best chance of doing just that.

Before he'd been kicked to death, Amin Latif had been the victim of a serious sexual assault. Semen samples had been taken from his body, had given up the gift of their DNA. Now, on a frozen slide in an FSS lab in Victoria, curled the double helix that might identify a killer; the sequence of letters on every rung of its elegantly twisting ladder just waiting for a match.

Downstairs, it felt like a bad wake after a good funeral; there was a sense of that sort of *desperation*.

In many of the rooms, bright against the darkness

that was descending outside, a decent enough effort was being made to generate a degree of conversation and activity; of ordinariness. To keep at bay the tide of gloom that threatened to rush through the house at any moment, as if a black and swollen river were about to burst its banks.

There were perhaps a dozen people in the Mullens' home, split fairly evenly between family and friends on the one hand, and police officers on the other. Thorne spoke through a cloud of cigarette smoke to Maggie Mullen and to a DS with a big mouth who drivelled on about a 'gang snatch in Harlesden that had gone monumentally tits up'. He had to spend five minutes talking football with Tony Mullen's brother, and fuck-all with the second family liaison officer, before he finally got the chance to speak privately to Louise Porter. He'd collared her as soon as he'd arrived back at the house and passed on what Carol Chamberlain had told him about Grant Freestone. That was half an hour ago, before he'd wandered upstairs and run into Juliet Mullen.

As soon as he saw the opportunity, he ushered Porter into a good-sized utility room that ran off the kitchen.

She grinned. 'This is all a bit sudden ... '

'I know what was wrong with the video,' Thorne said. 'What was bothering me.'

Porter leaned back against a large chest freezer and waited to be told.

'It's all to his mum.'

'What is?'

'Everything Luke says on the tape is aimed at his mum. He says nothing at all to his dad. I've got a transcript in my bag and I checked. Have a look if you like—'

'I believe you. Go on …'

'*Try not to worry, Mum. Nothing to get yourself worked up about, Mum. You know the stuff I mean, Mum.* Everything's for her. It's like Mullen's being cut out.'

Porter thought about it. Behind him, Thorne could hear the boiler clicking and then the rush as the pilot ignited the gas. 'Maybe Luke was punishing his father,' Porter said. 'For the argument they'd had.'

'It must have been one hell of a row, then, don't you think? If the kid's still bearing a grudge while he's being held hostage. While he's being tied up and drugged.' Thorne moved across and settled in against the freezer next to Porter. She shuffled along to give him room. 'Anyway, I talked to Luke's sister, and she's positive the row wasn't that serious.'

'I think you're reading too much into it.'

Thorne shrugged, acknowledging the possibility.

'Like you say, the boy's in trouble. So you're probably right – he's not likely to be thinking about whether he's fallen out with his dad – but it's perfectly natural for him to be thinking more about his mum, isn't it? He's only a kid.'

'Maybe. He's obviously trying to be brave for his mum because he doesn't want her to worry. But shouldn't there have been *something*, some message, for his dad? Everyone keeps banging on about how close they are.'

'He didn't mention his sister, either.'

That was a good point. Porter had a disconcerting habit of making them. 'It feels strange, that's all,' Thorne said.

'Maybe he didn't have a lot of choice about what he said.'

This was something Thorne hadn't considered. 'Are you saying it was scripted? You think he was told what to say? It certainly didn't feel like that.'

'Just thinking aloud,' Porter said.

They stopped at the sound of footsteps on the other side of the door. They listened, heard the fridge door swing open, and Thorne waited for whoever was helping themself to leave before he spoke in a whisper. 'Let's *keep* thinking,' he said.

Porter's mobile began ringing as they stepped out of the utility room; just when Tony Mullen walked into the kitchen. Mullen stared, his face giving nothing away, while, for reasons he couldn't immediately fathom, Thorne felt himself redden.

Mullen nodded towards the phone in Porter's hand. 'I think you'd better get that,' he said.

Porter answered, said nothing for a few seconds, but Thorne could see that whatever she was hearing was important. He glanced across at Mullen and could see that he knew it, too.

'Right,' she said. 'When?'

Thorne stared until he'd made eye contact, and saw nothing but concentration.

'I'll get back as soon as I can.'

Mullen stepped forward, asking the question calmly as soon as she'd ended the call. 'Have they found him?'

'Mr Mullen ...' Porter glanced at Thorne, then hesitated further when she saw Mullen's wife appear at her husband's shoulder. 'I'm sure you understand—'

Maggie Mullen clutched at her husband's sleeve, asked him what had happened. He didn't take his eyes off Porter, and when he spoke his voice was no longer quite so calm. 'And I'm sure *you* understand. So let's hear it.'

Porter took a second or two, then spoke quickly. 'It's good news,' she said. 'Apparently the people holding Luke aren't as clever as we thought they were.' Her eyes flicked to the screen on her phone, as if searching for more information, before she dropped the handset back into her pocket. 'We got a good set of prints off the videotape.'

'You've got a match?' Mullen said.

Porter nodded. 'We've got a name, yes.' She turned to Thorne. 'And we're working on an address.'

Investigating a murder rarely allowed those involved much of a private life, but the hours devoted to a kidnap case were even more brutal. For those few he'd been given to get his head down, Thorne was offered a room at a small hotel in Victoria where the Met had a permanent block booking, but he decided to make the trip back to Kentish Town instead. The travelling would cut down his free time between shifts, but he wasn't sleeping much anyway. He preferred lying awake at home to wearing out the thin carpet of an anonymous hotel room; to dunking teabags on strings, listening as the city coughed itself awake, and worrying about the fact that he hadn't fed the cat.

Perhaps if it had been a slightly *nicer* hotel . . .

He arrived home just after midnight, still early enough to call Phil Hendricks. Five minutes into their conversation and the last can of Sainsbury's lager, he was starting to relax. To enjoy telling his friend about the celebrated criminal history of a man named Conrad Allen.

'So he waves this plastic Magnum around . . .'

'I presume we're talking handgun here as opposed to ice-cream . . .'

'I'm not listening,' Thorne said. 'He waves it around, comes on like a hard case or whatever, thinks that's an end to it. But, unfortunately for Conrad, the other bloke's a little bit pissed off. He gets straight back in his car, dials 999, and fifteen minutes later an armed response unit's squealing up and Dirty Harry's face down on the Mile End Road, trying to convince some very pumped-up coppers that he was only having a laugh.'

'So how come he never got done for it?'

'Ask the CPS, mate. He was charged, but when it came to taking it any further, I suppose they just decided it wasn't worth the effort. But, luckily for us, he was fingerprinted and this was back in 2002 before they changed the law, so the prints never got destroyed after the charge was dropped.'

'What, and the silly bastard just forgot you had them?'

'Forgot that, forgot to wear gloves when he was handling the videotape . . .'

'Not the sharpest knife in the cutlery drawer.'

'I don't think this is his usual line of work, you know?' Thorne thought about another tape he'd seen a few hours before, back at Central 3000. 'Some of the boys on the Flying Squad are fairly sure Allen's the bloke who turned over half a dozen petrol stations and off-licences in Hackney and Dalston last year. Him, another gun that's probably plastic, and a woman, pretending to be a hostage. A lot of shouting and shit acting.'

'Sounds like an episode of *EastEnders*,' Hendricks said.

'It's a jump from that to kidnapping kids, though, don't you reckon?'

The tape of in-store CCTV footage had been biked over to the Yard from Finchley. As he'd watched, Thorne had struggled to equate its images with those on the tape that had been sent to the Mullen family. The picture of the big man in the ski-mask – the violence in his movements and language – failed to gel with that of the figure who'd walked towards Luke Mullen with a syringe. That action was equally violent, every bit as brutal, in its own way, but Thorne simply couldn't see Conrad Allen moving so easily on to something so clinical.

Something so *quietly* vicious.

Instead, he'd found himself watching the woman: staring at the screen as she screamed and begged for her life, pleading first with the robber and then with each terrified cashier and shop assistant to hand over the money before she was killed. If the man with the gun to her head *was* Conrad Allen, then the chances were that she was the woman who'd charmed a sixteen-year-old boy into her car. She might not be the greatest actress in the world, but Thorne had little trouble believing what she might be capable of. It was easier to imagine her as the driving force, as the one who'd come up with a way to make a lot more money than could be grabbed from the average till. Why she'd targeted Luke Mullen was a totally different matter ...

Thorne became aware of what sounded suspiciously like chuckling on the line. 'Is this the *EastEnders* crack? Are you laughing at your own jokes again, Hendricks?'

'One of us has to.'

'Good. I was hoping this would cheer you up a bit. I presume you do still need cheering up. You've not really given much away.'

Back when Thorne had first called, Hendricks had sounded reluctant to say a great deal about the Brendan situation. Now, as then, he seemed keen to talk about almost anything else. Just a grunt or two. A muted 'y'know' before a grinding change of subject.

'How's the back holding up?'

Thorne rubbed his calf. 'If anything, it's my bloody leg more than my back.'

'I've told you, it sounds like you've herniated the disc. You really need to get it sorted.'

'Not a lot of time at the minute.'

'It's a phantom pain in the leg, you know that, don't you? Where the disc's pressing on the sciatic nerve. Your brain's being told your leg hurts, but there's nothing really wrong with it.'

'Hang on ...' Thorne took a fast mouthful of lager. As time wore on, it was finally starting to taste of something. 'I thought it was the brain that did the telling.'

'Some parts of the body shout a bit louder than others,' Hendricks said. 'And of course, there's one or two with minds of their own.'

The cat wandered in from the kitchen, grumbled and was ignored.

Thorne sat there, thinking that although the 'part' Hendricks was talking about – *Thorne's* part at any rate – had been fairly subdued for a while, it had started speaking up for itself rather more than usual in the last couple of days.

# AMANDA

She was happy enough about it herself, but she knew
Conrad would be utterly thrilled that things were finally
moving. That it would all be sorted very soon. He was in
the bedroom talking to the boy, but she'd tell him as soon
as he came out. They'd need to get themselves together,
get ready to make a move.

The spoonful she'd been cooking up when the phone
had started to ring would balance her out a little ...

She'd screened the call, just as she'd been doing ever
since they'd got back to the flat on Friday after the pick-
up. All part of keeping their heads down, quiet as mice,
and it was mostly people phoning up trying to sell shit,
anyway. They'd given the kid enough stuff to knock out a
horse as soon as they'd had the chance: the minute she'd
driven far enough away from the school, pulled over and
let Conrad in. Then they'd waited until it was dark and

carried him inside, wrapped in the cheap picnic blanket they'd bought from Halford's and stashed in the boot. They'd made sure there was lots of food and booze in, so there was no need to go out, no need to talk to anybody. All they'd had to do was sit and wait it out, and now they were on the last leg.

She'd screened the call ... then, as soon as she'd recognised the voice, she'd grabbed at the phone, picked up and listened.

She was relieved, and pleased, that it looked like working out, looked like nobody was going to get hurt. She'd always insisted on that, even when they were pulling the hold-up thing. Nobody should get badly hurt if it could be avoided. She thought that this side of her, the side that wanted everyone to come out of a situation OK, said something good about her character. Something to be proud of. After all, with everything she'd been through, the shitty stuff she'd had to deal with when she was a girl, it would have been understandable if she'd turned into a vicious, vindictive cow; if she'd wanted others to feel pain just to make herself feel better. She knew people like that, and she despised them. No, she just wanted to have a good time and get enough of whatever she needed; to forget about all the bad stuff. And, while she was doing that, she was always happier when no one else was suffering. Not through any fault of hers, anyway. There'd been the odd idiot who hadn't played along, of course; there were always accidents. And there was that dealer she'd asked Conrad to sort out, but lowlife like him didn't count and deserved everything they got.

When bad things happened to bad people, she thought, there wasn't a whole lot to get upset about.

The boy, Luke, wasn't a bad person, and he didn't deserve any of what was happening to him, she was aware of that. He was just the means to make the money; he was their fake gun. She thanked God that, all being well, he would come out of it in one piece, none the worse.

Conrad had not been so certain, had said, 'Yes, but don't forget what he might go through later on. Don't forget about what could happen *mentally*.'

She'd turned, inched her body away from his, and pointed out that she was hardly likely to forget that.

Now, she was feeling a lot mellower, more forgiving. She sensed that she was starting to roll and relax, wondered if maybe she should tie the boy's hands again as things were going to start happening soon. Get him ready to go. Then, from nowhere, as the drug took her down, she began to imagine herself and Luke meeting up in ten years or so. They would run into each other at some trendy party or club and it would all be really nice. He'd be relaxed and pleased to see her. He'd be keen to tell her that it was all right, that, as it happened, he'd had a bit of a crush on her back then in that flat, and that a few sweaty nightmares were a small price to pay for a whole lot of perspective. She'd tell whoever she was with that Luke and her were old friends, and it would be cool as they shared a slow dance . . .

She was only dimly aware of Conrad coming into the room as she drifted away, Luke's arms around her neck, and his voice in her ear, thanking her for passing on her gift to him, for giving him a skin that little bit thicker than other people's.

# THURSDAY

# SEVEN

Half-past stupid in the morning, his third day into it, and the sun had struggled up just a little later than Tom Thorne ...

Its overnight absence had slowed things down, had seriously reduced the rate at which much-needed information could efficiently be gathered. It didn't matter how important your case was, how many bodies had been discovered, how imminent the threat to life and limb, who had been kidnapped. The simple fact was that most people, most *civilians*, at any rate, tended to knock off at five o'clock. Obtaining crucial intelligence outside office hours was always difficult. Gaining vital access to any secure or private database – at a local authority housing association, the DSS, Barclay's Bank or Virgin Mobile – was pretty much a lottery for as long as the M25 remained empty. It was often a question of tracking down a contact number for the person unlucky enough to be manning a twenty-four-hour emergency desk. Or the name of the *really* poor bastard who was going to get dragged out of bed in the middle of the night.

Finding an address for their main suspect had taken the Kidnap Unit four hours, and had come down in the end to Conrad Allen's love of cars.

Via M-CRAC, the remote-access search facility, officers had been able to access the CRIMINT system at Mile End and pull up all the details of Allen's original arrest in 2002. Running the number plate of his car through the national computer revealed that the vehicle had been sold the year before. The student who'd bought it – and who was still awake, honing his PlayStation skills – remembered Conrad Allen; remembered him describing in great detail the type of car he'd be buying next. An hour later, the owner of a small dealership in Wood Green was being asked to get up, get dressed and accompany the police to his less than organised office, where he grudgingly waded through a pile of less-than-kosher sales receipts. The dealer was naturally keen to help and go back to bed and, when prompted by a picture, he vaguely remembered Allen and the 'fit-looking blonde bird' who had been with him when he'd strolled on to the car lot. His memory of the car itself was better: he was able to give virtually every detail of the diamond-white Ford Scorpio 2.9i, its 24-valve Cosworth V6 engine and, rather more importantly, the address he'd delivered it to, after he'd banked the £1,200 in cash.

The dealer knew nothing about any Passat, black, blue or otherwise, so the team decided that the car seen near the school was probably the girlfriend's. Or maybe Conrad had decided that his boy-racer days were over, and had traded in the Scorpio for something a little more sedate.

Once the information had been obtained, Porter's team had shifted into top gear pretty bloody quickly. The first step was the establishment of an observation post. In the early hours – grateful for the cover of darkness as far as *this* part of the operation went – a dedicated Intel Unit had mounted one small camera on a lamp-post opposite an estate agent's just off the Bow Road, and another at the back of the building to monitor what looked like a rear entrance/exit. These immediately began feeding live pictures back to Central 3000, as well as to a mobile tech team which was cutting up and broadcasting the images from inside a fully equipped van two streets away. A dozen or more officers from the Kidnap Unit were scattered around the area: in empty buildings and unmarked cars and on the street; waiting alongside a Special Events team, a hostage negotiator, paramedics and a group from SO19, the Firearms Unit.

All waiting for word of one sort or another.

By the time he managed to slip into a nearby sandwich bar for an early lunch, Thorne had been stuck for the best part of four hours in a car with the same SO7 officer who'd bored his arse off the evening before . . .

He carried the tray over to the table; pushed a mug of

coffee and a plate across to the woman sitting opposite him.

'What do I owe you?' she asked.

Thorne took the top slice from a bacon and egg sandwich and reached for the ketchup. 'Let's hear what you've come up with first.'

He'd been surprised when Carol Chamberlain had rung up first thing, asking if they could meet. When she wasn't at the Yard working an AMRU case, it was all but impossible to prise her away from her husband and her home in Worthing, which Thorne took great delight in calling Euthanasia-on-Sea. She'd explained that after she and Thorne had spoken the day before, she'd spent the whole afternoon making calls and then caught the evening train up. She'd told him that she'd had dinner with one old friend and stayed overnight with another.

'Old friends?' Thorne had asked on the phone.

'A DCI I worked with on the Murder Squad for a few years, and a DS who retired same time as me. Both good blokes. Both useful.'

Thorne watched Chamberlain bite into a roll with rather more delicacy than he'd displayed himself. He was impressed by how quickly she'd got to work after they'd spoken. 'You don't waste any time,' he said.

'I didn't think we *had* any time.'

Thorne brought her up to speed, told her about the surveillance operation on Conrad Allen's flat. With the possibility of a child's life at stake, he knew that she was right to think that time was not on their side, yet, that

140

morning, every minute spent sitting and waiting for something to happen had seemed to warp and stretch until urgency had turned to inertia. The silence from radios had become deafening, and staring at the drawn curtains of the flat above that estate agent's had been like looking through the wrong end of a telescope.

'So, go on then,' Thorne said.

Chamberlain wiped crumbs from her fingers. 'I was right,' she said. 'Somebody should definitely have mentioned Grant Freestone.'

'Because of the threat he made to Mullen?'

'Because of that ... and because he's still wanted for murder.'

Thorne just looked, and waited for her to carry on. He could see that she was enjoying the moment of drama, that she relished the telling.

'In 1995 Freestone got ten years for child-sex offences. He served just over half his time, was paroled in 2000 and became one of the first ex-cons to be dealt with by a MAPPA panel.'

Thorne nodded. Though he had never been directly involved, he was well aware of the Multi-Agency Public Protection Arrangements. The scheme had been established as 'a statutory framework for inter-agency co-operation in assessing the most dangerous ex-offenders'. It was designed for those individuals who posed a serious threat to the public, 'to manage and monitor their reintroduction into the community'.

To keep a watchful eye on the bogeyman.

'Sounds like he was an ideal candidate,' Thorne said.

'He was, but I'm not so sure about the people who were supposed to be watching him. I don't know exactly how it all happened, but it's a wonder the scheme wasn't shut down there and then.'

'Teething troubles?'

'Ever so slightly. Freestone was given a flat in Crystal Palace, which is why Bromley Borough Council helped put this MAPPA panel together. Then he got involved with a woman called Sarah Hanley a few months after his release; a single mother with two young kids.'

'Ah. That would be a problem.'

'It would have been if a slightly bigger problem hadn't come along. In April 2001, Grant Freestone chucked her through a glass coffee table.'

'Nice.'

'She bled to death, and by the time anybody found her . . .'

'Freestone was long gone.'

'And still is,' Chamberlain said. 'Likely to stay that way, too, I would have thought. He's certainly the nearest thing to a prime suspect anyone ever came up with, but it's been so long I don't think anyone's looking for him very hard any more, or very *often* at any rate. He gets circulated once in a while, and the case notes are reviewed annually, but basically it's even colder than most of the shit I get given to try and warm up.'

A waitress came alongside, gathered up the plates, asked if either of them wanted more tea or coffee. Thorne told

Chamberlain he'd need to get back as quickly as he could, and handed over a five-pound note to cover the bill.

'Was Tony Mullen involved with this second case at all?' he asked. 'With the Sarah Hanley murder?'

Chamberlain said that he wasn't, that she'd spoken to the detective who'd headed that investigation and the subsequent hunt for Grant Freestone; the officer who, theoretically at least, still had the case. But Thorne was only half listening, having realised that he'd asked a redundant question. He knew that Tony Mullen could not have been involved, and he knew why.

'I've written down all this bloke's details,' Chamberlain said. She slid an envelope across the table. 'He seemed nice enough, though he was a damn sight more interested in finding out why I was asking than in telling me an awful lot.'

'Par for the course,' Thorne said.

'I suppose.'

'Aren't *you* still a bit touchy about the ones that got away?'

Chamberlain took a compact from her handbag and flicked it open. 'The older I get, the touchier I am about *everything*.'

'Thanks for this.'

'No problem, and I still owe you.' Her eyes darted momentarily from her mirror. 'I don't mean for the tea and a ham roll, either.'

Thorne picked up the envelope and pushed back his chair. He knew she was talking about the incident a year

143

before, when their questioning of a suspect had got horribly out of hand. He reckoned that each of them owed more than could ever be repaid. 'I'll let you know how everything turns out,' he said.

Carol Chamberlain nodded and went back to reapplying her lipstick as Thorne turned from the table. As he left, she shouted after him. Apologised for forgetting the stuff for his back, told him that she'd stick some in the post.

He walked quickly back towards the car. He stopped off at a newsagent's, bought two cans of Coke and a copy of *Uncut* without speaking a word. Thinking all the time, as he made his way back to the car, that Chamberlain had been right when she'd said that *someone* should have mentioned Grant Freestone. Someone ... One of the several coppers he'd spoken to, probably. Jesmond, almost *certainly*. And why hadn't Tony Mullen said anything?

His mind focused on Luke Mullen's father as he walked. On how – Thorne would double-check the month to be sure – he couldn't have been involved in the 2001 murder case and the hunt for Grant Freestone; the man he'd previously put away for twelve years; the man who had so publicly threatened him.

Because 2001 was the year that DCI Tony Mullen had resigned from the force.

The red Skoda was parked just south of the Bow Road, on a side street below the Blackwall Tunnel approach. Thorne was delighted to see that Dave Holland had arrived in his absence, and, ignoring the DS sitting behind the wheel, he climbed into the back seat alongside him.

The officer in the front seat turned round in a rustle of polyester. 'Please your fucking selves . . . '

Though Thorne had talked to Holland from the Mullen house the evening before, they hadn't seen each other since Holland's trip to Butler's Hall. Sitting in the back of the car, they talked about Adrian Farrell, about Holland's call to Yvonne Kitson and about whether there might be a connection between Luke's kidnap and the Latif murder.

'It's worth thinking about, certainly.'

'Not for too long though, right?' Holland said.

Thorne opened one of his cans. 'I can't see it to be honest.'

They sat in silence for five minutes after that. Thorne flicked through his magazine while Holland stared out of the window at a view Thorne had already decided was up there with the most depressing he'd ever seen. That said, he wasn't certain he could stomach the Taj Mahal for four hours at a stretch.

'It's fucking lovely round here, isn't it?' Holland said eventually.

'If you like concrete.'

The SO7 man took the chance to jump in, and pointed towards the Bow flyover. The permanently gridlocked slab of granite rose a few hundred yards to the north of them, lifting the A11 above the A12 and carrying traffic across the River Lea, towards Essex and away from the capital.

'They reckon that's where the Krays buried Frank Mitchell, you know? Inside one of the supports.'

'Right,' Thorne said. '1966.' He knew all about what the twins were supposed to have done with 'Mad Axeman' Mitchell, having made the somewhat rash decision to spring him from Dartmoor Prison. Though the Axeman's final whereabouts remained uncertain, with some claiming that the body had been dumped at sea, it was nevertheless slightly odd that, thirty years after Mitchell's disappearance, Ronnie Kray's funeral cortège should have crossed the Bow flyover. It was hardly the most direct route to Chingford cemetery.

The DS looked a little deflated. 'How come you're such an expert?'

'Too much time on his hands,' Holland explained.

'At least you knew where you were with those guys,' Thorne said.

Holland let his head drop back. 'Nice simple nicknames for a kick-off.'

'Right. Nobody got confused.'

'He's mad, he's got an axe. What shall we call him?'

'Er . . .'

And as they carried on, they could see the man from the Kidnap Unit clocking them in the rear-view mirror, desperately trying to work out if they were taking the piss.

At lunchtime, the Butler's Hall sixth-formers were allowed to leave the premises for one hour. Some took sandwiches into a nearby park, but most wandered towards the modest parade of shops on the Broadway. They browsed in the small branches of Game and HMV, or hung around outside the fish-and-chip/kebab shop, trying their best not to look like kids from a public school; to avoid getting caught doing anything that might reflect badly on the uniform they wore.

Yvonne Kitson sat in her car at the end of a road opposite the school entrance, watching the kids come out and waiting to get her first look at Adrian Farrell.

Next to her, DC Andy Stone flicked through the *Daily Mirror*. 'I still don't see why you didn't get DS Holland to come with you, Guv. To point out this little tosser.'

'Bored, Andy?'

Stone shook his head without looking up from the paper.

'Dave's a bit tied up with other things; and, anyway, I don't want him pointed out. I want to see if I can spot him. Fair enough?' She moved her thumb back to her mouth, chewed on the nail and stared out of the window.

Most of the time, it seemed to Kitson that you couldn't have it all; that if your life outside of work was going well, then the job itself would turn to shit. And vice-bloody-versa. A couple of years before, she'd been a high-flyer and she'd known it; the cases had been high profile, just as she'd been when she'd solved them. Then she'd been stupid enough to get involved with a senior officer, and while he had been forgiven by wife *and* top brass, she had watched both her career and her family life tumble into freefall. Now things were back on an even keel domestically – her kids were doing well, relations with her ex-husband were civil and she was seeing somebody – but work was another matter. Though she was grafting as hard as ever, the job just seemed to grow more maddening with each failure, each compromise. She'd begun to wonder if it might be down to her; if she'd lost the capacity to be satisfied.

Stone stopped whistling between his teeth for a few seconds. 'This is funny,' he said. 'They're dropping hints in here about some "popular daytime TV presenter" who's having it away with his male researcher. Who d'you reckon that is, then?'

The Latif enquiry had been as frustrating as any Kitson had known, and every murder case she'd caught since seemed to involve her running headlong into a series of brick walls. The wall she was supposed to be trying to get over that morning had built up around a disturbing rite of initiation into a Tottenham drugs gang. New members would drive around the streets in a car with no headlights on, and in order to prove they were worthy they would have to fire a gun into the first car that flashed its lights at them. It was brutal in its simplicity, in the casually random way that the unsuspecting victim was selected.

The first driver unlucky enough to try and be helpful.

Five days before, having been shot at for no obvious reason, the man behind the wheel of a Toyota Landcruiser had mounted a pavement on the Seven Sisters Road, killing himself and a young woman waiting at a bus stop. One of the city's newest gang members had moved straight from low-grade crack dealer to double murderer, and though Kitson and the team knew very well which gang was responsible, had spoken to half a dozen young men who knew equally well who had pulled the trigger, nobody was saying anything.

Sometimes the brick walls had wide smiles, and gold teeth, and enough attitude to make Yvonne Kitson want more than anything to punch them into the middle of next week.

She badly needed a result. For the way it would feel, far more than for the way it would look. And now, if Dave Holland's eyesight and instinct weren't both seriously screwed, she might achieve one.

Stone turned to the back page of his paper. 'No real surprise, though,' he said. 'I reckon a lot of those TV presenters are batting for the other side, don't you?'

Kitson mumbled something that could have been 'yes' or 'no', every committed part of her brain focusing on the group that was crossing the road, and on her first glimpse of Adrian Farrell. On the fact that she owed Dave Holland a very big drink.

'Is that him?'

Kitson held up a hand to silence Andy Stone, as though the boy they were talking about were no more than a few feet away; as though his hearing were as well developed as his arrogance. She watched him walk slowly down the main road, every bit as hard to miss as she had been led to believe. He was chatting idly with two other pupils, a boy and a girl. Although he would be off the premises for no

149

more than an hour, Kitson watched as he, along with most of those around him, went through the transformation that Holland had described. She watched as Farrell took off his blazer and tossed it over his shoulder; as he loosened his tie.

She watched, holding her breath, as he put in the earring. From school to cool.

A hundred yards or so from the entrance, Farrell eased away from his schoolmates and joined up with two new boys who were crossing the road fast towards him. These boys wore uniforms of their own: Nike caps; New Balance trainers; Kappa casuals. They moved like men but looked young enough to make Kitson question why they weren't in school themselves.

The three hailed each other, though it was impossible to make out the words being shouted. Fists were clenched and proffered. Kitson was reaching for the door handle as the knuckles kissed in greeting and the trio moved off together towards the shops.

'We on the move?' Stone asked.

Kitson opened the door. Stepped out, buzzing as she thought about Adrian Farrell's interesting new mates. His nice, white friends.

'Let's get some air,' she said.

Porter came through on the radio. She suggested to Thorne that they should meet somewhere between their two vehicles. Put their heads together.

They walked up Fairfield Road, crossing over the Docklands Light Railway towards Old Ford. 'Barry Hignett came down about half an hour ago,' Porter said. 'He was keen to get cracking.'

'Like the rest of us aren't?'

'I mean *really* on the hurry-up. So we sent a couple of the lads in to see if there might be any help around. See if we can get a bit closer.'

They stopped to let a lorry back out of a goods yard. The driver scraped a wall, pulled forward a yard or two and tried again. This time, they walked around, ignoring the exhaust fumes and the beeping of the reversing alarm.

'Thanks for telling me.' Thorne's tone made it clear that he wasn't the slightest bit grateful; that, in his opinion, he should have been told half an hour earlier.

'I'm telling you now, so there's no point getting snotty.'

'Hignett getting shit from your detective super, you reckon?'

'For definite,' Porter said. 'And I wouldn't be surprised if Tony Mullen had been on at him, too. Poor sod's got it coming from everywhere.'

'Is he still here?'

'Gone back to base.'

'Makes sense,' Thorne said. Which it did. As SIO, Barry Hignett would need to stay close to Central 3000. From there, he could monitor all events, could communicate with every member of his team, while staying within easy reach of the top brass. There was a buck in this case, same as in any other. It just flew around that little bit faster before it stopped.

Porter slowed outside a swanky-looking development of

flats. A map on the gate showed the location of the swimming pool, the sauna, the private shops. 'I could do with somewhere like this,' she said. 'My place is a shit-hole.'

'This is the old Bryant & May factory,' Thorne said, staring through the gates. 'Where the matchgirls' strike was.'

Porter shook her head.

'End of the nineteenth century.' He pointed towards the building. 'The girls in there went on strike for better pay and conditions. Turned into a national story. Kicked off the trade union movement, more or less.'

'Lit a match under it.'

Thorne was already thinking ahead and missed the joke. He turned around, pointed back towards the Bow Road like a tourist guide. 'You've got Sylvia Pankhurst's original campaign headquarters over there. Votes for Women and all that.' He tried to keep a straight face, but couldn't resist the crack. 'And *now* look where we are.'

'You asking for a slap?' Porter leaned into him as she stepped past and kept walking.

'So where's this flat of yours?'

Her mobile had barely begun to ring when Porter snatched at it. Thorne knew that the phone had a ringtone he would probably recognise, but he'd never heard enough of it to place the tune.

When the call had finished, they started back towards Conrad Allen's flat. 'Sounds like you got that help you were looking for,' Thorne said.

'We've got an old girl in the flat next door who's a major fan of ours. She got her front door kicked in a couple of weeks ago, and apparently the uniforms were *extremely* helpful. One of the tech boys is up there now setting some gear up.'

'Reckon they're in there?' Thorne asked.

Porter's look made it plain she hadn't the slightest idea. 'There's been fuck-all to see, so it's glass-against-the-wall time.'

They didn't say a great deal else after that. They just picked their feet up, jogged back around the lorry that was still trying to back out.

Andy Stone got the formalities out of the way. Made the introductions, waved the warrant cards around.

It was a very pleasant smile. Kitson wondered how much more of it she might be seeing in the days to come. 'We've already done this,' Adrian Farrell said. 'We spoke to a couple of officers yesterday after school.'

Kitson took a step closer, flashing a pretty decent smile of her own. 'It's not about Luke Mullen,' she said. 'We're investigating another matter.'

They were gathered outside a bakery and sandwich bar in a small, pedestrianised precinct off the Broadway. The place was busy, with workers from local shops and offices zigzagging between pushchairs to grab lunch or do a quick bit of shopping. Farrell and his two friends leaned against the window, eating sausage rolls from paper bags. They'd stopped talking, elbowed each other and stared as Kitson and Stone had walked up the gentle slope of a long wheelchair ramp towards them.

One of the boys in the baseball caps nudged his companion, nodding towards Farrell. 'They've finally come to get you, guy.'

'Yeah, the cops is well on to you for sure.' His friend spluttered the words through a mouthful of hot food and started to laugh.

Farrell grimaced at the pair of them. 'Shut it.' Then, back to Kitson: 'Sorry about them. Bloody rabble.'

'A student was murdered a couple of miles from here,' Kitson said. 'Last October, in Edgware, you probably saw it on the news.' Farrell's expression scrunched up, like maybe he *thought* he had. 'Ring a bell?' Kitson watched his eyes drop for half a second to her tits, then back up again. 'His name was Amin Latif.'

Farrell certainly looked as though the name meant nothing to him.

'You don't remember it? I'm quite surprised.'

'I remember our chaplain leading a special prayer in assembly. Right before the hymn. He does that, you know, for disaster victims, stuff like that. Yes, there was definitely one for some poor bugger who'd been murdered. It would probably have been around that time.'

There was loud music coming from the record shop opposite. Something cheery and pointless.

'So?'

'So what?'

Kitson tried hard to meet his eyes. 'Did you say a prayer for Amin Latif?'

Farrell sniffed and looked away from her, stepping aside

as a group of teenage girls came out of the bakery. One of his friends made a comment under his breath. A girl told him to piss off.

'Should you be talking to me?' Farrell asked.

'Sorry?'

'Without the presence of any legal representation. Without my *parents*.'

There was an impressed whistle from beneath one of the baseball caps.

'It's just an informal chat, Adrian.'

For the first time the boy looked slightly alarmed, though only for a second or two. 'How d'you know my name?'

'The police know everything,' one of his friends said.

The other pointed at Farrell, mock-serious. 'They know when you last had a *wank*, guy.'

Andy Stone stepped forward, corralled the designer-clad double act into an adjacent doorway. 'Why don't I get *your* names? Just so we don't feel like strangers.'

'You're seventeen,' Kitson said. 'Which makes you legally responsible.'

Farrell watched his friends, nodding his head to the rhythm of the pop song.

'Anyway, there's really no need to get worked up.'

'Who's worked up?' Farrell said.

'That's all right, then.'

'It's not true, though, is it?' He leaned towards her, con-spiratorial. 'You don't *really* know the last time I shook hands with my best friend?'

155

She smiled, not quite so easily thrown. 'As it goes, we'd be delighted to fix you up with whoever would make you more comfortable. A lawyer, if you want; your mum and dad. Maybe that nice chaplain of yours, if it would help. We could all reconvene at the station, do everything properly.'

'I don't actually have to do anything, though, do I?'

'No, absolutely not. We're just talking.'

'Fine then.' He put all his weight on one foot, preparing to leave. 'Nice to talk to you.'

'But when that happens, we just sit around and start asking questions. Of ourselves, I mean. We wonder why you don't like us. Why you're so reluctant to help. What you might be trying to hide.'

Farrell started to shake his head, grinning like he thought her efforts were clumsy and amateurish. 'I'm going back to school now,' he said. 'It's double history this afternoon, and that's my favourite.'

Kitson wanted to slap him stupid.

'Come on, wankers.' Farrell shouted across to his friends and started to walk away. Once there was breathing space between themselves and Stone, the other boys puffed out their chests, fell into step with each other and quickly caught Farrell up.

Stone moved across to Kitson. 'They're not afraid of very much, are they?' he said.

They watched the boys swagger down the ramp. As they reached the bottom, one of Farrell's friends tossed his empty bag towards a litter bin. The others jeered at the miss and the three kept on walking.

'It's easy when there's a few of you,' Kitson said.

Farrell glanced back, a couple of steps before he turned the corner; looked round as though he'd forgotten something, just for a second or two before he disappeared.

His hand was slapping the side of his leg in time to the music.

Kidnap or not, as operation posts went, the security was fairly relaxed. Thorne had taken part in plenty of intelligence operations – usually involving the Serious and Organised boys – where a steady stream of visitors to the target address had meant days on end in the back of a stinking van, pissing in plastic bottles and living on biscuits. In this instance, the surveillance provided by the cameras meant that there was no need for any vehicle to be located within direct sight of Conrad Allen's flat. So there was a degree of flexibility in terms of individual movements, and conditions within the team vehicles themselves were not quite as spartan.

Less than a minute on foot from Allen's flat, Porter had spent most of her morning south of the Bow Road, on a one-way street between Tower Hamlets cemetery and the tube station. After their brief meeting on Fairfield Road, Thorne had joined her in the back of a dirty Transit, its panels boasting the logo and contact details of a local roofing contractor.

That had been just after three o'clock. Nearly an hour before.

A trestle table ran down one side of the van. Two small

monitors displayed the black-and-white shots from the cameras front and back, while a scarred metal speaker broadcast communications from the assortment of unit vehicles in the vicinity. A strip of grubby brown carpet had been laid on the floor, and a plastic bag was wedged into one corner, bulging with Styrofoam containers, newspapers, empty cans and cartons.

'So what do we think?'

'It's been forty-five minutes since we went into the old woman's flat.'

'Longer,' Porter said.

Two other officers were sharing the space with Porter and Thorne. Kenny Parsons sat in one of two folding canvas chairs, with the other taken by a fat DS named Heeney – a gobby Midlander with a lazy eye and an attitude to match. Porter looked less than delighted at being harassed by either of them. She brought the radio handset to her mouth. 'How are we doing, Bob?'

There was a pause.

'I'm sure he'll let you know,' Thorne said.

Porter gave him a look like he wasn't helping a hell of a lot, either.

Then, from the speaker, with a hint of annoyance: 'Still nothing.'

'You've checked the equipment?'

'Twice. The equipment's fine.'

'Sorry ...'

It had been a stupid question. The microphones were about as high tech as they could ask for, and she knew that the technical operator had done his homework. They'd established that the flat was rented, had guessed correctly that the firm below it would have handled the letting and had gone in bright and early to acquire a diagram of the layout. A kitchen-diner, two small bedrooms and a bathroom, all leading off the single corridor. The listening equipment that had been set up in the premises next door would be more than adequate: nowhere in a flat that size would be out of range.

'Someone's going to have to make a decision here,' Heeney said. His accent turned 'make' into 'mek'; turned his opinion into complaint.

Thorne sat with his back to the van's doors and stared across at Porter, perched on the wheel-arch directly behind the driver's seat. She looked right back at him and raised an eyebrow. He thought she might be asking what he thought, but he couldn't be sure, and he was even less sure how she'd react if he told her. So he said nothing; failing to offer any opinion, because he didn't want to risk a row in front of the others. And because he didn't really have one to offer.

There were far too many questions that needed to be answered, boxes to be ticked, with no option to pass.

Were Conrad Allen and his girlfriend in the flat?

Was that where they were holding Luke Mullen?

Had they graduated from plastic guns to real ones, and how were they likely to react if a team of armed police officers smashed through their front door?

'If I had final say, I'd go in,' Porter said.

Thorne pulled up one knee, then the other, but he was

unable to find any position that wasn't painful. 'Would you want it?'

'The final say? Probably not.'

'Good call, I reckon. With great power comes great responsibility.'

'I didn't have you down as a philosopher.'

'It's from *Spiderman*,' Thorne said.

She lifted the handset. 'I need an opinion, Bob.'

From the speaker: 'There's nothing moving in there.'

'Fuck!'

'Sorry, but there it is.'

'Maybe the kid's drugged and they're both asleep.'

'What don't you understand? *Nothing's* moving. I can hear a clock ticking, and I can tell you which room it's in, if you want. I've got water moving through the radiators, and the rattle of pipes expanding, but I don't hear anyone snoring or turning over in bed. These mikes can pick up the sound of *breathing*, and I can't hear any.'

There was a snap of static, and another voice cut in: 'This is DCI Hignett.'

'Sir . . .'

'It's time to go in, Louise.'

It was suddenly as though the Transit had been wired up to the National Grid. Everyone jumped, looked hard at one another, and Thorne crouched straight back down by the doors as Porter gave all units the order to move in.

Thorne threw open the doors and jumped down on to the road. He felt Porter's hand on his shoulder; felt it dig in, and pull him back.

'Hang about, Tom. I don't want a crowd of us going in there behind the guns.'

'Are you joking?'

Porter wiped a fleck of Thorne's spittle from her lip. 'Look, Heeney's staying put as well, so don't get stupid about it.'

'Who's making these decisions?'

'You're only supposed to be helping out, remember. I haven't got time for this. Get back in the van and stay by the radio.'

Thorne watched her and Parsons sprint towards the Bow Road and climbed back into the van. Heeney was sitting again and looked at his feet as Thorne moved past him to take up Porter's place next to the monitors. The big DS mumbled something about Porter being 'on the rag'. Thorne turned away and tuned him out. He sat on one of the chairs, leaned closer and stared at the small screen, at the fixed and flickering picture of a black, metal fire-escape.

With only one door to get through, as opposed to a pair of them coming at the property from the front, the rear entrance was favourite. More importantly, when firearms were being deployed, keeping the action well away from the street was always desirable.

Thorne didn't blink.

For twenty, twenty-five seconds, the image was constant, then suddenly it filled with movement as a dozen or more figures began crowding in. Moving into the picture from the back and sides of a scrubby, unloved garden;

over and along the line of a crumbling wall towards the bottom of the steps.

Then a flurry of hand signals, and *up*; speed less important than stealth.

The team gathered around the door, and Thorne picked out what details he could, imagining those that were too indistinct to make out: the butt of an MP5 carbine; the MET POLICE logo on a chest thick with body armour; the dead geraniums in a plastic window-box . . .

In the van, a few murmured instructions came over the speaker.

Thorne could make out Porter and Parsons, and several heads he thought he recognised. He watched two figures move into the picture and knew – though he couldn't see it – that they would be fixing the rubberised teeth of a hydraulic jack to either side of the door frame. These were members of the Special Events team – the Ghostbusters – a civilian unit on call to any branch of the Met that needed to gain rapid entry to premises but wanted something rather more subtle than a ram or a size-nine boot.

The SE boys stepped away from the door, trailed the cables back to a small generator and signalled that they were set.

They looked towards Porter for the nod.

Got it straight away.

There was no sound from the monitor, but Thorne had worked with similar forced-entry equipment before. He imagined the sharp hiss of compressed air and the slap of the cables jumping against the metal floor. The crack as the frame was shunted wide, leaving the door with nowhere to go but in and down, forced hard to the floor by the feet of the SO19 officers who streamed across it into Conrad Allen's flat.

In a matter of seconds the shot was empty again, a flat shadow beyond the doorway, while its chaotic soundtrack was broadcast from half a dozen radios, exploding like bursts of gunfire from the speaker. Bouncing between the metal walls of the van: a collision and a curse; an order given to get out of the way; and an instruction to anyone on the premises to make themselves fucking visible very fucking quickly. A cacophany of grunts and shouts:

'Kitchen clear!'

'Armed police!'

'First bedroom and corridor clear.'

Thorne winced at each distorted spatter of voices and volley of breath, focused through every crackle of static. He pictured the officers running, freezing, pressing themselves against walls; sweeping the space through rifle-sights, moving sharply aside as other figures passed through shadows, barrelled in and out of rooms.

'Clear!'

'Clear and secure!'

Heeney muttered at Thorne's shoulder: 'The place is empty.'

'Shut up,' Thorne said.

A shout then, audible above the others. Just one word. Just the *crucial* word.

'Body.'

'Say again?'

'We've got a body.'

Thorne stands up, crouches, pushes his hands against the roof. He strains to hear more, to hear *anything* through the hiss, through elastic seconds of dead air.

'Where?'

'In here.'

'Where the fuck's "here"?'

'Back bedroom.'

And Thorne can see it when he closes his eyes. He's seen it before, or close enough: the sole of a training shoe, a mop of dark hair, a great deal of blood.

'Jesus,' Heeney whispers behind him, but Thorne is already moving towards the doors, putting a shoulder against them, and tearing across the road in the same direction Porter had gone just a few minutes before.

Pain blooming in his back and chest as he runs, and more pictures he could do without: fingers and thumbs, grubby on the barrel of a syringe; the tremble around Juliet Mullen's mouth.

A pair of armed response vehicles, three squad cars and an ambulance are already parked up on the track that runs along the back of the building, and the garden is thick with the Job by the time Thorne drops on to the other side of the low wall. Body armour is laid down, sweaty on the grass; stepped across by scene-of-crime officers, scrambling into full-body suits and hurrying towards the fire escape. There is conversation and clatter as a constant

164

stream of Met personnel shuttle up and down the metal staircase. A necklace of cigarette smoke curling past them towards a clear sky, and Holland at the bottom, turning to Thorne, his arms raised, asking:

*What the fuck's going on?*

'Tom . . .'

Thorne spun round and saw Porter moving towards him across the grass. Breathless and none too polite, he asked Holland's unspoken question for him, then asked another before she'd had a chance to answer the first.

'What about Luke?'

Porter shook her head.

'Alive? Dead? *What?*'

'We've got *two* bodies up there,' Porter said. 'Almost certainly those of Conrad Allen and his girlfriend. Both look like they've had their throats cut; to *start* with, at any rate. There's a knife.'

'So where's the boy?' Thorne asked.

In a hurry, or sick of being barked at, Porter turned and started to walk back towards the cluster of vehicles. She answered without bothering to look round. 'Right now it's impossible to say, and I can't see any point in speculating. I *do* know we've got a pair of dead kidnappers and a hostage who's nowhere to be found.'

# PART TWO

# ALL ABOUT CONTROL

# FRIDAY

# LUKE

Before, when he'd woken up, when he'd come out of it, it had been horribly slow. Like surfacing through water thick as glass. Seeing what was on the other side, but without the strength to kick hard and reach it quickly. But this time, when everything had happened, it was as though he were conscious in a second, and as soon as he'd opened his eyes he'd been alert and alive to every sound and sensation.

He'd felt his blood jumping.

He'd heard the shouting immediately; the grunting and the noise of things smashing in the next room. They were arguing. He'd heard them fighting before, a couple of times, but this sounded really serious, and he guessed it was what had woken him so suddenly. Something inside his brain, some weird survival instinct that never switched itself off, had roused him, was telling him that this might be his chance.

171

As usual, when he'd first opened his eyes, he'd had no idea whether it was day or night. The curtains had been drawn tight across. But for almost the first time he'd been alone, with his hands untied, so after a minute or two he'd got up from the mattress on the floor, crept over and pulled the curtains back an inch or two. It was dark outside, but in the tower blocks opposite he could see lights in some of the windows and the flickering of TV sets. He'd guessed that it was probably early evening.

Trying not to breathe, he'd stood very still in the middle of the room, listening to the screaming from down the corridor.

He'd mentally mapped out the whole place during those first few trips to the bathroom. It wasn't a complicated layout and he'd always been good at picturing stuff, at laying out diagrams on his computer and seeing how things connected. He'd known, standing there in the dark, that were he to take a left turn out of the room he was in, he would need to get through two doors before he was on the street. He knew that because he'd tried to run through one of them on the first day, which was when they'd started giving him the injections more often. Turning right would have been a better bet, but he knew that he would have had to go past their room, would have had to risk being seen, and he knew that there would still be a locked door between him and the back way out. He was fairly certain there was a way down through the kitchen: an old-fashioned fire escape like his nan used to have. He'd been almost completely out of it, but he could remember seeing the metal steps, hearing the man's feet ringing against them as they'd carried him in.

How many days ago was that?

Half a dozen times after he'd been woken, he'd decided that he'd have the best chance if he tried to get away right then, while they were distracted. If he went for it and tried to sneak past while they were still shouting and chucking stuff at each other. Half a dozen times he'd chickened out and told himself he was a shitty little coward. Shivering in the dark and pissing in his pants, afraid to make a run for it.

Then the shouting had stopped and he'd felt his feet carrying him from the room and turning to the right. The map in his head was bright and pulsing, and he was a glowing dot moving slowly along a dark line as he inched along the corridor, as he pressed himself against the wall and tried to move with no noise. And perhaps he wasn't quite as awake or alert as he'd thought, because things suddenly seemed to blur and shift when he glanced through the open doorway to the bedroom. When he saw Conrad and Amanda.

When he noticed the knife, and bent to pick it up.

Everything was very fucked-up and fuzzy from there on: from whenever the hell it was, to whenever the hell *this* was; from those incredible moments of light and colour to this newest, numbest darkness.

Memory came in beats and shocking flashes.

Explosions of clarity, like that moment in the horror

film when the power goes out and the stupid girl lights a match and sees the face of the slasher: the door as he ran at it, and his heart like a hammer; the klaxon of his breath; a woman's face at the window of a house moving quickly past him.

And the warm, wet memory of so much blood.

# EIGHT

Thorne stood in his dressing-gown, drinking tea and staring out at the garden as it grew lighter. His eye had been caught by a beer can he'd forgotten to bring in from the other night; then he'd seen the movement at the end of the garden and stayed to watch.

The fox was worrying at something, digging at it in the corner behind one of Thorne's recently purchased pots. Thorne wondered whether it might be a squirrel or a baby bird, then decided it was more likely to be an old burger carton or a discarded piece of KFC. Without turning round he called softly for Elvis, and relaxed a little when he felt the wetness of the cat's rheumy eye against his ankle.

Motionless, he stood with both hands wrapped around his mug, and tried not to think about what Russell Brigstocke might say, what he would be unable to *resist* saying, when Thorne saw him in an hour or so's time. He tried to think about the boy and not the bodies, but he was unable to separate the two. They'd have results on the knife and the blood by now, and perhaps the bizarre idea that some had begun to whisper the night before at the crime scene would have solidified into a genuine theory. Thorne was more comfortable with a very different notion, but his own idea was equally strange. And equally hard to explain.

A car alarm began to scream somewhere at the front of the house and Thorne watched the fox look up and freeze. He saw drops run along the animal's flank, the fur darkened and plastered to its bones by the drizzle. After a few seconds it turned back, unconcerned, to its meal.

Typical Londoner, Thorne thought.

He took a sip of tea, but it was almost cold, so he rinsed out the mug and wandered through to the bedroom to get dressed.

He ran into Brigstocke near the door of Central 3000, standing behind him in a short queue for the drinks machine. The chat was asinine enough: how it made the crappy old kettle at Becke House look a bit shit; how Spurs still needed someone who could put the ball in the net. Then, when Brigstocke had got his drink, he turned and leaned against the machine, spoke as Thorne stepped forward to stab at the buttons.

'Well, you've got those bodies you wanted.'

There it was . . .

Thorne could say nothing, could *do* nothing but

acknowledge the point with a look he hoped did not come across as sheepish.

They walked slowly towards the far side of the room, where two very pissed-off civilian staff were laying out many more chairs than Thorne had seen last time, when the team had gathered to watch the videotape of Luke Mullen.

'How's this going to work?' Thorne asked.

'I think that's what we're all here to try and work out.'

'Why here, though? Why not Becke House?'

'We tossed a coin.' Brigstocke blew across the top of his coffee. 'I lost.'

Thorne laughed, then realised he was the only one. 'You're not joking, are you?'

'The Kidnap Unit gets home advantage, and I get to make the speech.'

'Well, it's nice to see that this is all being handled so professionally.'

'That's the point,' Brigstocke said. 'None of us has handled anything quite like this before.'

'We've had FSS working their arses off overnight, and none of the blood found at the crime scene belongs to Luke Mullen. But we do know he was there. His fingerprints were all over the smaller of the two bedrooms, which is where he appears to have been held, and where we're ninety-nine per cent certain the videotape was shot. Luke Mullen's fingerprints have also been found on the knife which was used to kill Conrad Allen and his girlfriend, who, from the statement given by the car dealer in Wood Green, and from identification found on the premises, we believe to be one Amanda Tickell. Miss Tickell's mother is due at the mortuary any time now to identify the body formally.'

Brigstocke moved a pace or two to the left and right of centre as he spoke, his voice rather than his body language holding the attention of the fifty-odd men and women in front of him. Though the thick specs and the quiffy hair often lent the DCI a vaguely comic aspect, he could recite the phone book and no one listening would shuffle their feet. Toss of a coin or no, he commanded the attention far better than his opposite number at SO7. Thorne guessed this was why Barry Hignett was doing the listening, standing off to one side and trying to look like he endorsed everything that was being said.

Brigstocke gestured towards a black-clad figure in the front row. 'Doctor Hendricks is going to say a quick word about how the murders appear to have been carried out.'

Phil Hendricks stood up while Brigstocke stepped further across to stand next to Barry Hignett. Now there was movement, and a murmur or two, and a good deal of coughing as the changeover took place. Thorne took the opportunity to stretch his legs out, groaned quietly as the pain moved up and down in a wave from thigh to ankle. He was sitting in the same row as Holland, Kitson and Stone, while Porter, Parsons and the rest of the Kidnap crew were a couple of rows in front. Thorne read nothing into it beyond the usual demarcation of territory, the polite, run-of-the-mill 'fuck you'.

It was not quite seven o'clock in the morning, and, bar a nutcase or two, the rest of the huge room was empty beneath its coloured flags.

'"Appear" is the right word,' Hendricks said. 'The post-mortems aren't due to be carried out until later on this morning, so this is based on a cursory examination of the bodies, their positions at the crime scene, the blood spatter, the depth of the wounds and so on.'

Hendricks looked straight at Thorne, but no one could have guessed they were friends. Thorne had seen the professional side of his friend kick in on cue too many times to be surprised by it, but he still admired Hendricks' ability – especially given the hour – to turn it on like a tap. He was clear and concise, a real bonus when dealing with the average copper, and though he always looked the same, he even managed to soften those flat, Mancunian vowels when the situation demanded it.

'I'm guessing that although Allen may not have died first,' Hendricks said, 'he was the first to be attacked. He was taken by surprise, his killer probably coming at him from behind and reaching round to slash his throat.' Hendricks raised his arms to demonstrate, his right hand slicing through the air viciously. 'He might have taken a good few minutes to bleed to death, but from the moment he was attacked, he was out of the game. He'd've gone down and stayed there.'

'How tall would the attacker have been?' Hignett asked.

'I can't be exact ...'

'Be *in*exact.'

'From the angle at which the blade passed through the windpipe, I'd say he'd be about the same size as Allen. Around six feet.'

Hignett looked towards his team.

'Luke is five feet ten,' Porter said.

Hendricks glanced towards Brigstocke, got the nod to carry on. 'The woman died from a very different series of stab wounds,' he said. 'There are defence cuts on her arms and a far more haphazard pattern to the half a dozen or more wounds around her neck and chest. I'd say she was overpowered. I think she saw what happened to Allen, put up a fight and was just not strong enough.' He looked to where Hignett was standing, anticipating the next question. 'She wasn't a weakling; not for your average junkie, at any rate. There was decent muscle definition ...'

'Luke Mullen does a lot of sport at school,' Hignett said. 'I think we can assume he would be strong enough to overpower a woman, knife or no knife.'

Thorne had heard enough. 'Can we?' He clenched his jaw, but still felt the blood come to his face as heads turned towards him. 'Everyone does sport at that school, but it doesn't mean the kid was particularly sporty ... or strong. He'd had an argument with his father the morning he was snatched because he *hadn't* got into the rugby team.'

'We're just outlining possibilities,' Hignett said. 'If this were an explanation of events that we could possibly eliminate, we would.' He pointed at Hendricks, who seemed unsure whether he should sit down again. 'None of these are answers I want to hear, trust me.'

'Fair enough.' Thorne was trying hard to sound conciliatory. 'It just sounds like minds are being made up.'

Hignett nodded, but there was a nasty edge creeping into his voice. 'This unit's never had a case like this. We've had plenty of kidnaps turn into murders. *Plenty*. But in every case, the hostage has been the victim. It's not usually the kidnappers that wind up dead, so I hope you'll forgive us at this stage for considering all the options.'

'But you're *not* considering all the options—'

'You're the one who seems to have a closed mind on this one. You certainly don't appear to care too much about the evidence.'

Thorne could feel the eyes on him. Brigstocke's and Porter's. 'Yes, I do care. I'm not denying the fingerprints and all the rest of it, but I'm also wondering why the door to the flat was locked. Why Luke Mullen should suddenly decide to kill his kidnappers, then run off into the night, taking great care to lock the door behind him.'

'We're looking at that.'

'But most of all, I'm wondering where he is. Why he hasn't got in touch with us or with his family.'

An SO7 man, two rows ahead, piped up. 'Perhaps because he's just killed two people and he's scared to come forward.'

Porter cleared her throat. 'Or because he *can't* come forward.'

Thorne felt sure that Hignett was the type who would

have known exactly how to handle things were he speaking to his own team. As it was, he seemed a little unsure about how to deal with such an unfamiliar situation and looked to Brigstocke, as if they might smooth out the rough edges between them.

Thorne took it as a hopeful sign.

Brigstocke stepped forward again, ushering Phil Hendricks back to his seat as he did so, and making sure Thorne was given a good, hard look before he opened his mouth. Before he tried to move things forward. 'Like DCI Hignett said, this is a strange one for all of us. So it's going to be a case of suck it and see, and I'm sure we'll make mistakes. As to the direction we move in, we'll react to the evidence, same as we always do. With that in mind, we will have to look at the possibility that, for whatever reason, Luke Mullen killed his kidnappers. But we'll look just as hard at a scenario involving a third party, as yet unknown, who murdered Allen and Tickell, took Luke and is now holding him at another location.' He looked over at the SO7 man, who seemed to approve and was keen to press on.

'Right, practicalities,' Hignett said. He addressed his own officers. 'Good news for those of you who live a bit further north, shitty for the rest of us, but we'll be working mainly out of Becke House, up at the Peel Centre.' That got contrasting reactions, from the two sides of the room. Hignett held up his hands. 'It makes sense, I'm afraid. They're geared up for a major murder enquiry and, for what it's worth, Colindale's a damn sight closer to the

Mullen house. Some of you will still be working from here, but I want to avoid a stupid amount of toing and froing. You can spend half a day getting across town and we haven't got the time.' He turned to the area of the room in which Thorne was sitting; sarcastic but conceding a possibility at least. '*Luke Mullen* may not have the time.'

'We need to get this going,' Brigstocke said. 'That means we share information and pool resources, and I see no good reason why it shouldn't work out. We can afford to move in a couple of different directions if we choose, because ultimately they're bound to converge.'

Now it was Brigstocke's turn to direct a comment, but Thorne saw it coming and looked down before the DCI had the chance to catch his eye. He stared at his shoes through the rest of it.

'Because we're all agreed on one thing,' Brigstocke said: 'if we can find whoever killed those two up in that flat, one way or another we'll find Luke Mullen.'

'Well that was fun,' Kitson said.

Thorne and several others from the Murder Squad contingent had drifted towards the exit. Despite the somewhat fraught nature of the previous half hour, Thorne was in good spirits. He was pleased to see the likes of Kitson and Karim, happy that they would be working together again, albeit on an operation that no one had really thought through properly.

Thorne and Kitson lingered near the lifts.

'Define "fun",' Thorne said.

'OK. Relative to trapping your tits in a mangle.' Kitson smirked, but the lightness didn't remain on her face for long. Thorne thought she looked tired, and even further out of sorts than when he'd run into her at Becke House a few days earlier.

'How's this new lead on the Latif murder shaping up?' He asked.

'Early days ...'

It seemed to Thorne as though she was searching his face for signs that he was convinced, but seeing none.

'I fucked up,' she said.

'How?'

She took a few steps away from the lifts, and Thorne followed her. 'Ever since Holland came to me with this, I'd been thinking how strange it was that Farrell hadn't been looked at before. The E-fit that Amin Latif's friend came up with at the time isn't exactly a portrait – the hair's different for a kick-off – but it's very bloody close, you know? As close as I've ever seen. You look at this kid, Tom, and if you've got a good picture of that E-fit in your head, there's no question it's him.'

'Right.' Thorne had seen the picture, of course, but he hadn't been near to the case. It was one of those that the team had picked up while he was still working on the rough-sleeper murders.

'So I kept asking myself, "If it's so bloody obvious, why did no one call up and suggest we should be interested in Adrian Farrell?" That picture was in the *Standard*, it went out on *Crimewatch* ...'

'And?'

'And I checked ... Someone *did*. There were two calls logged in October last year saying that we ought to take a look at him, but we never did. He wasn't mentioned by name. It was more: "there's a kid in my son's class who looks like the picture I saw on the TV" sort of thing. But the school was named, and for some reason the tip was never acted on, the calls were never followed up. They got buried in the file and ignored, and ultimately, that's down to me.'

'Hang on, you weren't the one who ignored them. You never even knew about them.'

'I'll find out who *did* ignore them, but that's not the point. Whoever it was, they looked at that piece of information and dismissed it, presumably because it sounded like bollocks. Within the general framework of the case, the direction we were moving in, they looked like crank calls.'

'The obvious route is usually the right one, Yvonne.'

'Well, it wasn't this time.' Kitson had lowered her voice, but now it was growing louder, more strident. 'We had our heads up our arses, and when a posh public school four or five miles away was mentioned, it was ignored because we thought we were looking in the right place. Because we were far too busy talking to kids at the comprehensives in the shittier parts of Edgware and Burnt Oak. Knocking on every door on the Deansbrook estate, and on the Wallgrove ...'

Andy Stone came round the corner and Kitson trailed off. Stone nodded at the two of them, non-committal, and walked away again after a second or two. Thorne thought that Stone wasn't the greatest copper he'd ever known, but every so often his instincts were spot on.

Kitson spoke quietly again. 'Now that kid can afford to be a cocky little sod, because he knows he's got away with it. Because we let him. He can swan around, wearing the same earring he wore on the night he killed Amin Latif, because he thinks he's bulletproof.'

An officer by the lift kicked the doors, then walked briskly past them towards the stairs, announcing that he couldn't be bothered to wait, that he was desperate for a fag.

'I know all about fucking up,' Thorne said. 'I've done stuff that makes this look trivial.'

That got something to soften around Kitson's eyes. 'I'm not arguing,' she said.

'There wouldn't be any point.'

'I just want to put this right.'

'Well, that's the good part. Unlike most of the times I've fucked up, it sounds like you've got the chance.'

Now that they were out of the more dangerous territory, they returned to the lifts.

'Bearing in mind how we came across Farrell in the first place, are we chasing up a possible link to *this* case?' Kitson pressed the button. 'We're sure that he *knows* Mullen at least.'

Considering the strange turn that the case had taken in the previous twelve hours, Thorne now thought it even less likely that there could be a connection between the kidnapping of Luke Mullen and a six-month-old racially motivated murder. But he also remembered what he'd just said to Kitson about the most obvious route. 'It can't hurt to talk to him when you get the chance,' he said.

The lift arrived and they stepped inside.

'I certainly plan on getting the chance,' Kitson said. 'But he's not the easiest kid to talk to.'

'How are your three, anyway?'

The doors slid across as an officer from Serious and Organised slipped quickly inside. Kitson answered Thorne as though she were measuring her own children against others she might recently have met.

'Fucking *gorgeous*.'

On the ground floor, Thorne's phone rang as he moved gingerly through the revolving doors.

'This is Graham Hoolihan. You left a message ...'

Hoolihan was the DCI whose details had been passed on by Carol Chamberlain. He had led the investigation five years earlier into the murder of Sarah Hanley, believed to have been killed by her boyfriend, Grant Freestone. Thorne had left Hoolihan a message the previous afternoon.

'Thanks for getting back to me so quickly,' Thorne said. 'I don't know if Carol Chamberlain explained why we're interested in Grant Freestone ...'

She had, but evidently it hadn't been to Hoolihan's satisfaction. So Thorne went over it again. Outside Scotland Yard, the pavement was thick with people on their way to work, hurrying towards Parliament Square and

Buckingham Gate. Though the rain had as good as gone, there were still one or two umbrellas up, as it looked like it hadn't gone very far.

Hoolihan did not know Tony Mullen, and was unaware of any threats that might have been made against him by Grant Freestone. He was sure about one thing, though: 'Freestone's not a kidnapper.'

Thorne was consistently surprised by how ready people were to put criminals into boxes. Lazy or just unimaginative, it seemed strange to him. If a seemingly respectable doctor could be a serial killer in his spare time, why was it so difficult to conceive of a paedophile and suspected murderer kidnapping someone? 'Did you know him?' Thorne asked.

'I never *met* him,' Hoolihan said. 'Though I hope to have that pleasure one day.'

'I hope you do, too.' Thorne marked down the man on the phone as one of those who hated to fail, but guessed that it was the result – or the lack of one – more than any sense of injustice that needled him. Points or passion; it usually came down to one or the other.

'You could try talking to one of the people on Freestone's MAPPA panel. They *ought* to have known the bastard. They watched him for six months after he came out, didn't they?'

'Thanks, I'll do that.'

'I can't tell you who they were, mind you, except for the copper who was involved. I dug his name out before I called.'

Thorne reached into his jacket pocket and scribbled down the details on the back of a used Travelcard. 'He'd have the names of the others on the panel, would he?'

'I've no idea,' Hoolihan said. 'We certainly didn't have anything to do with them at the time. We just wanted to find Freestone. Once he'd buggered off, a bunch of social workers, or what have you, was no use to anyone. The whole thing was a waste of bloody time, if you want my honest opinion. Do-gooders who didn't really do a fat lot of good!'

'Why "do-gooders"?'

'They decide to tell Sarah Hanley about Freestone. About what he's like. They then tell *Freestone* what they're going to do, so he goes marching round there, him and Hanley argue, and he throws the poor cow through a coffee table.'

'You think it was the MAPPA panel's fault that Sarah Hanley was killed?'

Hoolihan paused, unwilling perhaps to go quite that far. 'The "PP" is supposed to stand for "Public Protection"...'

The chat didn't last much longer, with both men keen to get on with their days. Afterwards, Thorne sat on one of the concrete bollards and made four phone calls trying to get hold of DCI Callum Roper. Once he'd tracked down his quarry, he made an appointment to see him later that morning. During their brief conversation he outlined the Mullen case, taking care to drop the names Hignett, Brigstocke and Jesmond, and to stress the urgency of the situation. He never mentioned Grant Freestone.

Then he began heading towards Westminster tube station, exchanging nods with an armed officer he knew by sight. He watched as a kid with a Mohican posed next to the officer while his mate took a photo. The copper smiled politely and put a hand on the kid's shoulder. The kid grinned like an idiot and pointed towards the copper's machine-gun. Thorne turned at the clatter of heels on the pavement behind him.

'Hold on . . .'

Porter caught up, fell into step beside Thorne, and the two of them carried on walking. They had not spoken since the cursory exchanges the night before, at the crime scene.

'You move pretty fast for a short-arse,' she said.

They carried on in silence past Christchurch Gardens, originally part of St Margaret's, Westminster and burial site of the seventeenth-century Irish adventurer Thomas 'Colonel' Blood, who stole the Crown Jewels. In point of fact, Blood was buried twice, his body having been dug up by those keen to make sure that he was really dead before being interred again. Thorne had known one or two villains himself, happily no longer walking around, who it might have been worth checking up on . . .

'Thanks for speaking up at the briefing,' he said.

'About what?'

'What you said about Luke. About him not being able to get in touch. It's ridiculous, this idea that he killed anyone.'

'I'm not sure what I think, if I'm honest.'

Thorne looked surprised, and wasn't shy about letting her know just how sure *he* was. 'It's bollocks. Somebody's holding him.'

'Who?'

Thorne almost smiled. 'I don't have *all* the bloody answers.'

At the north end of Victoria Street the view improved, with the London Eye becoming visible through the grey, and the monstrous Department of Trade and Industry building giving way to the splendour of Westminster Abbey and the Palace of Westminster beyond. It was not much after eight o'clock, and the weather still looked like it could turn at any moment, but there were already plenty of snap-happy visitors being led around on overpriced walking tours by guides waving umbrellas.

'Why don't we just keep going up to Embankment?' Porter said. 'We can get the Northern Line straight up to Colindale. You can give me the tourist bit round Becke House.'

Thorne stopped, waited for a chance to cross the road. 'I'm not heading back there just yet. There's bugger-all else to do, so I'm going to chase up this Freestone thing.'

'Sounds reasonable.'

'Talk to someone who knew him.'

Porter stepped back from the kerb as a lorry overtook a car on the inside. 'Want some company?'

'Why don't I give you a shout a bit later?' Thorne said.

'OK.' Porter looked like she had a lot more to say than that.

Thorne saw a gap in the traffic and stepped into it. 'See where we both are after lunch?'

The rain had come again before he'd reached the other side of the road. He picked up speed as he turned towards the river and made for the tube station, feeling wetter, and more of a miserable shit, with every step.

# NINE

If the fixtures and fittings at Central 3000 had made
Thorne's shared cupboard at Becke House feel shabby,
DCI Callum Roper's office on the twelfth floor of the
Empress made it seem downright medieval.

Roper had read the look on Thorne's face as he was
shown in. 'It's only because we're new,' he'd said.

When it had been built in 1961, the Empress State
Building – a thirty-storey tower block in Hammersmith –
had been impressive enough to be named after a world-
famous skyscraper across the Atlantic. Back then, its
distinctive triangular footprint had seemed radical and
interesting, but forty years on it had been in dire need of
the eighty-million-pound refurbishment that had won several major awards and restored much of its former glory.
Though not quite as swish as the glass-and-steel Ark just
up the road, its fabulous new facilities had proved hugely

popular, with almost half of the office space behind the shiny, blue, solar-controlled double glazing being snapped up by the Metropolitan Police Service.

Thorne had stood in the vast atrium, gazed around as his ID card was swiped at the first of three separate security checkpoints. He'd been a little depressed by the fact that a building a year younger than he was had needed such a comprehensive facelift. How long before his own frame and superstructure would be in need of serious attention? He'd taken back his wallet and felt a spasm of pain as he'd reached round to tuck it into his back pocket. *What do you mean 'how long'?*

Though he worked at a desk that Donald Trump might have killed for, Roper had chosen to lead Thorne to the other end of his office, where four oatmeal-coloured armchairs sat around a low, glass table. Roper pushed aside a green file, watched as a young woman with lipstick on her teeth laid down a tray of coffee, and biscuits wrapped in cellophane. 'You know what coppers are like,' he said. 'This place'll be a shit-hole inside a month.'

Thorne smiled and nodded, but seriously doubted it. He'd taken in the man as quickly as the surroundings and decided that Roper was probably the type who liked to keep everything tidy. He was tall, and looked pretty fit for a man Thorne put in his early to mid-fifties, with hair that had been subtly coloured, and cut every bit as nicely as his dark blue suit. Not a man to let things slip, if he could help it.

When he'd said 'new', Roper had been talking about he

and his team, just as much as the facilities they occupied. The Special Enquiries team was an offshoot of what had once been the Fraud Squad, part of the SO unit that had become SCD6. Those on its roster had been brought together to tackle any case where the victim – or perpetrator – was deemed to be in the public eye. The SE team handled cases involving corrupt MPs, blackmailed TV personalities, drug-fucked pop stars and royalty behaving badly. It was widely thought of as a prestigious gig, and Callum Roper, for one, looked as though he thoroughly enjoyed being part of it.

The '*Sexy* Enquiries Team', Holland had called it once.

Thorne had pointed out that he and Holland spent their days dragging bloated bodies from dirty rivers, or trying to ID corpses so badly burned that they looked like Coco Krispies with legs. In comparison, issuing parking tickets sounded sexy . . .

'You'll have spoken to Graham Hoolihan then?' Roper had already helped himself to a biscuit and asked the question with his mouth full, like he'd suddenly remembered it.

'That's right.' Thorne was more than a little thrown, but hoped it didn't show. He tried to work backwards, to work out how Roper had made the connection to Freestone so quickly.

Roper leaned forward for his coffee and provided the answer before Thorne had had a chance to figure it out. 'I made a couple of calls. Found out you were thinking that your kidnapper might have previously made threats against Mr Mullen.'

Thorne made a mental note not to drop Trevor Jesmond's name into any more conversations.

'I can't remember the details,' Roper said, 'but I do recall Mullen's name somewhere in the original MAPPA case notes. Part of the probation report, I think. Grant Freestone issued threats against Mullen back when he was originally nicked, didn't he?'

Thorne told Roper as much as he knew; told him what Carol Chamberlain had witnessed in the courtroom. 'Did you know Tony Mullen?' he asked.

Roper shook his head. 'Not that it would have made any difference if I had. Any threats Freestone might have made against anyone, anything he'd done before, wasn't really relevant to what we were doing on the MAPPA panel. Our job was to monitor the way he lived his life *after* he was released. The slate was clean, you see?'

'Not entirely, no. How can what he'd done before not be relevant?'

'Well, of course, we knew what Freestone was capable of. I mean, that's why the panel was put together in the first place. I just meant that, generally, our brief was to look forward rather than back. In terms of any threat he might have made against someone, yes ... obviously, if he'd been spotted hanging around outside their house, we would have taken some action. Informed whoever we'd needed to.'

It was relaxed. It was coffee and biscuits and comfy-chairs casual. But Thorne could hear the tension and defensiveness in everything Roper said. The same way that a Parisian would always hear Thorne's London accent, however fluently he might speak French.

And Thorne had a fair idea why.

'What part do you think the MAPPA panel played in what happened to Sarah Hanley?'

Roper licked his lips, put down his cup. 'What does that have to do with your kidnapping?'

Thorne didn't even try to answer.

'Look, there were two decisions made. With hindsight, which we all know is a bloody wonderful thing, one of them was wrong.'

'The decision to tell Grant Freestone that you'd informed his girlfriend about his history?'

'That we were *going* to inform her,' Roper said. 'We never got the chance, did we? Freestone was informed of the panel's decision, but before Miss Hanley could be told anything, Freestone had stormed round there and killed her.'

Having ignored the cardboard croissants that had been passed around before the briefing, Thorne was suddenly starting to feel the absence of breakfast. He reached for a biscuit.

'Why did anyone think it was necessary to warn him?'

'He wasn't *warned*.' Roper sighed. 'It was our policy to keep the offender – the "client", or whatever he would be called now – abreast of significant developments. Clearly, that involved him being made aware of who had been told about his criminal record. The landlord he rented the flat from knew. So Freestone was told that he knew. Some people believed that it was his *right*.'

'Some people?'

Roper stared hard at Thorne. It was as though he was about to insist on a little respect and deference to rank; to point out that a 'sir' would not have gone amiss, irrespective of whether he was a high-ranking police officer. In the end, he seemed to decide that to ask for it might have appeared needy, more than anything else. 'It's a question of emphasis,' he said. 'If you were to ask those involved with MAPPA now, whether the arrangements were there to protect the public or to rehabilitate the offender, chances are you wouldn't get a straight answer. The party line is that one is very much dependent on the other, that each is part of the overall strategy.'

'But not back then, right?'

'There was a certain ... conflict between points of view. To some, it was all about a commitment to the victim, about the protection of *future* victims. Others had a more sympathetic attitude to the offender. Believed that once a sentence had been served the offender should be given every opportunity to rejoin the community; that they should perhaps be given the benefit of the doubt, rather than suspected at every turn.' Roper leaned back in his chair, folded his arms. 'Those people believed we could play some small part in helping Grant Freestone to do something decent. Others were just waiting for him to fuck up again.' He held up a hand at Thorne, then lowered it to his trouser-leg, where it gently smoothed out the material. 'And let's be clear. Which side of the argument I was on is *definitely* not relevant to your investigation, Inspector.'

It was as bleak a way of separating those who thought the glass was half full from those who believed it was half empty as Thorne had ever heard. 'How did you work these ... *conflicts* out?'

Roper's eyes flicked away from Thorne's face as he answered. 'We made compromises.'

'Who made them? Who took the decisions?'

'They were *discussed*.'

'Were they voted on?'

'There was nothing that formal. The opinions of certain departments carried more weight than others, perhaps. Look, I can't remember exactly who was responsible for which decision, or when, and I honestly can't see that it's of any interest now.'

'No, probably not.' Bearing in mind what had happened to Sarah Hanley, Thorne guessed that there was comfort to be gained from a fading memory.

From where he was sitting, Thorne could see a Met helicopter slowly circling a mile or so away; the same height from the ground as he was, perhaps even a little lower. He knew that any pictures it was taking were being fed live to Central 3000, and suddenly he had an image of the chopper's movements being dictated from long distance, as if it were a toy being flown by remote control. He imagined a commander's thumb whitening against a joystick, sending the helicopter round and round.

Roper turned to look. 'You been up in one?'

Thorne shook his head. It was right up there with bungee jumping or scrubbing a corpse.

'I went out in one the other day. It's a hell of a view.'

'Everything looks better from a distance,' Thorne said.

Roper turned back round to look at him, then down at his watch. 'I don't have much longer, I'm afraid ...'

'What do you think about Grant Freestone as a kidnapper?'

'I'm not even convinced he's a murderer,' Roper said.

Thorne had not yet had a chance to look over the case notes, but he could see Roper's point. It was hard to put 'throwing someone through a coffee table' down as a deliberately murderous act. 'You think it was an accident?'

'It's possible. I'm certainly not convinced he meant to kill her, which was the way some people were thinking at the time, but there *were* signs of a struggle. His prints were all over the show.'

'Who discovered the body?'

'A neighbour was on the school's contact list. When Hanley didn't arrive at pick-up time, the neighbour was called. She collected the kids, then went round to drop them off at home. She had a key, and the eldest child opened the door.'

'Jesus.'

'Accident or not, Freestone left the woman to die. I think manslaughter would have been the very least he would have been looking at, and with his record I can't see that he'd have come out again in a hurry. That's why he ran.'

The idea came at Thorne like a brick through plate glass. If Freestone had made threats against Tony Mullen before he'd gone to prison, wouldn't Mullen have been uncomfortable about his being released? With cause to fear for his safety, or for that of his family, it would certainly have suited him to have the slimy little sod well out of the way. Was it possible that Mullen could have had Grant Freestone fitted up?

Other thoughts, other *considerations* . . .

Mullen resigned from the force the same year that Grant Freestone disappeared.

If the motive for the kidnapping of Luke Mullen *was* based on a grudge against his old man, Grant Freestone might well have had a better reason than anyone thought for holding one.

It was Roper who brought Thorne down to earth with a bump.

'As far as kidnapping anyone goes, I really can't see it,' he said. 'If Freestone's been happily staying out of our way all this time, why would he suddenly make himself visible again? If it *is* because this kid's father put him away all those years ago or whatever, why risk being caught for something as stupid as revenge?'

Thorne had to agree that it was a bloody good point.

Louise Porter picked up the photograph, stared at the faces of the three boys, and lost herself for a moment or two.

In terms of its layout, the Area West Murder Squad HQ was a very different set-up from the one she was used to back at Scotland Yard. The Major Incident Room, on the third floor of Becke House, was an open-plan goldfish bowl, with smaller offices dotted along the corridor that curled around one side of it. It was into one of those occupied by Team 3 personnel that Porter had wandered looking for Yvonne Kitson.

An hour or so short of lunchtime, she felt as though she'd already put in a full day's work. Since arriving at Becke House, everyone had been going flat out; and though it was early days, and operationally a little ad hoc, things seemed to be rubbing along smoothly enough. In terms of the two units working together, both DCIs had been insistent on going in at the deep end. This was evident in the pairings that had been sent after the two men whose names had yet to be crossed off the original 'grudge' list: Holland had been teamed up with a Kidnap Unit DC to pay a call on a career armed robber turned mature student named Harry Cotterill; while Stone and Heeney were trying to track down a second-division pimp and occasional arsonist called Philip Quinn. The latter was a former snout, who Mullen had put away when he had outlived his usefulness and who had, at the time, been resentful enough to try to burn down Mullen's house.

While these four – and Tom Thorne – were on the street working the grudge angle, Porter and others were office bound, letting fingers do the walking at computer keyboards while a dead woman pointed the way.

One look at Amanda Tickell's wasted body – the skin like wax-paper where it wasn't covered in blood – had told Phil Hendricks that she was an addict, and he'd called twenty minutes into the post-mortem to confirm it, giving Porter and the others a direction in which to start moving. The rest of the morning had been spent making connections: talking to rehab centres and borough drug squads; chasing up her family and friends to try and shake loose the name of a dealer or fellow users; anyone who might give them a lead from Tickell to Conrad Allen, and from there to the possibility of a third party with whom, or at whose instruction, the pair had taken a major step up, and kidnapped Luke Mullen.

*The possibility . . .*

Without forensic evidence to the contrary, the idea that Luke Mullen had killed his kidnappers was still floating about, although Porter hadn't spoken to many who were completely convinced, or convinced enough to climb off the fence, at any rate. She, for one, was in little doubt that Allen and Tickell had been involved with someone else; that, for reasons she couldn't begin to fathom, this person had murdered them and was now holding Luke Mullen themself.

It was senseless, but the only explanation that made any sense. Porter wondered why she'd even bothered to hedge her bets when she'd been talking to Tom Thorne outside the Yard a few hours before.

She was still holding the photograph when she looked up and saw Yvonne Kitson in the doorway. She muttered an apology as she put the frame back on the desk. 'Nice kids.'

'Sometimes,' Kitson said.

Porter smiled and glanced back at the picture as she carried a chair across; painted faces and gaps where milk teeth had once been. 'I just came in so we could catch up, really.'

Kitson pointed back towards the corridor as she sat down. 'Sorry, I was just in with the DCI. As a matter of fact, I won't be around for a couple of hours this afternoon.'

'Hot date?'

'Not as such.'

Kitson hadn't said much to Porter that wasn't work-related since they'd met for the first time at that morning's briefing. But she'd taken a look, in the way that any female copper might size up another. Or any female. Short and dark, Porter was the exact opposite of Kitson herself, and, although she was not conventionally pretty, she had a figure it was hard not to resent a little. Kitson generally didn't mind her own body, she just tended to see it in one of two very different ways: 'vivacious' when she liked herself; 'mumsy' when she didn't.

She saw Porter glance around the office. 'It's nice, isn't it?' Kitson said. 'You must be green with envy.'

'It's fine.'

'The disabled toilet's bigger.'

Porter nodded towards the room's second desk, back to back with Kitson's and piled high with folders and box files, as though it were being used as storage space. 'You normally share with Thorne, don't you?'

'Normally, but everything's been a bit up in the air for a while. He'll probably be wanting it back now.'

'I can't imagine his side of the room being quite so homely, somehow,' Porter said. 'Photos of his kids or whatever.'

Kitson punched at her keyboard. 'Not even if he had any. Maybe the odd picture of Johnny Cash or Glenn Hoddle.'

'You're kidding. Johnny Cash?'

'Sometimes I think he just likes to be perverse.'

Porter opened the notebook she was carrying and began to leaf through the pages, looking for the bullet points she was keen to go over. 'Thorne's not the easiest bloke to suss out, is he?'

Kitson smiled. 'There isn't *nearly* enough time ...'

'You should be glad I never throw anything away,' Roper said. 'And that my wife knows where everything is.' He opened up the green folder and took out a piece of paper. 'I called her after we spoke on the phone and she copied these out of an old desk diary. It was the quickest way I could think of to get them. The only way, come to think of it.'

Thorne took the piece of paper and looked at the list of names:

DI C. Roper.
Mr P. Lardner.
Mrs K. Bristow.
Ms M. Stringer.
Mr N. Warren.

Roper shifted his chair closer to Thorne's, studied the list over his shoulder, pointing at each name in turn.

'I was just a DI back then with the CID at Crystal Palace; thought this would be a good thing to do, career-wise.' He shook his head at the stupidity of a slightly younger self. 'Never realised what a pain in the arse it was going to turn out to be, sitting round a table with half of bloody Bromley Borough Council once a month. Pete Lardner is the only one I've seen since, as a matter of fact. He was with the Probation Office, and I know he's still there, so it shouldn't be hard to get hold of him. 'Mrs Bristow. Scottish woman. Kathleen, Katharine, something like that. She was the social worker, and you'd work that out straight away. Liked to meddle and called it "caring". You know the sort, right? She tried to run the whole thing, and, to be honest, the rest of us were happy to let her. She was knocking on a bit, as I remember, so she might well have retired. *Ms* M. Stringer was from the local education authority.'

Thorne looked up, amused by the DCI's emphasis on the 'Ms', but also a little puzzled.

'There were four or five different schools within a few miles of where Freestone had been housed,' Roper explained. 'It was obviously a cause for concern.' He glanced back at the list. 'Warren was the drugs awareness bloke from the health authority. Freestone had developed something of a problem in prison and was attending a methadone clinic. Actually, I think Warren and Lardner had worked together before, but the rest of us didn't know one another from Adam.' He pointed again to the last name on the list, then leaned back and shifted his chair away again. 'Looked like he'd taken a few drugs himself, as far as I can remember.'

Thorne folded the paper and tucked it away. 'Thanks for this.'

'No problem, but I really do have to wind this up now.'

'Are there any minutes of the meetings?'

'Well if there are, I couldn't begin to tell you where they are now. God knows who kept them. The woman from social services would be my guess . . .'

Thorne wasn't hugely shocked, but it was more than enough to show on his face.

'We were the trial run for all this, remember?' Roper looked like he could remember perfectly well, and wasn't too thrilled about the fact. 'Now, it's structured. Now, the meetings are properly chaired and records are kept documenting every decision and responsibility for whatever tasks have been agreed. It's all properly buttoned up, with each agency cooperating with the relevant authority, sharing their information and so on. Back then, we were making it up as we went along. Now, there are "jigsaw teams" – local public protection units in each borough – so it's covered from both sides. There are "exclusion zones" and "action plans", and any factors that put public safety at risk are identified early on and addressed. All we could do was react to whatever happened.' He leaned forward, placed the flat of his hand against the coffee pot. 'Basically, we were guinea pigs.'

Thorne said nothing, and stood up, thinking that, despite the points Callum Roper had made, his final plea for mitigation had been a bit rich. It was definitely a bit bloody late. Some might have said that Grant Freestone was as much of a guinea pig as any member of that panel.

The woman he'd killed certainly was.

'I'll walk you to the lift . . . ' Roper said.

In the lobby, waiting for the glass lift with the posh speaking voice to glide up, Roper seemed keen to end their meeting on something of a lighter note. Thorne didn't see the need, but listened politely enough.

'You remember *Space Patrol*?' Roper asked.

'Sorry.'

'It was a kids' show in the early sixties. A science-fiction thing, with crappy puppets. Made *Thunderbirds* look high-tech.'

Thorne said he couldn't remember the show; that he'd only have been a couple of years old at the time.

'Anyway, back then, this building was pretty futuristic for its time, so they used a shot of it in the programme.' Roper raised his arms. 'This place was the original *Space Patrol* headquarters.'

Thorne couldn't think of anything to say. Puppets, science fiction, the Metropolitan Police. There were at least half a dozen different punchlines.

He'd switched off his phone before going in to see Roper. Once he was outside, he checked for messages and found two new ones. Porter's didn't seem to be about very much, while Phil Hendricks had rung to say that everything he'd suggested at the briefing – the way that Allen and Tickell had died – had been more or less confirmed by the post-mortems. Thorne called Hendricks back first, got an answering machine. 'What do you want, a bloody gold star? Seriously, Phil, it was a privilege to watch you doing some excellent mime work this morning, and I'd love to pat you on the back personally, but fuck knows when. Give us a call later, if you fancy a natter . . .'

Then he called Porter.

'*Touching base?*'

'It's just an expression,' she said. 'Calm down.'

'It's a stupid expression. Unless you're an American teenager and you haven't told anyone.'

'I was wondering what you were up to, that's all.'

'Well, I've stopped sulking. You probably noticed that I'd been sulking since the raid at Bow. But I've stopped now.'

'I didn't notice anything. I just thought that was what you were normally like.'

'If you're still keen, we could touch base after lunch.'

She ignored the dig so completely that he started to wonder if he'd really pissed her off.

'Where?'

'Have you got a pen?' Thorne waited, smiled at a uniform eyeing him with suspicion from the Empress's front entrance. 'Right, see if you can track down someone called Peter Lardner at the Probation Service. I'm not sure which borough. If you can, fix up an appointment for this afternoon and give me a call back.'

He could see a greasy spoon on the far side of the road and began walking towards it like a man in a trance. Coffee and Hobnobs had simply not been enough. It was gone midday, and right about then Thorne decided that a full English breakfast sounded like the perfect lunch.

It was madness, this dividing of himself.

He'd spoken and spoken, and been spoken to in this meeting and that. And all the time, while he was smiling or looking suitably serious, while he was getting on with normal things, he was thinking about the boy.

Thinking about what he'd done, and what he was going to do.

What he was doing was, literally, madness; a textbook example of it. But wasn't it a different type of insanity that had caused the problem in the first place? Wasn't that called madness by some people? In some languages it was, certainly, and with good reason. He'd been as mad as a March hare in that way, in the *good* way, for years now; long before he'd been driven to any of this.

Driven to stab. To steal children.

It was the way things went though, wasn't it? Swings and roundabouts, whatever you wanted to call it. Anything that felt good was ultimately going to hurt you. Cigarettes and chocolate. Sex and sugary deceit.

The door opened and someone came into the toilets, so

he turned on the tap, splashed water into his face to hide the tears.

He needed to get back to his office anyway. There was plenty to get on with.

As he pressed the paper towel to his face, he thought about the pithy slogan that dieters used, that he'd seen on a fridge magnet at his sister's place. The phrase so beloved of those keen to change themselves, to make their lives better. A simple reminder that to give into temptation was to pay for the rest of your life. He smiled at his colleague in the mirror, then turned away towards the door.

*A minute on the lips . . .*

# TEN

Peter Lardner worked as a probation officer for the Borough of Westminster, based in an office at Middlesex Guildhall Crown Court. The Guildhall was located on the north side of Parliament Square, which meant that Thorne and Porter met up again after lunch close to where they'd parted company five or six hours before. Porter moaned about having to come all the way south again, but at least the weather had improved since they'd last walked across the square. Thorne's leather jacket had dried out, and Porter tossed what looked like an expensive waterproof coat across her arm. Thorne thought it was the type favoured by that strange breed who trudged across hills of a weekend, pockets stuffed full of Kendal mint cake.

'Are you a walker?'

'Only as far as the car,' Porter said.

For all its gargoyles and ornate Gothic stylings, the

Guildhall was less than a century old, but it was an imposing building nevertheless, with a position as historic as any in the city. It had once been the site of the Sanctuary Tower, from where, ironically, the seven-year-old Duke of York had been dragged, en route to being murdered with his elder brother by the future Richard III. Four centuries later, Tothill Fields Prison had stood on the same spot, housing inmates as young as five years old in conditions only slightly less horrific than those a mile or two up the river in Newgate. And the building was still playing its part in constitutional history. Later in the year it was due to close, before reopening in 2008 as the Supreme Court, new home to a dozen fully independent law lords, and the single highest court in the country.

As Thorne and Porter climbed the stone stairs towards the Probation Service offices, Thorne decided that the Princes in the Tower killings would almost certainly be handled nowadays by Roper and his Sexy enquiries team. And that, although those sitting nervously outside several courtrooms were much older than five, he doubted that a single one of them was there because they'd stolen a loaf of bread ...

Though most of the seven courtrooms were as austere and darkly elegant as the fabric of the building itself, many of the offices attached to them were more basic. The room Thorne and Porter found themselves sitting in was dingy and utilitarian; and, if Callum Roper's appearance had been as immaculate as his shiny new home, Peter Lardner reflected his own, dowdier surroundings equally well.

He looked as miserable as the shittiest kind of sin.

'I know what Grant Freestone would say.' Lardner pushed his hands out in front of him. Slid his arms across the top of his desk, as if he wanted nothing so much as to lay his head down on top of them and go to sleep. He answered Thorne's question in a low voice, all but free from expression, speaking to a point on the coarse, grey carpet somewhere between his desk and the chairs in front of it. 'He'd deny it. Same as he'd probably deny killing the woman he pushed through that coffee table. He denied taking those kids as well, even after they found them tied up with gardening twine in his garage.'

'Had a problem facing up to stuff, did he, Mr Freestone?' Porter asked.

'He thought the world was out to get him.'

'It might well have been,' Thorne said. He knew a decent-sized corner of the world where they plastered pictures of alleged paedophiles on the front pages of their newspapers. Where the police might be waiting at Boots when you went to pick up photos of your child in a paddling pool. Where a paediatrician could have her house burned down, because some idiot got their words confused. If that world was going to get anyone, it would be a man like Grant Freestone.

'He certainly got a few good kickings inside,' Lardner said. 'He got used to the taste of tea with piss in it.'

'He must have been to our canteen,' Porter said.

Lardner nodded, acknowledging the joke, but not quite able to laugh at it. Later, Thorne and Porter would both admit to having had him down as someone who didn't find too many things funny, but they both conceded that if they had to spend as much time as Lardner did talking to criminals, they wouldn't have much to chortle about, either. Just trying to catch the buggers was enough of a pain in the arse.

Thorne put the man somewhere in his late forties. Though the hair showed few signs of grey, it was thinning on top, and the eyes were pale and bright behind metal-framed glasses. He wore what was, strictly speaking, a suit and tie, but the various items of clothing looked tired and pissed off with each other. He reminded Thorne of a teacher he'd liked at school, a man who would stop halfway through a geography lesson, tell them it was all a waste of time and read them stories instead. Sherlock Holmes and *The Thirty-nine Steps* . . .

'What do *you* think, though?' Thorne asked. 'You probably knew him better than anyone on that panel, and, obviously, we don't know anybody who's seen him since he did a runner. Do you reckon he's capable of taking a kid for an altogether different reason?'

'Do I see him as a kidnapper?'

They had not told Lardner anything beyond the basic fact of the kidnap and the suspicion about a long-held grudge. He knew nothing about the double murder at the flat in Bow. As Thorne asked the question, he was mentally putting a more complete version of it to himself, and the answer was unequivocal.

*Do you see Grant Freestone as a man who somehow*

*convinced two other people to do the kidnapping, then killed*
*them and took over the job himself?*

*Not in a million years . . .*

'I'm not convinced,' Lardner said. He straightened up, suddenly a little more energised than he had been. 'He wasn't what you'd call "organised". In the sense of getting your shit together, turning up on time and whatever. Or in the way they use that word to describe certain types of criminal.'

'Killers, usually,' Porter said.

'Right. Which, as far as Freestone goes, is something else I'm not completely convinced of. You've got to be organised, wouldn't you say, to carry out a kidnapping? It's not just something you do on impulse, is it? You don't just grab a kid off the street on a whim, even if you *are* pissed off with his father.'

'What about those kids in his garage?' Thorne said.

Porter tucked a strand of hair behind her ear. 'He seemed to manage that OK.'

'That was an urge he couldn't control,' Lardner said. 'That wasn't planned. Which is precisely why they caught him.'

Thorne and Porter shared a look; they both knew that was probably untrue. It was often those who did what they did instinctively – the rapists, the killers – who were the hardest to stop. Those who *thought* could make life too complicated for themselves eventually, end up thinking themselves right into Broadmoor or Belmarsh.

'Besides,' Lardner added, 'why would Freestone wait until now to get his own back? All this "dish best served cold" stuff is crap. I've had enough clients down the years with axes to grind to know that much. If you do these things at all, you do them in the heat of the moment. You don't wait years. It doesn't make any sense.'

But what Lardner was suggesting certainly did. Roper had said much the same thing, and it wasn't getting any easier to argue with. Even if someone like Grant Freestone were to decide, years down the line, to settle a score, was it likely he'd go about it in such a roundabout way? That he'd involve other people?

'Did Freestone ever associate with a Conrad Allen or an Amanda Tickell?'

Lardner looked blank. 'I don't recall the names. He didn't associate with a great many people, to be honest.'

It hadn't hurt to ask, but life was never that simple.

'Something you said before,' Thorne said, 'about Freestone not being a killer. It sounds like you don't think he killed Sarah Hanley. Like you're someone else who's going along with the accident theory.'

'Possibly.' Lardner suddenly looked a little uncomfortable.

'What did the others on the MAPPA panel think?'

'Excuse me?'

'Did you talk about it afterwards? People must have had opinions?'

'No.' More than a little uncomfortable now. 'We didn't talk about it.'

'You seem to be hedging your bets, that's all. Are you saying that Freestone didn't do it?'

'Oh, he did it all right. But there's a difference between pushing someone just to push them and pushing someone to push them through a sheet of glass, isn't there? I've got a client on my list right now who did four years because some drunk he shoved outside a pub one night happened to have an abnormally thin skull. Do you see what I mean? I've had countless similar cases over the years, and I still find the whole issue of "intent" a horribly grey area.' He held Thorne's eye for a few seconds before turning away again and shaking his head. 'I don't know ...'

Thorne saw his old teacher again. *It's all a waste of time.* He half expected Lardner to open a drawer and take out the John Buchan.

'What about the sister?' Porter asked.

'Well, that's something else entirely.'

'She gave Freestone an alibi ...'

Thorne looked over to Porter. His eyes wide, asking the question.

'*Sister* ...?'

'I think the police were right, on balance, to discredit her statement,' Lardner said. He raised a hand, swept what little hair there was straight back. 'If I remember rightly, the pathologist was a little vague about the time of death.'

'There was a two-hour window,' Porter said. 'And Freestone's sister claimed he was with her the whole time. Walking in a park with her and her kids.'

'The point is that she had also given him an alibi six

years before that. For the afternoon when the children were snatched.' Lardner smiled a little sadly. 'She clearly had the same problems facing up to stuff that her brother did.'

There was a knock at the door. Lardner stood and apologised, moved around the desk and explained that he had another appointment.

Porter said that was fine.

Thorne was still staring at her. Still asking.

On the way down the stairs, he vocalised the question somewhat more forcefully than he'd intended. 'What fucking sister?'

'Just what I said in there. Freestone's sister—'

'When did you find out about this?'

Porter couldn't suppress a smirk. 'I called up the case notes this morning. It wasn't a big deal at the time.' She leaned towards the wall as a fully kitted-up barrister charged down the stairs past them. 'You heard what Lardner said. They discredited her statement because she had a history of lying for her brother.'

They turned at the bottom of the final flight, into the busy corridor that ran alongside the two largest courtrooms. Into a scene they both knew well: anxious witnesses and bored coppers; relatives of those on trial and of those they were accused of defrauding, assaulting, abusing; men in new shoes and tight collars; women as glassy-eyed as Debenhams dummies, tensed on benches, desperate to puke or piss, high heels like gunshots against the marble.

All honing the truth or polishing up the turd of a lie. Sweating on the right result.

'He wasn't very happy talking about that whole MAPPA business,' Porter said. 'Made him very jumpy.'

Thorne agreed. 'Roper didn't like it much, either. He talked about it, but there was plenty of stuff he conveniently couldn't remember too well, that he was just a bit vague about. Know what I mean?'

'It's hardly surprising, is it? None of them were exactly covered in glory.'

You didn't need a degree in criminology to work out why anyone involved in the panel assembled to monitor Grant Freestone would be happier staying off the subject; keeping it as far behind them as possible. A project that had culminated in the death of a young woman – a death for which some thought the panel might be partly responsible – was hardly likely to merit pride of place on anyone's CV.

'I think the whole Freestone thing is probably a waste of time,' Thorne said.

'Can't say I disagree.'

'But I'll get Holland or someone to track down the other two who were on that panel. Might as well keep it tidy.'

'I had you down as a messy fucker.'

'Only when I can't find anybody else to clean things up.'

'So which of our white-hot leads do you fancy having a crack at next?' Porter asked. 'There are so many, I just can't make my mind up.'

'Why don't we have a look at the sister?'

Porter stopped, began rummaging around in her bag. 'But you just said—'

'Freestone's not a kidnapper, but something won't let me leave it alone.'

'And what would that be?'

'The fact that Tony Mullen never mentioned him.'

She produced a half-eaten tube of mints and dug one out. 'It couldn't hurt to go back via Arkley,' she said.

They stepped out into a square that was thicker with people, as the rush hour started to take hold; and darker, as the day began to dim, running out of breath while those hurrying through the streets at the arse-end of their nine, ten or more hours got a second wind.

Walking past the huge statue of Abraham Lincoln, Porter pointed back to the windows on the third floor of the Guildhall. 'His office was fucking horrible,' she said. 'Did you see the damp? And the mousetrap by the filing cabinet? I'd go mental working somewhere like that all day.'

Thorne said nothing, thinking she *did* work somewhere like that. All of them did, spending endless hours in other people's houses and shitty little offices. TV shows were fond of showing coppers, and those they needed to speak to, strolling slowly through the crowd at noisy dog tracks, arguing in meat markets, or blowing cigarette smoke at each other across empty warehouses in the early hours.

It was all about atmosphere, apparently . . .

But the truth was over-lit and dirty-white. It sounded like the hum of distant traffic and felt sticky against the soles of your shoes. It smelled of old blood or fresh bullshit, and no amount of gasometer-filled skylines was going to make it *gritty*. The atmosphere – in sweltering front rooms and shitty little offices – *could* make your guts jump for sure, and the hairs on the back of your neck stand to attention, but truthfully, it was rarely one of menace. Or of danger.

Watching people sob, and rant, and lie. Watching them tremble and gulp down grief.

It was more like embarrassment.

When he stepped off the bus, he looked pretty thrilled with himself; as though his journey home had been a riot of well-told jokes and stirring tales of sporting success. Yvonne Kitson was pleased to see that one look at who was waiting to meet him seemed to change the young man's mood in an instant. Pissing on Adrian Farrell's chips made her a very happy woman.

'Good day at school, Adrian?'

Farrell looked straight through her. He ignored the shouts and the waves of friends banging on the windows of the bus as it moved off and passed him.

'Did you have history today? I remember you said that was your favourite.' Kitson was talking on the move now, walking quickly to catch up as Farrell marched through spiky blots of shadow, cast by the trees planted every twenty feet or so along the broad pavement. 'Got anything planned for the weekend? After you've got your homework out of the way, obviously ...'

Farrell slowed a little, but he kept on walking, hitched his grey regulation rucksack a little higher on his shoulder.

'What sort of thing do you and your mates get up to on a Saturday night? My kids are still a bit younger than you, so I've really got no idea what goes on, except that I've got it all to look forward to. The taxi-service stuff, I mean.' She was ten, twelve feet behind him. 'Pub? Clubbing? What?'

Despite their pace, they were moving relatively slowly past a row of detached houses, many of them set back a long way from the road and some with gated drives. Kitson had to quicken her step to get the other side of a Jeep that reversed across the pavement without a great deal of attention.

'That student who was kicked to death. Remember, I told you about him?' Kitson said. 'He was killed on a Saturday night. Saturday, October the seventeenth last year. I'm sure you can't remember *exactly* what you were doing that night, but I bet you were enjoying yourself, whatever you were up to ...'

Farrell didn't stop dead, but he slowed to a standstill within a pace or two. He mumbled something as he turned, raised his arms and let them slap back down against his legs. It was a remarkably childish gesture of frustration and annoyance.

'Good,' Kitson said, as she drew close to him. 'Not that I couldn't have kept up with you all day long. Chasing after three kids keeps you pretty bloody fit.'

'This is ridiculous,' Farrell said. 'I talk to someone about this boy in the year below me who's gone missing. I answer

223

a couple of questions. Next thing I know I'm getting hassled for no good reason.'

'Nobody's hassling you.'

'Right. So nobody's following me into the precinct in the lunch-hour? You're not turning up outside my house after school, telling me about your kids?'

'I'm not here to talk about my kids.'

'Really?'

A jogger came past, his face twisted into a grimace, as though the song on the iPod he had strapped to his arm was particularly tuneless.

'I just wondered if you'd remembered anything else about Amin Latif,' Kitson said. 'Perhaps something came back to you.'

Farrell's expression was one Kitson knew well. He looked irritated, inconvenienced perhaps, as though he were being kept from some important TV show he really needed to watch. 'In terms of what, exactly? Have I remembered which hymn we sang in assembly?'

'Anything at all. Me talking to you about it might have helped you recall something that had slipped your mind.'

'It might have been "To be a Pilgrim".'

'How long have you known Damien Herbert and Michael Nelson?' The two boys Farrell had been with in the shopping precinct the day before.

'Are we changing the subject?'

'I didn't think we were getting very far with the other one.'

'A few months, I suppose.'

'*Six* months?'

'Did I know them on October 17th last year, you mean?'

'That's as good a date as any.'

Farrell nodded, understanding, and raised his eyes as though racking his brains. After a few seconds he snapped his fingers, grinned and pointed at Kitson. 'I think it was "Immortal Invisible, God Only Wise",' he said. 'I knew it would come to me.'

The urge to lay hands on him was getting harder and harder to ignore. Kitson pointed to the school crest, embroidered on the pocket of Farrell's blazer. 'What's it say on the badge, Adrian? What's the motto?'

'I'm really shit at Latin,' he said. 'Sorry ...'

She reached slowly into her bag, took out a piece of paper. 'So, without wishing to labour the point, we've established that the name Amin Latif doesn't really mean very much to you. Yes?'

'Not a great deal, I'm sorry to say.'

'What about Nabeel Khan?'

A shrug. 'No. I don't think so.'

'That's funny.' Kitson unfolded the piece of paper, turned it the right way up. 'Because he seems to know you. See?'

Farrell looked at the picture and the impatience suddenly gave way to panic, then genuine anger. He pulled the heavy bag from his shoulder, let it drop, and swung it back and forth in front of him. 'I'm not sure what you think *that* proves.'

'I'm not sure it proves anything,' Kitson said. 'I just

thought your parents might like to put one in a frame. Pop it on the piano.'

'I'm saying nothing more without a solicitor present.'

'Fine. Come to the station with me and we can organise one.'

'We already have one.'

For a second or two, Kitson wasn't certain who 'we' were. She wondered if Farrell meant himself and his friends. Then she realised he was talking about his family. 'Whatever you like,' she said.

'Are you arresting me?'

'Do I need to?'

'Definitely.' A twitch at the edge of the mouth; an aborted smile. 'If you want to talk to me again, I mean. I think that you *aren't* arresting me because, whatever you've convinced yourself I've done – and you've given me some fairly major clues – you don't have any evidence whatsoever to back your ideas up. None at all. I think you're worried, with fairly good reason, that if you *did* arrest me, you'd only end up giving yourself unnecessary paperwork. That all you'd have caused by the end of it was huge inconvenience to other people, and a lot of professional embarrassment personally. Is that about right?'

Kitson said nothing.

'*This* is lame.' He jabbed a finger at the E-fit. 'It's borderline mental, if you want to know what I really think.' If Farrell had lost his composure, it had been for only a few seconds; it *never* seemed to be any longer than that. 'Come to mention it, have you ever shown me any identification?

226

How do I know you're who you say you are? You might be some kind of nutter.'

Kitson stared at him: the wide eyes, the bag still swinging, like he couldn't decide what socks to wear. 'I think you should go home now,' she said. 'You should fuck off indoors to Mummy and Daddy, and have your tea.'

The shock at Kitson's language might have been genuine, might have been another mask. Having lost her own composure, she was suddenly finding him hard to read. Either way, Farrell didn't need a second invitation to turn on his heel.

He walked for fifty or so yards, then moved to the edge of the pavement and waited to cross. He looked left, then right and held it, making sure that Kitson was still looking at him. Thinking about it later, Kitson imagined that she saw that nice, polite smile again, just for a moment, before he hawked a ball of phlegm on to the pavement and jogged across the road.

As Kitson reached the spot where Farrell had crossed, a woman standing behind a large wooden gate caught her eye. She wore a green velour tracksuit and full make-up, and stooped to empty bottles from a plastic bag into the recycling bin at the end of her drive. The woman nodded towards where Adrian Farrell had disappeared round the corner. 'Dirty little sod,' she said. 'I would have been belted by a copper for that in my day. Not that you can find one of those buggers when you need one now . . .'

Kitson didn't answer. Just continued to stare down at the spit. Shiny, grey-green against the concrete.

The security light above the garage came on, and Maggie Mullen answered the front door as though she had been waiting on the other side of it. Her eyes moved quickly from Thorne to Porter. Seeing little need for concern, or relief, she waved them inside, through a curtain of cigarette smoke, then stared into the darkness that squatted beyond the bleed of yellow light, as if she were waiting for stragglers.

On their way along the hall, Thorne and Porter exchanged a word with Kenny Parsons, who emerged from the kitchen clutching a tabloid and a ballpoint pen. Their visit was unexpected and he searched their faces for news much as Maggie Mullen had done; and much as her husband did when they walked into the living room.

Mullen tossed a paperback on to the chair behind him. 'Do you want coffee or something?'

Thorne shook his head. Porter said no, that it was fine.

'Been a long day.'

Thorne wasn't sure if Mullen was referring to the day that had crawled past for himself and his family or to the one that the officers on the case had endured. Either way, there was little reason to argue.

Mullen sat down on the arm of the sofa. His wife came back into the room, walked past him to an armchair, grabbing cigarettes and ashtray from the mantelpiece as she went. 'I hope you're finishing better than you started,'

Mullen said. 'That certain people have taken their heads from out their arses.'

'Sir?' Porter lowered her bag to the floor.

'I'm presuming the idea that my son's murdered anybody has been kicked into fucking touch where it belongs. Yes?'

Now it was clear to Thorne that Mullen knew exactly how long a day it had been for everybody. He was plugged into the investigation just as much as the officers working it. Thorne wondered how many times a day he spoke to Jesmond, or called one of his other old mates, to get the inside track.

'There was evidence which had to be looked at seriously,' Porter said.

'Prints on a knife?'

Thorne decided that people were probably calling Mullen. He was being updated as comprehensively as if he were the SIO.

'That's enough to make you *seriously* believe that my son has gone from kidnap victim to some kind of killer on the run, is it? If that's what you're telling me, I'm *seriously* starting to doubt that the right people are on this.'

There was something like a sigh, something like a sob, from the armchair. Mrs Mullen was staring at the Chinese rug, as if she were mesmerised by the dragons and the bridges. Her hands were clasped in front of her and cigarette smoke rose straight up into her face.

'It's not what we think,' Thorne said. He spoke towards Mrs Mullen, the 'we' used as though he were talking about everyone on the case; though, in truth, he could vouch only for those in the room at that moment.

'Thank Christ for that.' Mullen walked across to Thorne, dropped a heavy hand on to his shoulder and let it rest. Both Thorne and Porter were given the benefit of a thin and not entirely convincing smile, before Mullen turned and went back to his perch on the arm of the sofa. It had been a strange moment: a gesture of solidarity perhaps, or gratitude, or something else entirely. All Thorne had understood was the booze he could smell on the man, and he began to hear the faintest trace of it, when Mullen spoke again.

'We need to move forward,' he said. 'Work out who contracted Allen and his girlfriend to do this. Why Luke was taken. We've got bodies now, and you can always get something from bodies, right?'

'We've been talking to people who knew Grant Freestone today,' Thorne said.

Mullen blinked.

Thorne spotted the movement and turned to see Maggie Mullen's arm move towards the ashtray; watched as an inch or more of ash dropped on to the rug. She didn't bend to brush it up.

'Well, *some* heads are obviously still up arses,' Mullen said. He was smiling but angry. 'A long way up.'

'Why didn't you give us Freestone's name when we asked you for the "grudge" list?' Porter said.

'God knows. I probably should have done, thinking about it. But I was hardly thinking straight, was I?'

'What kind of threats did he make against you?' Thorne walked across the rug and sat on the sofa.

'The usual. He was "going to get me". I was "going to be sorry". Stuff you've heard a dozen times. I was certainly no more worried about him than I was about the others on that list.'

'No?'

'What about them? Cotterill and Quinn? Have you eliminated them?'

Thorne and Porter had not heard back from Holland and his partner, nor from Heeney and Stone. 'Not as yet.'

'There you are, then. So why are you wasting so much time and energy on a pointless prick like Freestone?'

'Just trying to move forward,' Thorne said.

'*Jesus* . . .'

Porter opened her mouth to speak.

'Do you think this man kidnapped Luke?' The question came from Maggie Mullen.

All heads turned towards her.

'No, of course he doesn't.' Mullen stood and moved behind the sofa, looked hard at Thorne. 'Not unless he's one chromosome short of a special parking permit.'

Porter cleared her throat, but again failed to follow it up with anything. Thorne could feel Mullen's fingers digging into the back of the sofa behind him.

Mrs Mullen leaned down to stub out her cigarette, then looked up, smiling. 'Let's have some coffee,' she said. 'Who wants one?'

'I already offered,' Mullen snapped.

'Well, what about a glass of wine, then? Have you finished that bottle you opened when we had dinner?'

The colour was rising in Mullen's face. 'For God's sake, don't be so stupid. I put it back in the—'

'*Don't* talk to me like that.' Her voice was jagged, but her expression, and the finger she pointed, were fixed and severe. 'Like I'm a piece of shit.'

A few moments later, when Maggie Mullen flipped open the top of the cigarette packet again, Thorne dragged his eyes away and tried to find Porter's, but she was concentrating hard on those dragons and bridges.

*More like embarrassment ...*

# ELEVEN

The privileged few taking advantage of the Friday night lock-in at the Royal Oak were much the same as any other gathering of social, semi-serious or hardcore drinkers, save for there being one or two more women, fewer black and Asian faces, and the fact that the vast majority were carrying warrant cards. The Oak was an unofficial social club for anyone working at Colindale Station, or up the road at the Peel Centre, and though not a particularly attractive or friendly boozer, it had the advantage of being *close*, which was deemed more important than smiles or quiz nights. It also happened to be among those pubs less likely than some to be raided for after-hours drinking.

Thorne and Porter stared briefly into their own bit of space over pints of Guinness and lager-top. Letting the beer work at some of the rougher edges. Giving the tiredness elbow room.

'You reckon Mullen drinks that much normally?' Porter asked.

Thorne shook his head and swallowed. 'No idea. Same with her and the fags. Can't blame either of them for needing a bit of help, though, considering.'

By the time they had got back to Becke House from the Mullens' place, written up the work, been taken through a debrief and discussed the following day, it was after midnight. It was shaping up into an eighteen- or nineteen-hour tour, door to door, and though most of the team would be on again before the sun was up, the majority had decided that unwinding over a beer or two was worth an hour's sleep.

For Thorne, it hadn't been a tricky decision.

'Yeah, I suppose it's fair enough,' Porter said. 'If it was one of my kids, I'd be shooting up smack by now.'

'How many have you got?'

Porter shook her head. 'Oh, I haven't. I was just saying ...'

Holland stopped on his way to the bar, already a little ahead of them. They turned down his offer of a drink, happy to take things a bit slower, and to avoid getting involved in big rounds. Holland was sitting at an adjacent table, trading sick jokes with Sam Karim and Andy Stone. Heeney, Parsons, and some others sat a few feet away, on the other side of the fruit machine. Despite the operational insistence on cooperation, the Kidnap and Murder teams were keeping themselves to themselves now that they were off the clock.

'We should try and give the Mullens a wide berth tomorrow,' Thorne suggested. 'Once he sees the paper, he'll go fucking ballistic.'

'I'm happy to stay well clear of *that*.' Porter took a drink. 'Kenny Parsons will be back there first thing, so we'll get the highlights from him later.'

'Mullen will be straight on the phone to Jesmond, or somebody else he used to play golf with and then your bloke's going to get it in the neck.'

'Hignett's got some support on this.'

'Fine. Let the brass fight it out. We'll make ourselves scarce.'

Despite what Thorne had told Tony and Maggie Mullen a few hours before, the possibility that Luke Mullen was not being held against his will but had gone into hiding after killing his kidnappers was yet to be fully disregarded. Owing to the somewhat unusual turn that the case had taken, a decision had been taken partially to lift the press embargo and run a story the following day about Luke's disappearance.

It would not be front page.

It would not be scary stuff about children vanishing.

It would be a small story, about a teenage boy who'd gone missing after school, with a photo and an appeal to anyone with information as to his whereabouts to come forward. With an appeal to the boy himself, should he be reading the story, to do the same.

'You can't really blame Hignett.'

'Can I still think he's an arsehole?'

'He's just covering his bases,' Porter said. 'It's a straight-forward appeal for witnesses; plus there's a message for the kid if he's just hiding out somewhere, afraid to come home. Until we get evidence confirming that someone's taken him, Hignett's shit scared about ignoring the other possibility. It could seriously bite him in the bollocks if it turns out to be what happened.'

'It *isn't* what happened.'

'*We* can afford to be that sure. The DCI has to be more cautious, consider the unlikely scenarios as well. He's safe that way.'

'Safe, until the kidnapper sees tomorrow's paper and sends us a few of Luke Mullen's fingers wrapped up in it.'

Porter stared at him, her open mouth eventually creasing into a grin as she snorted in comic derision. Thorne was unable to maintain the over-earnest expression and laughed along with her. They drank, worked their way through four packets of crisps between them, and Thorne realised that Porter was probably right. As far as the newspaper coverage went, what Hignett was doing made political sense; and besides, apart from backing out of one dead end after another, there wasn't a fat lot else they could do.

Harry Cotterill had been on his way back from a booze cruise, his Transit stuffed with cheap Belgian lager, when Conrad Allen and Amanda Tickell were being carved up. No one had yet managed to track down Philip Quinn, but his girlfriend swore blind he was somewhere in Newcastle. She'd been pissed off enough with him to tell the police exactly how many different laws he was breaking while he was up there, giving her story, and his alibi, the depressing ring of truth.

As far as the murder victims went, nothing the team had discovered was helping a great deal. They'd put together a sketchy outline of Amanda Tickell's life: well-heeled parents; a car accident that killed her father when she was a child; adolescent rebellion spiralling out of control and into addiction. With what they already knew about Conrad Allen, a clear enough picture had developed of a third-division Bonnie and Clyde, but nothing pointed towards any figure for whom they might have been working. They'd spoken to a few likely dealers, working on the theory that Allen and Tickell had got into the kidnapping business to pay off a drug debt. From there, a more elaborate theory had emerged, in which the drug dealer, aware of what was happening, had seen a way to take all the money for himself and had muscled in by killing Allen and Tickell and taking Luke. But where was the ransom demand?

It was only the second-stupidest idea that anyone had come up with, and there was no point getting too stressed about 'what the brass were thinking'. Some coppers were just genetically programmed to hedge their bets, men like Hignett and Jesmond with fence-friendly arse-cracks who never left their Airwaves in a drawer.

'I need to say sorry to you,' Porter said.

'For what?'

'For playing silly buggers when we went into Allen's

237

flat. Cutting you out of that was nobody's decision but mine. It was just about territory, and I was a complete tosser about it. So, sorry.'

'Fair enough.'

'And you had every right to sulk.'

'I should have kept it up for longer.'

'*And* I wanted to say sorry for that comment the other day. For making that stupid joke about Alzheimer's.'

Thorne had to think back for a second or two. 'Don't be silly. It's not a problem.' He meant it, but, all the same, he wondered who Porter had been speaking to. He glanced towards the table where Holland, Karim and Stone were sitting.

'It's about a year, isn't it?'

'Just coming up.'

'It was a fire, someone said.'

Thorne took a mouthful of Guinness, licked froth from his top lip. 'A fire, yeah.'

'I lost my mum a couple of years ago. So . . .'

'Right.'

'I read somewhere it takes seven years to get over losing a parent. Seven years, like the itch. I don't know how they worked that out.'

'They probably didn't. It's just a number.'

Porter said she was sure he was right, then nodded towards him, asked where he'd got the scar.

Thorne instinctively traced a finger along the straight line that ran across his chin, paler than the flesh around it and stubble free. 'Shark-bite,' he said. The way things were shaping up, he was sure she'd find out soon enough.

Porter rubbed her own chin back and forth against the edge of her glass. She seemed happy enough with the only answer she looked like getting.

'I'm going to fetch another half,' Thorne said. He pushed back his chair. 'Do you want another of those?'

Porter handed him the glass.

On his way across, Thorne caught a glimpse of his father, propping up the bar at a family wedding a year or two before. Holding court, full of it, pissing himself laughing. Telling anyone too polite to walk away that the best thing about losing your marbles was that you could keep forgetting to buy anybody else a drink.

Thorne blinked slowly, and thought about what Porter had said. It sounded like a very long time to be stuck with the old bugger.

He ordered the drinks and moved along the bar to speak to Yvonne Kitson. She looked a lot happier than the last time he'd seen her, but then a few large glasses of wine could do that to people. 'How did it go?' he asked.

'I'd rather not get too far into it,' she said. She held a ten-pound note between her fingers and fluttered it in front of her face as though she were hot. 'But I'm hoping for some good news.'

'What did you do?'

She argued silently with herself for a few seconds. 'No, I don't want to jinx it. I'll know a lot more first thing in the morning. Can we just talk shit for a while?'

So they did, until Kitson's drinks arrived, and she turned away from the bar.

Thorne wondered just how much sleep his back would cost him later on. Deciding that he'd need some help, he changed his order from a half to a pint, then leaned on the bar and let his mind go walkabout.

Seven years of grief.

Seven years until you fell out of love and started looking elsewhere.

Could these emotions have sell-by dates? He knew as well as anyone that love was perishable and understood that grief might shrink to a half-remembered taste or smell. *Hate*, though, he imagined would outlast them all. It could be put away for later, like something frozen in a bag, to be thawed out, fresh and full-sized when it was needed.

He remembered a poem he'd had to learn at school, something about the world ending in fire and ice. A line about 'knowing enough of hate'. Then he thought again about his old teacher, and in turn about Lardner the probation officer, and there was all manner of crap bouncing around inside his head by the time he carried the drinks back to the table.

Tony Mullen wasn't sure how long he'd been lying there in the dark. Five minutes? Maybe fifteen? How long had it been since he'd lowered himself on to the bed and slid across next to his wife and daughter?

Maggie and Juliet were lying together, curled up like spoons, same as he and his wife had used to do. He'd snuggled in close, fully dressed still, on top of the duvet, lifted an arm right across the pair of them, squeezed them both when Juliet had briefly started to cry again.

The argument had not gone on for too long after Thorne and the others had left. It had run out of steam fast when he'd pointed out that the way he'd spoken to her wasn't really what they were fighting about; when she'd stopped screaming at him, and *remembered*, and gone very quiet.

Like she'd been looking the wrong way and had fallen down the hole where Luke used to be.

When she murmured to him from the other side of the bed, he had to ask her to repeat it, the pair of them speaking quietly across the body of their sleeping daughter.

'Why don't you go next door?' she said.

He was fairly sure they weren't going to start at each other again, but, still, he didn't want to ask her what she meant. If she didn't want to be lying there close to him, or if she just thought that things were a bit cramped with the three of them, that he'd have more chance of a decent night's sleep in the spare room.

It was academic, either way.

'I don't reckon I'm going to sleep anyway,' he said. 'I was thinking I might just go for a run.'

He waited another few minutes before lifting his arm and rolling away. By the low, green light of the digital clock, he could see that though his wife's eyes were closed, there was a tightness around her mouth; that sleep was a distant possibility for her, too.

He padded across to the fitted wardrobes, opened the door and bent down for his training shoes.

When Thorne got back to his flat just before two, he was surprised to walk into the living room and find a man asleep on his sofa-bed.

Hendricks opened his eyes and sat up. Elvis, who'd been curled against his chest, jumped to the floor and slunk away, yowling. 'It's late,' Hendricks said. 'I was getting so worried I almost called the police.'

Thorne walked around the bed towards the kitchen. 'I knew I should have asked for that key back.'

'You sound like you're about to break into "I Will Survive". You should probably have changed that stupid lock as well.'

'Do you want tea?'

Hendricks had spent a few weeks staying at the flat the previous year and Thorne had never bothered to get the spare key from him once he'd returned to his own place. He'd used it a couple of times since, but Thorne was fairly sure that Hendricks hadn't come over to feed the cat tonight.

'How long do you want to stay?'

Hendricks spoke a little louder, turning towards the kitchen. 'This is just a one-off,' he said. 'I wasn't going to stay overnight, but once it got late I just thought, Fuck it, and got the bed out.'

'It's fine.' Thorne walked back in, and headed over to the stereo. He put on a CD by Iris DeMent, a singer/ songwriter from Arkansas he'd first heard on Radio 2's

*Bob Harris Country.* These were mountain songs, about blessings and blood; simple and honest and suited to the hour. Thorne waited for the first few notes picked out on an acoustic guitar, adjusted the volume and went back to get his tea.

'I didn't argue with Brendan about "nothing",' Hendricks said.

Thorne sat down gently and pulled up his knee. 'I never thought you did.'

'The other day, I said I couldn't remember what we'd fallen out about, that it wasn't anything important, remember?'

'I remember you being a bit cagey . . .'

'We were arguing about kids.'

'What, did you finally get round to telling him that you couldn't have any?'

Hendricks smiled, but it was just punctuation. 'I *want* to have them. That's exactly the point. I know it's a fucking nightmare and we probably wouldn't stand a chance in hell anyway, but I wanted to talk about adoption. Brendan wasn't interested. He thinks I'm being selfish, that I should have told him when we first got together, but I didn't know I wanted them then, did I?'

The springs of the sofa-bed creaked beneath Hendricks as he shifted position. The guitar had been joined by a piano, and the voice, a rich Ozark twang, snaked between the two of them.

'So, when *did* you know?' Thorne asked.

Hendricks let his head fall all the way back, and spoke to

243

the ceiling. 'I went to that conference in Seattle last year, remember?'

'Round Easter, wasn't it? You were saying how cold it was.'

'There was a demonstration of some fantastic new mortuary facilities one of the days, and they had these viewing suites. Specifically, for viewing children's bodies, you know?' Hendricks cleared his throat. 'Anything from stillbirths to pre-teens in gangland shootings. We're starting to get these here now, but back then I'd never seen anything like it. Basically, it's about trying to minimise the trauma for the parent, to make the process less impersonal ... less *shocking*. So they lay the body out on a refrigerated bed. The whole suite's done up to look like a kid's bedroom, yeah? There's teddies and dolls and what have you for the very young ones, and there's music if you want it, and it's all geared towards making it seem like the dead child's asleep. Creating something peaceful, just for those few minutes, or whatever.

'Nobody's kidding anyone, you need to understand that. It's not cheesy and plastic. It really isn't like that at all, even if I'm making it sound like it is.

'So, they're showing us round, right? Giving us the tour. There's a bunch of us from the UK, from Germany, Australia, whatever and everyone's making notes and asking questions. "How is the temperature of the bed regulated? What are the set-up costs?" All sorts. And I'm just looking at the empty bed, at the racing cars on the duvet, at the soft toys, at the curtains ... And I'm seeing a child on the bed.

'A boy ...

'I'm seeing his face in real detail. How long his eyelashes are, and the hands crossed on top of the duvet and the perfect crescents of his fingernails. I'm seeing every strand of his hair, and I can see exactly how much colour they've put on his lips, and I think that *maybe* I can see an inch or so of the PM scar, red against his chest where the button's come undone on his pyjamas. I'm seeing all that, I'm *recognising* it, because for some reason I'm seeing through a parent's eyes and not a pathologist's.

'Does that make any fucking sense at all?

'That was all it took really; that was what changed. The child I'd imagined on that bed wasn't anonymous, wasn't a body I'd worked on. He was *mine*. I'd bought him those pyjamas with rockets and stars on them. I was the one who was going to have to bury him. I suddenly knew how much, I could suddenly *admit* how much I wanted a child. Because I knew how terrible it would feel to lose one ...'

Hendricks sniffed and cursed under his breath, but from low in his armchair there was no way for Thorne to see if that meant there were tears. He would have needed to stand up; and, truthfully, he had no idea what he would have been expected to do then. With Hendricks lying down in bed, it was hard. It was *awkward*. So he stayed where he was and felt bad, because he didn't know how to make his friend feel better.

And they both listened to Iris DeMent singing about

God walking in dark hills, and Jesus reaching, reaching, reaching down to touch her pain.

It was the biggest manhunt in Metropolitan Police history: the ongoing search for a serial rapist who had broken into nearly a hundred homes in south London since the early nineties, sexually assaulting more than thirty elderly women and raping at least four. The man, dubbed the 'Night Stalker', always worked in the same way. After breaking in, he would cut the victim's phone line and switch off the electricity before making his way to the bedroom.

She'd read extensively about the case over a number of years, disturbed by it yet fascinated. She'd had some experience of dealing with deviancy, with those in its grip and with those who had been its victims, so part of her was engaged on a professional level. But, more than that, she'd read about what this man's victims had been through, she'd watched the reconstructions on the television and she'd felt their terror as if it had been her own. The old women, many in their eighties and above, all described that same dreadful moment of waking, of seeing a dark figure at the end of the bed, and she couldn't help but ask herself what she would do in the same situation. How might she react?

She lived in a different part of London, of course, and she wasn't quite as old, *yet*, as this man seemed to like them, but still she'd sat and asked herself the question . . .

'I said don't move.'

She froze, her arm outstretched. 'I just wanted to put on the light. I wouldn't be as frightened if it wasn't so dark.'

'I like it dark,' he said.

Her heart was making the thin material of her nightdress dance against her chest, but she felt amazingly calm; clear-headed enough. There were ideas, pictures, words flying around inside her head like fireworks – *rape*, *scream*, *weapon*, *pain* – but there was still a strong, focused train of thought.

This was the way to deal with him. He needed to be engaged. She had to make him *care* about her.

'I'm sorry if you're frightened,' he said, 'I can't help that.'

'Don't be so silly, of course you can.'

'No . . .'

'You could just leave. I wouldn't tell anyone.'

She saw him lower his head, as though he were considering what she'd said, feeling guilty about it. She was doing very well, doing what the women who'd been confronted by this man in the past and had *not* been attacked had done. Those women had spoken afterwards about their appeal to something in him – to his conscience, perhaps – as being the moment when he'd changed his mind and decided to leave them be.

'What would your mother think?' one old woman had asked him.

He started to walk around the bed and she felt a surge of panic. He must have seen it in her, or perhaps she made a noise, because he told her to shush.

'I know you don't want to hurt me,' she said.

He moved closer.

'I can tell that you're caring.'

'Shut up now . . .'

'You've made me wet the bed.' She tried to keep her voice steady, as though she were scolding a child, but trying not to scare them. 'You should be ashamed of yourself.' But *she* was the one who was ashamed, then suddenly angry, and reaching across for the chain that dangled from the bedside lamp.

He swore when the light came on, started shouting, and in a second he was on her.

Her fingers dug into his forearms as he tried to reach behind her, but the strength went from them when she saw his face. It took her a second or two to place him. Then confusion took hold, and the fireworks in her head flew faster and hotter, but before she could formulate a 'what?' or a 'why?' her head was dropping back, and the soft shadow was rushing down at her.

She spoke his name twice into the pillow, but it was just a silly noise.


He was woken by the pain in his leg as he shifted across the mattress to make room for his father.

'Move your fat arse, for Christ's sake,' Jim Thorne said.

Thorne put the light on. 4.17 a.m. He reached across for the glass of water, pushed a couple of co-codamols from the blister pack.

'You're a fucking drug addict!'

There were two paperbacks next to the bed, both of which had been started several times over. Thorne couldn't summon the concentration to have another crack. There was a *Standard* in his bag, and two days' worth of unopened post on the table by the front door, but he didn't want to go through the living room and risk waking Hendricks up. So he lay there and tried to get comfortable.

Thorne's father had developed a decent line in good advice since his death. There were occasional words of wisdom, flashes of insight; at least once, the information Thorne had needed to catch a killer.

But it was not a source that anyone would call reliable.

For whatever reason, the old man was content on this occasion to do nothing but stare up at the ceiling and remind Thorne just how 'fucking-bastard horrible' his light fitting was.

# SATURDAY

# LUKE

He'd never got drunk. On those few occasions he'd tagged along with other boys on trips to the pub, he'd always drawn the line at a couple; stopped well before the one that would tip him over the edge. And however much he'd wanted to, however much he'd thought that he should, he'd always said no when those boys who were into it had slipped into the park for a joint after school. He knew that Juliet had done it. She'd told him that the first time you felt sick, but after that it was great, and you just felt really relaxed and mellow. That sounded good, but he'd never been quite brave enough to try it. To take the risk, knowing what might happen. How his dad felt about drugs.

He'd always been afraid of losing control.

But now, sitting against the wall in the dark, he imagined that this was probably what it felt like. To be completely off your head. He imagined that when you were pissed or stoned you got this sensation of being somewhere else, of everything swimming and twisted. Of losing touch.

The man had been down to see him, to bring him some food and tell him some things. He didn't know if the man had been in the house all the time, or if he came and went. He hadn't heard a front door open or close, but, of course, he didn't know how far away from it he was.

Luke had no idea if it was late at night or early in the morning. There was a narrow shaft of light coming down through a floorboard at the far end, but he couldn't tell if it was daylight or coming from a room on the floor above him. Whichever, it didn't allow him to see much. He was growing used to the darkness, though, and he was starting to map out the room, just like he'd done back in the flat with Conrad and Amanda.

It had been slow and difficult, feeling his way around, with the rope tying his hands together cutting off the feeling in his fingers.

He was in a cellar, maybe fifteen feet by twenty. There was a longer bit that narrowed and ran to a wall which sloped suddenly away from his touch and upwards. He was sure this was an old coal chute; he'd seen one before at a friend's house when they'd gone down to collect a bottle of wine to have with dinner. The walls at his friend's place had been plastered and painted, but these were rough, just the original brick, and the ceiling was only a few inches above his head. There were some shelves on one side, thick with dust where they weren't crammed with cans and open boxes of tiles. Beneath were rolls of paper, a heavy bag of hardened cement, what felt like picture frames leaning one against the other. He could smell paint and turpentine; could taste brick dust and damp earth in another corner. He heard something scurrying as he tried to get to sleep.

When the man had opened the door and stood at the top of the stairs, it had been dark behind him. He'd shone a torch to light his way down. He'd brought a hamburger and fries in a bag, a plastic cup of Coke. He'd crouched, ripped the tape from Luke's face, then let the torch beam drop to the filthy floor while Luke ate, and while he talked.

When the man had finished, he'd waited, staring at Luke as though he were expecting a reaction to what he'd said. To the mad, vile shit he'd said about everyone Luke loved. He'd raised the torch up to Luke's face.

But Luke had just sat, and wolfed down the food, and hated himself for wanting to cry.

Afterwards, the man had asked Luke if he thought he needed to put the tape back over his mouth. Luke had shaken his head. The man had told him that there was no point in shouting anyway because nobody would hear him, but that this would be a test. If Luke behaved himself, and didn't shout, then maybe next time the man would take the rope from around his wrists as well. The man was sure that Luke would pass the test. He'd said that Luke was a good lad, a sensible boy; that he *knew* what a very good boy he was.

Luke had nodded. Kept on nodding.

Now, sitting in the dark, he was trying to work it out. Was the man just talking, or did he *really* know? Did he know particular stuff about him? He certainly claimed to know the people Luke cared about very well ...

He was wide awake; as awake as he could remember being since this whole thing had started. Maybe it was because he hadn't been drugged again; not since the man had taken him from the flat and put him in the car. Maybe it was because he had slept, though Luke couldn't say for sure if he had, at least not for any length of time. Perhaps he was just at that stage beyond tiredness, where you started to feel fine again; where you could think clearly about something other than sleep.

He was thinking about survival.

He knew that his mother and father would do whatever the man wanted to get him back, but he'd seen enough films and TV shows to know that plans sometimes went wrong. As far as things between him and the man went, it was obvious that the key to getting through it was control. Control would give him his best chance.

He just didn't know whether that meant keeping it or losing it.

# TWELVE

Below the calendar, on the pale yellow kitchen wall, there was some kind of poem or story in old-fashioned copperplate. It was about a man walking along a beach and always seeing two sets of footprints: his and God's. Except for those dark periods of his life when he was unhappy or struggling with some great problem, when one set of footprints seemed to disappear. In the poem, the man is angry with God for deserting him in his time of greatest need, but God explains that although there was only one set of footprints on the beach, the man was never really alone. That it was at those very darkest of times, when God was *carrying* him ...

Heeney shook his head, nodded towards the large sitting room that was used as a therapy area. 'I never realised it would be, you know ... God Squad.'

Neil Warren finished stirring the last of the three teas

and lobbed the spoon into the sink. 'It isn't . . . necessarily,' he said. '*I* am, though.' He handed Heeney his tea.

'Right,' Heeney said.

'Most people need to find something that's more important to them than the drugs or the drink, you know? Something that isn't going to fuck their lives up in quite the same way. Then they make a choice.'

'Right,' Heeney said again.

'For me, it came down to God or cocaine.'

He handed Holland a mug, and Holland took it with a smile, enjoying Heeney's discomfort just as much as Warren clearly was.

Nightingale Lodge was a privately run halfway house, owned by an organisation called Pledge. It was a large, double-fronted Victorian place on Battersea Rise, where up to six recovering addicts at a time – those who'd completed eight weeks of rehab but were deemed to be 'still at risk' – could readjust to a drug-free way of life while waiting for permanent accommodation. Though Pledge was a registered charity, the residents of Nightingale Lodge paid a decent enough whack to live there, and it seemed likely that someone was making a profit. Neil Warren was one of two full-time counsellors and admitted to being a little unclear as to exactly who was paying his wages. He *did* know that they were a damn sight higher than those he'd been paid back when he'd worked for the London Borough of Bromley, several years before.

'Getting people off drugs is a boom industry,' he'd said when Holland had spoken to him on the phone first thing.

'There's no shortage of customers.' The voice was high and light, with a trace of a northern accent. Holland had imagined six foot something of emaciated hippy, in denim, with a ponytail.

Warren was in his late thirties, short and stocky, with dark hair shaved close to the skull. He wore a plain grey sweatshirt over khaki combats and Timberlands. He looked like he could handle himself.

'Might as well call this an official fag break,' Warren said. He produced a tobacco tin from his back pocket, took out a lighter and one of several prepared roll-ups. He offered the tin to Heeney, who declined but gratefully took it as a cue to reach for his own pack of Benson & Hedges. Holland shook his head.

'You talk about cocaine or whatever,' Heeney said, stuffing the cigarette between his lips. 'I can't even give these up.'

Warren lit up. 'Harder to quit than heroin,' he said.

'Cheaper, though.'

'Not by much . . .'

'That's the bloody truth.'

Holland looked at Heeney, leaning back against the worktop, with his fag and his mug of tea, like he was at home talking bollocks to his wife. It wasn't often Holland yearned to be working with someone like Andy Stone, but it would have been a joy by comparison. Perhaps it was the Brummie accent. It had seemed as good a reason as any to take against his newest partner almost immediately, and first impressions had proved horribly accurate. They'd quickly settled into a pattern that saw Holland doing most of the work while Heeney stood around, made facile comments, and tried to pick his nose while no one was looking.

'We'll talk in here,' Warren said. 'Some of the residents are having an unsupervised therapy session in the living room.' Heeney sniffed, and Warren saw it for the expression of disdain that it was. 'Therapy doesn't *always* mean "wanky".' The edge in his voice was clear. 'It's bloody hard work in here. They have to pull their weight and follow the regime, and if they don't, they're out. As it happens, I'm the nice cop. The other counsellor makes anyone who fucks up spend the day with a toilet seat round their neck.'

'How does that work?' Holland asked. 'You share duties with the other counsellor?'

'It's one on, one off.'

'Meaning?'

Warren slid the ashtray to within Heeney's reach. 'One of us is always here overnight and we each do a week at a time. I'm on days at the minute, so I get to sleep in my own bed.'

Holland looked at the Post-its stuck to the fridge door, the printed rota that had been laminated and pinned to one of the cupboards. 'It's how I imagine students live,' he said. 'Notes telling their flatmates to do the washing up and to keep their hands off the new pot of yoghurt. Like *The Young Ones* or something . . .'

'It's quite a lot like that,' Warren said, 'only with more violence and a lot less shagging.'

Heeney suddenly looked rather more interested. 'Why's that then?'

'It's single sex, for a start; not that *that* makes a lot of difference, of course. But residents are not really allowed to have any sort of relationship while they're here. Dependency isn't something we try to encourage, you see?'

'How long are they here for?' Heeney asked.

'Anything up to eighteen months.'

'Bloody hell.'

'Depends if they stick it, if a council flat becomes available, whatever.'

'I bet there's a lot of porn knocking about . . .'

Warren smiled as he took a long drag, but it was at the policeman, rather than with him.

Through the kitchen window Holland could see a long, narrow garden. There was a shed at the far end, a table and chairs. The grass badly needed cutting, and when a large magpie dropped, screeching into it from a fencepost, the bird all but disappeared from view.

'Why did *you* give up?' Holland asked. He glanced towards the calendar and the words beneath. 'What made you choose?'

'I wanted to stop from the day I started,' Warren said. 'Actually, make that I knew that I *should* stop. I was a drugs counsellor who was also a drug addict, so I knew exactly how much I was fucking myself up. But you don't stop until there's nothing else you can do. Until some part of your body packs in or something terminal happens in your

261

life.' Outside, a cat with long, matted fur jumped up on to the window sill. Warren leaned across and gently tapped on the window with a fingernail; watched as the cat rubbed itself against the glass. 'There's rarely a specific moment, to be honest,' he said. 'But if you want one, it was probably when my mum died, and my brother and sister wouldn't let me be alone with her body in case I nicked the jewellery off it.'

Holland noticed that even Heeney had the good grace to look at his shoes for a moment or two.

'Yeah.' Warren turned and stubbed out his cigarette. 'That was a decent-sized slap in the face.'

'That was when you decided to quit?'

'No, not even then.' He laughed gently at the ridiculousness of it all. 'But that was when the family *made* me quit.'

'Like an "intervention" sort of thing?'

'Well, a British version of one. My sister cut me dead and my brother beat the shit out of me.'

Holland could not help but be impressed by the man's openness, by his apparent honesty. He certainly seemed to be someone who'd given up hiding anything a long time ago. 'So, when was that?' he asked.

'I've been clean almost exactly two years, which is just about as long as I was on drugs.'

Holland did the maths and got an interesting result. 'So you started taking drugs when you were working on the MAPPA project.'

'I started taking cocaine seriously in 2001.'

'Around the time the panel was disbanded?'

Warren nipped a strand of tobacco from his tongue. 'Somewhere around there, probably. I could check, but I don't think "Took first line of charlie" appears anywhere in that year's diary—'

He was cut off by a burst of shouting from the next room, which grew suddenly louder as a door was thrown open. A few seconds later, a skinny teenage boy, who could not have been much older than Luke Mullen, stormed into the kitchen, gesturing wildly and cursing at the top of his voice.

The cat fled from the window ledge.

'Cunt Andrew grassed me to the group, fucking told everyone I'd been talking about gear ... about gear I'd taken like I loved it. Fucker wasn't even there ... cunt, saying shit to make himself popular with you lot. I swear, you better take all the fucking knives out of this fucking kitchen, Neil, I'm telling you that ...'

Warren led the boy to the small kitchen table. He sat him beneath a poster that said, 'THIS IS NOT A DRESS REHEARSAL', and talked to him as though Holland and Heeney weren't there. He spoke gently enough at first, until the boy grew calmer, then gradually his tone became firmer. He said that he understood how annoying it was to be grassed up, but that Andrew had done the right thing. Talking about drugs in a positive way was against all the rules; to talk about them as if they were something to be missed or mourned was not the way to move forward.

'It's stinking thinking, Danny, you know that. Stinking thinking ...'

The phrase rang a bell inside Holland's head. They were buzzwords, with the dreadful whiff of an American self-help course. But it struck a chord. Holland made a mental note to tell Thorne, who he was sure would find it funny.

*Stinking thinking.*

Without it, the two of them would be out of a job.

It wasn't panic but simple surprise that passed across Jane Freestone's face when she opened the door. Saw that it wasn't Jehovah's Witnesses who were ringing her bell at nine-thirty on a Saturday morning.

'I thought you lot had given up,' she said. 'Worked out you were wasting your time, started bothering someone else once a fucking year.'

It was the turn of those waving the warrant cards to look surprised, while Jane Freestone's features settled quickly into a resentful sneer. It seemed to Thorne that the Sarah Hanley case, certainly as far as Grant Freestone's involvement was concerned, had gone from cold to deep frozen. After a terse exchange on the doorstep, he and Porter were grudgingly ushered inside.

They walked down a narrow corridor with framed prints of sunsets and snowscapes on the walls. A sign saying, 'Billy's Room' was Sellotaped to a closed door. From behind it, Thorne could hear a television and the sound of toys being thrown around. He smelled last night's Chinese takeaway as they passed the kitchen.

Within a few minutes of standing in Jane Freestone's

264

flat – a two-bedroom maisonette on an estate in Brentford – Thorne's journey to work was starting to seem like a fond and far-distant memory. He'd left earlier than he needed to; slipped out of the flat without waking Hendricks and taken the longer route in through Highgate and Hampstead. The roads had been almost empty. Coming down towards Golders Green past the Heath, the sky ahead of him had been cloudless, and drowned with pink.

He'd thought, even then, that it would probably be as good as the day was ever likely to get.

The view from the window, below the M4 to the trading estate beyond, was only marginally bleaker than the one to be had inside, and the tenant's mood was more unpleasant than either. Thorne had pissed off some bad people in his time, but it had been a while since he'd felt quite so hated. The woman rarely raised her voice, but the tone was unmistakable; there was poison in every word, spat, spun or whispered. She told them she hadn't got long because she needed to get her kids dressed. They asked her what she'd meant when she'd answered the door, and she explained that there had been no annual visit the previous year; so she hadn't had to talk to 'one of you fuckers' for eighteen months. Porter explained that she and Thorne were fuckers of a different sort; that Grant's name had come up in connection with an entirely different matter.

'Something else you can fit him up for?'

'You think your brother was fitted up for Sarah Hanley's murder?' Porter asked.

Freestone shook her head, smirked like Thorne and Porter were as thick as pig-shit. She was somewhere in her early thirties, tall and large-breasted, with dark hair scraped back from her face and tied up. Thorne might almost have found her sexy in a hard-faced, brittle kind of way. If she were wearing a different dressing-gown perhaps, and he hadn't been laid in twenty years.

'Are you saying that a police officer, or officers, made your brother the prime suspect because they couldn't find anyone else?'

'I'm not saying anything.'

'Or that *they* were responsible for the murder in the first place?'

She took a crumpled tissue from her dressing-gown pocket, used one corner to dab at the inside of a nostril. 'There was the odd copper who wouldn't have been too gutted if Grant got sent down again.' She stuffed the tissue back. 'Put it that way.'

Thorne resisted looking across at Porter and sensed that she was doing likewise. 'I don't suppose you fancy naming this "odd copper",' he said.

She didn't.

Thorne and Porter were standing, but when they'd first come into the living room Freestone had dropped into an armchair and turned towards the large, flat-screen TV in one corner. She'd switched it on, then muted the volume, and spent much of the conversation staring at the screen.

'Why did he run, Jane, if he didn't kill Sarah?'

It was an obscure cable channel. Every time Thorne looked, someone was being shown around a house.

'Because he knew he was in the frame, and he didn't want to go back to prison, did he? Even though this was an unrelated offence, they had him marked down inside as someone who messes with kids.'

'*Marked down?*' Thorne said. 'Nobody planted those children in his garage.'

Freestone ignored the dig, studied the TV as though she could read lips.

'Don't you think he would have been better off staying put,' Porter said, 'if he really didn't do it?'

'Stop fucking saying, "*if*".' She turned suddenly, looking about ready to punch someone's lights out. 'Grant was with me when his girlfriend was killed. We were in the park with my kids.' She pointed back towards the corridor. 'Go and fucking-well ask them.'

The woman could easily make such an invitation, knowing it would never be accepted. Her eldest child was eight years old. Whatever they might say if asked now, neither he nor his little brother could be trusted to remember what had happened back when neither of them had been old enough to say much of anything.

Porter held up a hand, left a beat before trying again. 'Wouldn't he have been better off trying to prove he was innocent?'

The look Freestone gave Porter before she turned back to the TV made it clear that now she *knew* they were both stupid.

'Does Grant think he was stitched up?' Thorne asked.

'Have a guess.'

'Is that what he said at the time? Did you see him before he disappeared?'

'I haven't seen him in five years.'

'Nobody's suggesting that he's hiding under the bed, but the two of you must have been in touch, surely?'

'Must we?'

Thorne took a couple of steps towards the armchair. 'He's phoned you, written you letters, something. Is it what he still thinks?'

Freestone pushed herself up, waited for Thorne to move out of the way so she could get past. 'I'm going for a piss. Give you two a chance to have a good old nosy while I'm gone.' She pointed to a door. 'My bed's through there, in case you *do* want to check underneath . . .'

As soon as she had left, as soon as they'd heard the lock slide across on the bathroom door, Thorne and Porter did as Freestone had suggested. They moved quickly, and in virtual silence around the room, drew each other's attention to items of interest with a nod or a whisper. There were photographs on a low, glass table to the side of the TV: Jane Freestone and a man Thorne recognised as her brother, wearing smiles they'd been holding for a few seconds too long; a holiday snap of a well-built man with ginger hair and moustache sitting on a balcony in shirt and shorts, posing with his pint; Freestone's kids in a playground, running towards the camera. Porter looked at the magazines on a box below the window: *Heat*, *Auto Trader*,

*Nuts*. Thorne flicked quickly through the utility bills, fastened together with a bulldog clip next to the midi-system. He looked for any overseas numbers on the BT calls list and noted that the Sky subscription was for the complete films and sports package. He moved away to study the spines on the row of CDs when he heard the toilet flush.

When Freestone returned, she walked straight back to the armchair and sank into it as though there were nobody else in the room.

Porter nodded towards the photograph of the man with the beer. 'Is that the kids' dad?'

The laugh was short and bitter. 'He is now. Makes a damn sight better job of it than the real one ever did, that's for sure.'

Thorne wandered across and leaned down to look at the photo again. 'He lives here, does he?'

'Most of the time.' She sucked her teeth, answered like it was the question she'd been expecting. 'Which is why we've got Sky Sports and so many heavy-metal CDs.' She looked at Thorne, her eyes wide with mock concern. 'In case you were wondering.'

Thorne was wondering how many times this woman had had police officers in her house. 'Where is he?'

'Arsenal are away at Manchester United,' she said. 'Him and his mates went up on the train last night.'

Thorne looked closer and recognised the Gunners crest on the man's polo shirt.

'You going to get married?' Porter asked.

'What's the point? It's good for fuck-all, except making

it slightly easier for the CSA to catch up with them when they leave.'

In his head, Thorne fashioned a smartarse remark about how nice it was to see romance alive and well. He kept it to himself, thought instead about how vulnerable a marriage was; about those less-than-sturdy emotions with their in-built expiry dates. A marriage could survive if love became something else – companionship, perhaps – but if hate got its foot in the door, there would only ever be one outcome.

He thought about Maggie and Tony Mullen.

Hate did not appear overnight. It seeded itself. It sprouted and climbed from within the dark, damp subtleties of blame and guilt. Thorne could conceive of no better condition for such a twisted flowering than the loss of a child.

Thorne's eyes shifted back to Jane Freestone.

She was staring like she'd walked him in on the bottom of her shoe. 'What exactly is this "entirely different matter" you were talking about, then?' She was turning her head before she'd finished the question, her attention stolen by the sound of a child crying along the corridor.

'Bollocks,' she said.

Porter joined her as she reached the door. 'Can I use the toilet?'

'Why don't you just make yourself some fucking breakfast?' Freestone said, walking out ahead of her.

Left alone in the room, Thorne sat down on the sofa, deciding that as he got older and more experienced, he was becoming worse at reading people; at getting so much as an *idea* of what they were thinking. He could be close enough to see his own reflection in someone's eyes and still not be able to tell if they were sincere or running rings around him. There were days when he'd have the Pope down as a serial killer and Jeffrey Archer as an honest man . . .

He looked at the TV, saw more people being shown around more beautifully designed interiors. With the sound down, he tried to work out if the people liked the houses or not just from the expressions on their faces.

'I'd have to say Grant Freestone could be capable of almost anything.'

Holland, Heeney and Warren were alone again in the kitchen. Danny, the boy who had been so upset, had gone back into the living room to apologise to the rest of the group for his stinking thinking; to get back 'on the programme'. Warren had told him he should think a little more about what he wanted. That he should count himself lucky he wouldn't be spending the rest of the day with a bog seat for a necklace.

'I'd better qualify that,' Warren added. 'If he's still doing drugs, he'd be capable of anything.'

'You think he might be?' Holland asked.

'Who knows? He had a problem when he came out of prison, and I doubt it had completely gone away by the time his girlfriend was killed.'

It was an interesting choice of phrase. 'So maybe he was high when he attacked her?'

'I'm not going to speculate about that. Can't see the point. Make no mistake, though, even if Grant had been close to getting clean, that's exactly the kind of thing that's going to dirty you right back up again.'

Holland remembered when Warren himself had started taking drugs. Could guilt about Sarah Hanley's death have been the trigger for *his* addiction? 'You think?' he said.

It didn't receive much of a reaction, but enough to let Holland see the question had hit home. Warren turned to the sink and began to wash up the dirty mugs. 'You asked me if I thought Freestone was capable of kidnapping someone and I'm trying to be straight with you. If you get fucked up enough, you'll do whatever you have to.'

Holland nodded, waited for him to continue. He wondered, in this instance, if 'whatever' might include murder.

'There's a point you reach when you don't think about what you're doing. You think you're being clever when in fact you're doing something really fucking stupid. You're just focused on getting the money to buy what you need.'

Warren had been told no more than he needed to know. When Holland had begun talking about a kidnapping, the counsellor had made the natural assumption about the motive. He didn't know that, for all his speculation about what a junkie might do if he was desperate enough, the person holding Luke Mullen had yet to make any ransom demand. *Why* was still as much of a mystery as *who*, but it was starting to look like money had bugger-all to do with it.

All the same, the drug angle was interesting in at least one respect. 'Does the name Conrad Allen mean anything, Neil?'

Warren turned from the sink. Shook his head.

'What about Amanda Tickell?'

'Who?' Warren reached for a tea-towel, spoke again before Holland had finished repeating the name. 'I'm sorry, but there's really no point to this. I don't think you're asking if I play bridge with any of these people, and I can't discuss anyone who I may or may not know professionally.'

'Fair enough.' It was the first thing Heeney had said for a long while.

'Talking of which, I should get myself into the living room and make sure nothing kicks off.' He took a step away from the sink, the shift in his position leaving the sun shining straight into Holland's face. The cat was back on the window sill.

Holland narrowed his eyes against the glare. 'Is Freestone clever enough for this? I mean, I'm taking on board everything you've said: the desperation or whatever. But is he actually smart enough to pull off something like this?'

Warren thought about that one. 'Well, there's smart enough to get into Mensa, and there's smart enough not to get caught. They're very different things.'

'He might be both, of course.'

'He's no more than averagely bright in any conventional sense, but he's developed a few useful tricks. It's not so much clever as cunning.'

'Streetwise.'

'More than that,' Warren said. 'He knows how to get by, but to do the things he's done you also need to fool people for a while. What put him in prison in the first place, what he *is* ... You don't get away with that for long unless you can convince the rest of the world you're something you're not. You learn to pretend, and you get so good at it that it becomes second nature. Once you throw an addiction into that mix, something you need to keep secret from those around you, you end up being someone who spends most of their life hiding who they really are.' He chewed at a nail, tore, and ground it between his teeth. 'Yeah ... I think he's smart enough.'

Holland wasn't any more convinced than anyone else that Grant Freestone was their man, but he'd been given a job to do. He reckoned that as far as Neil Warren went, he'd about done it. He glanced at the wall, saw that it was someone called Eric's turn to cook dinner that evening and that Andrew was down to clean the bathroom. He looked at the poem below the calendar. It was still mawkish – and Holland was strictly a wedding, funeral and Lottery man when it came to God – but he couldn't help but hope that, wherever Luke Mullen was, he was leaving a single set of footprints.

They were still waiting for Porter.

The child who had been so upset – Thorne didn't know if it was Billy, or even if Billy was the elder – was now lying quietly in the armchair with his head on his mother's chest. The boy's face was expressionless as much as peaceful, but his eyes were wide, and fixed on the man standing by the window. If Thorne were letting his imagination run loose, he might have thought that the child had been taught to be suspicious of policemen nice and early. Or perhaps it was just men . . .

Freestone stroked her child's head. 'I don't appreciate your coming in here, using this place as a shit-house.'

Thorne glanced at the door. 'I'm sure she'll be out in a minute.'

'Your lot always does though, one way or another. Maybe she'd like to wipe her skinny arse on the curtains. Or some of my kids' clothes.'

'Now you're just being stupid,' Thorne said.

'It's about respect.'

Along the corridor, the toilet flushed.

'It's about you messing us around in the past: talking shit and lying to save your brother.'

'I didn't lie.'

'Who do you think took those kids, Jane? Did they tie each other up?'

'I didn't lie about Sarah Hanley. We were in the park.' She moved beneath her son, shifting his head from one side of her chest to the other. 'It was the last time he saw my kids.'

When Porter walked briskly into the room, there was a look on her face Thorne couldn't read. But something was different. She spoke to the back of Freestone's head. 'We should probably get out of your way,' she said.

'Nobody's arguing.'

'Sorry we disturbed your Saturday.'

'I still don't know what the fuck you wanted.'

Thorne looked at Porter, trying to work out what she was doing. He caught her eye for a second, but it told him nothing.

'Look, I'll be honest with you,' Porter said. 'You probably wanted us to be here about as much as we did, but the visit was actioned, so here we are. Because we do what we're told. Some idiot of a DCI with a tiny dick and an even smaller imagination thought this would be a good idea. Picked your brother's name out of thin air, as far as I can make out.'

'It wouldn't be the first time,' Freestone said. 'This is something to do with kids, right?'

'It's sod all to do with anything, if you ask me,' Porter said. 'It's about coppers making decisions based purely on what comes up on a computer screen, and all of us getting the shitty end of the stick. It's a waste of time, pure and simple.'

'If this is an apology, it's nice to hear. But you can still stick it.'

'I'll pass that on to our DCI.' Porter looked at Thorne, who did what he thought she would want, and smiled conspiratorially. 'Listen, just treat this as if it's the routine visit that Hoolihan's lot never got round to, OK?'

'Makes no bloody difference.'

'So, for the record Miss Freestone, just so I can tick a box to say I asked, have you seen your brother since the last time you were interviewed by the police?'

She closed her eyes, rubbed her child's back. 'I wish I had. More than anything, I wish I had. I've got no fucking idea if Grant's alive or dead.'

Thorne and Porter drove away without saying a word. At the end of the street, Thorne took a left, cut up a motor-bike and pulled hard into a bus stop.

Porter just looked at him, enjoying it.

'Are you going to tell me?' Thorne asked. 'I've no bloody idea what I was playing along with in there. What the fuck was all this "we're sorry for wasting your time" shit? "DCIs with tiny dicks ..."'

'I wanted her to think she had nothing to worry about. That she wouldn't be seeing us again. I don't want her warning her brother.'

'What?'

'She's a fucking liar. A good one.'

'Was this something in the bathroom? Don't tell me there was a floater in there with Grant Freestone's name on it?'

'I found stubble,' she said.

Thorne tried and failed not to sound patronising. 'Right. That'll be her boyfriend's ... '

'*Dark* stubble. She'd gone in and done her best to clean up, but I found it under the rim.'

'Why can't it be hers?'

Porter shook her head.

'She's got dark hair. Women shave their legs, don't they?'

'Yes, we do,' Porter said. 'But not in the sink.'

Thorne stared ahead through the windscreen, taking in what Porter was saying, considering the implications. 'Christ, do you think he was in there?'

'No. I sneaked out of the toilet and checked all the bed-rooms.'

'He may not have stayed there last night, or for any number of nights. That stubble might have been there for a while.'

Porter acknowledged the very real possibility, but there were others she found far more attractive. 'Or we might have just missed him. He could have gone out early for milk, to get a paper ...'

'We were there almost an hour,' Thorne said. 'There are shops in the next street.'

'Maybe he went to the supermarket. Maybe he went for a walk.' Porter was starting to sound tetchy, as her sugges-tions grew more desperate. 'It's a nice enough morning.'

Thorne watched a young woman on the pavement opposite, struggling with a pushchair and a wayward tod-dler. He remembered Jane Freestone pointing towards her children's bedroom, shouting: 'Go and fucking-well ask them ...'

'Did you see another child?' Thorne asked. He turned and looked at Porter, the idea taking hold, starting to jump in him. 'When you checked the bedrooms, did you see her other kid?'

Porter hesitated, as though a little unnerved by the intensity in Thorne's eyes. 'I just presumed she'd taken both of them into the living room with her. I never really looked when I came back in.'

Thorne started the car, pointed towards the glove compartment. 'There's an *A–Z* in there,' he said. 'Find the nearest park.'

He sat towards the end of the bench against which the boy's small, blue and white bike was leaning; so people would know he was looking after it. So they would know he was there with a child.

The boy jumped down from the roundabout while it was still spinning and ran for three or four steps before he stopped and waved across at him. He waved back, then stuck up a thumb. The boy grinned and ran towards a large wooden tree-house, with a rope bridge and a slide. He shouted across at the boy to be careful, but the boy showed no sign of having heard.

'I think you're wasting your time.' A woman who was leaning against the fence was smiling at him. She dropped her cigarette, stepped on it. 'Not scared of anything at that age, are they?'

'No,' he said. 'They're not.'

'It's nice, I suppose. That they're fearless, I mean. It's natural, isn't it?' She laughed, reaching into her handbag for another cigarette. 'But it does mean you can't take your eyes off the little buggers. Not my two, anyway.'

He smiled back, picked up the newspaper he'd brought with him and stared at the front page until the woman turned round again.

It was as nice a day as he could remember for a while; perfect for getting out and about. The playground was always popular, even when the weather wasn't so good, but this morning it was particularly crowded.

There were plenty of boys and girls for his nephew to play with.

Which was good for all sorts of reasons, not least because it meant that he'd been able to slip into the trees for ten minutes and smoke a little joint. He'd get into town later, buy himself something stronger for the weekend, but a bit of dope was a good start. Helped him enjoy the morning, enjoy the *view*, without getting too stupid about things.

'Excuse me ...'

He always kept a decent eye on what was happening, on stuff going on around him, and he'd seen the couple coming from a long way away. Hand in hand, honeymoon-period twats, smug and full of themselves. They'd stopped a few feet from his bench, and he could see the camera in the man's hand. He could tell that they were embarrassed to ask.

'Do you want me to take a picture of the two of you?'

'Would you?' the woman asked.

He stood up and the man handed over one of those cheap, disposable cameras, same as they sold in his local newsagent's. He put it to his eye and the couple posed, arms around each other with the playground behind.

'Cheers.' The man in the leather jacket stepped towards him.

He held out the camera, but the man grabbed his wrist instead, squeezed it hard, and took hold of his shirt at the shoulder, while the short woman with the dark hair opened up the warrant card and told him he was under arrest for the murder of Sarah Hanley.

After a minute or two of swearing and struggling, he nodded towards the playground and asked what they were going to do about his nephew. The woman told him that he needn't worry. That the boy would be taken back to his mother.

As the handcuffs were ratcheted around Grant Freestone's wrists, he glanced across at the woman by the fence. The cigarette drooped from her fat lips, and he couldn't help noticing that she'd happily taken her eyes off both her little buggers.

# THIRTEEN

They were getting used to this sort of meeting by now: ad hoc gatherings to take stock, to regroup, and jointly fight the temptation to panic or run around screaming for a while. To discuss the latest development in a case where surprises were being thrown up faster than dodgy kebabs.

The kidnap case with no ransom demand, two dead kidnappers, and a convicted paedophile arrested for a murder committed years before.

'Anything we haven't managed to get in yet?' Brigstocke asked. 'Freestone's still using, by all accounts, so we've got drugs covered. All we need now is a bit of prostitution, some gun-running maybe.'

Porter laughed.

'I'm serious. A bomb factory and one or two stolen library books and we've got the complete fucking set.'

Just after midday, and four of them were making a good

job of filling Brigstocke's office at Becke House: Brigstocke himself, Hignett, Porter and Thorne. The sun was struggling to find its way through a layer of thin cloud and the streaky patina of grime on the window. Thorne hadn't bothered to take off his jacket. Nobody in the room was sitting down.

'We should just step back and hand Freestone over,' Hignett said. 'Call in this Hoolihan, enjoy our pat on the back and get on with trying to find Luke Mullen.'

'Maybe Freestone can help us find him,' Thorne said.

Brigstocke stared at Thorne for a few seconds, as if looking for a hint before asking the inevitable question. 'Hadn't you more or less dismissed Freestone as a suspect?'

'More or less.' He was being more or less honest.

'But he's the closest thing we've got,' Porter said.

Whatever the various moods in the room – prickly, confused, determined – nobody could argue with Porter's assessment. Philip Quinn had finally been tracked down in Newcastle, and the assortment of crimes for which he'd been subsequently nicked had given him a cast-iron, if costly, alibi for the night Conrad Allen and his girlfriend had been murdered. With Quinn out of the frame, the only name on the list belonged to the man that Thorne and Porter had arrested in Boston Manor Park; the man now sitting in a cell five minutes up the road at Colindale station.

'Where did we get Freestone's name from anyway?' Hignett looked and sounded as if everything were starting to get away from him a little. Like it was all so much easier when people were snatched for cash. When an ear or two might be sliced off to bump up the price a bit, and everyone knew where they stood. He pointed towards Thorne. 'From some friend of yours, wasn't it?'

'An ex-DCI, now working on cold cases for AMRU.' Watching Hignett nod, as though this were significant, Thorne felt as though he had just been accused of something. Of chasing wild geese and landing the team with the horrible inconvenience of an arrest. 'She remembered Freestone making threats against Tony Mullen when she worked with him, and thought he might be worth pursuing. It seemed a reasonable avenue of enquiry, while you were busy looking at . . . other possibilities.'

The idea that Luke Mullen had committed manslaughter – that he had run amok with a knife and then vanished – thankfully seemed to have all but gone away. Thorne hoped that it had been as a result of certain officers coming to their senses, but couldn't help wondering if certain *ex*-officers had brought a degree of pressure to bear.

Hignett looked at his feet and rubbed his fingertip across the desktop, as though checking for dust. 'So, Freestone's name wasn't on the original list provided by Tony Mullen?'

'No . . . ' Thorne let the word hang and make its point. Then threw a 'sir' in on the end for good measure.

'It still seemed like as strong a possibility as any,' Porter said.

'You thought initially that he should be considered a suspect?'

'*Considered*, yes,' Thorne said. 'We began talking to one or two of those who'd been on the MAPPA panel that monitored Freestone when he was released from prison in 2001.'

'And as far as I understand it from your notes, those conversations persuaded you that he *wasn't* our kidnapper.'

'To a degree.'

'But you carried on talking to people, chasing it . . . '

'It was just a question of being thorough, sir,' Porter said. 'And, to be frank, we didn't have a fat lot else to chase.'

Thorne was grateful for Porter's help. He was hedging his bets, and sounding like it, and he didn't know how much longer he could fight shy of telling them why he really thought Grant Freestone was worth looking at. He'd spoken about it off the record to Brigstocke, but he couldn't be certain who else might have Tony Mullen's ear.

Brigstocke asked his question as if on cue: 'Do we tell Tony Mullen that we've got Freestone in custody?'

'No,' Thorne said immediately.

Hignett asked why not, and while Thorne bit back the urge to say, 'Because I don't trust the fucker', he came up with something more reasonable: 'We should think carefully before telling Luke's parents that we've made an arrest.' He looked at Hignett and tried to summon an expression that was close to deferential. 'I mean, I don't know how you usually do it . . . '

'There's no set procedure.'

'Obviously, I'm thinking more about *Mrs* Mullen,' Thorne said. 'We'd be raising hopes, *false* ones, probably. Causing a fair amount of upset.'

It was clear from Brigstocke's face that he couldn't help but admire Thorne's invention. His *cheek*. 'I understand that, but I think *Mr* Mullen might be fairly upset himself if he finds out.'

Thorne was in no doubt that he would, sooner or later. 'We'll have to live with it.'

'Hopefully Freestone won't be here that long,' Porter said.

Hignett had been shaking his head for a while, waiting for a chance to jump in. 'We've got nothing whatsoever to tie Freestone to this kidnap, and it's the kidnap we should be focusing on. Luke Mullen is still missing. We don't have time to piss about, so why are we even discussing this? Let's just hand him over to Graham Hoolihan, and find a real suspect—'

'Hoolihan fucked this up,' Thorne said. 'The Hanley case was not routinely reviewed. Christ knows when anyone from his team last spoke to Freestone's sister, or when they were planning to. Yes, we got lucky, but at the end of the day we've done him a favour, and he's the one who's going to be buying big drinks when we eventually hand Freestone over for the Hanley murder. Which, by the way, I also have serious doubts about—'

Hignett held up a hand to cut Thorne off, used it to point at Brigstocke and then himself. 'When you eventually hand Freestone over, *we*, Detective Inspector, not *you*, are going to get it in the neck from Hoolihan's boss for not doing so straight away.' He turned away from Thorne, spoke directly to his fellow DCI. 'I think this is a waste of time, Russell: talking to Freestone; even talking about talking to Freestone . . .'

'Why can't we have just one crack at him?' Thorne asked.

'Because you haven't got a single good reason to do so.' Hignett looked as though it were his last word on the subject. He stepped towards the door, which, after a perfunctory knock, opened as he reached for the handle.

Holland had saved Thorne's life a couple of years earlier, storming into Thorne's bedroom with an empty wine bottle as his only weapon. It was the night Thorne had received the scar across his chin, and one or two more that weren't as visible.

Holland's timing now was almost as perfect as it had been then. 'Looks like I've missed all the excitement,' he said.

'If you mean Freestone,' Hignett said, 'there's nothing to get excited about.'

Holland caught Thorne's eye as he moved further into the room. A silent exchange assuring Holland that he would be brought up to speed later.

'How did it go with Warren?' Thorne asked.

'Strange bloke: ex-junkie himself, turned to God. But I think we got something.' Holland had everyone's attention. 'He was concerned about client confidentiality, so he never actually *said* as much, but I had a very strong feeling

287

that he knew Amanda Tickell. That she'd been a client at some point.'

'Which connects her to Grant Freestone,' Porter said.

Thorne had been fired up by the morning's result, but had felt the energy pissing out of him ever since he'd walked back into Becke House. Now he could feel a buzz beginning to lick at his nerve endings, the ticking in his blood starting to build. 'They might have been clients of Warren's at the same time,' he said. 'If they did know each other, we've got a direct link between Freestone and the Mullen kidnap.' He looked at Hignett. Then, to Brigstocke: 'Sir?'

Hignett could do nothing but blink, like he'd just walked into something.

'Sounds like our *single good reason*,' Brigstocke said.

Having wrapped up the meeting, he asked Thorne to stay behind, announced that he needed a word about a death by dangerous driving case for which Thorne had done the pre-trial paperwork.

'Tony Mullen is already upset,' Brigstocke said, as soon as they were alone.

'He knows about Freestone?'

'Upset with *you*.'

'Ah ...'

'What the fuck happened at his place last night?' Brigstocke moved behind his desk, sat down like he didn't plan on getting up again for some time.

'Trevor Jesmond been by to say hello, has he?'

'He called.'

'I bet he's sorry he asked for me now.'

'Mullen says you were harassing him and his wife.'

'Talk to Porter,' Thorne said. 'She was there. To be honest, it was Mullen and his missus who were doing all the shouting.'

'He says you caused the trouble.'

'He's full of it.'

'I'm just telling you.'

Thorne turned towards the door. It always amazed him that a good feeling could disappear so fast you could barely remember having had it. 'Thanks, I'll consider myself told.'

Brigstocke hadn't finished. 'You shouldn't be making an enemy out of Barry Hignett, either.'

'Are you about to tell me that I've got enough enemies as it is?'

'No. It would be stupid, that's all. Hignett's not a bad copper and he's not a twat. He's just one of those strange fuckers who takes a position, you know? Who sticks to his guns, because he doesn't want to look indecisive. He's the opposite of that character on *The Fast Show*, the one who agrees with anything anybody tells him and keeps changing his mind.'

'Right.' Thorne knew who Brigstocke meant. The show had been one of his father's favourites. The old man had been fond of shouting out the catchphrases at inappropriate moments.

'It's good to have people like Hignett around,' Brigstocke continued. 'Sometimes he's going to be taking a *good* position and then you want him on your side. Chances are he'll be right just as often as *you* are.'

'More, I should think,' Thorne said. He reached for the door. 'Almost certainly ...'

You'd drive if it was pissing down, maybe, but by the time you'd negotiated assorted security barriers and wrestled with the limited car-parking space at either end, it was just as quick to walk between the Peel Centre and Colindale station. Thorne and Holland had made the journey often enough for their steps to be automatic. They crossed Aerodrome Road where they always did, walked at their regular pace, with Holland keeping to the left of Thorne, as usual.

They quickly completed the short conversation they'd begun wordlessly in Brigstocke's office half an hour earlier. Thorne told Holland what Hignett's objections had been and thanked him for his timely interruption. Holland said he was only too pleased to help, that it was another one up for the Murder Squad team, not that anyone was keeping score.

They never talked about the earlier incident, the one with the empty wine bottle, quite so easily.

'God told this bloke to get off the coke then, did he?'

'Apparently,' Holland said. 'Says a prayer instead of doing a line.'

'Knackering your knees certainly beats losing your septum.'

Holland lengthened his stride to avoid a spatter of dog-shit. 'If Warren *did* know Tickell, should we be looking at him, too?'

'Can't see any point,' Thorne said. 'Why on earth would he want to kidnap Luke Mullen? Unless God told him to do it, of course.'

Though there was no option but to walk all the way around, Colindale station was clearly visible – its three storeys broken up into units of brown and white – across the quarter-mile of bleak scrub that separated it from the Peel Centre. The station had been designed along the lines of an airfield observation tower, standing as it did on the site of the old Hendon aerodrome, and next door to the RAF museum. Signs along the edge of the land proclaimed it to be 'dangerous'. Thorne guessed that this was to do with the state of some of the disused buildings, but liked to imagine that it was something more sinister. He pictured London's criminal fraternity throwing a hell of a party when it was announced that one of the city's largest police facilities had been sited on top of a toxic-waste dump ...

'What about those two women on the MAPPA panel?' Holland said. 'Kathleen Bristow and Margaret Stringer. Do you need me to talk to them as well?'

'Only if you've really got sod-all else to do. Now we've got Freestone, we can get it from the horse's mouth. Whatever the hell there is to get.'

'Fair enough, but Porter told me you were banging on about being tidy.'

'Did she? What else did she say?'

'Nothing. It just came up, that's all ...'

Further along, sight of the station was cut off by newly

erected fencing. A sign on the gate announced the imminent building of 'luxury studios and apartments'. Having seen similar developments spring up in recent years, Thorne wasn't putting money on the view from his office window being significantly improved.

They turned right at the traffic island, where daffodils fought gamely for space with crisp packets and fast-food containers. For no good reason that they could fathom, two young women stood on the edge of the island, watching the cars move around it. Holland suggested that they were trainee WPCs failing a road traffic exam. Thorne wondered if they might be extremely misguided tourists who thought it was a small park.

'Kenny Parsons was telling me a few stories about Porter,' Holland said.

'Was he?'

'She's quite a character.'

Thorne stared casually up at the British Airways hoarding above them, and fought off the temptation to pump Holland mercilessly for everything he knew. The last thing he wanted was for anybody to think he gave a toss. 'I'm not that interested in gossip,' he said. 'I don't really think we've got time for it on a job like this, do you, Dave?'

Holland said nothing, just turned towards the road, but Thorne could see the trace of a smile and guessed that Holland hadn't been fooled for a second. He wondered if there was some kind of course you could take to make yourself less transparent when it mattered. He glanced back at the huge picture of a plane, shining above an ocean, and thought about going on holiday alone.

'I probably will follow up on Bristow and Stringer,' Holland said. 'When I get a minute. Just because I've already started.'

'I thought it was Andy Stone who couldn't resist chasing women.'

Holland smiled broadly this time, and continued: 'I've made a couple of calls and left messages. Waiting to hear back from Bristow and I'm still trying to get a current address for Margaret Stringer.'

'Can't you get it out of the education authority?'

As usual, traffic was heavy both ways. They had to raise their voices above the noise of cars and heavy police vehicles heading towards the tube station, or north to join up with the A1.

'The last one that Bromley Education Authority had for her was years out of date.'

'Typical,' Thorne said. 'I bet their council tax bills go out on time though.'

'No, she isn't working for them any more. She must have moved house after she left.'

'Which was when?'

'April 2001. And Kathleen Bristow retired just after that.'

Thorne remembered Roper suggesting that Bristow would have been around retirement age, but it was still striking. It was starting to look as if the lives of all those involved on Grant Freestone's MAPPA panel had been changed in some way by what happened to Sarah Hanley:

Bristow and Stringer had both left their jobs; Neil Warren had picked up a needle; Roper and Lardner certainly appeared to have *issues*.

Guilt and blame again. Poisonous and magical.

It seemed as though no one involved – however indirectly – with the death of a young mother in 2001 had come away unscathed. Thorne walked on, into Colindale station, to talk to the man accused of her murder. He had no idea how or why, and he still couldn't see Grant Freestone as a kidnapper, but he couldn't help but wonder if Sarah Hanley's killing was still fucking people's lives up five years on.

The interview was suspended before anyone grew too comfortable.

Freestone's legal representative had stood up two minutes in, insisted that proceedings be brought to a halt and demanded to talk to Thorne and Porter outside.

'Why the hell are you talking about a *kidnap*?'

'Let's get one thing straight,' Thorne said. '*Because* we are talking about a kidnap, we can't say too much.'

'That's bollocks. Don't forget who you're talking to.'

Thorne wasn't likely to.

Danny Donovan, like a lot of the legal reps working for solicitors' firms and sent along in similar situations to this one, was an ex-copper. Thrown off the force fifteen years earlier for drink-driving, what he lacked in legal qualifications – which were not strictly necessary for the job – he more than made up for in working nous and know-how.

He knew the system. He knew the difference between a loophole and a liberty. He knew his way round a police station, and most important of all, he knew the tricks that the likes of Tom Thorne played, because he'd played them all himself. This alone made characters like him unpopular with those still on the Job, but Donovan did himself no favours. When he wasn't aggressively reminding people that he'd been there and done that, he was prone to playing the old pals act: calling officers by their first names and swanning into one or other of the CID offices to put the kettle on.

He was fifty-something, and fucked. More than a few reckoned that his life as a 'legal' was about sticking two fingers up at the people who'd chucked him out on his ear. Thorne had thought this was a pretty harsh judgement, but he was ready to change his mind. What with Tony Mullen calling up to bad-mouth him to senior officers, Thorne had just about had a bellyful of bolshie ex-coppers.

'My client was arrested for murder,' Donovan said. 'Of which, as we have already established, he claims to be completely innocent.'

'Wouldn't expect otherwise.'

'"Murder". That's what it says on the arrest sheet; that's what it says on the disclosure papers; and, as far as I'm concerned, that's what you're going to be questioning him about.'

Thorne knew Donovan very well, but Porter had not had the displeasure. 'I'm sure you understand what DI

295

Thorne is getting at,' she said. 'We think that the murder for which your client has been charged, *might* be connected with a current case. A highly sensitive case.'

'Not my problem.' Donovan sniffed and bowed a finger across his nostrils. His hair seemed to have yellowed rather than greyed, and keyed in rather nicely with his light brown suit and sunbed tan.

'It's just a few questions.'

'It's a few too many. I conferred with my client on the basis of what I was presented with and now you're throwing stuff at us for which we're completely unprepared.'

'Come on, you know the game,' Thorne said. 'Sometimes "unprepared" is exactly the way they're supposed to be, right?'

The old pals act could work both ways.

Or not at all: 'Not from where I'm sitting,' Donovan said. 'Not when I haven't been given an indication of any evidence whatsoever.'

Porter tried to sound reluctant, as though Donovan were succeeding in dragging the disclosure from her. 'Look, there's a strong possibility that Freestone may have known the woman who was one of our kidnappers. They may have consulted the same drugs counsellor at the same time.'

'*A strong possibility ... may have.*' Donovan looked as though he couldn't decide whether to shout or piss himself. 'I'll tell you what you *do* have, and that's bugger-all. You must think I'm a mug.'

'We also have a sixteen-year-old boy,' Thorne said. 'Actually, someone else has him, and we're trying awfully

296

fucking hard to get him back. We could do with a break, Danny.'

'His dad's ex-Job, too,' Porter said. 'He's going out of his mind. Well, I'm sure I don't need to tell you ...'

Thorne knew that Donovan had two kids. He considered going down that road, but decided against laying it on too thick. For a second or two, it looked as though they might have got away with it; as though a simple, no-frills appeal to sentiment might have given them some leverage. But then, what Thorne had taken to be an expression of empathy – compassion, even – became something horribly like a smirk.

'Sorry. Unless you can come up with more than this very quickly, you know damn well what I'll have to advise my client to do.'

'Surprise me,' Thorne said.

'In his own interest, I'll tell him not to say a single word.' Donovan turned, walked back into the interview room and shut the door behind him.

A single word was all Thorne spoke, loudly, at the closed door. It wasn't a word he used very often outside a football ground, and he wasn't even sure that the man it was intended for heard it. But at that moment, it seemed like the only word that would do.

# LUKE

It was like being buried.

The smell of damp and dirt, and the floor above him.

It was dark, as always. Heavy, like the particles in the air would be big and black if you could see them. But he felt sure that it was daytime. If he listened hard enough, he could hear the hum of distant traffic. A motorway, maybe. And when the man had been down before, he'd brought breakfast stuff – tea and toast – and a lot more light had spilled in when he'd opened the door at the top of the stairs.

The man had done what he'd promised to do, and because Luke had not shouted when he hadn't had the tape around his face, the man had left the rope off his wrists as well. Now he could really explore.

His fingers dug into every crack and hole in the rough walls, his knuckles tearing on stone and nails, splinters slipping into his palms as he moved his hands through the cobwebs and across the ceiling above him. He felt along the shelves caked in grit and dust, and over the bags and sticky tins and picture frames. He added layer after layer of detail to the picture inside his head. He knew where everything was, and he could walk quickly from one side of the room to the other, his hands down by his sides until the very last second.

He thought it was a good sign that the rope and the tape had gone; that the man was starting to like him or something. If the man carried on being nice, and didn't say any more mad, horrible stuff, maybe he could ask him about sending another message. Maybe the man would let him say what he wanted, not like he'd had to do with Conrad and Amanda.

They were the ones who'd taken him, yes. But they'd not said any stupid, sick shit. They'd been OK with him most of the time, before they'd died.

He tried hard not to think about Conrad and Amanda, because every time he did, he saw them lying in the bedroom, with the blood underneath like the bright red lining of a jacket. Then he would get a lot more scared, because it was obvious that the man had killed them, and he started to believe that the man was going to hurt him, too, no matter how nice he was pretending to be.

Scared. Like that moron of a rugby coach had said he was for pulling out of a tackle; and like his dad had said he was for not sticking up for himself when the rugby coach had given him a hard time about it. Like Juliet said he was for not standing up to his dad a bit more . . .

The man was still in the house.

Dropping things ...

He heard them, whatever they were, falling to the floor somewhere above him. He began to cry. He just couldn't stop himself. He tried to be rational, to tell himself that the man was just moving stuff around, but he heard the noise as the objects hit the floorboards and he wept, as he imagined dirt being shovelled on top of him. He pushed himself up from the floor and began walking fast from one side of the cellar to the other. Gathering speed, bouncing off the walls and wailing.

Rattling around in the dark.

Like a stillborn baby in a big man's coffin.

# FOURTEEN

It was a contest, there was no getting away from it. Two of them on each side of the table, it was always going to be confrontational, no matter how touchy-feely you tried to make it; no matter how many beanbag sessions you sat through at seminars.

Thorne and Porter one side, up for it. Donovan looking ready for a scrap on the other, and Grant Freestone the only one in the room who seemed as though he didn't have much idea why any of them were there at all.

Like he still couldn't believe what had happened.

Thorne announced the time that the interview was recommencing, the location and the names of all those present in the room. He asked Freestone if he had been given something to eat; if he was feeling fit and well enough to be interviewed. Then he waited.

'You can answer *that*,' he said, eventually.

This was practicality and caution, rather than concern. The last thing they wanted was for Donovan to claim later that his client had been feeling sick or disoriented; that anything he might have said was unreliable, due to his not getting an aspirin or feeling weak through lack of a bacon sandwich.

'Are you feeling OK, Grant?'

Donovan smiled. He knew how little Thorne cared.

Thorne smiled back. 'For the benefit of the audio tape, Mr Freestone is nodding.'

It had been a very small nod; economical, like all his gestures. Freestone was a big man, thickset, but graceful and fine-featured. He was the right side of forty, with very pale skin, shoulder-length dark hair tied back, and a neatly trimmed goatee. Thorne said later that he looked like someone who should be discussing fringe theatre on Channel Four, while Porter said he reminded her in a *very* disturbing way of an ex-boyfriend.

They went over the facts of the arrest, of the custody record to this point, and of the death of Sarah Janine Hanley, whose body had been discovered by her neighbour and her own two children on 7 April 2001.

'Did you know Sarah Hanley?'

'Did you visit Sarah Hanley on April 7th, 2001?'

'When was the last time you saw Sarah Hanley alive?'

For fifteen minutes, Thorne and Porter asked questions, and for fifteen minutes Grant Freestone studied the table, as if the scars and scratches on its metal surface were the lines on some treasure map. There were long periods of silence, save for the occasional heavy sigh, or the hack of Donovan clearing his throat.

The accusatory approach was clearly going to get nothing other than a Trappist response, but questions about Freestone's alibi didn't fare much better.

'Your sister claims that you were in the park with her children when Miss Hanley was killed. Much as you were this morning, ironically.'

'Is that true, Grant?'

'Which park was it?'

'Come on, Grant. If you were there, why did nobody else see you?'

Donovan sat up straight in his chair suddenly and spoke as if he'd just woken up. Thorne couldn't be entirely sure that he hadn't.

'Lovely as it is to sit and listen to the pair of you, this is getting vaguely silly now.' He tapped the face of his watch. 'It might seem like time is standing still in here, but your clock's running . . .'

Thorne glanced up at the digital display above the door. Freestone had been booked in at just before half past ten in the morning. They were already three hours into their twenty-four.

'Thanks for the reminder, Mr Donovan,' Porter said.

'Pleasure.'

Sarcasm thinned Porter's lips a little when she smiled. 'And they say if you want to know the time, ask a policeman.'

'Why don't you talk to me, Grant?' Thorne said.

Thorne listened politely while Donovan told him he was wasting his time. Freestone looked up at him with an expression that said much the same thing. Thorne leaned in nice and close.

'Why don't you talk to me about the kidnap of Luke Mullen?'

Neither Thorne nor Porter had been given the chance to mention Luke Mullen's name during the first, truncated interview. Now that someone had, though, the reaction was obvious. Freestone's chin sagged momentarily, before his features reset themselves, tighter than before. Something came to life in his eyes. Though he might just have been opening his mouth and closing it again, it looked to Thorne like the man sitting across from him had said the first part of the surname to himself before he could think about it.

'That name obviously means something to you.'

Freestone looked to Donovan, who shook his head slowly. Freestone turned back, seeming genuinely confused for the first time. Frightened, even.

'What about Conrad Allen?' Porter asked.

Freestone swallowed.

'Amanda Tickell?' Thorne looked hard at Freestone, repeated the name, kept looking, even when Freestone lowered his eyes to the tabletop. 'I don't think that's a name you'd forget in a hurry. As a matter of fact, she's not a woman you're likely to forget in any way at all, so you might want to think back. Blonde, blue eyes. Sexy, if you like them fucked up.'

'And dead, of course,' Porter reminded him. 'Let's not forget that one.'

Freestone leaned away slowly, taking the chair on to two legs, gripping the edge of the table as he tipped back. He looked from Porter to Thorne, then dropped back down with a crack. 'No comment,' he said.

'It speaks!' Porter said.

Thorne looked at Donovan. 'Now we're getting somewhere.'

Donovan laughed, but put a hand on Freestone's sleeve and shot him a stern look once he had his attention.

'I'm sure your legal representative has given you excellent advice,' Thorne said. 'I'm sure you're in very capable hands. *Experienced* hands, certainly. But this might be a good time to remind you that keeping your mouth shut isn't quite the safe option it used to be. Should you find yourself in court at some point, the judge may direct a jury to draw an adverse inference from your silence. To read something into it that may not have been there at all. That's the risk you're taking, sitting there like Mr Bean. This is a chance to give your account of things, Grant, to get it down right, straight from the off.' He paused for a few seconds, as Freestone leaned across, raised a hand to shield his mouth and whispered to Donovan. 'So, bearing in mind that we're in something of a hurry, now would be a really good time to tell us anything you know about Luke Mullen. Anything that could help us locate him. I can't make promises, but I know that if you do give us information now, it can't possibly hurt when it comes to working out what happens to you later on.' He watched as the whispering continued. 'For the tape, the suspect is now conferring with his legal representative . . .'

'Or licking his ear,' Porter said, under her breath, 'we can't be sure.'

Freestone straightened and shuffled his chair forward a few inches. For the second time in twenty-odd minutes, Thorne wondered if his words might have made a difference; if they were about to hear something useful, or even just unexpected.

It wasn't like he was any stranger to disappointment.

Freestone laid his hands flat on the table and breathed out slowly. 'I didn't kill Sarah Hanley,' he said.

There were plenty of places where Thorne lowered his expectations as a matter of course: White Hart Lane, naturally; Trevor Jesmond's office; Irish theme pubs, and any part of London Underground. In the Colindale station canteen, it was best to have no expectations at all.

He cut through the crust of potato on top of his shepherd's pie. If there was any meat inside, it was heavily disguised. 'They're improving,' he said.

Porter had made what seemed to be the sensible decision to go with a sandwich. It was only moderately awful.

'This is slumming it for you, I bet,' Thorne said.

'Well, you can't get fresh sushi at the Yard, either,' Porter said, 'but it's better than this. Mind you, that's because we're more important than you are.'

'I think some people really believe that.'

She raised her eyebrows.

'Really, I think they do.' Thorne pointed with his fork. 'Because you're trying to save a life, because you're *proactive*. Whereas we just *react* to a body. Waste our time trying to catch the people who leave them lying around.'

'Well, we've got a bit of both on this one.' She had clearly been expecting a smile, or at least a softening. 'Look, anyone who seriously thinks that is just stupid.'

'*Very* bloody stupid.'

'I know. I said.'

'How many people who commit a murder might go on to commit another one?'

'I'm not arguing.'

'We save lives, too.'

Porter held up her hands in surrender and smiled, irritated now. 'What are you telling *me* for? I agree with you.' She pushed away the uneaten half of her sandwich. 'Christ, there are more chips on shoulders around here than there are going soggy on those hotplates.' She stood up. 'Do you want coffee?'

'Thanks . . . '

He watched her walk across to the till, wondering what his problem was, and why he'd taken it out on her. Whether he should go over and pay for the coffee. What she might look like naked.

When she returned to the table, he came as close to an apology as he was likely to, telling her that he hadn't been sleeping well. That his back was still giving him hell. She pulled a sympathetic face, then asked him where he thought they were with Freestone.

'We got a reaction,' he said.

'But to what? We know he had a problem with Tony Mullen.'

'He might still have one.'

Porter shifted to one side as two PCs put down trays and began to jabber about a 'muppet' on their relief. She lowered her voice. 'You seriously think Tony Mullen might have fitted him up for the Hanley murder?'

'No idea,' Thorne said. 'But maybe Freestone thinks he did.'

'None of which helps us find Luke, though, does it?'

Thorne knew that she was right. Throughout the rest of the interview, Freestone had said nothing to quicken anybody's pulse. He had just kept insisting that he hadn't killed Sarah Hanley. He'd given no indication that he'd played a part in the kidnapping of Luke Mullen, or that he knew anyone who had.

However, in the same way Thorne knew that something was bound to go wrong with his car sooner or later, or that getting pudding would be a serious mistake, he now knew that Grant Freestone had *something* to give them. A name, a place, a date; a whatever-the-fuck-it-was. He knew that it just needed digging up from wherever it lay, deep or barely hidden, and that everything would make a damn sight more sense once it had been.

Even if Freestone himself had no idea that he possessed it.

'I'm not sure what else we can do,' Thorne said. 'We could try to get a warrant, maybe. Force Warren to tell us if he treated Tickell at the same time as Freestone. But do we want to go through all the palaver of getting one?'

It might have been the coffee that made Porter grimace, but Thorne didn't think so. The 'palaver' he had referred to could involve anything from conclusive evidence of need to permission from the Home Secretary. 'You saw the state of Allen's flat,' she said. 'What this man's capable of. We can't take it for granted that the boy's got that long.'

For a few minutes after that, they just eavesdropped on the conversation next to them. By all accounts, the 'muppet' was only marginally less of a 'plonker' than the 'toerag' who spent all day 'crawling up the sergeant's arse'.

It was like listening to a lexicon of primetime plod-speak.

Thorne was still undecided as to whether coppers had begun to talk more like their television counterparts or if they'd always spoken like that and researchers on *The Bill* just did their homework. He suspected – he *hoped* – it was the former. The flash bastards on the Flying Squad had certainly started behaving a lot more like bouncers with warrant cards once Regan and Carter had begun handing out slaps and tearing around TV-London in their gold Granadas.

As he tuned into the conversation again, Thorne made a mental note to give Holland a list of words – to include 'muppet', of course, alongside 'slag' and 'snout' – with instructions to shoot him if he ever used any of them.

When Thorne took the call, it was the uniformed officers' turn to fall silent and try not to look like they were
earwigging. Thorne stared at Porter as he listened, then
thanked whoever had passed on what was clearly welcome
news.

'Go on,' Porter said.

'Mr Freestone fancies another chat, apparently.' Thorne
looked at what was left of his coffee and pushed back his
chair. 'Says he really wants to talk to us about Luke
Mullen.'

'I didn't kill Sarah Hanley.'

'Please don't tell me I've got indigestion for nothing,
Grant,' Thorne said.

'No, you haven't.' Freestone's south London accent was
not as pronounced as it might have been, and his voice was
soft, light even. It would have been tricky to tell him and
his sister apart from their voices alone. 'I just wanted to say
it again. I've never *stopped* saying it. It's just that no fucker's
ever started listening, you know?'

'You'll have plenty of time to talk to people about what
happened to Sarah—'

'I don't know what happened to her, all right? I just
found her.'

'OK, Grant.'

'She was dead when I got there, I swear.'

'It's not what we're here to talk about though,' Porter
said.

Freestone nodded slowly and took a series of short,

sharp breaths, like he was gearing up for something. Next to him, Donovan sat low in his chair, sullen and soured; boredom and resentment extinguishing any glimmer of curiosity about what might be said. Control had slipped away from him. Now that his client had chosen to ignore his advice, now that he was surplus to requirements, he would do no more than watch that precious clock of his for as long as he had to. Then he would pocket his firm's fee and go home to shout at his children for a while.

'I'm not going back inside,' Freestone said.

Thorne folded his arms. 'You asking me or telling me?'

'Doesn't matter if it's murder. Doesn't matter what it is. I could be banged up for forgery, or not paying my fucking income tax, but it'll always be about those kids once I'm inside. I'll always have to watch my back.'

'You looking for sympathy?'

'I'm not looking for anything.'

'Probably best.'

'You're just like everyone else ...'

'That's reassuring.'

'You need to tell us whatever it is you dragged us back down here for,' Porter said. 'That would be a good way to start. If you want people to think other things about you, to see a side that doesn't ... repulse them. You need to earn all that.' She sat back, leaving him to it; rummaged in her bag for nothing in particular.

Thorne watched the four small wheels moving round on the twin cassette decks. The tiny, spinning teeth ...

'I want to see Tony Mullen,' Freestone said.

311

Thorne and Porter said nothing. Exchanged a glance and tried to look as though Freestone had asked for no more than a cigarette, or a Kit Kat with his tea.

Freestone looked from one to the other, then spoke again, in case he hadn't made himself clear enough. 'Luke Mullen's father.'

Thorne nodded to indicate they knew exactly who Tony Mullen was. 'And I want to win the Lottery,' he said. 'But I'm not holding my breath.'

'That's it,' Freestone said.

'That's what?'

Porter looked tense, but her tone stayed reasonable, while Thorne's had become jagged at the edges. '*That's it*, as in you have no further requests? Or that's the end of the discussion?'

Freestone shook his head quickly, and waved his hands. 'That's all there is to it, that's the deal, if you want to look at it like that. I want him to come down here and I want to speak to him privately. Just him and me. No tapes, and not in here, either.' He looked up at the camera in the corner of the room. 'No video, nothing like that. So . . .'

Porter opened her mouth, but Thorne was quicker. 'Here's the thing,' he said. 'The only dealing that's going to be happening round here is in the office upstairs, where there's usually a game of three-card brag going on at the end of a shift, so fuck knows where you got *that* idea from. Second, and more importantly, if you have anything at all to say about Luke Mullen, you're going to say it to us.

Now. On tape. On camera. Broadcast live to the nation if the fancy takes us.' He stopped and smiled. '*So ...*'

Even Donovan was sitting up straight and paying attention.

'Mr Mullen is no longer a police officer,' Porter said. 'Obviously, he's not investigating this case.'

'He's the kid's father though, isn't he? That's more important, surely.'

'It's not happening,' Thorne said.

'Why not?'

'We don't have to give reasons.'

'Well, then, I don't have to tell you anything.'

'For someone who's so keen to avoid going back to prison, you're not doing yourself any favours.'

'There won't be any favours, whatever I say.'

'You might be right,' Thorne said, starting to lose it. 'But here's something else to think about. If you've got information about Luke Mullen, and you keep it to yourself, I'll personally make sure that when you do go back to prison, every nutter in there with an axe to grind will know you're coming.'

Freestone shrugged, looked to Donovan and back to Thorne, but he was thinking about it. It was almost a minute before he spoke again. 'I need to see Mullen.'

Thorne lifted his jacket from the back of the chair as he stood. He spoke to Porter, then to the cassette recorder. 'I'm going to finish my lunch. This interview is suspended at—'

'Just let me talk to him.'

'Tell us about Luke,' Porter said.

'Let me talk to his father first.'

'No.'

'I'm not asking for a fucking helicopter. I just want five minutes—'

'Give me one good reason,' Thorne said. 'Any reason at all why we should even think about arranging this.'

'Because it's going to get serious if you don't do what I want. If you don't start taking what I want seriously.'

Freestone's voice had changed now, and nobody around the table could fail to be shocked by the range and power of it. They'd listened to the voice that could cajole, that could charm children into garages. Now they were being treated to a voice they could only pray those children had never heard.

'Because, I'm the only person who knows where Luke Mullen is, and if you don't do what I'm asking, if you don't get it arranged, I'll just sit here like Mr *fucking* Bean and say nothing. I'll turn to stone, I swear to God, and you're going to have to carry the can for that. Fair enough? I'll sit here and say nothing for as long as it takes and you'll *never* find him. Not while it'll do any good, anyway.' He pushed himself away from the table, raised an arm to scratch at a shoulder-blade. 'If you don't do what I'm asking, Luke Mullen's going to die.'

# FIFTEEN

DI Chris Wilmot surveyed the footage of the suspect one final time, then went to work. The movements of the mouse around the mat were small, precise, but the cursor flew around the screen as he shifted and clicked, cutting and pasting using the specially developed software to call up, then select, subjects that would be a close enough match for the parade.

The traditional method, whereby an eyewitness might identify a suspect in the flesh, was rapidly becoming a thing of the past. It was time-consuming and expensive, with only a handful of stations capable of setting up and running a full parade. Wilmot was one of several roving officers who had been specially trained in newer identification procedures and, as such, he was able to oversee a video parade almost anywhere it was needed. He'd been informed well in advance of the impending arrest and had presented himself at Colindale within ten minutes of the suspect's arrival in the custody suite.

Wilmot drew from a database of several thousand individuals on video, using half a dozen different search criteria to narrow them down to those of a similar age and ethnic background; those whose height, weight and colouring were within acceptable parameters. After half an hour, he'd assembled the eight fifteen-second clips he would be using alongside the footage he'd already shot of the suspect. Now, it was simply a question of editing them all together into a sequence for the witness to watch. With random selection of the chosen extracts built into the software, Wilmot did not even have to think about it, and would not be aware of the running order himself until the finished sequence was shown to the witness.

Wishing all elements of the job were as straightforward, as *foolproof*, Wilmot pushed a button and let the computer do it all for him ...

Yvonne Kitson sat in the far corner, watching the ID officer make his final preparations. He was clearly efficient and cared about what he was doing, and there was no reason to think that things would not go the way she was hoping. Yet still she felt as knotted with nerves as she could ever remember. Getting everything right from this point on was hugely important to her, personally as well as professionally. Though she knew there was every reason to feel confident, she'd seen many cases a damn sight more buttoned up than this one fall apart at the last minute.

She wanted so badly to enjoy the reaction when she told Amin Latif's family that she'd found their son's killer; to see his mother's face when the right verdict was reached and a suitable sentence handed down. But she knew she'd have to wait a while, that she should assume nothing. And all the time, the very possibility that such things might not happen tied those knots a little tighter.

Despite the news she'd been given that afternoon by a contact at the Forensic Science Service . . .

She'd arrested Farrell at the parental home at 4 p.m., an hour after the call from the FSS. While Adrian was being taken to Colindale, she'd stayed on to speak to the parents. The encounter had been characterised by a great deal of shouting and crying; by the suggestion that Kitson was not up to her job; by patronising speeches and veiled threats from Farrell's father, which Kitson ignored, despite the huge temptation to stick him in the back of the car as well and do two for the price of one. When she'd finally been allowed to speak, Kitson had informed the Farrells that, aside from the solicitor they had already announced they would be sending to the station, they were not allowed to inform anyone of their son's arrest. This was not up for discussion. The identity of others who had taken part in the attack for which their son had been arrested was yet to be ascertained, and as police believed he was in a position to pass on those names, Adrian would be held incommunicado, with even the usual telephone call denied him. After listening to another rant from Mr Farrell – this time on the subject of the rights of those in custody – and a suggestion that Kitson was making a career-threatening mistake, she informed them that she would be back later with a warrant to search the house. Then she left, eager to get to work on Adrian Farrell, in no doubt as to where he inherited his confidence from.

Watching as final touches were put to the video parade, she wondered if the boy sitting downstairs in a cell was quite so confident now.

'We're about there,' Wilmot said.

Kitson opened the door, exchanged a few words with an officer on duty outside, and half a minute later Nabeel Khan was shown into the room.

He looked a little better than the last time Kitson had seen him, but that was hardly saying much. The bruises had healed, but she knew she was not looking at the teenager she imagined him to have once been. Before he and his friend Amin had stood waiting too long for a bus one night, six months before.

He took off his coat and nodded nervously in her direction. 'How you doing, miss?'

Kitson could talk to him now. For obvious reasons, until this point, she had not been allowed any contact with the witness. To ensure that any evidence he might provide could not be seen as tainted, officers unconnected with the original case had collected him from his home, then waited with him while preparations were being made. Now that the video parade was itself being videoed, and any conversation would be a matter of record, Kitson could speak freely to the boy.

'I'm pretty good, Nabeel,' she said. There was no need to ask how he was.

She talked to him as he took a seat next to Wilmot; told him that the whole thing would only take a couple of minutes, that it was all very simple and that he needn't worry. He seemed relaxed enough. He told her that he was much happier doing it this way, on the computer; that he was relieved he wouldn't have to stand in full view of anyone. He laughed when Kitson tried to tell him that wouldn't have happened; said he'd seen it on TV and knew all about the two-way mirrors and stuff . . .

Then Wilmot took over, began the official preamble, and Kitson could do little but sit back and watch.

Each short clip had the same basic shape. The subject sat in front of a white background, looking straight at camera, until a short bleep signalled that they were to look to their right. Five seconds later another bleep indicated that they should turn the other way. Finally, they turned back to the camera and stared at it until the clip ended. Then the next one began.

The expressions ranged from vacant to insolent. Though instructed to keep their faces as blank as possible, the subjects looked variously bored, fascinated or disgusted. Some looked contented, presumably because they'd just picked up eighty quid for a few minutes of their time, when they'd only popped into the station to produce valid car insurance or explain where their girlfriend had got her black eye and split lip. They were all between sixteen and twenty-one. All were blond, though the length of hair and its style varied, from flat-top to floppy. None of the young men wore earrings, the subject in the seventh clip having been instructed to remove a gold cross on account of the fact that it might be said to draw unfair attention to him.

When the montage had finished and the screen went blank, Wilmot asked the witness if he wanted to see the footage a second time.

The witness shook his head.

Wilmot then asked the important questions, as he had to, but Kitson didn't need to hear the answers. The face of the witness had remained more expressionless than many on the video, but Kitson had heard the noise begin towards the end of the sequence.

At around the minute and a half mark.

It continued now as Wilmot tried to elicit a response: the banging of bone against metal as Nabeel Khan's leg shook uncontrollably beneath the table.

'It's this business with the kids I don't get,' Porter said. 'How could Jane Freestone have let her brother come near her kids?'

'She may not have known back then. Not for sure, anyway.'

'She knows now though, right? And she's still happy enough to send them out to the park with Uncle Grant.'

'Apparently.'

'You stick by your family. I understand that. We've both seen people doing it, standing by relatives who've done some of the sickest fucking things. A lot of the time, however misguided they are, part of me even thinks that's *honourable*, you know?'

Thorne knew. He'd watched people eaten away from the inside by what those closest to them had done, while refusing to turn away. Insisting, despite everything, on being the only ones *not* to.

'But only up to a point, don't you reckon?'

'Children, you mean?'

'Right. It's got to be a different story when it comes to your kids. No matter how much you might love your brother or your father or your husband, you put the kids first and last, surely to God?'

'Maybe she genuinely thinks he's innocent,' Thorne said.

Porter was not convinced. 'I think Freestone's open enough now about what he did, isn't he? About what his preferences are. We're talking about his nephews here; kids whose trust he's already got, for heaven's sake.'

'I know . . .'

'What if there were other kids?' She said it like the ignorance was unforgivable. 'We don't know what he's been doing for the last five years.'

'Keeping his head down, I should think.'

'It's not his head I'm worried about.' She paused before asking the question, as if Thorne's answer was important to her. 'Do you think people like Freestone can change what they are?'

'Bloody hell,' Thorne said. 'Do we really need to get into this?'

321

'We're just talking.'

'Like you said, it's a preference, and whatever *they* might be, most of us are stuck with them.' He hesitated, feeling awkward, searching for a way to articulate it. 'I suppose ... I'm not convinced that you could make me start fancying blokes, however much therapy you gave me.'

'Right. And listen, I accept all the evidence about abusers having been abused themselves. It's just—'

'I know ...'

'I've been putting myself in her shoes, in Jane's shoes, and I couldn't do it. It's hypothetical, obviously, but I think I would have had to cut myself off from him. Me and the kids. I mean, Jesus, if you've got some of your own, you know what the parents of the kids he hurt have gone through, don't you? You've got that to live with as well.'

'I suppose so,' Thorne said.

She shook her head. Disgusted, adamant. 'I wouldn't have wanted him to come out of prison.'

They were sitting in one of the large CID offices on the third floor. Cut off from their own incident room back at Becke House, this was about the only place they could talk with any degree of privacy; to discuss progress, or the lack of it. To take a few minutes.

But they were still interrupted. Officers from various station squads moved in and out of the room at regular intervals, and the conversation was friendly enough. This was unusual, as ordinarily there was resentment between those who worked at Colindale full time and those, like Porter and Thorne, who were using it as little more than a facilities house. It was petty, territorial stuff: *our* interview room, *our* custody suite, *our* tea and biscuits. But, thus far, there had been only genuine enquiries as to how things were going, and both Thorne and Porter had been wished good luck on numerous occasions.

Word went round a station when there was a major case on the premises. It changed the mood of the place.

It was clear from many of the comments, passed openly or whispered too loudly in corners, that Grant Freestone's record – the crimes for which he had been convicted in the mid-nineties – was colouring opinion; preying on the minds of others just as much as it was on Louise Porter's. This certainly explained all those messages of good luck . . .

Thorne drank his tea and watched Porter work her way through a can of Diet Coke and her second packet of crisps. On the far wall, a large whiteboard was covered in names, pictures and numbered bullet points. Lines and arrows, up and across in red marker pen, linked a face to a blown-up section of the *A–Z*, a registration number to the photograph of a woman who had been severely beaten. Porter stared at the familiar map of an enquiry; the blood and beating heart of a case they knew nothing about. But Thorne knew that her mind was racing; was full of doubts and questions about their own case. Its fluttering, irregular heartbeat.

'Are we so sure this is the right thing?' Porter asked. 'We could just play safe and do what he's asking. Would getting Mullen in here do any harm?'

'It's not about *playing safe*. It's about refusing to be dictated to by a suspect, unless you're certain there are no other options.'

'So it's about who's in charge, is it?'

'I don't want Mullen in here.'

'I'm thinking about Luke.'

'So am I.' Thorne tried to sound thoughtful as opposed to plain sullen, but he wasn't certain he'd pulled it off.

'Well, then, can we afford not to do what Freestone's asking?'

'*Demanding*.'

'Does it matter?'

'He's pissing us around.'

'Well, hopefully we'll know soon enough.'

'Why is he insisting that he has to talk to Mullen in private anyway? Why all the secrecy?'

'Look, I don't trust him any more than you do, but—'

'I don't trust *either* of them,' Thorne said.

Porter rolled her eyes, but she obviously agreed, to some extent at least.

Thorne watched her lift up the packet, tip her head back and pour the remaining crisps into her mouth. Still chewing, she nodded towards the door and Thorne looked round to see Brigstocke and Hignett hovering, like funeral directors come to collect a body.

'Shall we get this done?' Brigstocke said.

The four of them took the stairs down to the ground floor, Porter and Hignett a few steps ahead of the two men from the Murder Squad. Thorne thought Brigstocke looked tired, guessed the DCI was probably getting even less sleep than he was.

As they stepped on to a small landing, with the other pair now a full flight below them, Brigstocke turned to Thorne. 'Any thoughts on how you and Porter are going to run this?'

'We thought we'd try to play it by ear,' Thorne said.

A few steps on, Brigstocke shook his head, mumbled, 'God help us . . .'

On the way to the custody suite, they met Yvonne Kitson coming from another direction. Thorne let the others go ahead.

'Crowded in here today,' he said. 'I heard you brought your schoolboy in.'

Kitson grinned. 'Sounds like you're not doing too badly yourself.'

'When either of us gets five minutes, we should drink to something.'

'All being well.'

'Have you had a chat with Farrell yet?'

'Just on my way,' Kitson said. 'Got him in the bin.' She brandished a sheaf of papers; passed them across for Thorne to take a look at.

Thorne studied the disclosure paperwork: a series of documents to be handed to the suspect's legal adviser; all at once, or strategically drip-fed if it was deemed to be useful. By law, the papers had to include everything from completed custody records to copies of the 'first description' –

in this case the statement given by Nabeel Khan at the murder scene and reproduced verbatim from the attending officer's pocketbook. Thorne flicked through copies of the incriminating E-fit and Farrell's arrest log, then pointed to a sheet outlining the results of the video ID parade. 'This should do you nicely,' he said.

'It wasn't very easy for the witness.' Kitson blinked away the memory of something, but managed to crank up the smile again. 'Should put the wind up his smartarse solicitor, though.'

'One of those, is it?'

'You know the firm: Smartarse, Posh and Fullovit.'

'I know them too bloody well . . .'

They moved on together, laughing, towards the interview rooms; through the door that separated the rest of the prison from the custody suite.

'Suite' was something of a misnomer, suggesting that the area was rather more comfortable and well appointed than it was. In fact, this was where industrial grey carpet gave way to concrete floors, where panic strips ran along the walls, and where an atmosphere of heightened awareness came close to one charged with aggression.

This was where the station became a prison.

A pair of custody sergeants, or 'skippers', sat on a raised platform at the centre, booking people in, working at computer screens and monitoring the CCTV images fed from cells and corridors. The 'cage' was off to one side, through which prisoners were brought in from the backyard, and where, if necessary, UV light would show up any property-marked items that they might be carrying. Corridors in two directions led to the twenty-seven cells which ringed the suite. Each was tiled from floor to high ceiling, with a metal toilet on one side and a blue plastic mattress along the back wall. A double doorway led through to an exercise yard, to which prisoners were taken if they needed air; or, more likely, nicotine.

Kitson slowed down outside the tiny kitchen, where the jailer on shift could make tea and coffee or prepare one of five different microwaveable meals for prisoners. She lowered her voice. 'I've got DNA as well, Tom.'

It took Thorne a couple of seconds. '*When* did you arrest him?'

'I acquired a sample beforehand, got it to the lab yesterday afternoon.'

'Right . . . ' He drew the word out, still thinking.

'It's only a preliminary result, obviously. Ninety-something per cent match so far. It doesn't eliminate him, which is what counts.'

'Twenty-four hours is still going some, though.'

Kitson reddened. 'Somebody at FSS likes me. Owed me a favour.'

'You flirted with him. I'm appalled.'

'With *her* . . . '

'You're fucking shameless,' Thorne said. He flicked quickly through the disclosure papers again. 'I can't see it anywhere in here.'

'Like I said, it's just a prelim. We've got two more runs before it's definitive.'

'You can still put it in here, though. Then you'll *really* put the shits up Farrell's brief.' Thorne looked up, saw that the colour in Kitson's face had deepened, and that it wasn't through embarrassment. 'When you say *acquired*?'

Kitson told him about the previous afternoon. She described her meeting with Adrian Farrell by the bus stop, the boy's reaction to her questions, and the way she'd scraped his spit off the pavement. Thorne stared, astonished and full of admiration. Then, much as he hated to be the one to do it, he pointed out that none of her forensic evidence would stand up anywhere.

'I've got a witness,' Kitson said, and she told Thorne about the woman in the tracksuit who'd seen Farrell spitting on the pavement. The woman who'd been kind enough to provide Kitson with a cotton bud and a plastic freezer bag when she'd needed them.

'Even so—'

'OK, look, I know I can't use it, and I took a kosher sample as soon as we booked him in, but I just wanted to be sure. D'you understand?'

Thorne handed back the documents. 'Probably right to leave the DNA stuff out then,' he said. 'For the time being.'

'Yeah.' She tapped a fingertip against the side of her head and grinned. 'But it's nice to *know*, isn't it?'

'Oh fuck, yes,' Thorne said. 'Every time.'

They walked round the corner to the interview room – the 'bin' – where Farrell was waiting. Thorne took a quick look through the small window.

Kitson nodded across to another room on the far side. 'You think you've got *your* man in there? For the kidnap, I mean.'

Thorne considered the question. 'I'm really not sure about anything,' he said. 'Right now, if you asked me what my name was, I'd only be able to give you a preliminary result.'

# SIXTEEN

'This room is different,' Freestone said.

Thorne nodded, as though he were impressed. 'Can't fool you for a second, can we, Grant?' He pointed to a red light on the far wall, informed Freestone that whenever it was lit the interview was being viewed remotely by other officers. 'You're very popular,' he said. 'Lots of people are keen to say hello, but we don't want to start cramming them into a small room like this, do we?'

Donovan was obviously eager to make his presence felt early. He leaned towards his client. 'And they don't want me claiming that you were intimidated by a gang of hulking great coppers.'

'Can't fool you, either,' Thorne said. He looked at Freestone for a second or two without speaking. 'Not that you look as though you'd be easily intimidated.'

'You can't afford to be, can you?' Freestone said.

Thorne understood perfectly well. He knew that Freestone had spent a long time on the receiving end of far harsher intimidation than anything *he* could dish out. 'You certainly can't,' he agreed.

Porter had been staring hard at Freestone across the table. 'You don't look too good,' she said. Then, to Donovan: 'Are you sure your client's well enough?'

Thorne glanced up at the camera through which he knew Hignett and Brigstocke were watching. He guessed they'd have approved of the question. Porter was right to allow for any eventuality at this stage.

'No, as it goes, he's far from well,' Donovan said.

Freestone began to nod quickly. 'I just need a bit of something. I'll be fine.'

It was obvious to all concerned what Freestone needed. Thorne did not know how serious the habit was, whether he was doing coke, heroin or both, but at best it would have been seven or eight hours since he'd taken anything. If the turkey wasn't yet cold, it was already tepid. 'We'll be as quick as we can, then we'll get a doctor in to sort you out. It's really up to you how soon that'll be.'

'This is the fourth interview with my client in as many hours,' Donovan said. 'And I still haven't seen much to justify a single one of them.'

'You were obviously asleep when he threatened a child's life.'

'He threatened no such thing—'

'When he confessed to holding a child against his will, then. That do you?'

Freestone, who didn't appear to be listening, pointed at the glowing red light. 'People are watching this, correct?'

'Correct,' Thorne said.

'Well, we can't meet in here, then. When Mullen comes in.'

'I think we're getting ahead of ourselves.'

'When's he coming? Is he on his way yet?'

'You have to talk to *us* first,' Porter said.

Thorne was shaking his head. 'There are no guarantees here.' He leaned his head close to Porter's. 'We're making no promises at all. We need to be agreed on that. Yes?'

Porter's expression made it clear that she understood. She turned slowly from Thorne to Freestone. 'We need assurances,' she said.

Freestone nodded again, like it was a reasonable request. One that he'd be happy to meet.

'We need to know about Luke.'

'What about him?'

'*Christ!*' Thorne said. 'Take a guess.' He raised his hands in apology at the sharp look from Porter.

'He's fine,' Freestone said.

'What about all that stuff you came out with before?' Porter's voice was low, not much above a whisper. 'You made it very clear that if we didn't find him quickly . . . '

'I was talking about a long time: months, whatever.'

'Is he somewhere with plenty of air?'

'What? I don't—'

'Does he have anything to eat? Is he tied up?'

'He's got food. I left him enough food.'

'What kind of food?'

'Burgers, that kind of thing. You know – stuff kids like.'

'You know all about what kids like.' Thorne leaned forward. 'Don't you, Grant?'

Freestone opened his mouth. Closed it again.

'Hang on,' Donovan said. 'There's never been any suggestion—'

Thorne pointed a finger and left it there. 'He tied two kids up in a garage. That's not a *suggestion*. How the hell do we know he hasn't stuffed Luke Mullen in a cupboard with gardening twine round his neck?'

'He's fine, I swear.' Freestone closed his eyes, rubbed the back of a hand across his forehead. 'When's Tony Mullen getting here? I need to see him.'

'Why did you take him, Grant?' Thorne waited until it was clear there was nothing coming back. 'Why no ransom demand? Do you just not need the money? Or did you miss the last bit of the kidnapping correspondence course?'

Freestone sucked his teeth, thought about it. 'I'll talk to Mullen,' he said.

Nobody said anything for a few moments after that, but when Porter started to speak, Thorne raised a hand to cut her off. 'How old is Luke Mullen?' he asked.

'I don't know exactly.' Freestone blinked. 'Fifteen? Sixteen?'

'Dark hair? Blond?'

'It's . . . dark.'

'What was he wearing when you took him?'

Freestone was growing increasingly flustered with each question Thorne fired at him, looking at Donovan more than once, and increasingly to Porter. 'School clothes ... '

'Can we stop asking quiz questions?' Porter snapped. 'We need to move forward here.'

Thorne's smile was ugly. 'It's all stuff he could have got from that newspaper story, anyway. He had a paper with him in the park.'

'We have to make sure Luke is safe and unharmed,' Porter said. 'That's the priority here.' She looked back at Freestone, making sure that he understood what was important as well.

'He's safe. I haven't laid a finger on him.'

'Luke's not the strongest of kids,' Porter said. 'We have to check.'

'I've been looking after him.'

'That's good. That helps.'

'You should really get Mullen now.'

'What about the asthma?' she asked. 'Has he had any attacks?'

Freestone shook his head, kept on shaking it.

'Shortness of breath? It's why I was asking about the air.'

'No, he's fine.'

'The family are worried because they're not sure if Luke had his inhaler with him, but it sounds like he wouldn't have needed it, right?'

'That's right.'

'Do you know if he has it? So I could at least tell them.'

Freestone closed his eyes again. Let the answer come to him. 'I think he said something about it.'

'Do you know what an inhaler looks like?' Porter started to mime it, pushing down on the imaginary pump.

'Of course I do. Jesus . . .'

'This is important, Grant. We need to know. Has he got one with him?'

A nod, small and fast, but frozen the second Thorne began to shout: '*Have you seen Luke Mullen's inhaler?*'

'Yes, I said so! I've seen the fucking thing.' The intense agitation on Freestone's face turned quickly to alarm when he saw Porter and Thorne relax. When the questions stopped. He turned to Donovan. 'What's going on?'

Donovan's former career gave him rather more insight than someone in his position might otherwise have had. 'I think you just gave them the wrong answer,' he said. 'Or the *right* one.'

Thorne looked at Porter, then up at the camera to share a small moment of success with the two watching DCIs.

Then he leaned back. Job done.

After Freestone had been taken back to the cells, they sat for a few seconds, relishing their newly acquired certainty. But each was aware that this feeling of having got something right would soon be replaced with a more familiar one. That of having nowhere else to go.

It was Thorne who broke the silence. '*Asthma?* That's fucking genius.'

'We both did a pretty good job,' Porter said.

They congratulated each other for a few minutes more on how well they'd played the nice-and-nasty routine. On how they'd let Freestone believe there was tension between them; that he was far better off answering Porter's questions than Thorne's. Making him think it was simple confirmation they wanted, rather than proof.

'He was so full of shit,' Thorne said. 'All that just to get a bit of leverage. So we'd agree to Mullen coming in.'

Porter raised her eyebrows. 'Now, there's a major question in itself.'

'Like we haven't got enough of those already.'

'Number one in the hit parade being: if *Freestone* hasn't got Luke Mullen ... ?'

And there it was. That familiar feeling ...

Thorne's first thought was that Brigstocke had come down to do his own bit of back-patting, but his face told a different story. As did the face of the man who appeared next to him in the doorway, then barged past into the interview room like he was a heartbeat away from cracking heads open.

'Why wasn't I told about Grant Freestone?' Mullen asked. His question was absurd, considering that he obviously *had* been told: he was *there*, after all. After a second of incredulity from the others in the room, he condescended to correct himself: 'Why wasn't I told *officially*?'

Thorne rose from his seat and exchanged a glance with Brigstocke. He was happy to handle this one, though even as he opened his mouth he had no idea *how* he was going to handle it. 'Your position as Luke's parent, and as an ex-officer, makes your role in this case tricky, to say the least . . . '

'Don't talk shit to me. Where's Freestone?'

'He's probably with the Force Medical Examiner by now, getting a dose of methadone.'

'I want to see him.'

'What you *want* is one thing,' Thorne said, 'and I do understand that you and Detective Superintendent Jesmond are . . . close friends. But I don't think that coming in here and trying to give anyone orders is particularly helpful.' He caught the look from Brigstocke, the warning to take it easy, but when his eyes returned to Mullen, the fury seemed to have cooled.

'However you'd prefer me to put it, then. I would *like* to see him. He's been asking to see me, so I think I have a right.'

'He hasn't got Luke,' Thorne said. 'He told us he had, but we're pretty sure he was just telling us what we wanted to hear.'

'*Pretty sure?*'

'We've got him talking to us about Luke being *asthmatic*, for Christ's sake . . .'

Confusion washed across Mullen's face.

Porter chipped in to explain. 'We asked him early on about Allen and Tickell and he blanked us. Later, he was just giving us stuff he could have picked up from the paper. So we needed to feed him something specific, something untrue. To catch him out with it.'

'He isn't our kidnapper,' Thorne said.

Brigstocke stepped towards Mullen. 'You probably don't know whether to feel relieved or not. It's hard, I know.' He held out an arm as though offering to lead him back out the way he had come. But Mullen wasn't about to go anywhere.

'I still want to see him,' he said.

Brigstocke lowered the arm which had been so studiously ignored. 'I'm afraid I can't see much point.'

'What about this connection to the dead girl?'

Jesmond was certainly keeping his friend very well informed. Thorne looked at Porter. They remained none the wiser about Freestone and Amanda Tickell. About the possibility that they'd both been treated by Neil Warren.

'It's only theoretical as yet,' Brigstocke said. 'And the community of addicts and counsellors is thankfully not as big as the *Daily Mail* would like to make out. If they *did* know each other, it may be no more than coincidence.'

Brigstocke had said it with conviction, but it wasn't enough to convince Mullen. Or Thorne. Coincidence played a greater part in many investigations than the writers of films and crime novels could ever hope to get away with, but he knew there was more to this than an interesting collision of names and dates. He knew that Freestone's connection to the kidnapping was important. But knowing counted for nothing. It wasn't going to put Luke Mullen in his mother's arms. While its true significance remained as elusive as it had been before they'd ever arrested Grant Freestone, simple coincidence was the much less frustrating explanation.

Mullen crossed to a chair, put his hands on the back of it, staking a claim. 'I'll see him in here,' he announced. 'Whenever the doctor's finished with him.'

Thorne tried to sound as though he hadn't forgotten that the man in front of him was missing a child. Thinking, as he spoke, that what had probably made Mullen a bloody good copper now made him a pain in the arse as a civilian. 'It's really not possible,' he said. 'Now we've eliminated Freestone from any active part in your son's abduction, there are others who want a crack at him. There's still the small matter of the murder case he was originally wanted for, and some people already think we've had him more than long enough.' He paused. 'The Sarah Hanley murder?' He looked for a reaction but saw none that told him anything useful.

'This room wouldn't have been any good anyway,' Porter said. 'He was insisting it was private. No cameras or tapes.'

'Was he?'

'Why do you think that was?'

'God knows.' Mullen's jawbone bulged beneath the skin as he gritted his teeth. 'Probably so he could threaten me again, without any record of it. But since when do the likes of him need a good reason to do anything?'

'Is that really why he wanted to see you, do you think?' Thorne asked. 'Just to make a few more threats?'

'I'd presumed it was about Luke. If Freestone had taken him, I thought he was going to tell me why. Tell me what he wanted.'

'Right.' Thorne nodded, but his face suggested that this was only one explanation.

'Well, what the hell else could it have been? Like you said, it was hardly so he could remind me I was off his Christmas-card list.'

Thorne didn't speak for several seconds. He just watched Mullen's knuckles turn white on the back of the metal chair. Finally, he said, 'We'll never know now, will we?'

At first, Thorne thought the noise was coming from the back of Mullen's throat. Then he realised it was the sound of the chair scraping against the floor. He watched as Mullen closed his eyes, lifted the chair a foot or so off the ground, held it there for a few seconds, then smashed it back down, shouting what might have been 'fuck' or 'no' as it hit the floor. Mullen took a few seconds to gather himself before turning slowly to look at the senior officer; seeking confirmation that there was no further argument to be had.

'I think you should go home, sir,' Brigstocke said.

In turn, Mullen gave Porter, then Thorne, the benefit of a flint-hard stare before spinning on his heel and striding towards the door. He stopped dead when he drew level with Brigstocke. Pushed back his shoulders. 'You know I'll take this higher, don't you?'

'That's your privilege,' Brigstocke said.

The older man took a step closer to him. 'How many kids have you got?'

'Three.'

Mullen snapped his fingers. 'Let's say it's two.' Snapped them again. 'Just like that, you wake up and one's gone. Imagine really hard for a few minutes what that would be like. Then try and lose that fucking sanctimonious tone.'

Thorne hadn't meant to follow Mullen. He wasn't seeing him off the premises or anything like that, but it was clear that others didn't view it in quite the same way. Thorne stood in the lobby, watching through the glass doors, as Mullen crossed the road and walked to a BMW somewhat newer than his own. Mullen opened the door and stared back towards the station. The orange from the street lamp and the paler wash from the car's interior cast enough light on his face to make the thoughts sculpting its expression clear enough.

Thorne didn't look away, but wondered if his own state of mind was equally transparent.

*Fuck. Bastard, bloody, fuckety-fuck . . .*

Lately, it was becoming hard to tell whether the voice in his head was his own or his father's.

As the BMW accelerated away and Thorne turned back to the access door, Kitson came through it on her way out. She gazed at the weather. The evening looked as though it would stay dry, but she still pulled on her coat. 'Better days?' she said.

Obviously he was as transparent as usual . . .

'Well, making the father of a kidnap victim want to rip my head off is not the cleverest thing I've ever done.' He

341

noted her reaction. 'I'll tell you later. How's things with the baby-faced Nazi?'

'Smartarse has done a pretty good job,' Kitson said. 'I can't get much more than a sick smile out of him, so I don't see him giving me these names in a hurry.'

'Knocked it on the head for the night?'

'Somebody else is having a crack at him, so I'm going back to poke around at Farrell Towers. We took a ton of stuff away and I'm still waiting on phone records, but there might be something we missed. It'll be a chance to have another lovely chat with his delightful parents, anyway.'

A teenager stood up from the bench in the small waiting area and sauntered over to them. He was probably around the same age as Adrian Farrell, but his skin, teeth and watery eyes could have belonged to someone fifteen years older. He stank of beer and smoke, as he leaned in close to ask Thorne and Kitson for a cigarette. They both shook their heads. The duty officer behind the screen told the boy firmly to sit back down; that someone would be out to see him in a few minutes.

Thorne gave Kitson the highlights of the most recent interview. Told her that, despite everything, he still believed that Freestone, or the Sarah Hanley killing, or both were somehow connected to Luke Mullen's kidnap and the murders of Amanda Tickell and Conrad Allen. They nattered for a few minutes. Kitson complained that it often got harder to see where you were going as you collected more information, as the map of a case became more detailed. 'Wood and trees and all that shit,' she said.

'Never mind,' Thorne said. '*You* might get lucky ... Find an address book at Farrell's place with a section marked "Others involved in murder". Maybe a nice pile of BNP leaflets under his bed. Then you can go home and get yourself an early night.'

Kitson smiled for a few seconds, then shook her head. 'I know the fact that Latif and Khan were Asian is crucial, and I'm not saying it wasn't a race crime *as well*, but I've always thought the sexual element of the attack was more important. It makes it something else.'

'It makes Adrian Farrell seriously fucked up,' Thorne said.

Kitson's smile returned, but it was the sort people made around hospital beds. 'I'd better get going,' she said. 'See where he gets it from.'

Thorne suddenly thought of something and stopped her. 'I know we talked about this, but it's still worth keeping one eye out for anything linking Farrell to Luke Mullen. Beyond them playing the odd game of football in the playground.'

'I was planning to.'

'Comes firmly under "clutching at straws", but you never know ...'

When Kitson had gone, Thorne took out his ID card, ready to swipe it through the reader on the access door, but he walked to the counter first. He was aware that the duty officer had been listening to the conversation he'd had with Kitson. He imagined that the young PC saw a career in plain clothes, on a murder squad, as a glamorous alternative to passing messages and getting shouted at. To dealing with people you knew damn well were just oiks and lowlifes, and doing your *own* bit of shouting when you'd had enough of it.

Thorne glanced at the teenager who was still sitting on the bench looking pissed off, then back to the uniformed officer, who he'd spoken to a couple of times and knew to be thick as a brick. 'You're better off where you are, mate.'

The officer straightened his back. 'Sir?'

Thorne tapped on the screen. 'You've got one of these. Decent bit of reinforced plastic between you and the rest of the world. Lose this and you're in trouble, because that's when you realise it's not spit or fists you've got to worry about.' He turned and walked towards the door. 'Once that screen goes, mate, you're stuffed.'

By midnight, the majority of the five hundred or so officers and police staff who worked at Colindale during the day had gone home, and the buzz around the station had faded to a barely discernible sputter. There was still a night-duty CID, of course, and a custody team, but as most of the rooms and offices had emptied, the place had taken on the slightly surreal atmosphere that many buildings acquired after hours: a thickening of the air and a humming in bright-white walls. Thorne remembered being in a school play once, rehearsing in the evening after he'd rushed home first to change out of his uniform. It had felt so weird and fantastic, so *invigorating*, to be in the building when it was empty. He'd run from classroom to classroom, charged into the gym in his Oxford bags and beetlecrusher shoes, and shouted swear words down the unlit corridors.

There was no such excitement in a police station once darkness fell.

Curiously, as the space around you increased, a feeling of claustrophobia took hold, while, outside, you knew only too well that crimes you would have to deal with the following day were taking place. Some types more than others, of course. Fraud happened during daylight hours, and drug-smuggling, and many kinds of theft. But night was when brutality flourished; when people suffered and died violently.

At night, in a police station, it felt like something was coming.

As far as the current cases went, the investigations had all but shut down until the morning. Adrian Farrell's solicitor had insisted that his client be allowed to return to his cell and get eight hours' sleep. Within the hour, Danny Donovan had demanded the same for Freestone and with the only lead on the Luke Mullen kidnap put to bed, there was nothing else that anyone could usefully be chasing. Now, there was little to be done but write the day up, drink too much coffee, then sit around feeling depressed *and* caffeined off your tits at the same time.

Russell Brigstocke walked into the CID room looking as though another cup or two of coffee wouldn't hurt. 'You two might as well piss off home,' he said.

'Beautifully put,' Thorne said. 'And I'm not arguing.'

Porter rose to her feet. 'Are you sure, Guv?' But she was already reaching for her bag.

'I'll need you back here in seven ... and rested. So I don't really want to see anyone getting nightcaps at the Oak.'

Thorne put on his leather jacket. '*See* anyone? You planning to go over there later then?'

'I'm planning to get home, eventually.' Brigstocke dropped into the seat that Porter had vacated. 'Not that there's much point.'

'When did you last see your kids?' Porter asked.

Brigstocke stared up at her in mock amazement. 'I've got *kids*?'

In the lobby, Thorne nodded to the uniform behind the screen, who nodded sheepishly in return and went back to being stumped by the *Sun*'s crossword.

'How are you getting home?' he asked Porter.

'I should just make the last train from Colindale,' she said. 'Be there in an hour, with a bit of luck. Cab, otherwise.'

Thorne realised he still didn't know where Porter lived. 'Where have you got to get back to?'

'Pimlico.'

'I'll drop you at the tube.'

'Thanks.'

Thorne waited until they were street-side of the automatic door. 'Listen, I've got a sofa bed. You're more than welcome ...'

'Right.'

They were walking towards the car. Thorne didn't want

to turn and stare, and in the shadow between street lamps it was impossible to see at a glance how Porter was reacting. 'I'm just thinking, you know, it's an hour back to your place and I'm only in Kentish Town, so it might make sense. Like I say, it's just a thought, but you'd probably get an hour or so's more sleep.'

Though Thorne couldn't see her face clearly, there was no mistaking the mischief in Porter's voice. 'Another hour in bed sounds good.'

'Great.'

'OK ...'

'Like I say, I'm only twenty minutes away. And, if you ask me, you'd be lucky to make Pimlico in an hour. So I reckon at least an extra hour's sleep.'

'You're not exactly making it sound like a lot of fun,' she said.

# SEVENTEEN

Maggie had always been the one to handle difficult questions. She had been the one who had dropped whatever she was doing when the homework emergencies had arisen. When Luke and Juliet had been younger, of course, her husband had simply not been around much, but even after he'd retired that sort of thing had come down to her. It wasn't about him not being clever enough. In most ways that seemed to matter, he was a lot brighter than she was, but aside from the maths – which Tony had always had an aptitude for – the responsibility for coming up with the right answer had usually rested with her. She knew the reigns of each Tudor monarch, could list symbols and atomic numbers for most chemical elements, and had drawn and labelled U- and V-shaped river valleys on two separate occasions.

She answered the other questions as well; the trickier

sort. The 'Where do we come from?' and 'What happens when we die?' and 'Why do boys and girls have different parts?' questions.

But Maggie Mullen had never been asked such a difficult question before: 'Is Luke going to be all right, Mum?'

She wasn't sure what destroyed her the most: not knowing the answer or not being able to do what she imagined most other people would do in the same situation, and lie about it to protect her daughter.

'I don't know, pigeon.'

It wasn't as though Maggie had any problem with lies in general. She told them when they needed telling. But she knew that Juliet would resent any clumsy effort to treat her like a child; to shield her from the painful reality of what was happening. It was hard, though, sometimes, knowing the right way to behave. Juliet was fourteen going on twenty-one, in the same way that she'd been nine going on fourteen. She'd been advising Maggie on how to dress, and what to eat, and which of her friends were worth a damn, for years, so there seemed little point in treating her as anything other than an adult now.

When the situation was so hideously *grown up* ...

And yet, there was something in Juliet's eyes, and around her plump, wet bottom lip, that made Maggie think of a doll her daughter used to cling to; that made her want to hold on to Juliet and squeeze for all she was worth. There was something that told Maggie how much Juliet *needed* to be held.

'Where's Dad, Mum?'

'He went out, pigeon. I don't know when he'll be back.'

Or perhaps Maggie was the one who needed to be held; who looked for comfort while giving it to her daughter when she couldn't find it elsewhere. She hated herself for the sudden, malicious thought; for judging him. She knew it was unwarranted, implying a lack of concern for her that should have been forgivable, considering.

She could see in every half look, in every glimpse of him moving across a doorway, how crushed he was. How shrunken. If he was focusing every ounce of love he had inside him to wherever Luke might be, then he could hardly be blamed for that, could he?

And whatever else he was, whatever could be held against him if you were taking stock ... Jesus Christ Almighty, she was hardly one to talk.

'Mum, if Luke is dead—'

'*Juliet!*'

'Please, Mum, listen. I've been thinking about this. If he is, we'll only lose the least important part of him. There's so much of Luke that's still here in the house. Can't you feel it?'

'He's alive, love ... '

'It's fine, honestly. I'm not being Goddy or anything – you know I can't be doing with any of that – but I really believe this. And it really *helps*. It'll be sad, of course it will, and we'll always miss him, and things will remind us that he was here. Like when we eat certain meals he loved or he couldn't stand, or we hear a piece of music or whatever, but we'll always have the important stuff. That won't go anywhere, I promise.'

In the days since Luke had been taken, Maggie had mastered the art of crying without making a sound. All she had to do was turn her head away, walk to the window, lift a newspaper. And though the tears came, the racking sobs and the gasps for breath were held inside, clutched tight behind her breastbone.

She did it because it wasn't necessary for anyone else to see. Because it wouldn't help.

Now, she wept in secret to be strong for the daughter who was trying to be strong for her. She listened to Juliet's words while tears that her daughter couldn't see ran under her chin and slipped below the collar of her nightdress. Lying on the sofa, her daughter's long legs stretched out across her own, watching something or other on TV, and thinking about her boy's smell and the way his hair was at the back of his neck. About the hole that had opened up at the centre of her, red and raw as a butcher's window.

Finding no comfort at all in the knowledge that Juliet was just about old enough, and independent enough, to cope with losing a brother *and* a mother.

The thought of leaving her was almost unbearable. But if anything had happened to Luke, the thought of not rushing to catch up with her firstborn was worse.

There was next to no traffic as they drove south towards Kentish Town, the empty roads being the only plus side to the stupidly early mornings and shitty late nights.

'Have you got any music?' Porter asked.

Thorne reached towards the button, began searching through the six CDs that were stored on the multi-changer he'd mounted in the BMW's boot.

'Any of that twangy-guitar country shit?'

Thorne looked over, in little doubt as to who she'd been talking to. He matched her smug grin with a couldn't-care-less one of his own. 'Holland's a dead man. You know that, don't you?'

'I like some country stuff, actually: Garth Brooks, Shania Twain ...'

Thorne grimaced, then tried to find one CD in particular. 'Right, since you took the piss, I'm not going to make things easy for you.'

'It wasn't Holland, by the way,' Porter said.

'So who was it?'

The music started: a delicate, plaintive guitar picked out below the mournful breaths of an accordion. Then the voice ...

'What's this?' Porter asked after a minute or so.

'Hank Williams. Sort of ...'

Porter looked confused, pained even. 'Is he not going to *sing*?'

As he got up to sixty between speed cameras, Thorne explained that Williams had made a series of records throughout his career under a pseudonym. As 'Luke The Drifter', he'd written and recorded a number of 'narrations' – spoken-word pieces over a simple musical background. Some were straightforward talking blues, but others sounded closer to prayers or spoken hymns. These moralistic recitations – deemed far too uncommercial for the jukeboxes and radio shows that were the great man's bread and butter – were bleak but compassionate, a long way from the hard-drinking renegade that country music fans had come to worship.

'It's bloody depressing,' Porter said.

'Serves you right.' Thorne put his foot down, made it safely through an amber light and swung left towards Belsize Park. 'Be nice to have an alter ego, though,' he said. 'Don't you reckon? Some other side of your personality that nobody knew was really you. That you could blame shit on and send along to do the stuff you didn't fancy.'

Porter agreed it sounded like a nice idea. 'What would yours be?' she asked.

Thorne considered it for a minute, then smiled. 'It'd be great to tell Trevor Jesmond he was giving the wrong man a bollocking. "Sorry, sir, I think you're confusing me with Kevin the Fuck-up. Or perhaps you mean Roger the Couldn't-give-a-toss." What about you?'

Porter thought too, but said she couldn't think of one, so they drove on in silence listening to 'Men with Broken Hearts', which Williams had proudly described as the 'awfulest, morbidest song you ever heard in your life'.

Thorne slowed a little as they approached the flat. Drew Porter's attention to shops and local landmarks; to pubs of interest. On Kentish Town Road he took care to point out the Bengal Lancer. 'Best Indian restaurant in London,' he said. 'You like Indian food?'

Porter nodded. 'I'm not sure they'll deliver to Pimlico, though.'

'I could take you.' Thorne glanced across, his eyes meeting Porter's for half a second on their way to the far-side wing-mirror. 'They'd look after us,' he said.

When they reached the flat, Thorne walked quickly inside, keeping a few feet ahead of Porter and tidying as he went. In the hall, he nudged discarded shoes towards the skirting board with the outside of his foot, straightened the rug, hung up a jacket that had been tossed across the back of a chair. Porter moved past him as he stopped to add the day's post to the pile on the table. When he caught up with her in the living room, she was leaning down to make a fuss of the cat, pretending not to look at the note that had been left on the sofa.

Thorne picked up the scrap of paper and read:

Don't worry, I was talking shit last night. I'd had a drink, and I was tired.

Feeling much better now.

I've eaten the last of your bread. Sorry . . .

'Who's your friend?' Porter asked.

'It's all right. It's a bloke.'

Porter raised an eyebrow. 'Now, *that* is even more interesting than the whole country music thing.'

'It's Phil Hendricks.'

'Right.' She stretched the word out. Left just enough of a pause. 'Hendricks is gay, isn't he?'

Thorne smirked, enjoying the wind-up, relishing the *attention*. He nodded towards the sofa. Elvis was curling up, making herself comfortable again. 'That's the sofa-bed,' he said. 'I'll get it out later.'

'I beg your pardon?'

He couldn't help but mirror her grin. 'Why do I feel like I'm suddenly in a remake of *Carry on Constable*? Isn't this where you tell me that anything I say will be taken down, and I say, "knickers"?'

She laughed. 'Is there anything to drink?'

Thorne tried to look stern. 'Seven hours until we're on again, remember. And *rested*.'

'One won't hurt.' She sat down on the sofa. 'Can't Roger Couldn't-give-a-toss go and get us a drink?'

Roger walked into the kitchen and squatted down in front of the fridge. He stared at its meagre contents, then realised that, as far as this woman he'd brought back to his flat went, he didn't have a clue what he was doing, or where things were heading, but he was loving every minute of it. He shouted back into the living room: 'Not much choice, I'm afraid. It's cheap lager or cheap lager.'

'Either's fine,' Porter said.


The 10 p.m. to 6 a.m. shift could be good news or bad news, depending on how hard you fancied working; and, more importantly, what night of the week it was. Early in the week, it could be fairly quiet. But round Shepherd's Bush, Acton, Hammersmith – *anywhere* come to that – things tended to get a bit livelier once people smelled the weekend coming.

PC Dean Fothergill knew that now and again, when

355

there were just the two of you, out and about in a panda, you could hide if you felt like it. For a while, anyway. You could try to stretch your hour's meal break into a couple if you'd not got enough sleep during the day. It was getting harder with the Airwaves, of course, but even if the powers that be knew where you were, they couldn't *see* you. Not yet, at least. So some of the lads had already figured out that as long as you kept moving, you'd look busy enough. Café to kebab shop to side street; half an hour with the paper in one place and a fag break somewhere else. Only on a slow night, obviously.

On a Saturday night, there was always something happening.

At a quarter past one in the morning, Fothergill and WPC Pauline Caulfield were up near TV Centre when they took the call.

'Some bloke's phoned through from Glasgow, says his sister was meant to have come up this afternoon and she never got there. She's sixty-odd, she lives alone, he can't get hold of her on the phone, didn't ring until now because he didn't want to worry us, blah, blah, blah. Go and check on her when you've got a minute, will you, Dean? I know you and Pauline are sitting around reading the paper.'

'We were dealing with that ruck outside White City tube, actually, Skip.'

'I believe you; thousands wouldn't. I'll send everything through on the MDT.'

As soon as the details started to come up on the screen

of the car's mobile data terminal, Caulfield swung the Astra round.

They took it steady towards Shepherd's Bush.

Fothergill shook his head. 'I bet you a fiver she forgot she was even meant to *go* to Glasgow,' he said.

'You're a good listener,' he said.

He raised the torch and trained the beam across the cellar, then lowered it when the boy squinted and turned his face away. 'I know that you're scared, so you'd probably listen to anything, but I can tell when people are really hearing what you've got to say and when they're not. I get a lot of that at work, and it can really wear you down. People just sitting there and letting what you say wash over them and not taking anything in. And it's harder for you, I can see that. Of course it is. It can't be easy listening to what I'm telling you. Just sitting there and hearing these hideous things and saying nothing.

'Do you *want* to say something? You can, you know . . .

'I know you maybe need time to take some of this stuff in, that's only natural. I'll leave you for a while to do that, but I want you to understand something first. I wouldn't be telling you any of this if I didn't think you could take it in. OK? If I didn't think you were old enough and bright enough. I know all about how clever you are, all about it. So I thought about everything carefully, and decided that you would definitely be able to process this information. Make sense of it. Not that you can make sense of all of it, because there are parts – I know you know which parts I'm talking about – that are so beyond what you and I, what *ordinary* people, perceive as normal that sense doesn't really come into it.

'Is that fair? Just nod if you agree with what I'm saying . . . Good.

'As long as you don't think I'm getting any pleasure out of this, that's all. You know I'm not trying to torture you with it, right? I mean, what possible reason could I have to do that? I've hurt you enough already; I'm well aware of that. Everything you went through before, in the flat, I mean. I suppose I just want you to understand that the motivation for telling you all this is . . . *decent*.

'Because you should know these things. Because not knowing would be so much worse. Because at some point you'll come to terms with it and be far better off in the long run. Do you see?

'Knowing what the ones you love are capable of is a terrible burden sometimes. But ignorance is a damn sight worse.'

He raised himself on his haunches when he heard the sniffing and crept a little closer to the corner in which the boy was curled. 'Don't cry, please. I really wasn't trying to make you cry. I'm sorry. I'll wait until you're a bit calmer. I'll go now, shall I?'

He moved back again. Waited. 'You'll forgive some of it, I'm sure. Not me, probably, and certainly not for all *this*. But some of it: those things, the less terrible things, we did for the right reasons. I know you won't be able to see that now, that right now you just want to lash out and scream or whatever. But they were the best reasons, I swear to you.

'Would you like to scream? Go on, it's fine, if you want to. Nobody's going to hear. That's why I took the tape off. Honestly, I can understand if you want to. Do you want to smash something? Do you want to kick my head in? Do you just want me to fuck off?'

He said nothing for a few minutes, then he raised the torch again and held its beam on the boy. 'You should really think about screaming, you know. It might be healthy if you did. Get it out.'

He turned the torch on himself, rested his chin on the lens and thought for a while. 'OK, maybe I've overestimated how much of it you've actually taken in. It's a heck of a lot, I know. A lot to ... *absorb*. Before I go, maybe I'll just run through some of it again. I'll try to make it simpler for you this time. Is that a good idea, do you think?

'Luke ... ?'

The joking had stopped the moment Caulfield had spotted the broken window. They'd already spent ten minutes knocking before Fothergill had scaled the side gate and they'd walked round to the rear of the house.

He'd called it in while Caulfield had gone back to the car for gloves, torch and their telescopic batons.

'Maybe we should just wait,' Fothergill said.

'For fuck's sake, Dean.'

Caulfield pushed her hand through and reached round until she could release the catch on the lock. Before she had a chance to open the door, a cat bolted past her and flung itself through a cat-flap and inside.

'*Jesus* ...'

She stepped into a darkened kitchen and shouted into the house. Fothergill shouted louder. Then they stood still and waited. If there was anyone in the house who shouldn't have been there, chances were that they'd hear some kind of movement, even if it was someone trying to conceal themself. Caulfield felt for a light switch, found it, and the two of them moved further into the room. There were dishes stacked neatly on a draining board. The cat roamed around near an empty bowl on the floor and rubbed its head against cupboard doors.

Caulfield bent down. 'Shush, it's OK.'

'You talking to me or the cat?' Fothergill managed the smile, but his voice was higher than normal.

They walked out of the kitchen and into a narrow hall-way with the front door at the far end. Streetlight filtered through small stained-glass panels, and stairs rose up from one side. There were two doors off to the right. They opened one each, turned on the lights in a small sitting room and a dining room.

'Dean?'

Fothergill put his head round the door and followed Caulfield's gaze. The dining table had been set for break-fast: an empty glass, spoon and napkin; a bowl already filled with cereal and covered in cling film.

'Come on ...'

There were watercolours on the wall running up the

stairs, and framed certificates, and photographs on a small table at the top, arranged around a large basket filled with pot pourri. Somewhere among the scents of vanilla and orange, though, there was a faint odour of something else. Something sharp and sad.

They turned on more lights, looked into a bathroom and a spare bedroom, then walked slowly towards the closed door of the only room that was left.

'Have you ever seen a body, Dean?' Caulfield asked.

'Come on, she might be anywhere. She might have gone away without telling anyone—'

'Dean?'

Fothergill shook his head. Took off his hat and held a sleeve to his forehead.

'It's fine, OK? Just stay calm, and don't touch anything.'

The smell was stronger when they opened the door. Each could taste it on the breath they sucked in before Caulfield turned on the light.

'Oh, fuck . . .'

She'd kicked the duvet on to the floor, and her nightdress had ridden up above her pale, hairless calves. One arm was thrown out to the side, hanging over the edge of the bed, while the other was tight against her side, a handful of the sheet clutched between thin fingers.

A lamp had been knocked from the bedside table. A paperback romance lay next to it on the carpet.

'OK, Dean?'

Fothergill had turned away and was looking across to

361

where more photographs were arranged on a dressing table. The same woman was posing in many of them: a young girl's hair gathered up in a black beehive; changing style and colour as the photos did; turning grey finally, and growing thin as the woman began to fade and shrink. Fothergill guessed the face was the same that lay twisted beneath the pillow a few feet away from him.

The cat had followed them upstairs. Caulfield reached down as it moved past her, but she was too late to stop it jumping on to the mattress, where it immediately began kneading at the dead woman's leg and purring loudly.

'Shit . . .'

Fothergill turned back to the woman on the bed. His face was the same colour as the stained white sheet beneath her.

'My mother was in a residential place for her last couple of months,' he said. 'It smelled like this.' He reached out a hand towards the bedstead, stopped, and nodded understanding when Caulfield repeated her warning not to touch. 'It smells like my mum's room.'

There had been a woman Thorne had slept with once, the year before, but he was still trying, for all manner of reasons, to forget that particular episode. Aside from her, Hendricks and the occasional plumber, he reckoned it had been quite long enough since he'd stood waiting for someone to come out of his bathroom.

He was sore, having strained his back fifteen minutes earlier, trying to assemble the sofa-bed. Porter had laughed when he'd sworn and cried out, then got up to lend a hand when she'd seen how much pain he was in.

'You should get that seen to,' she'd said. 'At least find out what's wrong.'

'I will.'

'Have you got health insurance?'

'No, but there's some money. From the sale of my dad's house, you know?' The money he'd not known what to do with; that he'd hated. He'd given some to Aunt Eileen, and a couple of hundred to Victor, but even after he'd handed the taxman his chunk, there was still plenty left. Maybe, a year on, he should spend it on something. Find some use for it that the old man would have approved of.

'Shame you didn't bugger up your back at work,' Porter had said. They'd lifted the metal bar beneath the cushions, pulled out the mattress and folded down the legs. 'Then the Job would have to cough up for it.'

She'd been close enough for Thorne to smell the beer on her. The one drink that had become a couple each.

They'd sat around and bitched about people at work, about the job in general. They'd given thumbnail sketches of parents and past relationships. Thorne had told her about the previous day, when he'd been thinking about bad marriages, and Maggie and Tony Mullen had sprung to mind. He'd been shocked that, for the first time he could remember, his own marriage hadn't been the first one he'd thought of.

Porter told him that was probably a good sign.

Now, standing outside the bathroom, he realised that he'd said far more about almost everything than she had. That – aside from the facts that she was funny and good at her job, and that he fancied the arse off her – he didn't know a great deal about Louise Porter.

Thorne could hear her through the cheap, thin door, making an odd humming noise as she brushed her teeth, and he decided he knew enough.

When she came out of the bathroom, she was carrying her own clothes in a bundle under one arm and wearing nothing but knickers under one of Thorne's T-shirts. She moved past him, reddening slightly, and began laying her blouse and skirt on the chair nearest the sofa-bed. 'I'll buy you a new toothbrush.'

'I should worry about explaining to people at work why you're wearing the same clothes two days running.'

'They're used to it,' she said. 'I'm such a slag.'

Thorne laughed, then coughed, then winced at the pain. Porter walked across and, without saying anything, began to untuck Thorne's shirt at the back.

'Hello,' he said.

She placed the flat of her hand against his back, low down, just above his belt, and began to rub. 'There?'

'Close enough,' Thorne said.

'Is that helping?'

'Oh yes . . .'

Then the phone rang.

He turned round and she removed her hand, and the look between them quickly became serious, with the phone demanding to be answered and both knowing very well it was unlikely to be a social call.

It was Holland. 'I think you'd better get out of bed,' he said.

'We haven't had the chance to get in yet.'

'*Sorry?*'

Thorne could have kicked himself. 'Get on with it, Dave.'

'Shepherd's Bush CID have got a body we should take a look at. I'll give you the address.'

Thorne looked around for a piece of paper. Porter appeared next to him with a notepad and pen, then walked back to the bed and began pulling on her skirt.

'I'm listening . . .'

'Remember that message I left for Kathleen Bristow?' Holland said. 'Well, somebody finally got back to me.'

PART THREE

# WHAT IT LOOKS LIKE

# SUNDAY

# LUKE

There'd been a kid, when Luke was a few years younger, who'd picked on him at school. He'd stolen things – a fountain pen, a watch – handed out punches to the shoulder and kicks to the ankle, and threatened to do a lot worse if Luke told anyone. Luke hadn't been the only one this boy had targeted. He'd watched the bully with others sometimes, and saw the same technique as had been used on him. The boy would smile, be nice, make out that he wanted to be friends, before dishing out the painful stuff. As though the pretend gentleness made the twisting and slapping that came afterwards more enjoyable for him.

Luke *hadn't* told anyone, had suffered until the boy had left the school, but he'd learned to recognise the smile that came before the pain, and he saw it with the man in the cellar. It sounded silly. It was obvious really, with what was going on, but there was something wrong with the man. Something out of control, lost, which made Luke feel as though the man himself didn't have much idea what he was going to do next.

The friendlier the man was – the more freedom he gave Luke, the more he told Luke how much he thought of him – the more frightening he became. And the more determined Luke became to try to help himself.

It was hard, trying to make himself concentrate on *doing* something when all he wanted to do was curl up and lie still, sleep until it was over. He'd spent hours since the man had last left, reciting poems in his head, lyrics to songs … anything to avoid having to think about what the man had told him; what he'd kept on telling him. It was poisonous shit, he knew that; like the lies that bully at school had once told him in a soft voice. The man was enjoying coming down with his torch and his filth. Spewing it out and messing with his head. Weakening him.

So Luke filled his head with as much other stuff as he could, trying to squeeze out the man's lies.

And he focused hard on the sting from a dozen cuts and bruises. He drove a fingernail across the graze on his knuckles until that pain became more important than the deep, dull ache that the man's words had left spreading through his body.

He climbed to his feet, feeling the pieces of discarded gaffer tape around him as his hands moved across the dirt floor. He tried to concentrate on the map of the cellar he had created in his mind: the low corners; the damp crannies and musty alcoves; the shelves thick with dirt; tins of paint, bags of cement and picture frames ...

If the man was still in the house, he would probably be down to see him again before too long. With more stories to tell ... or worse.

Luke stared into the thick, gritty darkness and made a decision.

He needed a weapon.

# EIGHTEEN

There was never a good time, of course. But when it came to working with a body, working *on* a body, the early hours of the morning were probably the least bad. During the day, a murder scene felt blatant and unashamed. There was something about the way daylight fell across a body that served to reinforce the brutality of the act; to hammer home the shocking truth that such things happened while the rest of the world went about its business. Walked around, shopped, sat bored at tills or desks, while others a few feet away bled, bloated and stiffened.

At night, Thorne could do what needed to be done and could extract a little comfort from the fact that he was performing a necessary, if ugly, public service by cleaning up the mess before dawn. In a bad mood he might consider such a night's labours as akin to shovelling shit uphill.

But tonight, standing over the body of an old woman while her neighbours slept, he felt like he was doing his bit to maintain a little of the bliss that ignorance afforded.

He'd already exchanged a few words with Hendricks as they'd climbed into the plastic full-body suits. It was a run-of-the-mill conversation, such as anyone might have before getting down to work:

'How're you doing?'

'Good. Didn't you get my note?'

'Yeah, but you'd probably say that anyway.'

'No, really. I saw Brendan.'

'How was that?'

'Well, there was no screaming, and I didn't try to smash his face in, so pretty good, I think ...'

Now, forty minutes or so into it, the dialogue had taken on a more businesslike tone. The talk was of lividity and core body temperature; of traumatic asphyxia and cadaveric spasm. As Hendricks dictated a few notes into a small digital recorder, Thorne watched the team of scene-of-crime officers move around Kathleen Bristow's small bedroom. As always, seeing them work, he felt something nagging at him; irritating, like a rough seam scratching his skin inside the plastic suit. He had come to realise over the years that it was envy: of their certainty; of the scientific boundaries which he imagined must give them the kind of reassurance he had rarely felt himself.

Theirs would be the evidence for the likes of him to label and box up and get to court. Without it, the best he had to offer was guesswork and speculation.

'So, when are we talking, Phil?'

Hendricks took one of the woman's dead hands in his own. The flesh was mottled, bluish against the cream of his surgical glove. 'Rigor's just starting to fade, so I think we're talking a little over twenty-four hours. The early hours of yesterday morning, probably. Maybe late the night before.'

The night before they'd nicked Grant Freestone.

But Freestone couldn't be the killer, could he? They'd already established that he hadn't kidnapped anyone, and it would have been too much of a coincidence for Kathleen Bristow's death *not* to be connected to the abduction of Luke Mullen.

'I reckon he broke a rib or two as well,' Hendricks said. 'Pressing down on top of her. Kneeling on her chest, maybe.'

When Hendricks reached forward to push a finger inside Kathleen Bristow's mouth, to rub a cotton bud across the tears inside her lip, Thorne turned away. He walked out of the room, and downstairs. A SOCO he knew well was working in the dining room, moving methodically around the small table on top of which sat a telephone and answering machine. It was from here that a DI from the on-call Murder Team had phoned Dave Holland, having listened to the message he'd left for Kathleen Bristow. As Thorne headed towards the back door, he exchanged a joke with the officer, but he was thinking of how the old woman's face had seemed to collapse when Hendricks had removed her false teeth.

Outside, Thorne pushed back the hood of the plastic suit, walked over to where Dave Holland, similarly attired, was leaning against the wall next to the kitchen window. A generator hummed at the front of the house and a powerful arc light brightened the half of the garden nearest the kitchen door.

Holland took two quick drags of a cigarette, held it up to show Thorne, raised his eyes towards the top floor of the house. 'All this seems a good enough reason to give in and have one, you know? But then you feel guilty for enjoying it.'

In direct contrast to most people, Holland had taken up smoking *after* his child was born. He'd smoked secretly, at work, until his girlfriend had found out and gone ballistic, since when he'd done his best to knock it on the head. But, like he said, there were times when it seemed reasonable to weaken.

'Doesn't Sophie smell it on you?'

Holland nodded. 'But she understands that nine times out of ten, there's a bloody good reason, so she doesn't usually give me a hard time.'

Thorne pushed himself away from the wall and strolled to the rear of the garden. Holland followed him into the shadow, beyond the arc light's reach. They sat on a small, ornamental bench.

'You reckon our kidnapper did this?' Holland asked.

'If he didn't, I haven't got a fucking clue what's going on. Not that I've got much of an idea anyway.'

'Maybe we're getting close to him.'

Thorne looked back towards the house, stared at the SOCOs inside, moving back and forth past the bedroom window. 'It's hard to feel too excited about that,' he said, 'right at this minute.' He stretched his feet out in front of him. The grass smelled as though it had been mown only a day or two before. It looked grey against the white of the plastic overshoes.

'I haven't seen DI Porter for a while,' Holland said.

'And . . . ?'

'Nothing. I just wondered where she was.'

'Right. She was talking to the photographer, last time I saw her.' Thorne leaned forward, looked at Holland, daring him to give anything away.

'*What?*'

'Don't even think about smirking,' Thorne said. 'Just shut up and finish your fag . . . '

'I was only asking.'

'Or I'll call your girlfriend and tell her you're back on twenty a day.'

Holland did as he was told, and they sat in silence for a few minutes. The smoke drifted away from them towards the light, disappearing at its edge, where moths and midges danced in and out of the beam. When he'd finished, Holland stubbed out his fag-end on the bottom of the bench and stood up. 'Best get back in there,' he said. 'I reckon they'll be bringing her out in a minute.'

This was the other advantage of working a murder scene at this hour: save for the occasional insomniac dog-walker or crazed jogger, Kathleen Bristow could leave her home for the last time without an audience. During the day, there would be no shortage of gawpers, standing silently, shifting from foot to foot, formulating the story they would tell later around the dinner table or in the pub. Whenever Thorne listened to traffic updates on the motorway, he wondered why the announcer didn't just tell the truth; why they didn't come clean and say that the tailback was the result of drivers slowing down to get a good look at the accident.

He raised his head at the rustle of plastic trouser-legs moving against each other and shifted across to let Porter sit down.

'Holland giving you a hard time?' she asked.

'He knows better.'

Thorne thought Porter probably had more to say about what had nearly gone on at his flat, but he made it obvious that he wasn't too keen to get into it. He couldn't help but wonder how he'd feel about discussing it if anything had actually happened.

'I spoke to Hendricks,' she said. 'So I suppose we should at least ask Freestone where he was on Friday night.'

'Can't see the point.'

'Well, how about because we haven't got anyone else even resembling a suspect?'

Thorne shrugged. 'We can *ask*.'

'A tenner says he was with his sister anyway, right?'

'Probably. But whether Freestone's got an alibi or not, this is the same man that killed Allen and Tickell. Has to be. The same man who's holding Luke.'

A light came on in an upstairs window of the house next door. Looking across, Thorne saw that there were downstairs lights burning on the other side, too. So much for the absence of an audience. In London, he supposed, there was usually *someone* watching. There would probably be a house-to-house later that morning, and they could only hope that someone had been equally watchful twenty-four hours earlier.

'OK, seeing as *who* is pretty much a non-starter, any bright ideas about *why*?'

*Bright ideas?* More like guesswork and speculation . . .

'Did you look in the spare room?' Thorne asked.

He had noticed the three battered, metal filing cabinets in the second bedroom and remembered something Callum Roper had said about who was most likely to have kept any records of the MAPPA meetings back in 2001. He ran the idea that had begun to form in his mind past Porter.

Her response suggested that, as pieces of speculation went, it wasn't the most outlandish she'd ever heard. 'You think she was killed because of something she knew?'

'Or something she had. Perhaps without even knowing she had it. It's just a thought . . . '

'The problem is that without us knowing what was in those filing cabinets, I don't see how we're going to work out what might have been taken.'

'I had a quick look in one of them. There's a ton of stuff in there, going back years. We can go through it all later, when scene of crime's finished. If there's nothing there about Freestone, or the MAPPA project in 2001, I think we should try and find out if there ever was.'

'We'll need to get back on to whichever social services department she was working for then.' Porter winced, like she'd just remembered what day it was. 'Won't have a lot of luck on a Sunday, mind.'

'I wouldn't bank on them having copies of these records themselves,' Thorne said. 'Not if what Roper said is true. But they might know what Bristow took with her when she retired, or at least confirm that she kept her own records.' Even as Thorne said it, the idea was starting to sound vague and flabby; time-consuming at the very least. Though they now had three murders to investigate, there was still a missing boy whose safety, whose *quick* recovery was, theoretically, their prime concern.

A boy who, theoretically, was still alive.

Porter, though, seemed energised by Thorne's idea. While Thorne himself could only hope that he didn't look as bad as he felt, her face showed no sign of the fact that she was approaching what must have been twenty-four hours without sleep.

'Maybe it's Freestone's connection to this MAPPA business that's important,' she suggested. 'Not the threats he made before he went to prison.'

*Three murders ...*

'Well, something's *seriously* important to someone,' Thorne said.

'What about Luke?'

There was guesswork and there was speculation. And

there were some things that just became horribly obvious. 'He'll kill Luke if he has to,' Thorne said.

Porter nodded, like Thorne had confirmed what she already knew. She lifted her feet on to the bench, wrapped her arms around her knees, and said, 'I've only ever lost two.'

For a minute or more, Thorne searched for something to say, but before anything suitable could come to him Porter had chased away the need for reassurance and was getting to her feet.

'We need to get a fucking shift on,' she said. 'Maybe coming at it from this new angle might help.'

'Maybe.' Thorne hauled himself upright, hoping that her optimism would prove justified. There was no doubt that the map of the case was being freshly laid out on memos and whiteboards; was redrawing itself in Thorne's head. But as lines snaked in new directions and intersected for the first time with others, one name – whatever else was happening – kept drifting towards an area where it should not, by rights, belong. It kept floating away from that part of the map reserved for victims and witnesses and heading towards an altogether murkier, unlabelled zone.

Tony Mullen.

A wave from just inside the kitchen door indicated that the body of Kathleen Bristow was being brought out. Porter started walking back towards the house, with Thorne a few paces behind her.

The joking always stopped at this point, for a few minutes at least, until the mortuary vehicle had driven away. Then the bagging and the scraping, and the banter, could resume; with the volume cranked up a notch or two.

Once the body had gone, the murder scene could let out the breath it had been holding.

Thorne watched as the stretcher was lifted over the step at the back door and into the garden. Holland came out after it, then Hendricks, who began to clamber out of his plastic suit in readiness for following the body to the mortuary. The stretcher was taken through the gate, the arc light illuminating its path along the side of the house towards the road.

Thorne walked back into the house, thinking that cigarette smoke wasn't the worst thing you could go home stinking of.

Custody reviews took place six and fifteen hours into the twenty-four. Thirty minutes earlier, at 8 a.m., Kitson and Brigstocke had reviewed the ongoing custody of Adrian Farrell for the second time. Now, she was cheerfully passing on the news to the prisoner himself: that should matters not proceed to her satisfaction, she and her DCI would be going to the superintendent to seek a six-hour extension.

Smartarse, the solicitor – who preferred the name Wilson – was less than impressed. 'And this is on the basis of a video parade, is it?'

'A positive identification from an eyewitness who says he watched Mr Farrell and two others murder Amin Latif on October 17th, last year. Sorry … I should say, "murder Mr Latif after seriously sexually assaulting him", if we're being accurate. Although, that said, I think the murder will probably be enough, don't you?'

Wilson began scribbling something, then casually slid his forearm across the top of his notepad, like a schoolboy protecting his answers.

Kitson watched him write, thinking that it might just as well have been a shopping list, for all the help it was going to be to his client. Next to her, Andy Stone did up the buttons on his jacket. Stone was just there to make up the numbers, and seemed happy enough with his role.

'You warm enough, Adrian?' he asked.

The interview room was cold, which was probably a good thing, as someone brought in overnight after a knife attack outside a bar had thrown up in the corner. Heating would almost certainly have made the stench of stale puke and disinfectant unbearable.

Judging by the expression on Adrian Farrell's face, the smell was bad enough as it was.

He looked very different out of uniform; away from school and everything that went with it. He wore jeans, and a red hooded top with 'NEW YORK' emblazoned across the chest. The blond hair was messy, but had certainly not been styled that way, and the face it framed showed every sign of having spent a night as uncomfortable as those in the cells were supposed to be. He was trying to look bored and mildly irritated, but lack of sleep was obviously affecting his ability to keep up the act. Where previously she had caught only glimpses, Kitson was starting to get a better look at the fear, and at the dark, quiet anger which settled across his features, like scum on the surface of still water.

'I know what'll cheer you up,' she said. 'A bit of a history quiz.'

A laminated list of prisoner's rights had been fixed to the desk. Farrell was picking at an edge of it. He looked up, shrugged. 'Fine.'

'History's your favourite, isn't it?'

'I said *fine*.'

'Good on dates? What about February 28th, 1953?'

Farrell tapped a finger against his lips. 'Battle of Hastings?'

'Why don't we ask the audience?' Kitson said. 'Mr Wilson?'

Wilson did a little more scribbling. 'I doubt you'll get any kind of extension if you waste the time you've got playing silly games.'

'It was the day that Francis Crick and James Watson worked out the structure of DNA.' Kitson slowly drew a figure of eight on the desktop in front of her. 'The double helix.'

Farrell looked as though he found this genuinely funny. 'I won't forget it now,' he said.

'I bet you won't. We should have a preliminary result by the end of the day, and I know it's going to be a match.'

This time, Kitson was talking about the result of tests carried out on an *authorised* DNA sample, taken the previous day at the station. Farrell had refused to give

385

permission for this, so Kitson – as she had every right to do in the case of a non-intimate sample – had taken it without consent. As several strands of hair were removed by the attending medical officer, with Stone and another DC providing the necessary restraint, Kitson had seen flashes of an anger a lot less quiet than the one she sensed, simmering inside Adrian Farrell now.

She stared across the table, turning up the heat. 'And *you* know it's going to be a match, too, don't you?'

'I know all sorts of things.'

'Of course you do.'

'I know that you can't decide how best to talk to me so as to get what you want. I know that you're either patronising me or pretending that you think I'm *really* clever and *really* mature, but all the time you're steering a clumsy course between the two you're just sitting there hating my guts.' He cocked his head towards Stone. 'And I know that he just wants to climb across this table and get his hands on me.'

Stone returned the stare, like he wasn't about to argue.

Kitson caught the look, like a poker player spotting a tell. The puff of the cheeks from Wilson told her he was resigned to the fact that whichever way he'd advised Farrell to behave, the boy thought he knew better. That the fat fee he was doubtless being paid by his client's parents would be earned without a great deal of effort. Kitson turned back to Farrell, convinced that his solicitor was already thinking about future, fatter fees. Those that might be earned appealing against a guilty verdict.

'You're not walking away from this,' she said.

'You seem very sure of yourself, but you're still not charging me, are you?'

'Who were the two other boys with you when you attacked Amin Latif?'

'When I *what*?'

'Give me the names, Adrian.'

'Now, you say you can't promise anything, right? But if I help you, you'll see what you can do about getting my sentence reduced. Or maybe you'll just try to appeal to my conscience, because you're sure I've got one somewhere, and that deep down I want to do the right thing.'

'What about Damien Herbert and Michael Nelson?' Kitson asked. 'Shall we talk to them? You can bet *they'd* give *you* up in a second.'

It was as though Farrell simply hadn't heard her. 'Isn't this where you slide a few pictures of the dead boy across the table?'

Kitson looked to Wilson, then to Stone. The pause was less for effect than to suck up saliva into a mouth that had suddenly gone dry. It was coppery with adrenalin. 'You've got a lot of confidence, Adrian,' she said. 'A lot of charm. I'm sure you're a big hit with young girls and old ladies. But all the charm in the world won't sway a jury if it's looking at an eyewitness ID and a DNA match.'

'*I'm* confident? If you ask me, you're the one who's counting all the chickens. It's an eyewitness ID six months after the fact. And you keep talking about this DNA match like you've already got it.'

387

Kitson couldn't resist a smile, remembering the one Farrell had given her, just before he'd spat on to the pavement.

Stone shuffled forward on his chair. 'I'll tell you who else you'll be a big hit with,' he said. 'One or two of the lads you're likely to find yourself banged up with.'

Wilson groaned in distaste.

'Are you serious?' Farrell asked. He held up a hand, apologising for finding what Stone had said so funny. 'Sorry, I swear I'm not trying to wind you up . . .'

'It's a last resort,' Wilson said. 'Sordid scare tactics of that nature are only ever made when a case is nowhere near as strong as is being made out.' He looked over at Kitson, pleased with himself. 'It's barrel-scraping.'

'It's quite appropriate, I would have thought,' she said. 'Bearing in mind what happened to Amin Latif.'

A bubble of fear, or fury, rose to the surface and broke across the boy's features. He reached for Wilson's notebook, tore back a page and jabbed a finger at something the solicitor had jotted down earlier.

'My client is unhappy about the confiscation of some of his property.'

'My training shoes.'

'They've been taken away for forensic tests,' Kitson said. There had been no footwear prints or casts taken at the Latif murder scene, but it was standard practice nonetheless. 'It's a routine procedure.'

Farrell pushed his chair away from the table, stuck out his feet. 'These are bloody ridiculous.' He raised one of the black, elasticated plimsolls with which almost all prisoners were issued. 'They don't even fit.'

'Everyone gets them,' Stone said.

'Why can't I have another pair of my own brought in?'

'Sorry. It's part of the uniform. There's no Latin motto, but—'

'Those trainers cost a lot of money. They were customised.'

Wilson raised his pen. 'Can you assure us that they won't be damaged during any chemical examination?'

Kitson decided there and then to end the interview. She stood up and instructed Stone to complete the formalities: to stop the recording and seal the cassette within sight of the prisoner. Looking back from the door, she could tell that both Farrell and Wilson were taken aback by the abruptness with which she'd brought proceedings to a halt.

'I'm investigating the sexual assault and murder of a seventeen-year-old-boy,' she said. 'And I will do whatever it takes to get the names of the people who were there with you when it happened. To make sure that all three of you stand trial for brutalising Amin Latif, then kicking him to death.' She reached behind her, aware of the slightest tremor in her hand as it closed around the door handle. 'But I will not sit here and argue with you about fucking shoes.'

Ten minutes later, standing just inside the cage, Kitson saw Farrell's solicitor in the backyard, enjoying a cigarette. She walked out to join him.

He offered her the packet but she shook her head: 'Got anything stronger?'

'You seemed a little wound up in there,' Wilson said.

'Well, he's quite a lad, isn't he?'

The solicitor didn't bite. He took one last, deep drag, then flicked the butt towards a pair of police motorbikes. 'Any thoughts on when you might be bringing him up again?'

'Not specifically, but I wouldn't go too far away.'

'I was wondering if that pub up the road does a traditional Sunday lunch later.'

'The Oak? It does lunch, but I'm not sure their definition of "traditional" is the same as yours.'

She walked back inside, deciding that once she'd sorted out the paperwork with the custody skipper, she'd grab some breakfast. Then she'd try to track down Tom Thorne. Everyone had heard about the overnight development on the Mullen case, and Kitson could only guess that Thorne had not yet had a chance to pick up the memo she'd left in his pigeonhole, or return the message she'd left on his mobile.

Compared to the discovery of a body, what she had to tell him was hardly particularly urgent.

# NINETEEN

That was why people stopped to look at accidents: the vicarious thrill without the inconvenience of being doused in blood or dressed in twisted metal. It was almost certainly the same principle that made watching three senior officers arguing with one another so exhilarating.

It was the row that Hignett had predicted, and it was only surprising that Graham Hoolihan had taken as long as he had before coming down and throwing around some of his considerable weight.

'I was cooperative when DI Thorne first contacted me. I was more than helpful. And, unlike anyone on this case, I showed a bit of common fucking courtesy.'

'There's no point chucking insults at people.'

'Why not? You clearly don't understand how the proper channels work.'

Thorne had decided not to get involved, but just to stand there at the back of Brigstocke's office and watch. Maybe chip in every now and again.

'I found out about this in the *pub*, for crying out loud,' Hoolihan said. 'Because your chief superintendent was at some function or other with mine, and just happened to mention it over the gin and tonics.'

Thorne pictured Trevor Jesmond with one trouser-leg rolled up, clutching a tumbler and talking shop over the clinking of ice cubes.

'Look,' Hignett said, 'we'd certainly have been making contact with you today. But then we picked up a murder in the early hours and other things became somewhat more important.'

It sounded convincing enough. Brigstocke picked up the baton. 'As it was, we'd only had Freestone in custody a little over twelve hours anyway.'

'And there was every reason to believe he could help us with an ongoing enquiry into a kidnap and double murder. So ...'

'So it wasn't as though we were trying to keep the fact that we had him a secret.'

Brigstocke and Hignett were making a decent job of putting on a united front. Thorne was impressed by Hignett's stance in particular. Under the circumstances, the DCI from the Kidnap Unit could have been forgiven for jumping up and down, pointing the finger elsewhere and telling everyone that he'd wanted to hand Grant Freestone over straight away.

'Why didn't anyone call me when he was brought in?' Hoolihan asked. 'Just as a common courtesy.'

Brigstocke and Hignett looked at one another, each trying to formulate a nice, polite answer.

It had all kicked off towards the end of the morning's briefing, which had naturally concentrated on the discovery of the body in Shepherd's Bush. As ever, the first twenty-four hours were the most crucial, so all efforts would now be channelled into investigating the murder of Kathleen Bristow. Though this was clearly the best chance they had of making progress on the main case, too, the kidnap itself had barely been talked about.

It had not escaped Thorne's attention that Luke Mullen's name was being mentioned less and less as the days went by. Spoken more quietly, when it was. There were the murders to work on now, he understood that; other angles that might prove more productive. But Thorne knew that wasn't the only reason.

As the briefing had broken up, Graham Hoolihan had appeared, and a heated discussion had rapidly reached boiling point, until a sergeant from another squad had ushered them all towards Brigstocke's office, like an irate landlord escorting drunks from the premises.

'You should know that I've got written authority to take Freestone back with me to Lewisham.'

Lewisham, Sutton, Earlsfield. The three places Homicide South were based on the other side of the river.

Hoolihan reached down for a briefcase, then swung it

on to Brigstocke's desk. 'My guvnor got it signed by Commander Walker first thing this morning.'

From where Thorne was standing, it looked as though Hignett and Brigstocke couldn't quite decide whether to bristle or shudder. Clive Walker was head of Homicide Command, London-wide. He was one of the few men who could make Trevor Jesmond seem like one of the lads.

'So let's not waste any more time,' Hoolihan said. 'Do you still have every reason to believe Freestone can assist with your enquiries?'

There seemed little point pretending there was any reason whatsoever. Freestone had been questioned earlier that morning, and had claimed to have been tucked up in bed at his sister's flat when Kathleen Bristow was having a pillow put across her face. Predictably, Jane Freestone had confirmed her brother's story, and, though she was hardly the world's most reliable witness, the alibi would be tough to dispute.

Not that Thorne could see any reason to even bother trying. He knew that Freestone had no more murdered Kathleen Bristow than he had Amanda Tickell or Conrad Allen; any more than he was behind the kidnapping of Luke Mullen. He thought back to when he and Porter had nicked Freestone in the park the morning before. He hadn't looked happy, of course, why would he? But he *certainly* hadn't looked like a man being arrested for a murder he'd committed only a few hours earlier.

The hesitation that followed his question seemed to give

Hoolihan the answer he desired. 'Right, well, let's get a move on, then.' He tapped the lid of his briefcase. 'We'll have plenty of paperwork to push at each other.'

Thorne felt himself stepping forward, then heard himself speaking. 'For someone who obviously sets so much store by courtesy, I was thinking that maybe a "thank you" might be in order.' Brigstocke threw him a look, but Thorne ploughed on, making a mental note to adjust his definition of 'chipping in'. 'OK, we may not have handled things exactly as you'd have liked them, but the fact remains we did you a bloody big favour.'

Hoolihan pulled his briefcase to his chest, folded his arms around it and waited for Thorne to continue.

'You'd taken your eye off the ball as far as Grant Freestone was concerned, or given it up as not being worth the effort. Somebody rubber-stamped the review paperwork once a year, but you weren't doing much of anything, as far as I can make out. The fact that you're going to get a nice, fat feather in your cap is down to us. We may not have been as *courteous* as we should have been, but I still think you should be fucking grateful.'

It was the F-word that did it; that caused the colour to rise to Hoolihan's face. Though he pointedly refused to respond to what had been said, it was clear that Thorne would no longer be getting any favours from anyone at Homicide South.

After losing what was only a half-arsed staring contest, Hoolihan turned back to Brigstocke and Hignett. 'It's not like I'll be taking Freestone very far,' he said. 'We'll get him up in front of a magistrate within a day or two, so he'll be on remand somewhere, if you need to speak to him after that.'

There was some shouting once Hoolihan had left, but not too much. Hignett once again showed restraint in his decision not to gloat or say, 'I told you so.'

There were more important things to be discussed.

'We got a preliminary PM report from Phil Hendricks,' Brigstocke said. He picked up a piece of paper from his desk, and read: 'Asphyxia due to suffocation, obviously . . . three broken ribs . . . a broken nose. That's from where he's put his weight on the pillow, Phil reckons . . .'

A second or two of looking at feet, and walls, and a sky that couldn't make its mind up.

'You still think he was after something?' Hignett asked.

'It's a possibility,' Thorne said. 'Porter's going to have a good look through those filing cabinets later. I think she'll be at the mortuary for a while yet.'

'Whatever it was, he obviously wanted it badly.' Brigstocke took a last look at the PM report. 'Or else he's just rattled.'

'Not *too* rattled, I hope,' Hignett said.

Thorne knew what Hignett was saying, the dreadful possibility it would be stupid to ignore. He noted that, yet again, the point had been made without any mention of the boy's name.

The Major Incident Room seemed just a little busier than it had the day before. Conversations were less likely to go round the houses. People moved from desk to desk, from phone to fax machine, with greater urgency. It was not even twelve hours since Kathleen Bristow's body had been discovered, but Thorne knew that unless those doing the chasing were quick enough, murder cases could be away and out of sight long before that. He exchanged quick words with Andy Stone and a couple of the Kidnap boys, then spent a few unwelcome, but necessary, minutes talking admin with DS Samir Karim, who was also office manager. Thorne liked Karim, an overweight, gregarious Asian with a shock of prematurely greying hair and a thick London accent. But the smile that was normally hard to shift was not much in evidence this morning.

'Everything's fucked up,' he said.

Thorne nodded, without really needing to know exactly what Karim was talking about.

Dave Holland seemed as focused as anyone, but up close his eyes betrayed a man who hadn't slept the night before.

'Pissholes in the snow,' he said, 'I know, but still slightly bigger pissholes than yours.'

Thorne looked down at Holland's computer screen: a page from the Borough of Bromley website displaying various contact telephone numbers and email addresses.

'There's an out-of-hours contact service,' Holland said, 'which is fine if a water main bursts or you see someone fly-tipping, but not much use for anything else. I've spoken to a couple of people at home, but I'm not getting anywhere. As far as any records Kathleen Bristow might have kept, I think we'll have to wait until tomorrow morning, talk to someone at social services who's got access to the files. Even then, I'm not sure it'll be a five-minute job.'

'Get hold of the other people who were on the panel with her,' Thorne said. 'Roper and the rest of them . . .'

Holland left the website and quickly accessed the Crime Reporting Information System. CRIS was updated constantly, with every detail of the case to that point logged and catalogued for the entire team. He entered the case number, searched the files, then called up the names and contact details of those on Grant Freestone's MAPPA panel:

*Roper, Warren, Lardner, Stringer, Bristow.*

Holland tapped a finger against the screen. 'I never managed to track Stringer down first time round.'

'See what you can do,' Thorne said.

'Right. It'll be interesting to see how they react to the news about Kathleen Bristow. Maybe one of them can confirm she had the records.'

'Roper thought she probably did,' Thorne said. 'But that's not why I was suggesting it.' He looked at the list on Holland's screen, the cursor blinking beneath the final name. 'While we're still not sure exactly why Kathleen Bristow was killed, it can't hurt to make sure each of the other people on that panel is still walking around.'

Thorne had been in the backyard when they'd eventually brought out the prisoner. He'd been leaning against the van that was waiting to take Freestone south, talking about a recent Spurs–Crystal Palace game to one of the DCs sent to fetch him.

Hoolihan had walked past Thorne without a word and climbed into an unmarked BMW, ready to follow the van down to Lewisham.

Freestone himself had been considerably keener to chat.

'What the fuck's going on?'

'It's time to answer for Sarah Hanley, Grant.'

'I didn't kill her.'

'Keep telling them that,' Thorne said.

'You're a fucking genius . . .'

Freestone was cuffed, an officer on each side marching him purposefully towards the open doors at the back of the van.

Thorne ambled after them. 'I'll give your best to Tony Mullen.'

'You should get him down here,' Freestone said.

'Can't see any point now,' Thorne said. 'He's got nothing to do with the Hanley case.'

'I saw him.'

'*What?*' Thorne picked up his pace. '*When* did you see him?'

But Freestone was already being bundled into the back of the van, and pushed on to a bench between his two escorts. He turned to look at Thorne, but there was no time to register the expression before the doors were slammed shut. The Crystal Palace fan shrugged an apology and walked round to the driver's side.

Thorne took a step back as the van started up. Parked alongside it, Hoolihan raced the BMW's engine; impatient probably, but perhaps also hoping to send a fatal dose of carbon monoxide Thorne's way.

As he walked back in through the cage, Thorne saw Danny Donovan loitering near the custody skipper's platform. A uniformed PC was leading a young woman by the arm. As Thorne approached, he watched Donovan engage the woman in conversation, then hand her something just before she was led towards the cells.

'Still here, Danny?'

'Can't seem to tear myself away.'

'Someone else going to be looking after Freestone now, then? One of those people with qualifications?' Thorne held out a hand. Waited until Donovan handed over one of the business cards he was cradling in his fist. 'Touting for business? You cheeky fucker.'

'What's the problem?'

'The problem for you is that you've run into me. And that *this*' – he held up the thin, cheaply produced card – 'really pisses me off.'

'Fuck's sake.'

'Away you go ...'

Thorne was already moving towards the exit, arms wide, shepherding Donovan in the direction of the metal doorway.

'You want to get out of this game sharpish, Thorne.' Donovan stepped backwards into the cage, half turned as if to leave. 'It's sending you a bit mental.'

Thorne approached Donovan fast, backed him against

400

the side of the cage. 'You really should fuck off now,' he said. 'And next time you're in here, if I so much as see you helping yourself to a teabag, I'll nick you for theft.'

Donovan waited for Thorne to step back. 'Things carry on as they have been, you'll probably be desperate for any sort of result by then.'

When the ex-copper moved to walk past him, Thorne reached out both arms and pushed him hard against the wall. Donovan slammed into the metal, which gave a little, then bounced back, dropping the handful of business cards as he reached out to retain his balance.

There was a shout from inside the custody suite and Thorne yelled back that everything was fine. Donovan squatted and tried to pick up the cards, but Thorne was quicker. Breathing heavily, he slapped away the other man's hand, grabbed as many cards as he could, and threw them, fluttering out into the backyard.

A pair of uniformed beat officers appeared at the doorway on their way into the station. They watched for a few seconds, then stepped around the two men scrabbling around on the floor.

Thorne's heart was still beating faster than normal when Kitson found him in one of the CID offices on the first floor.

'Did you not get my message?' she asked.

Thorne gulped down his tea. It wasn't quite twelve yet, and he was wondering if it was too early to get some lunch. 'Sorry, it's been a pig of a morning.'

'I heard.'

'Actually, the murder scene was a doddle,' Thorne said. 'There wasn't any blood spilled until we got back here.'

Kitson's shoes were new. She kicked them off when she sat down next to Thorne. Began to rub at tender heels and toes through her tights. 'Listen, I've got Adrian Farrell's phone records.'

'Any help?'

'Not yet. But there are plenty of numbers to check out, so we might get lucky. There was something, though. Remember I said I'd look for any connection to Luke Mullen . . . ?'

'What have you got?'

'There was nothing on Farrell's mobile, but when I checked the landline the Mullen number came up. More than once.'

Thorne's heartbeat accelerated even more. 'Why not the mobile? I thought these kids were never off their bloody phones, sending text messages or whatever.'

'He's got a pay-as-you-go, right? But he's also got a phone in his bedroom. I reckon he was just trying to save money. He can use the landline from his room and make private calls whenever he likes on Mum and Dad's bill.'

'When you say *more than once* . . . ?'

'Half a dozen calls in the three weeks before Luke was taken. More before that.'

Thorne sat back, trying to take in what Kitson was saying. 'When Dave talked to the kids at the school, Farrell

402

told him he hardly knew Luke Mullen. He knew he'd gone missing, but that was about it, right?'

'Right, but I don't have to tell you that he's a very good liar.'

'Hang on. Are we sure this was *Adrian* Farrell making the calls? Maybe Mrs Farrell and Luke Mullen's mum both work on the PTA committee or something.'

Kitson shook her head. 'I checked with his mother, and the parents hardly know each other. A few words over coffee at a school concert, nods at the school gates, no more than that.'

'OK . . .'

Thorne's mind, dulled by fatigue and hunger, tossed around possibilities like a tumble dryer on its last legs. Could Luke Mullen's kidnapping be connected with Farrell, or some of Farrell's friends? Was he taken because of something he knew about them? If that were the case, why was the video sent to Luke's parents? And what the hell could any of it have to do with the murder of Kathleen Bristow?

'These are not quick calls either, Tom,' Kitson said. 'Ten, fifteen minutes.'

'What does Farrell say?'

'I haven't gone at him with any of this yet. I wondered if you fancied coming into the bin with me and having a bash yourself.'

Thorne grunted a yes as ideas continued to tumble and tangle.

'One more thing.' Kitson said it as though it were an

afterthought, an irrelevance. 'When you're talking to Farrell, if you could squeeze out the names of the other two who helped him kill Amin Latif, there's half a shandy in it for you.'

They enjoyed the moment, and sat there, and took a minute. Rubbing at sore feet and cradling paper cups of tea, like any other pair of workers on a break. Catching their breaths.

Thorne sensed that it might be their last chance to do so for a while. There had been times, on previous cases, when it had felt as if he were on a collision course with whoever he was trying to catch. As though the speed had increased until in the end it had just been a question of where the crash was going to happen.

This case felt different.

There was the same inevitability, like something rising from the guts into the mouth, the same sense that the end was coming. But it wasn't a question of getting closer, or even of something gaining on *them*.

Thorne simply felt like they were running out of time.

He hadn't meant to hurt the boy.

That didn't excuse the fact that he had; that he'd known his words were like slaps, like punches. But he genuinely hadn't wanted to. Everything was more complicated than that, of course; *and* more simple. It was someone else he wanted to hurt. Someone who would see how much a child they loved had suffered and would feel that pain a thousandfold.

That would make them see sense, wouldn't it? Would make them look at things a little differently.

It had been such a straightforward idea, but from the moment he'd started to put it into practice he'd felt it going away from him. Now he honestly didn't know if things were going to work out as they'd been supposed to. It had all got out of control. *He* was out of control.

But at least he wasn't so far gone that he couldn't recognise what was happening. He was still aware. He'd seen it too many times himself: car accidents on two legs who had ruined lives – their own and those of everyone around them; fuck-ups and hard-luck merchants whose tears were real enough, whose anguish could suck the air out of a room, but who couldn't seem to grasp that it was not an excuse.

*I didn't mean to hurt anyone . . .*

He knew very well that he'd done terrible things. That good intentions counted for nothing with blood on his hands and the noise from the cellar. And that, although he had no idea *how*, it *would* end.

There were bells ringing across the field.

He sat and thought about engineering some sort of resolution himself. If he just opened the door and stood back, things would sort themselves out quickly enough. The boy would run towards the sound of the bells, towards a place where there was a phone, and it would all be over.

But that was hypothetical nonsense, because too much had happened now for everything to finish as simply as

405

that. The slate could no longer be wiped clean. But it felt good to know that he wouldn't be the only one paying the price.

When the bells finally stopped, he could hear the sobbing again. Coming up through the floor: a stutter, a desperate beat; rising every few breaths to something cracked and sore.

He closed his eyes, tried to forget how stupid he'd been, until he could almost believe that what he heard was only the sound of water and rust, and the pipes expanding.

# LUKE

The religious stuff was sort of taken for granted at Butler's Hall. It wasn't a church school, as such, but there were hymns in assembly every day, and, even though it wasn't forced down your throat in RE lessons, the presumption was that anyone whose parents had not stated otherwise was C of E.

He knew that the chaplain would have made speeches. Something about lost sheep, most likely. That teachers would have lined up on stage and bowed their heads, and that prayers would have been said for him every morning.

Now he'd started saying them himself.

He'd been filling his head with all manner of rubbish, trying to force out the stuff he couldn't bear to have in there. Thinking about whatever else he could while the man was talking to him; and later, when it had finished and the man had gone. Sequences of streets and underground stations; rules of games he'd played with Juliet when they were younger; the names of his old soft toys ... *Anything*.

Now God had elbowed His way in there as well.

Neither his mum nor his dad was big on church, save for the odd nativity play or whatever, and Juliet seemed actively drawn to Satanism, if anything. But he'd always liked the basic idea of it, of what it stood for. It was hard to argue that love and compassion were *bad* ideas. And some of the stuff in the Bible stood up OK, as long as you took it as nothing more than a cracking story.

He'd seen a programme on TV once, about why bad things happened to good people; about a bloke who did tons of work for charity then got some horrible disease, and a couple who went to church every five minutes and whose daughter had disappeared. They all said that suffering was part of being a Christian, and that everything they were going through was just a test of their faith. He'd watched it, thinking that they probably *had* to say something like that. He'd decided that if he believed in God, and was ever tested to the same extent, that he'd fail miserably.

But he didn't believe, not really. And anyway, he knew what he was going through was nobody's fault but that of the man on the other side of the cellar door. So a prayer couldn't hurt, could it?

He guessed that the school chaplain might have something to say about praying at the same time as harbouring such violent thoughts; while clutching the carefully prepared means to put those thoughts into practice, if need be. But he also remembered that some of the stories he'd read in the Old Testament made *Grand Theft Auto* look tame. He knew that God had no problem with blood and thunderbolts, and striking down those who deserved it.

Thinking about it, perhaps the most appropriate thing he could ask God for was to be given the chance.

So he prayed for a while, because he knew that's what people did as a last resort. Then he wiped away the tears and the snot. Went back to the distraction of memories and mental gymnastics.

The names of every child in his class, alphabetically, forwards and backwards. Planets and moons. Stars and satellites. His toys.

A dinosaur. A Bugs Bunny. A brown bear named Grizzle ...

# TWENTY

She made it a rule never to look at the faces.

It wasn't about the pain. Porter was used to seeing the rifts and fissures that pain could gouge across a face; she worked with it most days. But there was hope in those faces, too: that the nightmare would soon be over, that she or someone like her would do a good job and bring their loved ones home again. There were times, if that hope were misplaced, when it was terrible to see, but nothing was as dreadful as its absence.

When it came to identifying a body, the hope was often there right until the very last second. Hope that there had been a terrible mistake; that the police had got it wrong; that their wife/husband/child was still alive somewhere. On occasions, of course, when there was a genuine element of doubt as to identity, it was her *job* to look. But not once, even then, had she ever seen that hope rewarded. She'd watched it die and seen it buried in a blink; gone before the breath had been fully caught.

So Louise Porter didn't look any more. She dropped her eyes for that moment when hope was extinguished.

Afterwards, she sat with them on a brown plastic bench near the mortuary entrance. Francis Bristow and his wife had caught the early train from Glasgow. Clutching tight to overnight bags, they looked like bemused tourists who'd taken a wrong turn.

'Have you got anywhere to stay?' Porter asked. 'Any other family?'

Joan Bristow was sitting on the far end. She looked to her husband, who was seated in the middle, then leaned forward slightly to look along at Porter. 'We didn't really know what we'd be doing. How long we'd be here, or anything.'

'I'll see if we can get something sorted out for you,' Porter said.

'We didn't know, you see . . .'

The woman had a smart woollen coat folded across her knees. Next to her, Kathleen Bristow's brother sat stiff-backed, staring straight ahead, as if studying every bump and crack in the primrose-yellow walls. He wore polished brogues and a jacket and tie. His hair was thick, cream-coloured, and his eyes were the same blue as his wife's, wide and watery behind his glasses. He was probably in his early seventies, a few years older than his sister, but it was impossible for Porter to say if there was any family resemblance. She hadn't had a good look at the photographs in

411

the bedroom and she could not compare any living face with the one she'd seen on Kathleen Bristow.

The old man spoke suddenly, as if he'd been able to follow Porter's thoughts. 'I don't understand why there was all that bruising across her nose,' he said. 'All black, like someone had hit her.' The voice was quiet, and the Glaswegian accent strong, so Porter had to listen hard. He began to wave a finger in front of his face, pointing towards it. 'And there was something else going on *here* ... something not right with her mouth.'

The couple had been told how Kathleen Bristow had died and had been warned before the identification that her face was marked. Porter hesitated, unwilling for a variety of reasons to explain to Francis Bristow exactly what had been done to his sister's face during her murder.

Joan Bristow's accent was less pronounced than her husband's. 'They can't tell us that kind of thing, Frank.' She squeezed his hand and looked at Porter. 'Am I not right, love?'

Porter nodded, grateful for the escape route, and stared at the finger, which still circled slowly in front of the man's face. 'What I was saying about family? We called you first because you were the one who reported her missing. We're presuming there were no children ...'

'No children,' Bristow said.

The words were then spoken a third time by his wife. She shook her head and talked softly, as if this were another, smaller tragedy. 'Kath was never married, you see? She lived with a "friend" for many years.' She looked at Porter, in case the understated inverted commas she'd put around the word 'friend' had not been obvious enough.

Porter had understood perfectly well. 'Right, well, maybe we can get those details from you later, if you'd like us to inform this friend of hers.'

'I don't think we've got them, to tell you the truth.'

'Kath kept herself to herself,' the old man added. 'She was very private about things.' He picked at something on his lapel, remembering. 'She'd come home once a year or so; or maybe we'd get the train down here for the week-end.'

'It's hard when you live so far away,' Porter said.

'Right enough. But still, there were things we didn't really talk about, you know?'

'Shush, don't think about all that now, love.'

'Bloody stupid, when you stop and think about it.'

'Spent all her time at work getting involved in other people's lives and kept her own very quiet, you see?' Joan Bristow leaned close to her husband, trying hard to elicit something like a smile, concern for him bleeding through the powder and thick foundation.

They sat and watched a woman with an electric floor-polisher; listened to the vague buzz of a one-way phone conversation, and, incongruously, to gales of laughter coming from a room down the corridor. Porter opened her mouth, desperate to say something and disguise the noise, but Joan beat her to it.

413

'Was it one of those nutters, then?' she asked. There was a pained expression on her face, and pity in her voice. 'One of them as gets released from somewhere when they're still poorly. You read about that sort of thing all the time.'

'It's too early to say.'

'Kath dealt with her fair share of headcases over the years. Could it have been one of them, d'you think?'

Genuinely, Porter had no idea. Whoever had murdered Kathleen Bristow and the others was certainly a headcase, as far as she was concerned, though others would determine later whether he was suffering from an 'abnormality of mind'. She found the procedures for deciding such things bizarre to say the least. A solicitor had once tried to explain the rules for establishing mental competence by telling her that if a man threw a baby on to a fire believing it to be a log then he was insane and could not be criminally responsible. This, according to the law, would not be the case if he threw the baby on to the fire knowing it was a baby. Porter had found this preposterous, and had said so. To her mind, the man who knew the baby was a baby was *more* insane; was obviously as mad as a box of frogs. The solicitor had merely smiled, as though that was exactly what made the whole issue so complex ... and so fascinating.

She remembered what the probation officer, Peter Lardner, had said about intent. If *that* were a grey area, then diminished responsibility came in a thousand different shades.

'You've still got to ask why, though, haven't you?' Bristow said.

414

'What's the point, love? It's bad luck, that's all it is.'

The old man shook his head. His voice was suddenly thin, and falling away. 'Whether he's a nutter or no, you still want to know what was going on inside his head.' He rubbed a hand across his chin, rasping against the silvery stubble. 'What made him choose our Kathleen.'

Porter didn't look at their faces when they saw the body, and she didn't make speeches. She said no more than she had to. She told Francis Bristow that, as things stood, they were all wrestling with that question, but she would do her very best for them, and keep them informed.

She also made a promise to herself; the sort of promise the likes of Tom Thorne made, broke and lived with.

Getting Luke Mullen back remained her first priority, of course. When there was still a life to be saved, that was a given. But however the kidnap investigation turned out, she would do whatever she could to give the man sitting next to her a definitive answer. She would tell him *exactly* why his sister had died, and she would find that out from the man responsible.

Porter was just about to start making noises about needing to get on and making sure that someone would be along to take care of them when she felt the hand slip into hers. When she looked, Francis Bristow was staring straight ahead again, blinking away the tears.

She followed his gaze, and all three of them sat and looked at the woman with the floor-polisher for a while.

\*

415

'DC Holland?'

'Speaking . . .'

'DCI Roper at Special Enquiries. You left a message.'

Holland put down the sandwich, 'That's right,' took a swig from a bottle of water to clear his mouth out. 'Thanks for getting back to me so quickly, sir.'

'I've only got five minutes.'

'We just wanted to let you know that the body of Kathleen Bristow was discovered in the early hours of this morning.'

The pause might just have been the time it took Roper to recall the name. Holland couldn't know for sure.

'Poor woman,' Roper said, finally. 'Christ . . .'

'She was murdered, sir.'

Another pause. This one definitely for effect. 'Well, I hardly thought you'd be calling to let me know that she'd popped off peacefully in front of *The Antiques Roadshow*.'

'Right.'

'How was she killed?'

'Someone broke in and suffocated her.'

'Nice.'

'It looks like she held on to a lot of records,' Holland said. 'Filing cabinets full of stuff from her old cases and what have you.' Holland took another small bite of his sandwich while he was waiting for a response. He could hear classical music playing softly from another room.

'So you think this is connected to your kidnap, do you? To Grant Freestone? To Sarah Hanley, maybe?'

'We're keeping an open mind at the moment.'

416

'And you just called to keep me informed, did you?'

'Sir . . . ?'

With the music in the background, it was like being put on hold.

'Not even going to tell me to make sure my doors and windows are locked?'

'I would've presumed you'd do that anyway, sir,' Holland said.


'Present for you . . .' Thorne dropped the plastic bag on to the table in front of Adrian Farrell.

'Your twenty-four's up in a little over ninety minutes,' Wilson said.

Kitson glanced up at the clock. 'At four thirty-eight.'

Farrell looked weary, suspicious. He reached forward and dragged the bag towards him as Thorne and Kitson took their seats.

'As it happens, I've already spoken to my superintendent,' Kitson said. 'Assured him I'm carrying out my duties in regard to this case diligently and expeditiously . . .'

The solicitor made a winding gesture with his finger, urging her to get on with it.

'Basically, I've got a six-hour extension.' She smiled at Farrell. 'He's here until twenty to eleven, if I fancy it.'

Farrell's face darkened as he pulled out the contents of the bag.

'Don't say we never do anything for you,' Thorne said.

The boy pushed Thorne's 'present' back across the table. 'You're hysterical.'

Thorne picked up one of the cheap, black plimsolls and examined it. Each had had a Nike-style tick drawn on the side in Tippex. 'Suit yourself.' He put the shoes back in the bag.

The interview room was one that had recently been upgraded to CD-ROM. Kitson unwrapped and loaded the fresh discs, made the speech and began the recording.

Thorne didn't waste any more time. 'How well do you know Luke Mullen?' he asked.

Farrell appeared to be genuinely confused. 'The kid who disappeared?'

'You told officers that you barely knew him when they spoke to you at your school.'

'So what are you asking me again for?'

'Well, let's just say that as you haven't been entirely honest with us about other matters, we're thinking that you may have been full of shit about this as well.'

Farrell was chewing gum. He held it between his top and bottom teeth, pushed at it with his tongue.

'This is relevant to your murder enquiry, is it?' Wilson looked at Kitson. 'I certainly hope so.'

'Perhaps you know him a little better than you told us you did,' Thorne said.

Wilson began writing in his notebook. 'I think it might be best to say nothing, Adrian.'

Farrell lifted a hand. He pushed a comb of stiff fingers through his hair and began tugging strands up into spikes. 'It's fine,' he said. 'He was the year below me, so we never had much to do with each other. We weren't in any teams together; not even in the same house. Maybe exchanged a word in the playground, but that's about it.'

'You never phoned him at home?'

'*No.*' He looked horrified, as if he'd been accused of something terminally uncool.

'You might want to think about this, Adrian.'

It looked as though Farrell were doing exactly what Thorne had advised. He blinked and fidgeted, and though the expression stayed defiant, there was much less confidence in his voice when he spoke again. 'Maybe I called him once or twice, yeah.'

'Why would you do that?'

'He was a clever kid, wasn't he? Maybe I just needed a bit of help with some homework, or something.'

'I thought *you* were a clever kid.'

'It was just once or twice.'

Kitson took the printed phone logs from her bag, traced a finger down to the items marked with a highlighter, and read: 'November 23rd, last year: 8.17 until 8.44 p.m; November 30th: 9.05 until 9.22. January 14th this year, February 12th. Then a call lasting nearly an hour on February the seventeenth ...'

'You must have needed a lot of help,' Thorne said.

Farrell's expression started to catch up with his voice. He leaned away from the table, reddening, the desperate smile looking ready to slide off his face at any moment. 'This is bollocks,' he said. He turned to Wilson. 'I'm not saying anything else.'

'It seems a very odd thing to lie about, that's all.'

Farrell studied the tabletop.

Thorne glanced at Kitson and understood at once from her expression that this was as rattled as she'd ever seen Adrian Farrell.

'Maybe we'll come back to that,' Thorne said. 'We wouldn't want Mr Wilson saying that we bullied you.'

Wilson just sat back and clicked the top of his expensive ballpoint.

'Is there much bullying at your school?' Thorne asked. He didn't wait long for an answer. It was already clear he would be having a more-or-less one-sided conversation. 'There's always *some*, isn't there? Can't get rid of it completely, because one or two kids are never going to like themselves very much.

'They reckon that's why bullies do it, don't they? Because of how they feel about themselves. Same for those who take it outside school, if you ask me. The ones who try and make themselves feel better by giving people a kicking on the street. The ones who attack complete strangers because they've been looked at the wrong way or imagine they've been "disrespected"; who maim, or cripple, or kill someone for no other reason than they're black, or gay, or wearing the wrong kind of shoes. Then tell themselves they're being honourable by refusing to grass anyone up when they get caught.'

'Just tell us their names,' Kitson said. 'Tell us and we can stop all this pissing about.'

'The thing is, I can even understand it, up to a point,'

Thorne said. 'You can call these crimes "wicked' or "evil" or whatever you want, but it usually comes down to plain ignorance in the end, and none of us is immune to that, right? There's a *scale*, though, isn't there?' He traced a line along the tabletop with his finger. 'I think I'm tolerant, of course I do. *Most* of us do. But every now and again stuff comes into my head I wouldn't dream of saying out loud. I don't know where it's come from, how it got in there, but I'd be a liar if I didn't put my hand up to it. I'd never *do* anything, and I think the people who perpetrate these crimes are shit, scum, whatever ... but I know *why* it happens. I understand that they're just more ignorant than I am.'

He paused for a few seconds. Watched the red numbers change on the digital clock above the door.

*43 ... 44 ... 45 ...*

'What happened to Amin Latif, though?' Thorne shook his head. 'That's about something else. It's got to be. I'm not even sure I want to understand why anyone could do that. The first bit's not too hard to fathom: it's the sort of thing I've just been talking about. It's ignorance, and trying to make yourself feel better, plain and simple. Amin and his friend are standing at that bus stop and not looking away when you and your mates try to stare them down. *Saying* something maybe. So they get a kicking, right? Or at least Amin does, because his friend manages to get away, which leaves three against one. Good odds for hard men like you and your mates, right?'

421

Farrell was bent forward in his chair. He mumbled something. His hands were fists, hanging at his sides.

Kitson leaned in, her head low, trying to catch Farrell's eye. 'Just the names, Adrian. Get it over with.'

'You're not a virgin, are you?' Another rhetorical question. Thorne cracked on immediately. 'Christ, I *presume* you're not; not at seventeen. You know what sex is *supposed* to be about, right? Love, in an ideal world, course it is. Lust, more often than not, if we're being honest. And habit, and booze, and boredom now and again ... But what happened to Amin Latif wasn't any of those things, was it?'

*36 ... 37 ... 38 ...*

'Let's imagine for a minute that you weren't there that night, in the rain, at that bus stop. I'll tell you what happened, what we *know* happened from Nabeel Khan's statement and from the other evidence. I'll tell you, and you tell me if you've got any idea at all what it was about. OK? You see, the job's done, that's the strange thing. The Paki bastard's half-dead in the gutter, right, so why don't the three of them just piss off? Maybe one or two of them are ready to go, but someone else is calling the shots and he's got other ideas. He really wants to teach the cheeky fucker a lesson. So he drags him back on to the pavement and turns him over on to his belly. He undoes Amin Latif's belt and pulls down his jeans. Are you following this OK?'

Farrell's breathing was heavier, *wetter* ...

'Then he pulls down his own trousers, and pants, and

422

by this time I'm guessing that his two mates have backed right off. They want nothing to do with any of *this*. Maybe they're shouting at him to leave it, telling him he's a fucking perv, but he doesn't care by this point. He's not thinking about anything else. He's got carried away and he's already getting his tiny little dick out ... He's already dropping down to his knees ...'

'You're being stupid for no reason ...' Kitson said.

'Trying to stick it into Amin Latif.'

'If we pull in Damien Herbert and Michael Nelson, and it turns out to be them, they're going to think it was down to you anyway.'

*12 ... 13 ... 14 ...*

'But the Paki bastard – which was how he was described during the initial attack – he puts up a fight. At this point, all he's got are a couple of broken bones. At *this* point, the shitbag kneeling behind him can walk away and be looking at a lot less than life imprisonment. But he chooses not to. And Amin Latif makes his own choice: he struggles, and refuses to raise his arse up off the pavement; refuses to submit to this animal who's trying to rape him, who's trying to prove how much of a man he is. So the animal eventually gives up. He gets back to his feet and takes hold of himself. And, while his mates laugh, he masturbates. And even before he's finished coming, he's begun kicking his victim in the side and in the head, and he doesn't stop until Amin Latif is completely still. Lying in the gutter. Covered in rain and blood and cum ...'

When Farrell looked up suddenly, it was clear that he'd

423

been crying for a while without making any sound. The neck of his sweatshirt was already darkened with tears. The sobs exploded from him as he began to curse and thrash in his chair like someone burning. He called them bitches and cunts, and pulled away violently when Wilson reached over and tried to put a hand on his arm.

Neither Kitson nor Thorne could be sure if the hatred was aimed solely at them; for what was happening, for the state they'd reduced him to. The tears that flew off his face as he jerked and spat out his insults certainly pointed to something aimed at least partly at himself, for what he'd done.

For what he *was*.

Kitson had to raise her voice to terminate the interview.

Farrell was still swearing, hoarse and red-faced, when they sealed up the discs and called the jailer into the room.

It was pleasant enough for people to be enjoying a late afternoon pint outside the Oak, or pottering in the tiny front gardens of the estate next door.

Thorne and Kitson made their way back towards the Peel Centre, in silence for the first couple of minutes. Thorne could see that Kitson was smarting at the continued failure to get the names she was after. He, too, was thinking about the extreme manner in which the interview had ended, but also about the boy's even stranger reaction to being questioned about the calls to Luke Mullen.

'Where does all that come from?' Kitson asked. 'What he did to Latif. What he tried to do.'

'You thinking he might have been abused?'

'I don't know. You just look for something that makes sense, don't you?'

'What about the father?'

'I didn't exactly take to him, but I wouldn't know beyond that.'

They crossed the road, taking out IDs as they approached the security barrier.

'What you said in the interview, about stuff in your head.' Kitson looked at him. 'Were you just making that up?'

'I suppose so, yeah, for the most part. But none of us are saints, are we?' He showed his card and walked on. 'If I see someone with a scar on his face, I think about where he might have got it, and I tell myself he's probably aggressive, violent. I never see him as a victim. Is that really any different from a woman seeing a young black man coming towards her at night and worrying that he's going to mug her?'

'The job makes you see the worst in people,' Kitson said.

'It's still a sort of prejudice though, right?'

They stopped for a few seconds before they walked into Becke House, watched a group of recruits in gym kit kicking a ball around on the sports field. All of them full of piss and vinegar. All up for it.

He caught Porter in her car, on her way back to the Bristow murder scene in Shepherd's Bush.

'Hang on, I'm not hands-free ...'

Thorne could hear a siren. He guessed that she'd lowered the phone, knowing that to nick a DI for driving without due care and attention would make the average uniformed copper's afternoon.

'Right, I'm all yours again.'

He told her about the interview with Adrian Farrell, about the boy's cagey response when he'd been confronted with the phone records. 'It was cock and bull,' Thorne said. 'I just wish I had a fucking clue what any of it means.'

Porter said something, but the signal broke up and Thorne caught only fragments. He asked her to say it again.

'Maybe it wasn't Luke he was calling.'

'We already looked at the parents—'

'What if the racist thing runs in the family? Maybe Tony Mullen's a closet BNP member and Farrell's old man is calling him up to organise meetings or whatever.'

'Kitson checked. They hardly know each other.'

'He might have been calling the sister, of course: Juliet.'

Thorne sat a little straighter at his desk. They hadn't considered that. 'OK ... but why would he bother lying about it? He's been cocky as fuck about being accused of murder, even now he must know we've got him. Why react like he did in the bin? Why start making shit up, just to avoid us finding out he's seeing Juliet Mullen?'

'Because she's fourteen,' Porter said. 'If he's having sex with her, that's *exactly* how he would react. It's a machismo thing, about respect or whatever. If he gets sent down for the Latif murder, he goes down all guns blazing, doesn't he? He keeps quiet, he's a hero to his mates, to the other idiots who think the same way he does. Sleeping with an underage girl doesn't exactly fit in with that image.'

There was a twisted logic that made as much sense as anything else in the case so far. Thorne told Porter that he'd talk to Juliet Mullen. Porter suggested that he do so in person, so he said that he'd try to get over to the Mullen place later on. Then he asked her what she was going to be doing, if they would see each other.

'I'm not sure how long I'm going to be at Kathleen Bristow's. I'm hoping SOCO will be about done, and I want to have a good go at those filing cabinets. Maybe what's in there can give us a clue about what might have been taken.'

'How did it go with the brother and his wife?'

It took no more than the sigh and the traffic noise, a second or two of the pause before she began to answer, for Thorne to realise that he'd asked cleverer questions.

# TWENTY-ONE

A makeshift stage had been set up in his old man's front room.

Sitting on the solitary chair, Thorne could hear the voices from behind the hastily rigged-up curtain, as his father and his father's friend Victor got themselves ready. Thorne glanced over at his mum's old clock on the mantelpiece. He needed to get back to work and didn't really have time for this.

'Are you going to be much longer?'

His father yelled back from behind the curtain, 'Keep your fucking wig on!'

Thorne froze as he saw the smoke curling underneath the thick, black material. He got up and ran for the curtain, but found himself unable to reach it. He clawed at fresh air and shouted to his father on the other side, screaming at him to get out.

'Relax,' his father said. 'Sit down. We'll be ready in a minute.'

'There's smoke . . .'

'No, there fucking isn't.'

'Stop swearing.'

'I can't fucking help it.'

The curtain rose and Thorne fell back in his chair as his father and Victor stepped forward through waist-high dry ice.

Jim Thorne grinned and winked. 'Told you it wasn't smoke, you big cock!'

The show itself wasn't bad.

Victor walked across to a piano and started to play. Thorne's father began to sing, but the cheesy rendition of 'Memories' fell apart when he forgot the words almost straight away, mugging furiously as he gave it up as a waste of time. Then they went into the patter . . .

'Do you know they've spent more money on developing Viagra than they have on research into Alzheimer's?'

'That's terrible,' Victor said.

'You're telling me. I'm walking around with a permanent stiffy and I can't remember what I'm supposed to do with it!'

Then more of the same. All the usual jokes, reeled off one after the other, with Victor playing straight man and cheerily feeding the set-ups to his old friend. Stuff from Thorne's father about how Alzheimer's wasn't *all* bad: how at least he never had to watch repeats on TV, and how he could hide his own Easter eggs, and how he was always meeting new friends.

'As long as you don't forget your old ones,' Victor said.

'Of course not.' Beat. Look. 'Who are you again?'

Thorne enjoyed every minute of it, thrilled to see his father so happy. He forgot about the time and about the work he should be doing as those expressions of loss and confusion he had always dreaded seeing were transformed into something comical, as his father stared out at him in *mock*-bewilderment, his eyes bright.

Thorne laughed, and applauded another badly timed gag. The noise of his clapping faded on cue as his father turned to Victor and stage-whispered from the side of his mouth: 'I'm killing 'em.'

'You're on fire, Jim.'

'Too bloody true I am!'

Thorne whistled as the old man turned, revealing the elaborate and colourful flame design that had been embroidered on to the back of his jacket. He stamped his feet as Jim Thorne began to dance, as he moved his hips and rolled his shoulders, so the flames appeared to be climbing slowly up his back.

'Dad ...'

His father turned to look at him. 'Don't panic, Son. It's not what it looks like.'

But, suddenly, Thorne knew that the flames were real; that they were burning through his father's polyester suit and eating away at the flesh beneath.

He could smell exactly how real it was.

He reached across to slam down the large red button by the side of his chair and a bell began to ring; deafeningly loud, but fading, just as his applause had done, each time his father said something.

'That is *so* rude.'

'What is?' Victor asked.

'Fancy not turning off your mobile phone during a show!'

Thorne's hands were over his ears. He couldn't hear himself screaming at his father to shut up and get out, or begging Victor for help.

'Bloody funny-sounding ice-cream van,' Jim Thorne said.

'It's a fire alarm, you stupid old bastard.'

'Don't jump to conclusions.'

'We need to leave now. It's a fire alarm.'

His father's smile was visible in flashes through the crown of flames. The mischief in his voice was clearly audible above the spatter, and the crackle of burning hair.

'Is it, Tom? Are you sure?'

Thorne lifted his head and reached for the phone, wiped away the string of drool that hung between his cheek and the desktop.

'Were you *asleep*?'

'No ...'

'You're such a shit liar,' Hendricks said. He recognised something in Thorne's tone, or in the silence. 'Same dream?'

Thorne sat up straight, then rose slowly to his feet. 'More or less,' he said. He groaned, rolling his head around. His back was complaining and he felt as if someone had been standing on his neck.

'I wish *I* had time to take naps,' Hendricks said.

'It's been a very long day.'

'For you and me both, mate.'

'Yeah, sorry. I almost forgot you were there this morning.'

'Trust me, I'd rather not have been. There's times I wish I'd never gone into medicine. When I think I should have listened to my parents and studied hard to be a ballerina, like they wanted.'

Spoken in Hendricks' flat, Mancunian accent, such comments rarely failed to improve Thorne's mood. The dream was already fading, though the *smell* was still strong enough . . .

'No surprises on the PM?'

'None at all in terms of cause of death. I found a large tumour in Kathleen Bristow's stomach, though. I've no idea if she even knew about it.'

The woman was dead, so there was no real reason for Thorne to find this as depressing as he did.

'What time d'you think you might be getting away?' Hendricks asked.

Thorne looked at his watch. It was nearly half past seven. He'd slept for around half an hour, but it had been light outside when he'd closed his eyes and now it was starting to get dark. He'd check with Brigstocke, but bearing in mind he'd racked up back-to-back eighteen-hour shifts, he didn't think there'd be much objection to him heading off. 'I've got to shoot up to Arkley, but that shouldn't take too long. Home by nine-thirty, ten o'clock, I would have thought.'

'Fancy a late one in the Prince? Couple of games of pool?'

Thorne still didn't know if he'd be seeing Porter later, but he reckoned Hendricks wouldn't mind being stood up if it came to it. 'Yeah, why not? I won't sleep much anyway . . .'

'As long as you don't use the bad back as an excuse when I thrash you. Fiver a frame?'

The door opened, and Yvonne Kitson marched across to her desk with a face that said she was an inch from chucking it all in. She dropped her bag, switched on the light, then walked over and leaned against the wall. She looked like she wanted to talk; like she wanted Thorne to know about it.

'I'd better go, Phil. I'll call when I'm nearly home.'

'Right. See you later.'

'Everything OK?'

'Yeah, I'm great,' Hendricks said.

As a liar, he was no better than Thorne.

'You're getting far too worked up about this whole case, because you think you fucked it up last time,' Thorne said as he replaced the receiver.

'Wrong,' Kitson said.

'Which bit?'

'I *know* I fucked it up last time.'

Kitson was wired; pacing the small office as though she couldn't decide whether she'd prefer a shoulder to cry on or a face to punch.

'You'll get the other two,' Thorne said. 'You *will*. If Farrell won't cough, you'll just have to do it the hard way, that's all.'

She stopped, looked hard at him, as though he hadn't heard a word. 'I really *want* these two, Tom. I know Farrell killed him, but the others just stood there and watched him do it. The CPS are telling me they can stick all three of the fuckers in the dock for murder. It might get knocked down to GBH in court, but we can have a bloody good try.'

'So bring in Farrell's mates, Nelson and Herbert, like you told him you would. It's probably them anyway.'

'I've had another idea,' Kitson said.

'If it's early retirement, I might join you.'

'I fancy stopping the clock, bailing Farrell to return tomorrow. We could get some surveillance organised and see if he gets in touch with anybody. He just might contact the other two to let them know he hasn't said anything.'

Thorne thought it sounded like a reasonable enough idea and told her so. Then he repeated himself, as he wasn't sure she'd believed him the first time. 'You've done a good job on this, Yvonne.'

'I went round to see Amin Latif's parents,' she said, 'to tell them about Farrell.'

'I bet that felt good.'

434

'I didn't tell them how we found him.' Shame and resignation passed across her face in quick succession. 'That we should have found him six months ago. I know it'll come out and we'll have to deal with it then, but sitting there with Mrs Latif in her living room, I didn't want to spoil that moment. For them, I mean. Really, for *them*.'

Thorne just nodded, and straightened one or two things on his desk.

'I'd better go and talk to Brigstocke about setting up the surveillance.' She started towards the door. 'Getting the bail paperwork together ...'

After Kitson had gone, Thorne watched as rain fell through the darkness. He was grateful for a minute or two alone; for the chance to let what was left of his father's performance roll around in his head for a while.

*Don't panic, Son. It's not what it looks like.*

Smoke that wasn't smoke, and a fire alarm that was really a telephone.

*Don't jump to conclusions.*

He walked to the doorway of his office, from where he could see Kitson talking to Karim and Stone in the Major Incident Room. As he watched, an idea sparked and flared, took hold as quickly as flames on polyester.

His father's face was smothered in red and gold as Thorne stepped out into the corridor.

'I'm afraid I'm not at liberty to say how she died, sir.'

'Don't you think that's a bit ridiculous?' Lardner asked. 'You call to tell me a woman's been murdered, but then I

435

have to sit here wondering if she was shot, stabbed or drowned in the bath.'

'It's probably a *bit* ridiculous, yeah,' Holland said. 'But that is the procedure, so . . . '

'She was a nice enough woman, as far as I can remember. Fond of sticking her nose in a bit, but I suppose that went with her job. Like journalists drinking . . . or coppers and probation officers being cynical.'

Holland sipped his tea and grunted.

'Right, well, not a lot else to say, I suppose.'

'We were just concerned that you should know about Mrs Bristow's death.'

'Should *I* be?'

'Sorry?'

'*Concerned*. Are we being targeted, do you think?' Lardner barked a humourless laugh. 'Perhaps Grant Freestone's come back out of hiding and is going to slaughter us all one by one.'

'I don't think you need to be concerned about *that* . . . '

With lunch having been just as piss-poor as Kitson had promised it would be, Wilson had scuttled away to dinner as soon as he was informed that Farrell was being bailed, having agreed to meet his client back at the station the following day.

Kitson stood with Farrell in front of the platform as the custody skipper took him through the release procedure. The sergeant was a wily old sod, and he'd looked sideways at Kitson when she'd presented herself and Farrell, being well aware that she'd been ready to charge the boy a few hours earlier. He knew she was up to something, but knew enough to keep it to himself.

After first checking the next day's 'Bailed to Return' schedule, Farrell was informed that bail had been authorised conditional upon his return at four o'clock the next afternoon. That he was being released into the custody of his parents.

Farrell seemed to have recovered himself, to have put what happened in the interview room behind him. He just nodded each time he was asked if he understood what was being said to him. Then he asked again when they were going to return his three-figure Nikes.

'You should shut your mouth before we change our minds,' the custody sergeant said.

Farrell signed for the return of the property that *was* handed back to him. He made a great deal of slipping on his designer watch and checking there was nothing missing from his wallet. Then he signed to confirm that he'd been shown his custody record and that it was complete and accurate. He signed the release form and the declaration that he fully intended to return at the specified time.

'I presume you'll be keeping an eye on me,' Farrell said.

Kitson said nothing, just glanced up from her paperwork.

'You must think I'm stupid.'

'I know you're not,' Kitson said.

'You know *nothing* about me.' Farrell turned his face from hers, concentrated on finishing the procedure.

'These copies are for you to keep.'

Farrell took a sheaf of papers from the custody sergeant.

'Shall we phone your mum and dad? Get them to come and fetch you?'

Farrell looked away and shook his head, snorted like it was a ridiculous idea.

'Right, I'll call you a cab. Be a couple of minutes. If you haven't got enough cash, they can take it from your parents at the other end. Will that be a problem?'

'I think they'll manage ...'

As the sergeant picked up the phone, Kitson thanked him for his help. He nodded, a look on his face like he hoped she knew what she was doing. Kitson escorted Farrell out of the custody suite, and led him through the station towards the main entrance.

She briefed the officer on the front desk before she left Farrell to wait for his taxi. She swiped her pass and yanked open the door to go back in. Then she turned back to Farrell. 'You're sure there isn't anything you'd like to tell me before you leave?'

Farrell's smile was still engaging enough, but his eyes were slits. 'Nothing you'd want to hear,' he said.

When Kitson had gone, Farrell took a step towards the automatic doors, which opened as he approached. The desk officer suggested that he should wait inside. Pointed out that it was pissing down. Told him he could suit his fucking self when Farrell said he'd rather get wet.

Outside, Farrell stood beneath the overhang and stared out at the road.

It hadn't been much more than a day, but it felt like a lot longer: like ten years' worth of change, of major fucking upheaval. And he knew that it hadn't really started yet.

His mind and his heart were racing, but he knew he needed to stay calm, that he should breeze back through the door as though nothing had happened. Despite the way he'd played it with the twat on the custody desk, he wanted to get home and see his mum and dad more than anything. He wanted to be back where it was warm and safe, and where he knew that, whatever happened, there was only ever one side they were going to be on.

He stared through the rain. Still able to recall the taste of it as he and the others had walked towards that bus stop six months before. It had been a little colder than this, maybe, but otherwise exactly the same sort of night . . .

A dark Cavalier drew up and a thickset Asian man climbed out, leaving the engine running.

'Minicab?' Farrell shouted.

The man turned back towards the car.

Adrian Farrell pulled up his hood and jogged after him.

# TWENTY-TWO

'Sunday's a pretty busy day round here,' Neil Warren said. 'It's changeover day, so it's always a bit bloody frantic if there are new tenants coming in or anyone going out. Plus I've got family business and church stuff, and I organise a small service here in the house for anyone who's interested ...'

'It's really not a problem,' Holland said. There was a block of multicoloured Post-its on his desk. He scratched a tick next to Neil Warren's name.

'I just wanted to explain why I hadn't returned your call sooner.'

'I understand.'

'Now, of course, I feel fucking dreadful.'

'I'm sorry,' Holland said.

'You meet people, they drift into your orbit, and then ... life moves on, you know? You go in different directions or whatever, and most of the time you never give them another thought. Kathleen Bristow hadn't crossed my mind in five years until you came round here talking about Grant Freestone, and now she's dead. And I think I should probably feel more upset than I do ...'

'Like you said, you hadn't thought about her in a long time.'

'I'll ask people here to remember her in their prayers.'

Holland looked at his watch: it was five past nine. Once this was done with, he'd see about getting away. Chloe would be in bed, but it would be good to have an hour or so with Sophie before one or both of them flaked out.

'I take it you don't think it's a coincidence,' Warren said.

'Sir?'

'That you start asking people about what happened back then, about Freestone and all that, and someone on the panel gets killed.'

'I think it's probably unlikely.'

'Have you spoken to the others?'

'Most of them, yes.'

Warren said nothing for ten or fifteen seconds. When Holland heard the click of a lighter, he guessed that Warren had been rolling a cigarette. There was a long exhalation, another pause. Then Warren said, 'Did she suffer very much?'

Holland would normally have said something pat, something reassuring, at this point. Beyond knowing that Warren was plain-speaking himself, that he didn't seem enamoured of bullshit, Holland couldn't really say where his answer came from.

'Yes,' he said. 'I think she probably did.'

It was only twenty minutes from Hendon to Arkley. Half a dozen Gram and Emmylou tracks had done wonders for Thorne's mood, but all their sterling work was undone with one glance at Tony Mullen's face.

After their last encounter, Thorne hadn't been anticipating the warmest of welcomes, but there was more to this than a predictable antipathy. There was resignation in the man's expression, and in his posture as he stood aside to let Thorne in without a word. Tony Mullen looked like a man who was no longer expecting good news.

As a parent, there would always be hope until there was a body to bury, but as an ex-police officer, Thorne knew that Mullen would be painfully aware of how the timescales worked. How quickly realistic chances became slim ones. How quickly they faded away to nothing.

It was now nine days since Luke had first gone missing; almost five since the video had been sent; seventy-two hours since Luke had been taken a second time, without word of any kind from whoever was holding him.

Thorne could still see rage in Mullen's eyes, but there was next to no fight left in him.

'Whatever you want, I hope it's quick,' Mullen said. 'We're all tired.'

'Actually, I've come to have a word with Juliet.'

'Why?'

Thorne took a second and decided it couldn't hurt; that it might even build a bridge or two. 'We've been talking to a boy from Butler's Hall about a completely different case. It's almost certainly unconnected with this one. With Luke . . . '

'*Almost* certainly?'

'We think he's lying about knowing Luke, for some reason. We know he phoned here on several occasions and we want to make doubly sure it was Luke he was calling. I just came to check that he wasn't calling your daughter. I don't think I'll be more than ten minutes.'

'What's this boy's name?'

Thorne took a little longer this time. 'Farrell.'

There was no obvious reaction, but Thorne wondered if he'd seen a flicker of something before Mullen turned his head, looked away and spoke to his wife.

Thorne hadn't noticed Maggie Mullen. She was sitting ten or so feet above them at the top of the stairs, on a small landing before further flights curved up to the second and third floors. She was wearing dark tracksuit bottoms and a brown sweater. Her hair was tied back, much of it the same grey as her face, and as the cigarette ash that Thorne presumed filled the saucer between her feet.

'You'd better give Jules a call,' Mullen said.

His wife stared, as though she hadn't heard him, then glanced at Thorne. He smiled and nodded. Both gestures were small and both felt slightly patronising even as he made them; as though he were reassuring someone very old or very sick.

'Has she done something wrong?'

'No, nothing like that,' Thorne said. 'It'll just be a couple of questions.'

Mullen stepped past Thorne, leaned against the banister at the foot of the stairs. 'Just give her a shout, will you, love?'

Maggie Mullen picked up the saucer and got to her feet. She brushed a few stray ashes from her lap, turned and walked up and out of sight towards Juliet's room. After half a minute, Thorne heard the faintest of knocks, then a muffled exchange, one voice raised above the other. He heard a door shut and the tread of four feet moving down the stairs.

As he waited in the hall, Thorne studied the family photographs on a table by the front door, then looked at the wallpaper instead when he became uncomfortable. Next to him, he heard Mullen's head bump gently against the wall as he let his head drop back; heard him say, 'fuck' quietly, to no one in particular.

Farrell presumed that the cab firm had been given the address by the custody sergeant when the car had been booked. The driver certainly seemed to know where he was going. The miserable bastard said nothing as they drove, but that suited Farrell well enough. He didn't want to chat. He wanted to close his eyes and gather his thoughts.

He leaned his head against the window and listened to the rain slapping on the roof and to the squeak of the wipers. It stank of oil in the back, and one of those pine air-fresheners shaped like a tree. Piece of shit probably didn't even have insurance; the Asians always tried to avoid paying anything if they thought they could get away with it. It was like the joke a few of them had about the Asian kids at school. They used to say that their dads were the ones who owned chains of newsagents', and posh curry houses, but still went to the headmaster's office to try and haggle over the fees . . .

When the car pulled over, Farrell thought that he must have nodded off and slept through most of the journey. It seemed like only five minutes since they'd driven away from the station.

A door opened on either side of him. When they'd closed again, he was sitting between two Asian men.

'What the fuck's going on?' But even as he was asking the question, the answer was settling in his stomach and starting to boil.

They didn't speak to him.

They didn't look at him, or at each other.

The driver flicked his indicator up and eased slowly into the stream of traffic. He turned on the radio, tuned it into a bhangra station. Moved ahead nice and steadily.

Farrell was still pretty certain that the police had bailed him just so they could watch him for a while; see if he got in touch with either of the others. Wedged tight between the men on either side, he wasn't able to turn round fully, but he craned his neck as much as he could, desperately hoping that he might be proved right and see a panda behind them. But all he saw was rain, anonymous head-lights, and, when he turned round again, the eyes of the driver in the rear-view mirror. They were cold and flat, and yellowed for a second as the Cavalier passed below a street light.

The digital clock on the chrome range read 21.14. Juliet Mullen sat perched on the black, granite worktop with a can of Diet Coke. Her Converse Allstars bounced gently against the cupboard beneath.

'He's the twatty sixth-former with the spiky hair, right?'

'That's a good description,' Thorne said.

'Fancies himself.'

'Not a friend of yours, then?'

'No ...'

Thorne sat at the kitchen table. Fresh coffee had been made and he'd helped himself. 'He's a good-looking boy, though, to be serious. Wouldn't you say? I bet some of the girls in your year like him, don't they?'

'Maybe some of the sad ones.'

'But not you?'

She threw him a look drenched in pity. Thorne was convinced. He knew precisely the reaction he'd get were he to ask Juliet Mullen if she'd ever spoken to Adrian Farrell on the phone. 'What about your brother?'

'What about him?'

'Is he a friend of Farrell?'

She took a swig from her can, swallowed the belch. 'I don't know all his friends – not that he's got too many, to be honest – but I seriously doubt it.'

'Why?'

'Like I said, Farrell's a wanker. He's a poser and Luke's really good at seeing through all that shit. If someone like Farrell was being matey with Luke, it would probably just be so he could take the piss. Or because he wanted something.'

'Any idea what that might be?'

'Not a clue. Help with homework, maybe?'

Thorne nodded. It was the first thing she'd thought of, the most obvious explanation. It was the first thing Farrell himself had thought of, too, when he'd been groping for a lie to explain the phone calls.

Juliet squashed the empty can, dropped down from the worktop and opened a cupboard where there was a recycling bin. 'Is this to do with what's happened to Luke?'

'I don't think so. I'm not sure . . .'

'Do you think Luke's still alive?'

Thorne looked up at the girl. Her image was designed to project a generalised angst and tension, frustration and despair at nothing in particular. In that moment, though, brightly lit and brutal, there was only a pudgy-faced child whose breathing was suddenly ragged above the low hum of the fridge. Thorne could see beyond the dark make-up and the bitten nails to the consuming pain beneath.

And he could see that lying would not ease it.

'I'm not sure about that, either.'

Juliet nodded, like she appreciated the honesty. 'I am,' she said.

447

# TWENTY-THREE

'Amin Latif was my nephew,' the driver said. He nodded towards the men in the back seat. 'And these are my sons: Amin's cousins.'

Finally the men on either side of Farrell looked at him. One had a goatee and wore a leather jacket. The other was clean-shaven, with small, round glasses and hair that flopped down across his forehead. Neither of them looked like hard men, Farrell thought. But they both looked hard *enough*, and intense, like they had something burning in *their* bellies, too.

'You look like you're going to shit yourself,' the one with the goatee said.

Farrell had spent the ten minutes since they'd climbed in next to him imagining the worst. He'd pictured the car pulling off the road, driving on to some deserted industrial estate. He knew for certain that the men would be carrying knives.

'How does it feel?' the one with the glasses asked.

In fact, the driver had steered the Cavalier into the large car park of an entertainment complex. Farrell thought he recognised the place; that maybe he'd been bowling here one night or gone to the pictures. The car had eventually stopped in a far corner behind a Pizza Hut, away from any other vehicles. Out of the light.

'I could have such a good time using a blade on you.' The man with the glasses was inches from Farrell's face. Farrell could smell the chewing gum on his breath. 'Not quick, either. There are halal butchers in our family. You understand what that is?'

'He knows how to bleed an animal properly.'

'And you still wouldn't have paid for what you did to Amin . . . nowhere near. For what you did before you killed him.'

Farrell heard himself say, 'please'. Felt the heat that was rising inside him spread out and bubble across every inch of his skin.

The driver, a big man, heaved himself further round in his seat. 'OK, let's calm down. Nobody's using knives on anyone.' He pointed a finger at Farrell. 'You're going to prison, don't be in any doubt about that. *That's* how you're going to pay for Amin. With years and years of stale air, and shitting where you eat. Of worrying what might happen every time an Asian face stares at you in the canteen or across the exercise yard. You clear about that?'

Farrell nodded. Ahead of him, through the rain-streaked windscreen, he could see a small crowd of people two hundred yards away, milling around outside the cinema.

'But there is a choice you have to make: you can go to prison, or you can go to prison after you've had the shit kicked out of you.' He looked to the men on either side of Farrell, then back to the teenager. 'Because I *will* let them beat you. In fact, I will probably *help* them beat you. So there you go . . . It's not really much of a choice, if you ask me.'

Hearing the tremor in his voice as he started to speak only made it worse for Farrell. The fear was growing fat inside him, feeding on itself. 'What do you want?'

'There were others with you,' the driver said. 'Two others, the night you killed my nephew. They could have stopped you but they chose to stand by and watch. The police will probably catch them eventually, but even if they do, those two bastards won't get what they deserve. If they get clever lawyers, maybe even clever *Asian* lawyers, to go down well with the jury, they won't be sent to prison for murder. They may get a few years, but it's not enough.'

'They're as guilty as you are,' the man with the glasses said.

'Fucking *worse* than you, man.'

The driver waved his hand until there was quiet. 'We want to see them before they're arrested, that's all. If the law won't deal with them properly, then we'll sort things out ourselves. So, obviously, we need to know who they are.' He stared at Farrell, brought a thumb to his mouth and chewed at a nail. 'You can say nothing, that's up to you, but why the hell would you want to take a beating for them? You get prison *and* a good kicking, and what do they get? That seems stupid to me. What thanks do you get for protecting these fuckers?'

'If you're stupid, whatever happens to you tonight can happen again, many times, once you're in prison.' The man with the floppy hair took off his glasses. He untucked his T-shirt and wiped the lenses. 'We can get to you in there. If we want you hurt, we can make it happen, any time we like.'

'Tell us their names,' the driver said, 'we drop you off near a police station and that's it.'

Farrell wanted to be sick. And to shit, and to cry. If he told them what they wanted, how did he know that they wouldn't hurt him anyway? He knew that if he asked the question, the beating would probably begin.

'Two names. Say them quickly and it's finished.'

Farrell closed his eyes and shook his head. For a wild, unthinking second or two he *wanted* them to hurt him. He wanted it over and done with, and being beaten seemed better than waiting.

Than not knowing . . .

'I won't allow any weapons,' the driver said. 'And it will be over quickly enough. But if you make the wrong choice, and it comes down to it, you need to understand that violence is never precise. It's hard to keep things . . . reined in. You must know better than anyone what damage can be done with a kick or two, right?'

'Amin tried to protect his head and it didn't help.'

'And there was only *one* person doing the kicking.'

'Swings and roundabouts, though.' The driver stuck the key back in the ignition, turned it some of the way. 'If things get out of hand, I mean. If you end up damaged in some way and in a unit that's designed for prisoners with special needs, it'll probably be harder for us to get to you later on.'

'Tell us their names. Last chance.'

Farrell's mouth felt dead and scorched inside. He prised open his lips and panted, gulped and choked as he tried to dry swallow.

'Silly,' the driver said. '*Very* silly.' He swung himself around again and started the car.

Farrell screamed over the radio and, once the music had been turned down, he started to gabble, breathless, in a whisper that struggled not to become a sob. He said the names over and over until they ran into one another and became meaningless; babbling until he felt hands on his face, closing his mouth, and voices telling him to shush.

Telling him that he was still scum, still a prick and still a murderer. But at least he was not a *completely* stupid one.

Porter knew that she should knock it on the head. There was little point in ploughing on when she was so tired that she might well be overlooking stuff anyway. But she really wanted to get it done.

There were hundreds of files, each containing sometimes

452

dozens of reports and assessments. There was clearly no need to read all of them, or even the majority, but it had quickly become apparent that even skimming through Kathleen Bristow's records wasn't going to be a five-minute job.

Client files had been organised alphabetically, and while searching under 'F' for Freestone, Porter had found herself reading case notes that she knew were of no real interest. She supposed that even though these were ex-clients of a dead woman, there were still issues of confidentiality. But that didn't stop her. She was fascinated, and, on occasion, appalled. Francis Bristow had been right when he'd said that his sister had worked with more than a few 'head-cases'.

The documents relating to Grant Freestone put a little unpleasant meat on the bones of what she knew already, but there was nothing that seemed significant. There were transcripts of interviews conducted in prison, and statements from a number of healthcare professionals who'd treated him during his sentence, but there was nothing in the file relating to the Multi-Agency Public Protection Arrangements that came into force after he was released.

Porter was alone in the house. She'd brought a radio upstairs from the kitchen and tuned it to Magic FM. When the songs had become a little too soporific, she'd retuned it to Radio 1, nodding her head in time to the music as she'd hauled out batch after batch of brown and green suspension files.

She hummed along with a dance track she recognised

and wondered if Thorne had managed to get away yet. Earlier, on the phone, when he'd asked her what she would be doing, it had sounded like more than just a casual work enquiry, but she'd decided not to push it. She sensed he wasn't completely relaxed about what had nearly happened, but in that respect he was probably just an average bloke: happy enough to get into her pants but not very comfortable talking about it, or, God forbid, what might happen afterwards.

Porter finally found the MAPPA stuff in the section of files that was organised by year. There were half a dozen well-stuffed folders relating to Grant Freestone's 2001 panel. She squatted down and sorted them into piles: 'Risk Management'; 'Domestic Arrangements'; 'Community Sex-Offender Treatment Programme'; 'Drugs & Alcohol'. She picked up the folder marked 'Minutes' and took out a sheaf of papers held together with a bulldog clip. Kathleen Bristow had been as meticulous as always, and the documents, most of which were handwritten, had been filed in strict chronological order. Porter flicked through to the last sheet: the minutes of the meeting that had taken place on 29 March 2001.

She recognised the names under 'In Attendance'. There were none listed under 'Apologies for Absence' ...

Porter stared at the date.

Sarah Hanley had been killed on 7 April, nine days after the meeting. The panel had met weekly until this point and there was no record in these minutes of the decision to tell Hanley about Freestone's past; the decision that was widely regarded as the reason she had ended up dead. Porter went through the sheets again, sensing that there should have been one more, checking that she hadn't missed it.

Of course, after what had happened, Kathleen Bristow might have decided that the final meeting was one for which she wanted no record.

It might also have been what her killer had been after.

Porter made a mental note to check with Roper, Lardner and the others, to confirm that a meeting *had* taken place on 5 April, two days before Sarah Hanley's death.

Energised suddenly, but still as knackered as she'd felt in a long time, Porter sat back against a filing cabinet. She reached for the folder marked 'Drugs & Alcohol', thinking that either would be more than welcome.

Farrell felt a jolt of something like hope when the car drew close to Colindale station. He'd held his breath for most of the journey back, but suddenly started to believe that his ordeal would soon be over.

The place he'd been so happy to walk out of an hour or so before now seemed like a sanctuary.

But the driver slowed, crept past the front entrance, then took a sharp left.

'Please,' Farrell said. 'Here is OK.'

The driver ignored him, moving along the side of the station and stopping at a security barrier. He wound down the window, leaned out and punched at some buttons.

'I don't understand . . .'

The barrier started to rise.

Farrell finally thought he saw what was happening. Anger spread and hardened, cracked into a series of low curses, which grew harsher as the Cavalier turned into the backyard and he saw the officers waiting.

Saw Kitson exchanging nods with the driver as they drew to a halt.

Samir Karim slammed the car door and pulled on his jacket. He let out a long, slow breath as he walked towards Kitson. She put a hand on his arm and left it there as they exchanged a few words; watching as the two young men in the back seat moved away from the car, and uniformed officers leaned in to drag out Adrian Farrell.

Farrell struggled and swore as the handcuffs were put on, his body straining towards where Kitson and Karim were huddled, twenty feet away, near the back entrance. 'You told me you were a cab driver, you fucker. You told me.'

Karim turned, equally angry, but marshalling it. 'That's bollocks. I said nothing. You took one look at me and you *presumed* I was your driver.'

'Nobody made you get into the car,' Kitson said. 'You jumped to conclusions.'

*Just like Thorne had said he would.*

'They threatened me.' Farrell looked from face to face, repeated the accusation, making sure every copper within earshot was under no misconception. 'They fucking *threatened* me.'

Backs were still being patted, hands shaken, as Kitson walked across to the prisoner and stood, waiting for him to stop shouting. After a few moments she gave up and got on with it, spoke the words she had no real need to think about.

Charged Adrian Farrell with the murder of Amin Latif.

As she made the speech, she thought about how much persuasion Thorne had needed to employ on her. He'd reminded her about her 'acquisition' of Farrell's DNA; pointed out that, as she'd already taken several steps in an unorthodox direction, it couldn't really hurt to take a few more. 'Welcome to the slippery slope,' he'd said.

'... but it may harm your defence if you do not mention, when questioned, something which you later rely on ...'

She knew that there would be fallout: questions raised, evidence discounted. Thorne had mentioned Farrell's solicitor and Trevor Jesmond. He'd offered to open a book on which of them would be the more apoplectic.

But she didn't care.

She looked at Farrell and she knew she'd got him, that, whatever happened, there was more than enough to put him *and both his friends* away. She pictured the face of Amin Latif's mother, and decided that she could live with a slap on the wrist.

She followed a step or two behind as officers escorted Farrell through the cage. When she entered the custody suite she watched as they led him towards the skipper, walking slowly, *deliberately* slowly, past Samir Karim and his 'sons' – the two Asian DCs Kitson had 'borrowed' from CID.

Farrell glared, and got it back in spades.

The DC with the goatee sucked his teeth. 'And they reckon you don't see white dog-shit any more . . .'

Thorne was being shown to the door by Juliet Mullen when his phone rang. She walked back towards the kitchen once he'd answered; when he turned away and lowered his voice.

'Dave?'

'Where are you?' Holland asked.

'I'm at the Mullens'.'

'Jesus—'

'How did it go with Farrell?'

Holland sounded flustered, thrown, spluttered an answer: 'Kitson got the names. Sir, this is important.'

Thorne listened. Holland didn't call him 'sir' very often.

'I thought I was going mad,' Holland said. 'Thought I was just overtired, that I'd looked at the wrong list or something.' He explained that he'd finally been able to track down the missing member of the MAPPA panel; that the people living at Margaret Stringer's old address had finally got back to him. They'd been away, but had dug out a phone number they'd been left when they'd bought the place five years before. 'When I called, I just presumed I'd got confused and dialled the wrong number . . .'

'What's the matter, Dave?'

'How long have you been at Tony Mullen's place?'

'I don't know ... half an hour or so.'

'You must have heard the phone go, then,' Holland said. 'A couple of times in the last fifteen minutes?'

Thorne *had* heard it, when he was with Juliet in the kitchen. Both times the call had been answered from the sitting room next door.

'First time, when I realised who I was talking to, I didn't know what to say. I just talked some shit about a courtesy call. Second time, when I rang again to check, I just hung up.'

'OK.' Thorne was only half listening now; trying to put it together.

'What the fuck's going on?'

Thorne had no idea, but he was in the right place to find out. He had already worked out that a lot of women worked under their maiden names. And he knew what Margaret shortened to ...

When he'd hung up, Thorne went back to the kitchen and told Juliet Mullen to go back to her room. Then he walked into the sitting room and sat down without being invited.

Maggie Mullen put down the book she was reading and her husband, somewhat reluctantly, turned off the television.

'Have you finished?'

'I haven't even started,' Thorne said.

# TWENTY-FOUR

'Did it not occur to you for one minute that this was going to come out?' Thorne spoke to them, and looked at them, as if they were children. 'How could you think we wouldn't find out about this?'

'It's not a big deal,' Mullen said.

'Isn't it?'

'It was an affair, that's all. People have them. You'll just have to forgive us for trying to keep some tiny part of our fucked-up lives private.'

But Thorne was in no mood to forgive anyone. He'd listened with a growing sense of disbelief and anger as Tony Mullen had explained why he'd taken the decision not to mention Grant Freestone. How they'd jointly decided that there would be little point in revealing the affair that his wife had had while serving as an officer of the local education authority on Freestone's MAPPA panel in 2001.

'You lied because of *this*?' Thorne said. 'We're trying to find your son and you lie because of a bit of screwing around? Whose embarrassment were you trying to save? Your wife's or your own?'

'Both,' Mullen said. 'Either. Does it really fucking matter?'

'You messed us around—'

'Does *any* of it matter?' Mullen looked ready to scream, with frustration, exhaustion, rage. 'Christ, my wife made a mistake years ago. *One* mistake . . .'

Mullen was sitting on the sofa, facing the fireplace and the TV. Thorne and Maggie Mullen were opposite each other in the armchairs to either side. Thorne stared at the woman across the Chinese rug, her feet curled underneath her, same as he'd seen her daughter do. She was still, and had spoken barely a word since Thorne had entered the room.

He was unable to tell if she wore a stunned expression or a defiant one.

'So who did you make this mistake with, then?'

She shook her head slowly, as if she were being asked to submit to something unspeakable.

Mullen groaned. 'Does it matter?'

'No more secrets,' Thorne said.

So Maggie Mullen named the man with whom she'd had her affair. Thorne thought about it for a moment. He could see why it would have upset Tony Mullen so much.

'You're obviously enjoying this, Thorne,' Mullen said. 'Enjoying our . . . discomfort.'

461

'You think you can claw back one single bloody inch of the moral high ground?' Thorne asked.

Mullen said nothing, looked across at his wife.

'You *should* feel uncomfortable. Jesus. You're ex-Job, for crying out loud, and your son is missing. *You withheld information.*'

'*Irrelevant* information.'

'You sure?'

'Considering everything that's going on, do you really think that who my wife slept with five years ago is remotely important?'

'That depends,' Thorne said. 'Does "everything" include another member of the MAPPA panel being murdered this morning?' He looked from one to the other. It was clear from Tony Mullen's expression that he hadn't known. That, despite his connections, this development in the case hadn't been relayed to him five minutes after it had happened. 'Someone broke into Kathleen Bristow's house and killed her, and nobody's going to convince me that it wasn't the same person who took your son, so . . .'

Maggie Mullen began to cry.

'I wonder if you still think the fact that your wife was on that panel is unimportant. If it's *irrelevant.*'

Mullen stood up, held out his arms towards his wife, but she didn't move. She sat and wept and looked anywhere but at Thorne or her husband, until Mullen moved across to her. He gathered her up and pulled her back with him on to the sofa, pressing her head to his chest until she had to break free to suck in a breath.

'I don't understand how you could have been on that panel in the first place,' Thorne said. 'Wasn't there a conflict of interest, with your husband having put Freestone behind bars in the first place?'

Mullen looked at his wife. She was in no fit state to answer. 'She didn't know,' he said. 'Not to start with at least. We didn't discuss cases and she'd never even heard of Grant Freestone until she joined that panel.'

'So what happened? "Not to start with", you said.'

'She saw my name on Freestone's probation report, the stuff about the threats he'd made, so then she told me and we discussed it. She talked about resigning, but there was really no need. What had happened in the past was of no concern to Maggie and the others on that panel, so there was no conflict.'

'Of course not. Still, it must have been handy to have someone who could keep a close eye on Freestone for you. Someone who had a nice professional reason to know exactly what he was doing.'

Mullen shook his head. 'You're talking crap. My wife just did her job.'

'Right, and plenty of overtime, by the sound of it.'

It was a cheap shot, and it got the reaction it deserved. Mullen sat up straight, clutched his wife's hand and spoke quietly, each word clearly intended to be definitive; weighted with loathing for both subject *and* listener.

'This *man* was someone Maggie worked with closely, only because she believed in doing things properly. She trusted everyone on that panel, had every reason to

463

think they had the same dedication to the work that she had.'

Next to him, Maggie Mullen sat, stiff and shaking, the tears coming more slowly now. Her face reacted to the jolt of each sob, and twisted as her husband spoke, as though in distaste, in horror at this woman he was discussing that she did not recognise.

'Men like him can mistake a close working relationship for affection. They look for it, desperate, and search for any way to exploit it, to turn it into something sordid it was never intended to be. They're leeches. That's what he was.'

Next to him, Maggie Mullen spoke her husband's name quietly. It sounded like a plea to stop.

'He was needy,' Mullen said, 'terminally needy, and he twisted my wife's sympathy into something different. He took advantage of her.'

Maggie Mullen was shaking her head, insistent now, her words spoken and repeated in tandem with the movement. 'That's not what happened. That's not what *happened* . . .'

'Calm down, love—'

'Don't be so *fucking* stupid,' she shouted. She turned to Thorne, focused, spoke quietly. 'He's got Luke.'

Thorne felt the prickle at the nape of his neck, a buzz that began to build and creep . . .

'Who's got Luke?'

She said his name again. The name of the man with whom she'd had the affair.

Mullen took hold of her other hand and put his face close to hers. 'Sorry, love, I don't—'

She screamed the name into his face, scored it in spittle across his cheek and into his eyes.

'He took Luke,' she said. 'He got those people, that couple, to take him as a warning. To convince me, I suppose. The affair didn't finish when I told you it did. I tried to end it, but he wouldn't let me.' Mullen tried to say something, but she continued over the top of him, quickly, as though, if she stopped, she might fall to pieces. 'We carried on, but I was dying every time I looked at Luke or Juliet. I was dying with the guilt. So, a few months ago, I decided I was going to end it and I told him that this time I wasn't going to change my mind.' She paused, remembering. 'He took it badly . . .'

Thorne was out of his seat. He couldn't keep the astonishment and the disgust from his voice. 'So he kidnapped your son?'

'I was stupid,' she said, clutching at her husband. 'I was so stupid to do it when I did. He'd just lost his mother and he was in pieces, and I thought it would be a *good* time, you know . . . to tell him, because he would have other things on his mind. But he went completely off the rails.'

Thorne stared, thinking, *You're telling me.* He waited for the rest.

'And, God help me, I mentioned Sarah Hanley.'

'*What?*'

'We never talked about what happened. It was just like a film we'd seen or something. But I wanted him to accept

465

that it was over and leave me alone, and I said something about how terrible it would be if anyone ever found out. It was just something I said, because I was desperate and I didn't know what else to do. I wasn't *trying* to threaten him.'

'*What* was it that happened?' Thorne asked.

Mullen just gasped out his wife's name.

'I was there when Sarah Hanley died,' she said.

Tony Mullen got slowly to his feet and, as both of his wife's hands were in his, she rose with him. Their fingers twisted, whitened, and the tension grew in their arms until they were pushing at each other, standing in front of the sofa, straining and searching for some leverage, a low moan somewhere in the throat of one of them ...

Thorne was out of his chair, fearing violence, but the moment passed and Mullen dropped back on to the sofa as if he'd been gutted. Thorne stared at the two of them. Took a few deep breaths as a hundred questions careered through his mind.

Knowing that he could wait for the answers, he took out his phone and began to dial.

Maggie Mullen saw what was happening. She stepped towards him and reached out a hand. 'Please, not like last time,' she said. 'Don't go in there like you did at that flat. Don't charge in there with guns. I don't know how he'll react. I've no idea what he'll do.'

Thorne nodded and raised the phone. 'I need a home address.'

She gave it to him without a second thought. 'Please,'

she said again. 'Luke's unharmed ... so far. He's fine. Promise me you won't do anything stupid, that you won't go in there with guns ...'

The number Thorne was calling began to ring. He looked at Tony Mullen and followed the man's wide eyes to those of the woman who was pawing at his sleeve. 'How do you *know* Luke's unharmed?'

Her eyes left his. 'I've spoken to him.'

Mullen's voice was hoarse. 'You've spoken to Luke?'

'No,' she said. 'Not to Luke. I haven't spoken to Luke.'

Porter answered her phone.

She'd just started driving back from Kathleen Bristow's house in Shepherd's Bush. She pulled over to take down details as soon as Thorne had her attention and began to take her through it. He gave her an address in Catford, the other side of the city from him, and still a good distance south-east of where Porter was.

'How soon do you think you can get a team there?' He asked.

'They'll be there before I am,' Porter said. 'Almost certainly.'

Thorne passed on Maggie Mullen's concerns: her belief that the kidnapper's reaction to an armed entry was highly unpredictable; her plea for them to be cautious.

Porter sounded dubious. 'I can't make any promises,' she said.

When Thorne hung up, he told her Porter had assured him that she'd do her best.

He didn't feel bad about lying to her.

467

# TWENTY-FIVE

You think about the kids.

First and last, in that sort of situation, in that sort of *state*; when you can't decide if it's anger or agony that's all but doubling you up, and making it so hard for you to spit the words across the room. First and last, you think about them ...

'Why the hell, why the *fuck*, didn't you tell me this earlier?'

'It wasn't the right time. It seemed best to wait.'

'Best?' She took a step towards the man and woman standing on the far side of her living room.

'I think you should try to calm down,' the man said.

'What do you expect me to do?' she said. 'I'd really be interested to know.'

'I can't tell you what to do. It's your decision ...'

'You think I've got a *choice*?'

The other woman spoke gently. 'We need to sit down and talk about the best way forward—'

'Christ Almighty. You just march in here and tell me this. Casually, like it's just something you forgot to mention. You walk in here and tell me all this . . . shit!'

'Sarah—'

'I don't know you. I don't even fucking *know* you . . .'

For a few seconds there was just the ticking, and the distant traffic, and the noise bleeding in from a radio in the kitchen . . .

'I'm sorry.'

'You're *what*?' Sarah Hanley smiled, then laughed. She gathered the material of her dress between her fingers as her fists clenched at her sides. 'I need to get to the school.'

'The kids'll be fine,' the man said. He looked at the woman who was with him and she nodded her head in complete agreement. 'Honestly, love. Absolutely fine.'

' . . . that's when she came at him,' Maggie Mullen said. 'When she came at both of us, scratching and spitting and swearing her head off. He only raised his hands to protect his face, because she was out of control. He didn't mean to push her.'

'She was thinking of her children,' Thorne said.

'So were *we*. That's why we were there, why the decision was made to tell her about Grant Freestone's past.'

'And it never occurred to anyone that she might not take the news very calmly?'

Maggie Mullen had slunk back to the armchair. Her arms were wrapped around each other at the waist as she spoke. From the sofa, her husband watched, ashen-faced, as though all but the smallest breath he needed to stay alive had been punched out of him.

'We were trained to have these conversations,' Maggie Mullen said. 'We tried to be sensitive. Everything just ... got out of hand.'

'What happened afterwards?'

'We panicked. There was such a lot of blood. We didn't know what the hell to do, and in the end we just decided to leave.' She looked at Thorne. 'I can't remember whose idea it was, really I can't, but it was all such a mess. It was just a stupid accident.'

'An accident for which you knew Grant Freestone would probably get blamed.'

'We never thought about that,' she said. 'I didn't anyway, I swear. When he *did* get blamed, we talked about it, but we didn't know what to do for the best. It was too late to come forward by then, to try and explain.'

Thorne moved slowly around to the back of her chair. 'Was she still alive when you left?' he asked.

Maggie Mullen lowered her head, shook it.

Thorne stared down at hair that had gone unwashed for days. Only she and the man she'd been with in Sarah Hanley's house that day knew if she was telling the truth. 'You know that her children discovered the body, don't you?'

'Yes ...'

470

Tony Mullen's hands were trembling in his lap. He swallowed hard, then muttered, '*Christ . . .*'

'So, you just walked out,' Thorne said.

She nodded, but kept her eyes down. 'Yes, we walked out, and we hoped nobody had seen us.' She looked up. 'And nobody had. We went to Kathleen Bristow, who'd assigned us the job of making the visit, and told her that we'd had to cancel it, that we'd never gone. We made up some story about me being poorly. Then, when the body was discovered, it all got forgotten anyway, and it looked like we were safe.'

'Is that why he killed Bristow?' Thorne asked. 'Did she keep a record of the fact that you were due to have visited Sarah Hanley?'

'I suppose so. She certainly knew that he and I were involved with each other. She caught us together in a pub once after one of the meetings. Maybe her knowing that was enough to scare him.'

'But why *now*?'

She shifted in her chair, let her head fall back and talked to the ceiling. 'I don't know what's in his mind. I can't pretend to know why he's done any of this.'

'Maybe you should have asked him,' Mullen said. 'During one of your cosy little chats on the phone.'

'Please, Tony . . .'

'I can't believe that you knew he had Luke, but you said nothing. He had our *son* and you said nothing.'

Thorne looked at what was left of Mullen, and despite everything he'd felt about him until this point, he was

471

overwhelmed by sympathy for the man. He'd lied by omission, thinking only that he was covering up simple adultery, unaware that there was so much more at stake.

'At the beginning I thought he was just trying to frighten me, you know? Because I'd told him we were finished, and I'd talked about the Sarah Hanley business. He knew this woman from somewhere, paid her to take Luke from the school, and I thought it would just be for a day or something, that he was just making sure I got the message.'

Thorne knew then that he'd been right about the video; about how strange it was that nothing had been addressed to Luke's father. The boy had been told what to say. The words had been aimed solely at his mother because the message was meant for her and no one else.

'What did he say?' Mullen asked. 'After he'd taken Luke, what did he say when you spoke to him?'

She looked as though this was the hardest answer she'd had to provide so far. 'He said he was doing it because he loved me so much.'

'*Sweet Jesus!*'

'It's what he believes. He's not well.'

'Why didn't you sort this out straight away?' Mullen was reddening, breathing noisily. 'Why didn't you agree to everything, anything, *whatever he wanted*, so that he'd let Luke go? You saw that video, you saw what they were doing to Luke.'

'He said he didn't want to make it *easy*. He promised not to hurt him, told me that the drugs weren't doing him

472

any harm. He told me he wanted to be sure I knew how serious he was.'

'*Serious?*' Thorne said.

'Then, after the first few days, there was nothing I *could* do. I was terrified because everything had escalated.'

Mullen bucked in his seat, punching at the chair around him, swinging at nothing. 'He killed people. He started fucking killing people.'

'That's what I mean,' she shouted. 'I knew that he'd lost control, that I couldn't predict what he was going to do or how he was going to react. He said he wouldn't hurt Luke, but I didn't know what would happen if I told the police.' She glanced at the telephone. 'I still don't. All I could do was keep talking to him, make sure that Luke was still all right.' Her hand rose to her head, closed around a clump of hair and began to pull. 'I fucked it all up, I know I did, but it went so completely mad that I didn't know what to do.' She looked wildly from her husband to Thorne and back again. 'I was thinking of Luke all the time. But ...'

Thorne nodded. He did not want to listen to any more. There were no more tears left, but Maggie Mullen's face looked as though it were made of cracked plaster. He remembered the words she'd used when she'd described what had happened on the day Sarah Hanley died. 'Everything just got out of hand,' he said.

An hour or more passed as slowly as any Thorne could remember. The minutes crawled by on their bellies, each through the glistening, greasy trail of the one before, as he watched Tony and Maggie Mullen damage themselves and each other. Screams that sliced and flayed. Accusations swung like bludgeons, and the silences burning away the flesh from the little that was left between them.

Drawn from the top of the house by the noise, Juliet had appeared in the doorway. Demanding to know what was happening, and understandably reluctant to go upstairs again, she had begun a shouting match with her mother that was just starting to get nasty when Thorne's mobile rang. Tony Mullen moved quickly to manhandle his daughter from the room as Thorne took the call.

When it was over, Thorne turned back to them. He raised a hand quickly, a gesture to reassure them that the news was not the worst they could have been expecting. 'Nobody there,' he said. 'They went in five minutes ago and the flat's empty.'

Mullen's expression was one Thorne had seen several times since he'd first got involved with the case: relief that washed briefly across a mask of panic, then unthinkable fury.

Maggie Mullen was breathing heavily. 'They went in there very quickly. How could they be sure it was safe?'

'They decided that they couldn't afford to wait,' Thorne said. 'Going in fast is always iffy, but waiting might have been riskier, and it certainly didn't help last time. There was an armed response vehicle close by and they took the chance.'

'You said there'd be no guns.' She pointed a shaking finger, spat out the words. 'You *promised*.'

'No,' Mullen said, cold. 'No, he fucking didn't.'

'Is there anywhere else?' Thorne asked. 'Anywhere else he might have taken him?'

Thorne could see that as soon as the idea presented itself to her, she knew it was the right one.

'His mother's house. She had a cottage somewhere near Luton, in the middle of bloody nowhere.' She couldn't look at her husband. 'I went there once.'

'Call him,' Thorne said.

She closed her eyes and clamped a hand across her mouth, which muffled the end of her refusal.

'*Call* him . . .'

It took a few minutes before Mullen and Thorne saw her walk across to her bag, take out her phone. Watched her gather herself, and dial.

Then speak to the man who had kidnapped her son.

She told him that she needed to talk; that she knew it was late but that she was coming to see him. She insisted. She said she knew where he was and swore that she would be coming alone.

She pressed back fresh tears and took a deep breath before she asked how Luke was.

Then she hung up.

Nodded . . .

Mullen was face to face with Thorne before he had completed a step. 'I'm coming with you,' he said.

'No.'

'Just try and fucking stop me.'

Thorne looked into Mullen's eyes and knew that if he

*did*, and it got physical, he would be in serious trouble. 'It's really not a good idea,' he said, brandishing his mobile. 'Don't make me get a uniform over here.'

Mullen took a few seconds, but finally stepped away. When Thorne asked where his car keys were, Mullen handed them over. Looking at him, Thorne suddenly remembered what Hendricks had told him about seeing the child on the bed that was really a mortuary slab. Thorne saw a man who knew that his son's life was in somebody else's hands; and that his own pride and stupidity might have helped put it there.

He led Maggie Mullen to the front door and opened it. She walked out without looking back and moved towards the car. Thorne turned to see Juliet Mullen sitting halfway up the stairs and her father climbing towards her.

'It'll be all right, sir,' Thorne said.

# TWENTY-SIX

Thorne drove, glancing down every now and again at the road atlas open in his lap. At the square of country-side between Luton and Stevenage that Maggie Mullen had identified as their destination. Swallowing up the tarmac in Tony Mullen's Mercedes, the A1 almost empty as it neared eleven o'clock, it wouldn't take much more than another twenty minutes to get there.

If they could find it.

He spoke to Porter again as he pushed the car north. Telling her where he was heading, talking her through his likeliest route. Porter sounded tense, knowing she could do little but take her team in the same direction and wait for more specific instructions.

'Goes without saying that you keep me up to speed, right?'

'So why say it, then?'

'Tom—'

'You'll know where as soon as I know,' Thorne said. '*If*
I know ...'

Another glance down, once he'd hung up, and one
more at the woman in the passenger seat. They'd barely
spoken since they'd left the house in Arkley. Maggie
Mullen had spent most of the time staring hard out of the
window, not wanting to risk making any kind of contact
until she had to, unwilling, or afraid, to catch Thorne's
eye. To engage.

They drove on in silence, save for the low hum of the
big engine and the hiss of the tyres against a still slick road,
though the rain had stopped. It would have been wrong, of
course, horribly inappropriate, but just for a second or
two Thorne had considered reaching for the stereo, as the
atmosphere in the car grew more uncomfortable with
every minute and every mile.

He wondered what Tony Mullen's taste in music might
be. The trivial nature of the thought was a welcome relief
from the darker ones that sloshed around in his brain. The
blackness spreading, discolouring the contents. He
thought about Tony Mullen waiting back at the house.
Had he got on the phone to Jesmond or any of his other
friends in high places yet? What on earth would he have
said to them if he had?

Thorne touched 110 in the outside lane. Hoped the
Hertfordshire traffic boys were a long way away.

'You think I should have spoken up?' she said
suddenly.

Thorne focused on the tail-lights ahead of him. 'Fuck, yes.'

'I was trying to protect Luke.'

'You're well aware how ridiculous that sounds, aren't you?'

'I don't care.'

'That's obvious ...'

'I knew he wouldn't hurt him.'

'You still sure?'

She hesitated.

'And are you sure that keeping all this to yourself had nothing to do with Sarah Hanley? With the fact that you'd be in just as much trouble as he was if it came out?'

Her answer wasn't quick in coming. 'He said we'd both go to prison for it.'

'Right. Turned your stupid threat back on you, didn't he?'

She closed her eyes. 'Yes.'

Thorne grunted, satisfied. 'You didn't want to go to prison ...'

'He asked me what it felt like, being without my son,' she said. There was an edge to her voice, and a hardness in her expression when Thorne glanced across. 'He asked me how I thought I'd feel if I lost *both* of them. If I spent however many years it might be inside, while they grew up without me.' She straightened out the seat belt across her chest. 'No, I didn't want to go to prison.'

'It's no excuse,' Thorne said. 'You said yourself that you

479

didn't know what was going on in this man's head. That you were scared, that he was out of control.'

'I talked to him,' she said. 'I tried to keep him calm, to reassure him, if you like, but it was all for Luke ... '

The thought struck Thorne with such force that Maggie Mullen slid away from him, inching towards the passenger door when he turned and looked at her again. 'What did you tell him about the case?'

The silence was answer enough.

'You told him that we had the fingerprints, didn't you? That we got Conrad Allen's prints off the videotape. That we were close to an address.'

'I thought he'd stop it if he knew the police were coming. I wanted him to give up.'

'What about Kathleen Bristow?' Thorne was asking himself as much as he was asking her, working through the chronology in his head, putting the pieces in the correct order. Had Kathleen Bristow died before or after her killer had been interviewed? 'He knew we were coming to see him, didn't he? You told him we were asking about Grant Freestone, that we'd be talking to members of the panel ... '

'It was all going to come out anyway,' she said. 'What had happened, I mean. I thought if I could make him understand that, he would let me have Luke back.'

'You thought wrong.' Thorne was forcing the accelerator to the floor, squeezing the wheel. 'He killed her, same as he killed Conrad Allen and Amanda Tickell. It sounds to me like those three deaths are down to you.'

'Please ...'

'Three *more* deaths.'

She turned away. Leaned her forehead against the window.

'Whatever you *thought* you were doing, you were just pushing all the buttons.'

'I didn't mean to.'

'I hope Luke's alive, that he hasn't been hurt; more than anything, I hope that. But if he isn't ...'

She moaned, her head sliding against the glass.

'It's probably no more than you deserve.'

Thorne drove on, past signs for Welham Green and Hatfield, past the turn-off to St Albans that he'd taken so many times when his father was alive.

The water on the road was like a long, lonely *shush* beneath them.

Without turning, Maggie Mullen said, 'She was dead when we left. Sarah. She'd lost such a lot of blood.'

Thorne thought she sounded pathetic. He felt numb, cold, without anything even close to sympathy. Knowing what might be waiting for him when they arrived at their destination, he thought it was probably the best way to be.

'Right. And you watched her die.'

They turned off the A1 just past Welwyn Garden City. That much she could remember. But from there on it was hit and hope. There were some fragmented memories of the village they were looking for – a large house on its outskirts, a church – but no more than that.

Within five minutes, it was a different world.

The overhead lighting had gone, and even the catseyes disappeared at the end of the slip road, which quickly narrowed as A route became B, with high hedges on both sides and barely room enough for one vehicle to pass another.

Thorne drove as quickly as he was able, full beam cutting through the black, which twisted away ahead of him.

They moved slowly through a village called Codicote: Tudor houses, pubs, a village green; Maggie Mullen searching desperately for some clue that they might be in the right place. Thorne sped out the other side, past the sign that thanked him for driving carefully, back into the dark necklace of lanes that strung these villages together, a mile or two apart.

He swore and dipped the headlights as another car came around a corner, braking too hard and wrestling the Mercedes into the verge. He tried to look at the other driver as the car went past, but he could see nothing. Back on full beam, the lights caught yellow eyes, low in the undergrowth, and something flashing across the road fifty yards ahead of them.

'All these roads look the bloody same,' Maggie Mullen said.

They drove through Kimpton and Peter's Green. Stopped and turned the car round when they got within a mile of Luton airport and a sign told them they were entering Bedfordshire. Heading north again, they passed through Whitwell, crossed over the River Maran and entered the village of St Paul's Walden.

'*Stop* . . .'

Thorne jumped on the pedal and put out his arm as Maggie Mullen shot forward in her seat. 'What?'

'That's the big house.' She nodded towards a pair of wrought-iron gates. The outline of a grand mansion was just visible in the distance. 'We visited it once. Something to do with the Queen Mother. Keep going . . .'

At the other end of the High Street she told Thorne to stop again. Pointed to a church. A spike rising up from a turreted tower, vivid against the night sky.

'You can see that tower from the cottage,' she said. 'Across the fields.'

'There are fields everywhere,' Thorne said. 'Which direction?'

She looked around, unsure.

Thorne picked one.

Driving out of the village, they both started when Maggie Mullen's phone rang. She looked at the display. The phone was shaking in her hand.

'It's him . . .'

She said, 'yes' a lot; told the caller that she was nearly there and that she just wanted to talk. She asked how Luke was, begged the man on the other end of the phone not to hurt him.

'What did he want?' Thorne asked when she'd hung up.

'He wanted to know where I was. If I was close.'

'You said, *Yes I am; it's fine.* What was that?'

'He was worried,' she said. 'Told me that if I was driving, he hoped I was hands-free.'

Thorne accelerated into the countryside again and smiled grimly. 'He knows you're not alone . . .'

Five minutes later he turned on to a narrow track. It was overgrown and pitted with puddles. The car rattled across a cattle-grid, then followed the track down and to the right, until its lights picked out the house a few hundred yards away.

'That's it . . .'

It wasn't what Thorne had expected. Not a cottage in any usual sense of the word. It wasn't particularly small, and didn't even look that old. But it was certainly isolated. Not exactly chocolate-box, but in the ideal position for some purposes.

Thorne slowed to a crawl as he approached. There were lights on in two rooms downstairs, at the front.

'What are we going to do?' Maggie Mullen asked.

'Well, *you* are going to knock on the door. Go and say hello to your boyfriend.'

'What about you?'

'I have absolutely no idea,' Thorne said. He stopped the car, climbed out and moved away without shutting the door. From the shadows fifty feet from the house, he watched Maggie Mullen go to the front door. Saw it open and watched her walk inside, slow and stiff.

Then he moved quickly towards the back of the building.

He was in virtual darkness almost immediately. He pushed slowly through a low wooden gate whose top edge felt damp, rotten beneath his fingers. It opened into a knot

484

of bramble. Stepping across, there was coarse, wet grass around his knees. As his eyes adjusted, Thorne could just make out the wall – higher in some places than others – that separated the garden from the fields beyond.

He kept close to the side of the house, moving away from it only when he needed to step around a long metal trough and what looked like an old butler sink full of earth and stones. He caught his hand on something as he edged along the wall, sucked in air fast, and wiped away the thickening beads of blood on his damp trouser-leg.

At the back of the cottage was a rusted table and chairs. An arrangement of bird tables. A rotary washing line that barely protruded above four feet of couch grass and thistle below it.

Thorne pressed his face against the window of a small extension. He could make out plates and pans on a drainer, the digital display on a microwave oven. There was a sliver of light at floor level from somewhere inside the house.

The back door was open.

He thought about Porter waiting for his call. About the phone sitting on the front seat of the car . . .

In the second or two between feeling the handle give and pushing, he considered all those times when he'd faced a similar decision. When he'd been torn between doing the sensible thing or saying, 'Fuck it.' When, on almost every occasion, he'd made the wrong choice.

He pushed.

And he stepped into the dark kitchen. Moved quickly to

the door beneath which the light was coming. And listened. Though he could not hear voices, there was something about the quality of the silence from the other side of the door that told him there were people in the next room.

He waited.

Five seconds ... ten.

Then a voice he'd heard before: 'For heaven's sake, stop pissing about and come in.'

Thorne did as he'd been invited, slowly. His pace slowed even further once he saw what was waiting for him. One step at a time, though his mind was racing, processing the visual information, asking questions.

Where's the boy?

Man, woman, rope, knife ...

*Where's the fucking boy?*

# TWENTY-SEVEN

'I knew she was lying.'

'Peter ...'

'About coming on her own.' Lardner nudged his glasses with a knuckle. 'I could hear it in her voice, clear as a bell.' Laughing. 'I mean, I've heard her lying often enough, haven't I? Stretched out next to me, naked, telling her old man she's tied up in a meeting ...'

The buzzing in Thorne's head had faded enough for him to formulate a response. 'She's lied to a lot of people,' he said. He glanced towards a dustsheet-covered armchair in which Maggie Mullen sat directly ahead of him, beneath a small window. She didn't return Thorne's look. Her eyes moved back and forth every few seconds between Lardner and the brown panelled door a few feet away.

Lardner was sitting on the floor against a covered

sofa that had been on Thorne's right as he'd entered the small living room. He was wearing jeans and a rust-coloured shirt, and his legs were drawn up to his chest. His hands dangled between his knees, a carving knife held loosely in one of them. The other clutched the end of a rope which ran away from him, straight and taut, disappearing around the edge of a door beneath the stairs.

Cellar. Had to be.

Thorne asked the question even though he'd known the answer a second after stepping in from the kitchen: 'Where's the boy?'

There was a noise from somewhere beneath them. The rope shifted against the white painted floorboards.

Luke Mullen was alive.

Lardner turned his head towards the door and shouted, 'Come on now, son, I told you I want to see this rope stay taut. You stay where you are, and come up here when I'm good and ready.'

Maggie Mullen leaned forward in her chair. Her fists were tight around the material of her sweater, pulling at it, wrenching. 'For pity's sake, Peter . . . '

'You need to shush . . . really,' Lardner said. 'We've talked about this.' He sounded tired but relaxed. He looked back to Thorne and rolled his eyes, as though another man would understand how exasperating all this nagging was.

Thorne nodded gently, tried to smile.

Lardner raised the hand that held the knife, rubbed it

across the top of his head. The few wisps of dark hair were all over the place and he hadn't shaved for a day or two. 'Silly,' Lardner said. 'All so bloody silly.'

A board moaned beneath Thorne's feet as he shifted his weight, and he saw Lardner's eyes fly to him, *target* him, in a second.

Not relaxed at all . . .

'*You* should sit.' Lardner nodded towards a low pine trunk next to the fireplace.

Thorne moved back until his calves met the edge of the box and dropped down slowly. He looked around, like someone who might be considering renting the place. The ceiling was Artexed: stiff spikes and whorls like hardened icing. A small landscape in a lacquered frame; a wooden barometer; a row of hardback books without jackets on shelves to one side of the front door. In the hearth, an arrangement of dried flowers poking from a stone vase, thick with dust.

'Why are we here?' Thorne said.

Lardner looked a little confused. 'I don't remember inviting anybody.'

'You know what I mean. Why *any* of this?'

'Well it's a fair question. Because it *is* all senseless, all of it, but I'm not really the right person to ask.' He drew a foot of the rope towards him and twisted it around his wrist. 'I don't want to sound childish, really I don't, but I'm not the one who started this.'

'Oh Jesus, Peter.' There was suddenly anger in Maggie Mullen's voice. 'You can't lay any of this madness at my door. All I wanted to do was get out of a relationship. I didn't do anything wrong.'

It was as though he hadn't heard her. 'She made a mistake. And everything went haywire from that point, I suppose. I couldn't believe she was trying to hurt me as much as she had. I convinced myself she didn't know what she was doing . . .'

'Yes,' she said, 'I *did* know.'

'Losing a parent isn't easy, we all know that. You can understand how hard it is.' He looked at Thorne, wanting a response. 'Yes?'

Thorne nodded.

Lardner's tone was chatty again, conversational. 'So to do what she did when I was still suffering the loss of my mother was . . . an *error*. That's what I'm going to call it. And, yes, I was desperate, I don't mind admitting that to you. I don't think that means I'm weak or less of a man or whatever. I didn't want to lose her, I still don't want to lose her, so I clung on for dear life. Which was when she started talking about the Sarah Hanley business, dredged all that up and made stupid suggestions, and I decided something needed to be done.'

'I just wanted to get out,' Maggie Mullen shouted. '*I* was the one who was desperate.'

Thorne looked at the rope. At the knife. It felt as though the skin was tightening across every inch of his body.

Lardner continued to address Thorne; to ignore the woman who, for one reason or another, had caused so much to happen. 'I should really have taken the boy

490

myself,' he said. 'But it was difficult, with work and what have you. It cost me every penny I had to pay those two, I can tell you that. Maybe if I'd sold this place after Mum died, but that was never going to happen.'

Thorne knew most of it, but he was still curious. They'd thought Neil Warren's professional relationship to Amanda Tickell was the link to Grant Freestone. But now Thorne remembered what Callum Roper had said about Warren and Lardner knowing each other. 'Did Neil Warren introduce you to the woman?'

Lardner smiled. 'Neil's very conscientious,' he said. 'He has regular get-togethers for some of his old clients, even though most of them have long since gone back on the smack or the coke or the booze. He gives them a few nibbles, talks about God, that sort of thing. All very jolly . . .'

The rope was frayed and dirty, an old tow rope, by the look of it. Thorne tried hard not to think of the boy on the other end. Of the state he might be in.

'I met Amanda and her boyfriend at one of Neil's parties,' Lardner said. 'And when I was working out how best to snatch the boy, I knew she had it in her. She was always desperate for money.'

The knife swung slowly back and forth, its handle gripped between Lardner's thumb and index finger. It looked as though it came from the same set as the one he'd used to kill Allen and Tickell.

'Why did anyone have to die?' Thorne asked.

'I shan't say that it seemed like a good idea at the time, as that would be flippant. In fact, it seemed like a very *bad*

491

idea. I've no wish to be disrespectful, and I'm very sorry about Kathleen, but same as with the other two, there wasn't a great deal else I could do.' For the first time in a few minutes he looked across at Maggie Mullen. 'Mags was telling me what I needed to do . . .'

Maggie Mullen was almost out of her chair. '*What?*'

'There were hints,' Lardner said. 'We talked on the phone, talked in secret . . . and when she told me about what the police were doing, about Freestone and so on . . .'

'I wanted you to finish it, to know it was pointless—'

'I knew she was *really* telling me that I needed to take steps to protect myself.'

'*No!*'

The wash of a warm smile. 'That's when I knew her feelings for me were still as strong as they'd ever been.'

'You're fucking *mental*, Peter.' She'd known it before, obviously. But here, seeing it acted out in front of her, the shock and the sadness were evident on Maggie Mullen's face. 'You've completely lost it . . .'

Lardner looked at Thorne, shrugged and smiled. Then wound in another foot or so of the rope.

There was a thump from the cellar: a shoe against a wooden stair.

'Let the boy go,' Thorne said. 'I'll stay.'

Lardner looked at him.

'We'll *both* stay. But you could just let Luke walk out of here.'

Another tug, and more rope dancing in. Another thump

from behind the door, and a voice; indistinguishable, but clearly that of someone in pain.

An equally agonised sound broke from Maggie Mullen. She spluttered, '*please*' and '*don't*', then her head dropped forward until her knees muffled her voice, and the terrible sound of her begging became something grunted, animalistic.

Lardner stared at the woman he claimed to love, as though something else, something he didn't understand, was responsible for her pain.

She lifted her head, held her breath and searched for some compassion in his face.

Thorne didn't look away from Lardner. He wondered how much of his attention was really focused on the woman. Then he glanced down at the knife in the man's left hand. Was Lardner left-handed? He thought about making a move but did nothing.

'Right . . . come *on.*'

As soon as Lardner stood and began hauling in the rope, all three were on their feet: Lardner dragging the rope towards himself with one hand, twisting the arm quickly, coiling the rope between elbow and fist, while the other hand continued to point the kitchen knife; Thorne and Maggie Mullen staring – hopeful, terrified – at the small, brown door.

The silence between the bumps and cracks of feet on the stairs felt like hands over Thorne's ears, and his skin continued to shrink; to feel as though it were constricting across his bones. He imagined pressure building on the muscle and the creamy layers of fat as they were squeezed; the blood rushing, searching for the easiest way to burst through the flesh that stretched and thinned. For one strange, disconnected moment he thought he felt it gathering, about to gush from the small wound in his hand, and he pressed the palm hard against the side of his leg.

The rope was high off the ground now, and taut.

The noise on the stairs grew louder ...

Maggie Mullen's hands were steepled in front of her face. They had flattened, been pressed tight across her mouth, by the time the door to the cellar was shouldered open, crashed back against the wall, and her son stumbled into the room.

She screamed when she saw that his face had gone.

# TWENTY-EIGHT

'Yes, I'm sorry about that,' Lardner said. 'But he got a bit excited when I told him you were coming. Got very noisy.' He pointed the knife at Maggie Mullen when she took a step towards her son, then twisted the blade to point out his handiwork. 'I did it in a bit of a hurry, but I made sure he could breathe, obviously ...'

The black gaffer tape had been wrapped clumsily, round and round Luke Mullen's face, and in such haste that what remained on the roll hung down, knocking awkwardly against the boy's shoulder as he moved; against the rope that had been looped around his neck and now stretched tightly to where Lardner stood next to the sofa.

Luke stood, swaying on the spot.

Brick-dust streaked his hair, and the navy-blue Butler's Hall blazer was torn at the pocket and ghost-grey with dirt. One hand stayed stiff against his side while the other clutched at the rope around his neck. Thorne could see that the backs of his hands were almost black with filth, and bloodied.

The boy strained instinctively towards his mother, his neck pulling forward against the rope, moaning, *growling*, when Lardner dragged him back. The word had sounded sung almost, from behind the tape. It was impossible to make out clearly, but easy enough to guess at.

Two syllables, definitely.

'*Mummy . . .*'

Maggie Mullen tried to say her son's name but lost it in the sob. She mouthed it as she moved across to Thorne, reached out a hand and took a handful of his leather jacket at the elbow.

Thorne remained still. Whatever she had done, or been responsible for, it had become impossible not to feel *something* for this woman. Seeing what she was seeing; watching the misery carve itself deeper into her face.

Luke swayed and shouted again.

His nose looked obscenely pink and fleshy through a gap in the thick mask of tape. The crooked line of gaffer stopped below his eyes, which had been blinking furiously, widening since he'd stepped from the dark of the cellar into the living room.

Lardner hauled the boy closer to him, more brutally this time.

He pointed with the knife again, first to Luke's face, then to the cellar door. 'It's stupid, really,' he said. 'There's a perfectly good light down there, but the bulb needs replacing. Actually, it went just before Mum died and she asked me to change it for her. I said I would, but you know how you never get round to doing these things. So . . . ' He saw something in Thorne's face. 'Now you think there's some kind of Norman Bates thing going on, and I'm trying to keep everything the way it was, don't you?' He smiled. 'I haven't got my mother stashed upstairs, you know.' He reached out a foot towards the sofa, flicked it against the edge of the dustsheet. 'These things are purely practical, I promise you . . . '

'I lost my father a year ago,' Thorne said. 'Almost exactly a year.'

Relief flooded into Lardner's face. 'So you *know*.'

'I know it's hard. But nobody else has to pay for it.'

'She's not paying for *that*.'

'What then?'

'You can't treat people the way she did. Not the people who love you.'

'She ended it because she felt guilty,' Thorne said. 'She was thinking about her family.'

Lardner found this funny. 'She never thought about them before.'

Next to him, Thorne felt Maggie Mullen's grip on his arm tighten. She spoke softly to Luke, told him that it was going to be all right. That it would soon be over.

Luke nodded, then staggered as he was pulled to one side. He took a step and regained his balance, his hand scrabbling where the rope was biting into his throat.

'Whatever else happens,' Lardner said, 'she'll be thinking about them a damn sight more from now on.'

Thorne looked at the distance between himself and Lardner.

No more than eight feet. At the end of the rope, Luke was another five or six away, to Lardner's right.

'It sounds to me like it was just about shitty timing,' Thorne said. 'That's all. Probably nobody's fault . . .'

Lardner held the knife out hard in front of him. His arm was tense, shaking with the effort and the intent, but his tone when he spoke was tender, regretful.

'I've thought of little else but her for five years, and it was instant, you know? Well, it was with me, at any rate. Maybe what happened with Sarah Hanley bound us together, made what we already had stronger.' He turned the grip of the knife slowly in his fist. 'She tried to end it once, back when her husband found out, but I knew she was only doing what he wanted. So I didn't know she meant it this time, either. I didn't know how serious she was . . . serious enough to do it *when* she did. I didn't know she could be so completely *fucking* heartless.'

Maggie Mullen's eyes stayed on her son, but she shook her head.

'And I didn't know how hard it was going to hit me. You don't, do you, even if you see these things coming? And I didn't see either of them coming. Mags or Mum. They were like car crashes, both of them right out of the blue. You kid yourself that you've walked away unscathed, but there's a delayed reaction.

'It was like everything was happening to someone else, and all I could do was watch this other person's life slide away, out of control. Even while I was contemplating terrible things – even while I was *doing* them – I couldn't get hold of anything ... I couldn't reach it. There was no way to pull back.'

The knife turned faster in his fist as his speech slowed. 'Everything just gets away from you. Can you understand that? Your grip, your respect for yourself, for other people's lives. *Everything*. Changing a bloody light bulb ... '

His lips were still moving, just a little, and he stared along the blade of the knife as if he were trying to work out what it was for. Suddenly, he looked lost.

Thorne was the only person in the room not crying. He looked at Lardner and willed away any hint of compassion.

He focused on the boy.

Thought of Kathleen Bristow's body. Her stained nightdress. Her sparrow's legs, twisted ...

'Let Luke go,' he said.

Lardner shook his head. Thorne could not be sure if it was a refusal or the gesture of a man who was unsure, *distracted*. There were no more than a couple of paces between them ...

He tensed. A heartbeat away. Lardner had not been afraid to use the knife before.

Thorne knew he would be lucky to come away unscathed.

He had no idea what Lardner's response would be to an

attack. Would he lay down his weapon and throw in the towel? Or would he take a child's life as easily as he'd taken that of an old woman? Whatever his appearance, however beaten and confused he seemed, the unpredictability of the man opposite made him as dangerous as any gangland enforcer or flat-eyed psychopath Thorne had ever faced.

A few years earlier, in a similar position, he'd frozen while a man had held a knife to the neck of a female officer. He had done it by the book, afraid that heroics would cost the officer her life.

Then he'd watched her die anyway.

The boy himself had become completely still and silent. His eyes had closed. Then the words of Luke's mother – calling his name, asking him repeatedly if he was all right – seemed to snap Lardner back into the moment.

'He's fine, really,' Lardner said. 'We've become good mates, haven't we, Luke?'

The boy opened his eyes.

'We've had some good old chats down there, I reckon.'

'No . . .'

Thorne saw the spasm of panic around Maggie Mullen's eyes.

'Talked about all sorts.'

'Like what?'

A shrug. 'Family, you know. The important things in life . . .'

'Don't.'

Luke Mullen moaned, a long, desperate 'no . . .' from behind the tape.

'I wasn't planning on bringing any of it up here,' Lardner said, 'but now that you mention it . . .'

It was no more than a couple of paces, but Thorne knew Lardner could have the knife at Luke's throat before he reached him.

'What did you tell my son?'

'Want me to repeat it? Even police officers can be shocked, you know. But he looks up to it.'

'Stop it!'

'Should I tell him what the pair of us got up to in bed? Or how about why you started having an affair with me in the first place?'

If she rushed towards her son, if she could distract Lardner for just a second, he'd have a chance. There was just no way to let her know what to do.

'Luke, listen to me. I don't know what he's been telling you.'

'We'd better not pretend it was my looks.'

'He's sick. You know that, darling, don't you? You *know* he's sick.'

Thorne would need to go for the left hand, for the knife. Maybe if Luke was quick and moved away at the same time, Lardner could be caught off balance . . .

'Driven into my arms,' Lardner said. 'I think that's a fair description.'

'*Twisted.* What he's been saying.'

'Certainly driven out of her husband's.'

'Please look at me, Luke.'

'I think we all know each other pretty well by now. A home truth or two can't hurt, can it?'

'Luke. *Please!*'

There would be no perfect moment. He just needed to pick one . . .

'Why don't you tell the inspector all about it?' Lardner's mouth was firm, grim, but there was gentleness in his eyes. 'Why you can't bear to let him touch you . . .'

The sound was unearthly, as the howl of rage and horror vibrated against the gaffer tape. Luke lurched towards his mother, and, as he was hauled back, he let his momentum carry him fast and hard into Lardner, taking the two of them down on to the sofa.

Thorne saw what was happening too late.

Saw the hand that the boy had kept pressed against his leg come up high. Saw the light catch something in his fist. Heard the sigh as the flesh was pierced, and the snap.

Then everything was happening at double speed. Crowded with screams and coloured red.

Thorne found himself at Lardner's feet, staring at the broken shard that Luke had dropped. Its edge was bloodied, and the gaffer tape, wrapped around one end as a makeshift handle, was slick with sweat.

Picture-glass, it looked like. Thin, easily snapped.

He looked up for the piece he knew was embedded in Peter Lardner's neck, saw that it was already lost beneath a bubbling spring of scarlet.

Maggie Mullen was on her knees, whispering, one arm wrapped tight around Lardner's neck, both of them slick with blood. Her other arm was reaching desperately for Luke, the hand flapping, trying to grab the son who stood a few feet away, still screaming as though it were a language he had just mastered. The boy's eyes were saucers, wild with horror and exhilaration.

And with something else Thorne could not name, something more shocking than all the blood that flowed into the cracks between the chipped and flaking boards.

# MONDAY

# TWENTY-NINE

They'd had wine and a glass of whisky each before getting back to Thorne's flat. A fair amount of lager since. And their first kiss.

It was a little after six in the morning, and getting light outside.

They lounged, laughing on the sofa, arms and legs moving against each other, and bed clearly on the cards at some point, once a different sort of excitement had burned itself out.

'I wonder if Hignett and Brigstocke have started arguing about credit yet?' Porter said. 'Worked out how this is going to get divvied up.'

Thorne was grinning like an idiot, same as Porter, but he pulled a mock-thoughtful face. 'Well, *we* get the three murders, obviously. Four, if you count Sarah Hanley. Your lot can have the kidnap. How's that?'

'Oh, *can* we?

'Plus any little extras that come up: out-of-date tax discs, that sort of thing ... '

'Very generous of you.'

'*Bloody* generous, if you ask me.'

Porter raised her eyebrows.

'If Lardner had been at that flat in Catford and your lot had collared him, I bet you'd be claiming the bloody set.'

'Fair point.'

'Too right it is,' Thorne said. 'Now shut your face.'

She smiled, the pissed kind of smile that spread a little slower, and wider. 'So ... You charging into that cottage then, not bothering to let me, or anybody else, know ... '

'Hardly "charging".'

'How would *you* describe it, then?'

'There wasn't time to call. I didn't know how close you were ... '

'You didn't bother to find out.'

'I took a decision, same as you did when you went into the flat.'

'I didn't go in on my *own*!'

'Look, she was terrified about a firearms unit going in there, after what happened in Bow. I was just ... ' Thorne puffed out his cheeks, gave up. He knew she had him.

'Maybe you were getting your own back for being left in the van when we went into Allen's place?'

Thorne looked shocked. 'You really think I'm that bloody petty, do you?'

'It crossed my mind.'

'You're right, obviously. I'm *very* petty.' He leaned across. 'Vindictive. Vengeful. I'm a nasty piece of work ...'

They kissed again. Longer, the second time.

'Sorry about the smell,' Thorne said. 'They only had that soap, you know? The medicated shit. Little green slivers.' Thorne had showered at the hospital.

'It's *five* murders,' Porter said. 'You said "four".'

He nodded.

*Picture glass. Thin, easily snapped ...*

Peter Lardner had died in an ambulance which had taken twenty-five minutes to reach the cottage.

'One more reason not to live in the countryside,' Thorne had said.

Porter reached down, felt for the lager can on the floor. 'So what about Luke?'

Thorne could not shift the picture of the boy's face when they'd finally unwrapped the tape. Red from the adhesive, and wet with tears and sweat, but still that crazed expression around his eyes.

*Crazed*, just like words scrawled in rage on the wall behind a poster.

'He's alive, which I suppose is the main thing. But he won't be able to wake up tomorrow and just get on with it, will he? That's going to be who he is now. Getting over that kind of thing's all about support, and there's not much of a family for him to go back to.' He clocked Porter's expression. '*What?*'

'I meant what about the case against him?'

509

Thorne shrugged, picked up his own can. 'Fuck knows. They'll have to charge him ...'

They each took a drink. Thorne asked Porter if she was hungry, and she told him that she wished she'd eaten something before they'd started celebrating. Thorne got up and went into the kitchen to make them both toast.

They talked easily about nothing through the open door, letting the dirt settle. Like they'd been out all night dancing, or at a party.

Like nobody had bled to death.

Thorne turned from monitoring the grill when he heard Porter get up and watched her walking across the room towards the stereo. He told her to put on some music, apologised for the absence of any Shania Twain. He checked on the toast, flipped over the slices of bread on the grill-pan, then felt her fingers against his shoulder.

She was leaning into him as he turned round, one hand on his face and the other fumbling with the buttons on his shirt.

'We'll leave the toast then, shall we?' Thorne said.

Her tongue tasted sweet and boozy in his mouth. He bent his knees to press his groin against hers, and they staggered away from the cooker, lips pressed back hard against gums and teeth banging together.

She leaned back against the kitchen table and he went with her. Then he felt the pull and the pop, and the dizzying rush of pain, slicing deep from thigh to ankle.

He waited until they'd broken the kiss before he cried out.

# PART FOUR

# A PICTURE OF
# THE DAMAGE

# THIRTY

Thorne lay perfectly still in the tight, white tunnel and tried to listen to Johnny Cash.

The music was faint in his headphones, and all but drowned out by the noise of the MRI scanner that was slowly putting together a picture of his spine. Of the state of it. The sound, like a pneumatic drill, made it seem as if he were listening to some radical, techno remix of the Man in Black, but it was still better than the alternative. They'd told him he could choose one of their CDs for the twenty minutes or so he'd be inside the chamber, but Thorne had decided to take no chances and brought *The Man Comes Around* along with him. Good job he had. Even the little he could hear was preferable to some of the shit on the laminated list he'd found waiting for him in the changing room.

Jamie Cullum, Katie Melua, Norah bloody Jones.

He lay, quite still as he'd been instructed. Straining to hear. His hand around the rubber panic button he'd been told to squeeze if he felt uncomfortable or alarmed for any reason. If he wanted to stop the procedure.

The rhythm of the machine, the repetitive clatter, like a buzz that had been slowed, began to fade. The noise relaxed him. He started to drift and reflect, savoured the luxury of the time, the *space* inside his head. Like slipping between pristine sheets after too long in a bed that was stained and stinking.

Six days since the end of it. The end of *part* of it, at any rate.

Everything now would be in the hands of judges and lawyers. All Thorne and the rest of them could do from hereon was present those people with the material, and hope they made decent decisions.

They'd already made a couple of very brave ones.

Luke Mullen had been charged with the murder of Peter Lardner, though there was good reason to believe that when it eventually came to trial, the jury would not convict. Thorne was happy to take the stand as a defence witness, and believed that the extenuating circumstances which would probably see Luke Mullen acquitted – along with the fact of Tony Mullen's former position – probably accounted for why the magistrate had decided to release the boy into his father's custody. There were strict conditions, of course: Luke would need to report to a police station at regular intervals. He would not be going back to school.

It had been an equally brave decision to remand Maggie Mullen for trial in Holloway Prison.

Although, in the end, the magistrate had been left with little choice. The charge of attempting to pervert the course of justice, relating to the death of Sarah Hanley, certainly warranted bail, and a surety of fifty thousand pounds was set. However, once Tony Mullen – the only person in a position to act as guarantor – had refused point-blank to do so, prison had been the court's only option.

Thorne remembered Mullen's face in the sitting room as his wife had made her confession, and guessed that *his* decision to see her jailed had probably been easier to make than the magistrate's.

What had Thorne said to Porter that night?

*Not much of a family for him to go back to ...*

And unbidden, as Thorne remained motionless, different voices started to make themselves heard. Drifting in from nowhere and demanding attention.

A series of remarks and suggestions that began to curl around or lie across one another; to tease and illuminate.

Insisting ...

*I've always thought the sexual element of the attack was more important.*

*Listen, I accept all the evidence about abusers having been abused themselves.*

*Maybe it wasn't Luke he was calling.*

*We already looked at the parents.*

Until one single, big idea crowded out all the others, and the noise in Thorne's head was louder, harder to ignore, than that coming from the machine.

And what Lardner had said. The *last* thing he'd said:

*Why don't you tell the inspector all about it? Why you can't bear to let him touch you . . .*

Thorne pulled off the headphones and began to squeeze the rubber button.

Jane Freestone had stood up and wandered away when she'd seen him coming. Thorne watched her walk to the fence, spit and light a cigarette. Then he sat down next to her brother on the bench.

The same one Grant Freestone had been sitting on when Thorne and Porter had nicked him a week earlier.

'Fuck's sake,' Freestone said.

'Calm down.'

'I'm here with my sister, all right?'

Freestone had been released from custody in Lewisham on the same day that Maggie Mullen was charged. Now, aside from the compulsory rehab clinic, and weekly visit to sign the Sex Offenders Register, his life was more or less his own again. Though Thorne would soon inform those who needed to know just how often that life seemed to involve sitting in a local park, on the bench nearest to the children's playground.

'You shouldn't be so arsey,' Thorne said. 'If it wasn't for some of us, you'd be on remand for Sarah Hanley by now. Watching your back in Belmarsh or Brixton.'

'*Thanks*. But let's not forget you're the fuckers who nicked me in the first place.'

It was a fair point.

'All worked out, though,' Thorne said.

There was a breeze, but it was a warm afternoon. Thorne took off his jacket and laid it across his knees. Petals of cherry blossom drifted gently along the path, and an ice-cream wrapper clung to the side of the litter bin next to the bench.

'I couldn't believe it when I heard,' Freestone said. 'That woman, I mean: Tony Mullen's missus. And her boyfriend.'

'Did you ever meet her? Back then, when she was Margaret Stringer?'

'I only ever really had dealings with the social worker, Miss Bristow.' He turned to Thorne. 'I was upset to hear about her. She was all right. Bloke that killed her deserved everything he got, if you ask me.'

Thorne shifted his position slightly, and again, until the pain had subsided. 'So it was a surprise, then, when you found out what really happened to Sarah Hanley?'

'Big one, yeah.'

'Surprised to hear that it was Tony Mullen's wife, and not Tony Mullen himself, right?'

'*Sorry?*'

'I'm guessing you thought that Mullen had set you up for it. I'm not saying you thought he did it himself, but maybe he was happy enough to put you in the frame for it. He would have been well chuffed to get you out of the way. That's what you thought, isn't it?'

Freestone shrugged, worried at his goatee.

'There's no good reason not to tell me, Grant. Mullen's in no position to do you any damage now. Or to do you any *favours*.'

This was where Thorne found himself, the series of jumps he'd made. A sequence of bleak possibilities that pointed into the dark, lit the blackest corner of it . . .

If the nature of Adrian Farrell's crime had been, at some level, a reaction to his own abuse, might he have suffered that abuse at home?

If the calls from the Farrell house to the Mullen house had been from father to father, rather than son to son, what would they have had to discuss?

And what was Maggie Mullen so afraid that Peter Lardner would reveal? Or had *already* revealed, whispering home truths in the dusty dark of that cellar.

Thorne might never know for sure if he'd got there by the correct route, but he felt like he was in the right place. Felt fairly certain that in not mentioning Grant Freestone, it was more than just his wife's affair that Tony Mullen had been trying to cover up.

Only Freestone could tell him for sure.

'You don't look like someone who fancies kids to me,' Thorne said.

Freestone turned, his lips whitening across his teeth.

'You *don't*. That's just a fact. I've no more idea what someone who's into kids looks like than anybody else.' He nodded towards two old men, deep in conversation a couple of benches along, then at a younger man jogging towards them alongside a young woman. '*They* don't look like paedophiles ... *He* doesn't.' Thorne pointed at a skinny man, looking the other way while his dog defecated on the grass verge. 'Now, see, *he* does, and what's the betting I'm way off the mark?'

'What am I supposed to say?'

'Most of us have no real ... sense of it; that's my point. We can't recognise someone who has these drives, or desires. We can't pick up the signals, the signs, presuming there *are* any.' He straightened his leg, pushed back his shoulders. 'But I wonder if you can?'

Freestone said nothing.

'You didn't threaten Tony Mullen with violence,' Thorne said. 'You didn't make promises to get him, or members of his family. You threatened to *expose* him. You knew what he was.'

They waited, watched as the joggers passed.

'It wasn't like I could just *tell*,' Freestone said. 'Any more than you could. That's bollocks.'

'So what was it like?'

'I'd met him before, hadn't I? Sunday afternoon barbecue round at a ... third party's place. We talked about stuff, a few of us; there was an exchange of material later, upstairs. Nothing too heavy. But *he* definitely knew a lot of the people. He knew where all the best websites were ... not that there were too many back then. I never realised he was a copper, obviously, but he was hardly likely to broadcast the fact, was he?'

'Not really.'

'He nearly shat himself when he walked into that interview room and saw me looking back at him.'

'So you made threats?'

'Didn't do me any fucking good, did it? Mullen said I could say what I liked. Told me he'd just claim he'd been working undercover off his own bat, getting in with a known paedophile ring, gathering evidence, whatever.'

'He would have had a hard time pulling that off.'

'That's what I thought. But he wasn't bothered anyway; he had other options. He told me he'd make sure I got seriously worked over inside if I said anything. Now, I knew he could get away with *that*, so I just kept my mouth shut.'

'Different business when you came out, though,' Thorne suggested.

One of Jane Freestone's kids, the one who had been there when he and Porter had first gone round, came running over, asking if he could have some sweets. Freestone told him maybe later, and the boy turned away unconcerned, as though he couldn't even remember what it was he'd asked for.

'He came to see me,' Freestone said. 'Not quite so full of himself. A bit more of the politics, or whatever you want to call it, now he was a chief inspector.'

Thorne couldn't help but smile at that.

'He told me there were things he could do to help if I kept certain information to myself. Said that he had some influence on how everything worked out for me.'

'Because his wife was on your MAPPA panel.'

'I didn't know that at the time, did I? I had no idea what he was on about. But then all the shit happened with Sarah, and it didn't matter. I was away ...'

'So *did* you think that was down to Mullen?'

He sniffed. 'It crossed my mind. But it didn't make any difference in the end, did it? I wasn't going to hang around and try and convince anybody.'

'This "material" ...' Thorne said.

Freestone shut his eyes for a few seconds. 'You know: photographs, some tapes, whatever.'

*Whatever ...*

'Does the name "Farrell" mean anything?'

Freestone shook his head. 'Are you going to nick Mullen?'

'How would you feel about it if we did?' Thorne asked. 'I know you've got good reason to not like him, but aren't you at all ... sympathetic? Do you think he's actually guilty of anything?'

Freestone slumped a little, let out a long breath like he'd had enough, and stuck out his arms. 'Look, it's a nice day, OK? I come here for the scenery.'

'You'd better be talking about the trees,' Thorne said.

He watched Freestone walk away towards his sister and nephews. There was cherry blossom stuck to the soles of his shoes.

# THIRTY-ONE

It was just starting to get dark, just starting to spit with rain.

Thorne sat in the BMW opposite the house. He rubbed his neck – aching from where he'd turned his head to face the front door – and looked at his watch. He knew what time SO5 had been planning to knock.

They'd already been in there an hour and a half.

He imagined that Mullen had been unconcerned at first, even bored. He'd got used to being shown warrant cards on his doorstep. Thorne wondered how quickly the expression had soured when the officers had explained which unit they were from.

When the door opened, it was Mullen himself Thorne saw first. Then Luke, pulling at his father's tracksuit top, clearly distraught.

*Jesus . . .*

The boy disappeared from view, eased gently back inside the house, and the door half closed again, before two officers – a man and a woman – stepped out. They began leading Tony Mullen down the drive towards the cars.

There were no handcuffs.

Just questions, at this stage ...

Thorne knew that there would be three or four more officers still inside. That they would start bringing out paperwork, computers, boxes of videotapes and DVDs, once all the occupants of the house had left.

A few minutes after Mullen had been driven away, they brought out the kids.

Thorne watched Luke Mullen move like a sleepwalker down the drive, his sister's arm around his waist, the hand of a WPC resting gently on his shoulder. He wondered again, never *stopped* wondering, about Tony Mullen and his children.

Thorne remembered Adrian Farrell's desperate excuses in the bin, when they'd questioned him about the phone calls. Thorne had come to realise that Farrell, in spite of what they now suspected he'd been through, had been trying to protect his father, rather than himself.

Thorne could not say whether Tony Mullen's children had suffered at the hands of *their* father. It was wishful thinking, obviously, but it made some sense that at least one of them had escaped abuse at home. Maggie Mullen had been terrified by the thought of what Lardner had told her son; she had seemed convinced that Luke had not already known.

*Denial. Belief.*

Maggie Mullen was ravaged by both . . .

'Why stay with him?'

'I did leave once. Years ago.' Maggie Mullen scratched at the scarred surface of the table with what was left of her fingernail. It was chilly in the Legal Visits Room, and Thorne hadn't taken off his coat, but the prisoner didn't seem bothered by the cold. 'I didn't stay away for long.'

'Why did you go back?'

'The children, of course.'

'You could have taken them. You'd have got the kids in any divorce.'

'They love their father,' she said. 'He loves them too, more than anything . . .'

Thorne had not gone to Holloway Prison because he thought it might help the case against Tony Mullen. He had no idea if Mullen would even face a trial. It was out of his hands now.

The answers he'd gone there after were for nobody's benefit but his own.

'Tony never touched our children,' she said. 'Never.'

Thorne wanted to ask if she was sure, how she could ever *really* be sure, but the pause was filled with a plea for him to ask no such thing.

'You saw what it did to Luke,' she said, 'what Lardner told him. He loves his dad. So does Juliet.'

'What about you? I can't see how you—'

'I did love him.' Her expression made it clear that she

524

didn't know if she was being a martyr or moron. 'I pity him, because he's broken. He hates what he did ...'

'*Did*. Past tense.'

'Past tense ...'

Thorne waited.

'It was just pictures,' she said. 'Some pictures of little girls, years ago. There was nothing else.'

Again, Thorne wanted to ask how in God's name she could be certain, but he knew there was little point. It was a question she'd have asked herself plenty of times.

Like the question Thorne had been asking himself about Chief Superintendent Trevor Jesmond. About why *he* had never mentioned Grant Freestone. Thorne still could not decide whether to voice his concerns to those who might act on them. Could not be sure if the question sprang from gut instinct or from something more malicious ...

Maggie Mullen pushed back her chair. Ready to go.

'You loved Peter Lardner, though,' Thorne said. 'Didn't you?' He'd seen it at the end. Seen it in the blood that had bubbled and flowed across her as she'd cradled her former lover. Now, for the first time since she'd been led into the small, cold room, Thorne saw a softening in the woman's features. Saw the pain in her eyes and around her mouth.

'I was obsessed by him, once. As obsessed as he was.'

'But you could have been together. That's what I can't understand. You and Lardner, and the kids ...'

Grief and desperation took up residence again, settled

525

back into the folds of her face, while she thought of something to say. 'Have you always done the right thing?'

The lie came easily. 'Always,' Thorne said.

Maggie Mullen gave little sign of believing or disbelieving him as she dragged herself slowly from the chair and walked past Thorne towards the door and the waiting prison officer. Eyes wide, fixed front.

The same eyes as her son's . . .

Eyes wide and fixed front, Luke's face was grey beneath the peak of a baseball cap. Thorne watched as he was led to the far side of the car, as he bent to climb inside.

Thorne looked back and found himself staring straight at Juliet Mullen. It was for only a few seconds, and there was no more expression on her face than there had been on her brother's, but Thorne saw only an accusation.

He started the car and turned up the music.

Asked himself why, nine times out of ten, doing the right thing felt so bloody awful.

# EPILOGUE

Thorne regained consciousness thirsty and dribbling, with tears in his eyes.

He'd seen the old man knocking around while he was under. Not saying a lot, just there at the edge of it, keeping an eye on things. He felt as if his father had been drifting, shadowy, same as he was. When he came out of it, Thorne had the powerful sense that he'd said goodbye to more than just the pain.

Like both his phantoms had left at the same time.

He sat up on three pillows and stared at the TV screen. Watching the coverage of a criminal trial was something of a busman's holiday, but it was irresistible. In the United States, one of the world's most recognisable celebrities was facing a major prison sentence, and the past three weeks had been taken up with the farce of jury selection. Candidate after candidate was rejected on the grounds that they knew who the defendant was and would therefore make assumptions. The prosecution demanded to know where they were meant to find jurors who *didn't* know the mega-famous celebrity and what he was alleged to have done.

Thorne, still sleepy, closed his eyes and conjured a wonderful picture of a jury consisting of an Eskimo, a Kalahari Bushman, one of those African tribesmen with a saucer in his bottom lip . . .

*Assumptions.*

Boys and girls from *nice* homes and *good* schools don't become racist murderers. Don't grow up and snatch kids.

The ex-copper must be the parent being targeted when his child is kidnapped.

Children are safe with those closest to them.

He knew that everyone had prejudices and preconceptions. That they made fucking idiots out of good people as well as bad. That most of them were based on simple experience. But still ...

When it came to matters of guilt and innocence, of trust or misgiving, Thorne knew better than most that making assumptions was a dangerous thing.

It was *stinking thinking*.

The door opened at the far end of the room and Hendricks stepped out of the bathroom, wiping his hands. 'Nice facilities.'

Hedley Grange was a private hospital and convalescent home on the banks of the Thames, near Kingston. It was where the Met sent all officers injured in the line of duty; where Thorne would be recovering from an operation on the 'back injury' he'd received when rescuing Luke Mullen from the cottage in St Paul's Walden.

'Might as well get something out of it,' Holland had said.

Hendricks came around the side of the bed. 'Let's have a look at the mess they've made.'

Thorne eased himself on to his left-hand side. He moved gingerly so as not to disturb the stitches, or the tangle of tubes by which he was wired up to a saline drip and a syringe-driver delivering welcome shots of morphine whenever they were needed.

It was too early to tell if the operation to sort out the herniated disc had been a success. It was still very sore, though the surgeon had suggested that the pain might just have been post-operative. Either way, Thorne had hit the button on his syringe-driver several times in the three hours since he'd come round.

Hendricks lifted the sheet, drew in a sharp breath.

'What?'

'I'm kidding,' Hendricks said. 'It all looks fine. The plastic pants and DVT stockings look pretty sexy as well.'

'Piss off.'

Hendricks walked back to his chair at the end of the bed. He examined the floral tributes on the table: the customary small bouquet from the Commander; the slightly bigger one, with a printed card that said, 'Get Well Soon'. That was signed, with kisses, from 'Louise'.

'You were going to tell me what happened with her,' Hendricks said.

'Nothing, as yet,' Thorne said. 'Hopefully, if the back's sorted out ...'

'Easy, tiger. I wouldn't start swinging from the chandelier just yet.'

Thorne smiled. 'I'd settle for a cuddle, tell you the truth.' The smile widened. 'Maybe a handjob.'

'You reckon it might work out?'

'It'd be good, wouldn't it?'

'She's nice,' Hendricks said. 'Doesn't take any shit.'

531

They could hear voices from the corridor. The clatter of a trolley. Tea or medication.

'What about you and Brendan?'

Hendricks leaned back on the chair; held it balanced on two legs. 'We're getting on fine.' He looked out of the window. 'He hasn't said anything, but I think he's got someone else knocking around.'

'You OK with that?'

Hendricks said he was, and looked as though he meant it. 'I'm going to find someone who wants the same as I do. It can't be *that* hard.'

'Kids, you mean?'

The chair dropped back on to four legs. 'What about it?' Hendricks said. 'You and me. Why fight it any more? Let's adopt.'

'I'm not sure I'd make a very good father,' Thorne said.

Hendricks didn't miss a beat. 'You mean "mother". I'm the butch one.'

Thorne laughed, then wished he hadn't. He pressed the syringe-driver a couple of times until he floated away from the pain and couldn't remember what it was he'd found so funny.

Until he couldn't remember much of anything.

# ACKNOWLEDGEMENTS

For very good reasons, much of the procedure involved in the investigation of a kidnap is, and must remain, highly sensitive. As a result, I had to dig deeper than usual for any information I could get, and had little choice but to employ a good deal of licence in fictionalising it. Such things as I *was* able to find out have left me in no doubt that those who investigate kidnapping – in all its many forms – in the UK, are kept extremely busy.

The inner workings of the Kidnap Investigation Unit aside, I have, of course, to thank a number of police officers for a great deal: Detective Chief Inspector Neil Hibberd was, as always, generous with his time and good advice; the staff of Colindale Police Station were unfailingly helpful; and I am especially grateful to Detective Sergeant Georgina Barnard in her capacity as tour guide, and tireless answerer of stupid questions.

I apologise in advance for having *plenty* more ...

I am consistently grateful to a number of fellow writers both at home and in the US for their support and friendship, and on this occasion would like to say a particular 'thank you' to Linda Fairstein, whose expertise in the workings of Deoxyribonucleic acid rescued a particular strand of this novel's plot from an early grave.

I want to thank Filomena Wood and Cecilia Duraes for their hard work when I'm not doing any two-fingered typing, Yaron for his mastery of the Web, and Hilary Hale for making the entire process – from line one to launch – so hugely enjoyable.

And of course: Mike; Alice; Wendy; Michael; and the real Mr Thorne.

And Claire, Katharine and Jack, for so much.

Now read on for the beginning
of the next Tom Thorne thriller,

# Death Message

He could tell they were coppers the second he clapped eyes on them, but it was something in how they stood, in that formal awkwardness and the way their features set themselves into an overtight expression of concern, that drilled a hole straight through to his guts; that sucked the breath from him as he dropped into the chair the female officer had advised him to take.

He drew spit up into his dry mouth and swallowed. Watched as the pair of them tried and failed to make themselves comfortable; as they cleared their throats and pulled their own chairs a little closer.

All three winced at the sound of it. The dreadful scrape and its echo.

They looked like they'd been dropped into the room against their will, like actors who had wandered on to a stage without knowing what play they were in, and he felt almost sorry for them as they exchanged glances, sensing the scream gathering strength low down inside him.

The officers introduced themselves. The man – the shorter of the two – went first, followed by his female colleague. Both of them took care to let him know their Christian names, like that would help.

'I'm sorry, Marcus, but we've got bad news.'

He didn't even take in the names, not really. Just stared at the heads, registering details that he sensed would stay with him for a long time after he'd left the room: a dirty collar; the delicate map of veins on a drinker's nose; dark roots coming through a dye-job.

'Angie,' he said. 'It's Angie, isn't it?'

'I'm sorry.'

'Tell me.'

'There was an accident.'

'Bad one . . . '

'The car didn't stop, I'm afraid.'

And, as he watched their mouths forming the words, a single, banal thought rose above the noise in his head, like a distant voice just audible above the hiss of a badly tuned radio.

*That's why they sent a woman. Because they're supposed to be more sensitive. Or maybe they think there's less chance I'll break down, get hysterical, whatever . . .*

'Tell me about this car,' he said.

The male officer nodded, like he'd come prepared for this kind of request; was happier to be dealing with the technical details. 'We think it jumped the lights and the driver couldn't brake in time for the zebra crossing. Over the limit, like as not. We didn't get much of a description at the time, but we were able to get a paint sample.'

'From Angie's body?'

The copper nodded slowly, took another good-sized breath. 'We found it burned out the next morning a few miles away. Joy-riders . . . '

It was sticky inside the room, and he could smell the recent redecoration. He thought about sleeping, and of waking up from a nightmare in clinging sheets.

'Who's looking after Robbie?' He was staring at the male copper when he asked the question. Peter something-or-other. He watched the officer's eyes slide away from his own, and felt something tear in his chest.

'I'm sorry,' the woman said. 'Your son was with Miss Georgiou at the time of the accident. The vehicle struck them both.'

'They were both pronounced dead at the scene.' The male officer's hands had been clutched tightly together. Now he loosened the grip and began to spin his wedding ring around his finger. 'It wasn't drawn out, you know?'

He stared at the copper's thumb and forefinger working, shivering as his veins began to freeze and splinter under his skin. He felt the blood turning black and powdery, whispering beneath his tattoos and his yellowing flesh, like the blood of something that had been dead for a very long time.

'OK, then,' the female officer said, meaning: Thank Christ for that. Now can we get the hell out of here?

He nodded, meaning: Yes, and thanks, and please fuck off before I smash my head into your face, or the wall, or the floor.

Walking back towards the door, where the warder was waiting, it was as though each one of his senses were suddenly working flat out; heightened in a momentary rush, before everything began to shut down.